Praise for Pen

'A rural story that has it all ... sim... ....
intrigue, a complex heroine and a swoon-worthy hero. What's not to love?'

—Karly Lane, bestselling Australian author, on *Clouds on the Horizon*

'When reading a Janu novel, one expects several things: a feisty heroine, gorgeous rural settings, and a passionate, captivating romance. She delivers all that here, in spades.'

—*Better Reading* on *Clouds on the Horizon*

'Encapsulates everything I love about the romance genre and so much more. A go-to author for rural romance for the head as well as the heart ...'

—Joanna Nell, bestselling Australian author

'Endearingly quirky and utterly charming. Funny and sweet and wonderful.'

—Amy Andrews, *USA Today* bestselling author, on *On the Same Page*

'Penelope Janu's fresh, bright, funny new twist on rural romance is an absolute delight. Her wit is as sharp as a knife. She is one of my absolute must-read authors.'

—Victoria Purman, bestselling author of *The Nurses' War*, on *Up on Horseshoe Hill*

'Intriguing characters and a colourful setting: if you like romance and a little mystery, get ready to enjoy this novel.'
—Tricia Stringer, author of *Keeping Up Appearances,* on *On the Right Track*

'Take a break from the news and spend time in Horseshoe Hill. Well written, interesting and filled with heart, *Starting from Scratch* is the perfect weekend read.'
—*Better Reading*

'Oh, how I do love reading a novel by Penelope Janu, it's always an absolute pleasure and I find them hard to put down. *Up on Horseshoe Hill* is no exception, I read until the early hours of the morning and picked it up again as soon as I was awake.'
—*Claire's Reads and Reviews*

'*Up on Horseshoe Hill* is a novel that I would recommend for animal lovers, for rural romance lovers and for those seeking an engaging read.'
—*Great Reads and Tea Leaves*

'Penelope Janu succeeds in delivering fans old and new an engrossing tale. *Up on Horseshoe Hill* is a novel that awakens our sense of hope that love can prevail, even when life deals you with a series of devastating setbacks to overcome.'
—*Mrs B's Book Reviews*

'*On the Right Track* by author Penelope Janu is on my unputdownable fave reads category. There was humour, tension, chemistry amongst a backdrop of family drama that just keeps the pages turning.'
—*Talking Books Blog*

ABOUT PENELOPE JANU

Penelope Janu lives on the coast in northern Sydney with a distracting husband, a very large dog and, now they're fully grown, six delightful children who come and go. Penelope has a passion for creating stories that explore social and environmental issues, but her novels are fundamentally a celebration of Australian characters and communities. Her first novel, *In at the Deep End*, came out in 2017, followed by *On the Right Track*, *On the Same Page*, *Up on Horseshoe Hill*, *Starting from Scratch* and *Clouds on the Horizon*, as well as a novella, *The Six Rules of Christmas*. Penelope enjoys riding horses, exploring the Australian countryside and dreaming up challenging hiking adventures. Nothing makes her happier as a writer than readers falling in love with her clever, complex and adventurous heroines and heroes. She loves to hear from readers, and can be contacted at www.penelopejanu.com.

Also by Penelope Janu

In at the Deep End
On the Right Track
On the Same Page
Up on Horseshoe Hill
Starting from Scratch
Clouds on the Horizon
The Six Rules of Christmas (novella)

PENELOPE JANU

Shelter from the Storm

Penelope Janu ♡

First Published 2023
First Australian Paperback Edition 2023
ISBN 9781867223597

SHELTER FROM THE STORM
© 2023 by Penelope Janu
Australian Copyright 2023
New Zealand Copyright 2023

Except for use in any review, the reproduction or utilisation of this work in whole or in part in any form by any electronic, mechanical or other means, now known or hereafter invented, including xerography, photocopying and recording, or in any information storage or retrieval system, is forbidden without the permission of the publisher.

This book is sold subject to the condition that it shall not, by way of trade or otherwise, be lent, resold, hired out or otherwise circulated without the prior consent of the publisher in any form of binding or cover other than that in which it is published and without a similar condition including this condition being imposed on the subsequent purchaser.

All rights reserved including the right of reproduction in whole or in part in any form.

This is a work of fiction. Names, characters, places, and incidents are either the product of the author's imagination or are used fictitiously, and any resemblance to actual persons, living or dead, business establishments, events, or locales is entirely coincidental.

Published by
HQ Fiction
An imprint of Harlequin Enterprises (Australia) Pty Limited (ABN 47 001 180 918),
a subsidiary of HarperCollins Publishers Australia Pty Limited (ABN 36 009 913 517)
Level 13, 201 Elizabeth St
SYDNEY NSW 2000
AUSTRALIA

® and TM (apart from those relating to FSC®) are trademarks of Harlequin Enterprises (Australia) Pty Limited or its corporate affiliates. Trademarks indicated with ® are registered in Australia, New Zealand and in other countries.

A catalogue record for this book is available from the National Library of Australia
www.librariesaustralia.nla.gov.au

Printed and bound in Australia by McPherson's Printing Group

*To my grandsons Harrison and Darcy,
who love to read books and tell stories*

CHAPTER 1

A grey gum towers over the windswept scrub that borders the path to the beach. The shadows are deep in the moonlight, but my watch lights up when I push back the cuff of my wetsuit: ten forty-five. An hour has passed since I ordered the recruits to join me at the tree. *Yes, lieutenant. Sure, lieutenant. We won't let you down, lieutenant.* They've probably gone back to sleep.

The breeze is light, whispering through the foliage and warming my skin. Dropping my backpack at my feet, I pluck a leaf, fold it in half and then in half again. Summers in the country, long sunny days, starry skies at night. The scent of eucalyptus, the sharp and the sweet, always takes me back.

Distant applause rings out from the parade ground. HMAS Creswell is hosting an environmental summit and the delegates, seated at tables in a marquee, are attending the opening night dinner. Amplified voices suggest the speeches have started. I check my watch again: ten fifty-two, and still no sign of the recruits.

It's a fifty-metre walk to the beach, where small but busy waves, like silver-edged ribbons, rush to the shore before dashing out again. A jetty, a solid timber structure where naval craft are moored, juts out from the wide strip of sand, and a breakwater, an artificial outcrop a hundred metres long, shelters the beach from the ocean. Four tall poles mark the end of the break, and two broad banners hang between them.

The recruits, drunk on shots and high on exam results, rowed to the breakwater at dusk, took down the official banners and strung up alternatives. In the first banner, a whale and calf float lifelessly in the water. In the second, a koala, her joey clinging desperately to her back, falls from a tree. The images are underlined with bold black text. *Our leaders have blood on their hands.*

How could the recruits have been so stupid?

Particularly as everyone on the base had been instructed to treat conference delegates—environmentalists, scientists, industry leaders and politicians—with discretion and respect. We're hosts. This is a demonstration of community engagement. *No controversy.* I couldn't *strictly* be blamed for something the recruits did off duty, but …

When I discovered they'd switched the banners, I should have reported them.

I didn't.

If I get caught, I'll be in trouble too. But …

The recruits shouldn't lose their careers over this. *Technically* they're adults, but they're barely out of school. Which was why they let themselves get talked into trouble. Was I ever so fun-loving and idealistic?

I doubt it.

I glance towards the marquee, just visible at the top of the rise. Can they see the banners from there? Kicking off my thongs, I store them in the backpack alongside the banners that should be on the poles. *HMAS Creswell. Welcome to Jervis Bay.* Single handed, I won't be able to rehang them, but I can take down the offending ones.

Leaving my backpack by a post of the jetty, I walk to the water and splash my face. I untie my ponytail, comb through my hair with my fingers, twist the curly lengths into a bun and secure it at my nape with the band. Whitewash gathers at my ankles as a blanket of lightning brightens the sky. Thunder follows, rumbling from the east. The waves on the jetty slap a beat. One two three. One two three.

There's another sound as well.

'Hey!' The voice is male and close—on the beach on the far side of the jetty.

I'm a sitting duck out here. And if I'm caught, I'll have to explain what I'm up to. My body pings with adrenaline as I run, ducking behind the post closest to the shoreline. I risk a glance at the man rounding the jetty twenty metres away. My view is obscured, but he's tall and well-built. He has a long stride.

He's walking directly towards me.

Is he another officer, or part of the summit's security contingent? Has he seen the banners? If he has, I won't want to answer the questions he'll have. I push back my shoulders and step out of the shadows.

'Identify yourself!' My voice is brisk and assured.

He stills for an instant. 'Imp?' And then he keeps on walking, stopping only metres away. Square jaw, straight nose, nice mouth. There's not an ounce of fat on him. *Confident, athletic, capable.*

'Hugo.' Tightness cramps my chest. 'What are you doing here?'

His dark blond hair is shorter than it was, the sun-tipped ends less marked. I can't see the colour of his eyes, but I know them so well I could never forget them.

Clear and bright. Sea-green like ocean.

'I'm a delegate at the climate summit.' When he folds his arms, his shirt pulls at his shoulders. 'How about you?'

'I work here.'

He indicates the banners. 'Who put them up?'

I lift my chin. *Push back the memories.* 'This is a restricted area. You'd better get back to the marquee.'

He looks me up and down. 'Small. Barefoot. Trouble. Are you involved?'

'I could have you removed.'

'Imp?' He scrapes a hand through his hair. 'What's going on?'

'Don't call me that.'

'Lieutenant Patience Cartwright.' His eyes narrow. 'Is that what you want?'

'I want to know why you're here.'

'I've already told you.'

'You weren't on the list of delegates.'

'A colleague roped me in.'

'What kind of work are you doing?'

'Biodiversity, habitat, amphibians.' He's wearing a collared white shirt. He rolls up the sleeves and loosens his tie. 'How about you?'

I focus on the cuff of my wetsuit, pulling it over my watch. 'I have a temporary posting on the base. I train the new recruits.'

'Last I heard, you were a maritime warfare officer, navigating ships at sea.'

'I'll be back on my ship after Christmas. And I really need to—'

'That's ten months away.' He smiles stiffly. 'Where's your uniform?'

'I'm off duty.'

'And swimming in the dark.'

'There's nothing new in that.'

When he was still at school, Hugo's mother drove hundreds of kilometres from Horseshoe Hill so he could swim with other squad members at the Olympic pool in Dubbo. Almost three years older than me, popular, tousle-haired and easy-going, he was the swim club captain. Anti-social, argumentative and small for my age, I was a town kid swimmer, one of the many who looked up to him.

'The banners.' His brows lift. 'Who put them up?'

'I'm going to take them down.' Before I can block him, he swoops, grabbing my backpack and yanking it out of reach. 'Give that back!'

'Tell me what you're up to.'

I grasp a strap of the backpack, but he holds fast. Our fingers touch. 'Oh!'

When we let go of the backpack, it falls to the ground between us. His eyes stay on mine as he bends at the knees to pick it up. Immediately he stands, I grab the strap and yank the bag free, dropping it behind me.

'Leave, Hugo.'

When he holds out his hand, I take a hurried step back. Frowning, his hand drops to his side. He opens his mouth and shuts it again. And then,

'There are environmentalists and scientists here, but also economists, mining representatives, lobbyists, politicians. Anything controversial or overtly political,' he indicates the banners, 'we lose the collaboration.'

'I get it.' A bolt of lightning highlights his features, the planes of his face, the shades in his hair. 'That's why I'm taking them down.'

Now. Right now. Without delay. Immediately. Yet my feet stay firmly on the sand. My lips open. No words come out.

'How are your sisters?' he asks.

'They're well, thank you. How is Greta? And Derek? Your brothers?'

'It's been a year since you were in Horseshoe. They ask about you.'

I'm a hundred and fifty-two centimetres to his one eighty-six. I lift my chin. 'I was back for Phoebe and Sinn's wedding last month.'

'Two days in Warrandale.' He squares his shoulders, stands even straighter. 'This naval base. Is it your home?'

'It's where I belong.'

'It wasn't always.' He jerks his head towards the sea. 'Out there on your ship. Is that home too?'

'It's like the song.' I smile sweetly. 'Home is where I lay my hat.'

Hugo is glaring when I see Commander Ruddock, the executive officer at the base, standing at the end of the track. Middle-aged but fit and dressed in naval whites, he holds out his torch, throwing an arc of light onto the sand. Scooping up my backpack, I dart around Hugo and into the shadows.

'Hugo!' I hiss. 'I don't want him to see me.'

He crosses his arms. 'I noticed.'

'Come over here. Stay till he's gone.'

'Tell me what you're hiding.'

'Shhh.'

'Imp!'

Ruddock turns off the torch as he crosses the soft sand to the harder sand at the shoreline. He's at least thirty metres away. He's increasingly short-sighted, but hates wearing glasses. Does he know that Hugo is here? That he's with someone? Has he seen the banners?

I glance longingly at the scrub that borders the beach. If Ruddock saw me running towards it, he could recognise my height, my build. Even if he didn't, I'm not dressed for a formal dinner—Ruddock would want to know what business I have being here. And if he gets close enough to ask …

He's been looking for an excuse to get rid of me since I arrived.

I grab Hugo's arm, tugging until he faces me. 'Stop looking at him!'

Hugo speaks through his teeth. 'I have nothing to hide.'

'I don't want Ruddock to identify me. You're …' I consider his build, the breadth of his shoulders. His tawny hair isn't quite short enough for the military. 'He'll know you're not navy. A few of the delegates have partners here. If Ruddock thinks I'm one of them,' I drop my backpack at my feet, 'there's a chance he'll go back to the marquee.' Ruddock walks along the sand in the opposite direction. He peers towards the cliff on the far side of the beach.

Hugo swears under his breath. 'What are you afraid of?'

'Please, Hugo.' I focus on his tie and the unfastened button at his neck. 'Pretend we're together.'

'I don't pretend.' Immoveable. Unwavering. He could be a statue. A tall bronze statue on a stormy summer's night.

I glance around him. 'If Ruddock sees us, he'll leave. You're thirty. I'm twenty-eight. Why can't we pretend?'

'You're twenty-seven.'

'Almost twenty-eight. And I'm trying to put things right. Please, Hugo.'

'Tell me what you're up to.'

'After Ruddock has gone, and if you swear not to tell anyone, I'll brief you about the banners.'

Another frown. 'You're dictating terms?'

'I said I'd explain.'

'You never do.'

I put my hand over his mouth. 'Shhh.'

His breath is warm on the palm of my hand. And then, all of a sudden, I'm warm all over. The nape of my neck, my face and my breasts. There's heat in the air that blows on my skin and in the waves that sweep on the sand. When I draw in a breath, he does the same. My breasts so close to his chest; the touch of my hand on his face.

I pull away, take a backwards step, and hold out my hands. 'Take them. That's all you have to do.'

When he finally does as I ask, holding my hands in a cool firm grip, our eyes lock. Do I imagine the deep green of his? I must. Because there's not enough light for—

He pulls me closer. 'Oh!'

For a heartbeat, he stills. 'Do you want this or not?'

I look past him to Ruddock, still staring out to sea. 'Yes.'

Head lowered, he threads our fingers together. His thumb slides over the back of my hand. 'There's salt on your skin.'

My breath hitches. My heart tumbles.

Breathing and tumbling.

When we swam together, Hugo taught me how to breathe to the side, and helped me with tumble turns at the end of each lap. He didn't laugh or turn away when I sucked in water or coughed until my nose bled. He'd pull me out of the pool, wrap a towel around my shoulders and tell me to stop trying to do everything at once. *Don't be so impatient.* Then he'd hand me over to one of the swimming mums and dive back into the pool. He was tanned, tall and mature for his age. He had a face that people looked at twice—as if the first time around they might have imagined how attractive he was.

They hadn't.

Nothing has changed.

Ruddock's phone rings and he answers, walking towards the treeline before turning and facing the ocean again. He's closer than he was, but still twenty metres away.

When I pull Hugo further into the shadows, the sand is wet under my feet. He's looking at me, but I look out to sea, the sparkles of light on the ocean.

Hugo swam like a fish. *A merboy.* We often argued, but I looked up to him. He'd grin and praise my tenacity. And when I stood back at the social events at his family's farm, he'd encourage me to join in with the others. Greta, his mother, was kind, paying me to help in the kitchen when Derek employed itinerant workers to labour on the farm. Hugo scrubbed the roasting trays and saucepans. He treated me the same way he treated the other kids, but I imagined I meant more to him than they did. In any case, I'd made up my mind. I wanted to be with him.

I was nineteen the first time we kissed.

The last time we kissed.

Now?

Breathing.

Tumbling.

The waves on the beach whisper to the shore. An owl calls two shrill hoots. 'Is Ruddock still there? Is he looking this way?'

'Yes.' He squeezes my hands. 'And no.'

Need and sadness all mixed up. I swallow, focus. 'Do you think he knows we're here?'

When he looks into my face, what does he see? Parted lips, wide eyes. Does he recall the blue in the way I recall the green? His breathing is deeper than it was, but his body is rigid. He lowers his head, my stomach flips.

'He's unlikely to leave,' he says quietly. 'I should have warned you.'

Real sounds come back. Cicadas. The slosh of water on the posts of the jetty, the rush of the waves on the shore. Distant thunder.

The jangle of the keys on Ruddock's belt.

CHAPTER 2

'Hugo! He's coming!'

'The banners.' He keeps hold of my hands. 'Tell me.'

Pulling free, I take hurried steps backwards. 'What did you mean, you should have warned me?'

'Dr Halstead?' Ruddock, torch extended, calls out. 'Is that you?'

Tight throat. Sore heart. When I rub my face with my sleeve, the neoprene smells of rubber and salt. I gather my thoughts and pull the ends tight.

'He knows who you are.'

'We met at dinner.'

As if guided by the beam of the torch, a dainty little crab with a speckled brown shell skitters on the sand to a hole at my feet. Lightheaded, a little disoriented, I take another step back, turn my ankle in the sand.

'Imp?' Hugo touches my arm.

My eyes sting. From the momentary pain in my ankle or something very different? 'Don't touch me!'

He drops his hand.

Spine straight, shoulders back, chin up. I know the drill. *I've been here before.* 'You knew this would happen.'

'I saw the banners and asked him about them. He had a call, I got here first.'

My voice is stronger than the waves and the crickets. *It has to be.* 'You knew he'd stay and wait.'

'It was possible.'

Dot, dot, dot. Dash, dash, dash. Dot, dot, dot. 'Why didn't you warn me?'

'Imp! For fuck's—'

'Why take my hands?'

His lips are tight. 'You asked me to.'

Breathing and tumbling.

Uncertainty. Heartache. Confusion.

Hugo.

When I drop my shoulder and shove him out of the way, he mutters a string of curses. Ruddock pulls up short. 'Lieutenant Cartwright?'

I salute. 'Commander.'

He takes in my wetsuit, the backpack at my feet. 'What are you doing here?' He points to the banners. 'Are you responsible?'

'No, sir.'

Hugo's gaze goes from Ruddock to me. 'She's taking them down.'

'Stay out of this!'

'Cartwright!' Ruddock glares. 'Apologise.'

Hugo crosses his arms. 'She doesn't have—'

I look through him. 'I'm sorry, Dr Halstead.'

'Accepted,' he finally mutters. 'Now can we go?'

'The other banners.' Ruddock glances at the backpack. 'Where are they?'

'I'll see to this, sir.'

'Answer the question!'

'I'll remedy the problem.'

'Open the backpack.' The backpack is only half unzipped when Ruddock snatches it and pulls out a banner. He shakes out the folds and throws it on the sand. Forming a barrier between Hugo and me, he quietly spits out words. 'I'll have you charged.'

'I'll take down the banners now. I'll rehang the others at dawn.'

He turns to Hugo. 'What did she tell you?'

'Patience?' The second button of Hugo's shirt is undone. 'You said you could explain.'

'Cartwright!' Ruddock again. 'Who else was involved?'

'I believe it to be members of my division, sir. I'd like to deal with them myself.'

'That's not your call!'

Hugo curses under his breath. 'She said she'd—'

'Thank you for bringing this matter to my attention, Dr Halstead,' Ruddock says. 'This is now a disciplinary issue.' He nods towards the track. 'Your colleagues will be waiting.'

Hugo looks from me to Ruddock. 'I'm in no hurry.'

'This is a restricted area.'

'Patience?' As Hugo steps closer, Ruddock is forced to move back. 'Do I stay?'

No sun-bleached scruffy hair from early morning swims. No dust-streaked boots. No smiles that go straight to my heart. The wind plays with the waves and blurs the silver lines.

'Why would I want you to do that?'

As Hugo stalks away, Ruddock, hands behind his back, shoves his face into mine.

'Your failure to report in the incident log constitutes negligence in the performance of your duty.'

'This isn't fair!'

'Insubordination!' Chin out, hands still behind his back, he walks a circle around me. 'You're not fit to lead or serve. It's why you were discharged from your ship.'

There are no sharks in this bay. *There's danger on the land.* 'I was assaulted.'

He shakes his head dismissively. 'You withdrew the allegations.'

'Lieutenant Commander Grantham is a bully.'

'Withdraw that!'

I look somewhere over his shoulder. 'No, sir.'

'You're a disgrace,' he spits out.

The crabs are back, marching in a line. 'May I take down the banners, sir?'

'It's a mark of a leader to *lead*, Cartwright, not score points by protecting rule breakers.' He snorts a laugh. 'Your academic credentials, your so-called mathematical *brilliance*, won't save you this time.'

The four speckled crabs at my feet scamper over the sand in a diagonal line. If each crab laid thirty thousand eggs every year for three years, but only twenty-eight per cent hatched, I could work out the survivors in a moment. *100,800.*

Ruddock finally stops circling. 'You're a liability.' He leans in close, every word articulated. 'I want you out of the navy.'

Water on the posts. *Slap. Slap. Slap.* Burning throat and stinging eyes.

I didn't cry for Hugo. I won't cry for you. I lift my chin. 'I'll take down the banners.'

'Now!'

The push and pull of the current, the shimmer of shallows and darkness of depths, the taste of salt on my tongue. *Hugo said I had salt on my skin.* When a shoal of fish swim towards me, I open my fingers, feel the rush of their bodies. I swim a hundred metres until I'm halfway to the breakwater, then I tread water and look back. Beyond the strip of sand is a blurred black line, the trees that fringe the track, and above them the lights on the parade ground. Is Hugo up there? Waiting for a lift to his hotel? Why should I care?

I alternate between backstroke, freestyle and breaststroke to the breakwater, then climb onto a half-submerged boulder. Shallow waves with frothy white caps wash into the rockpools and gather round my feet. Clambering from rock to rock, I reach the level bitumen strip that curves around the coast towards the land. I could have rowed out here like the recruits did, but thought I'd be less likely to draw attention to myself, and it'd be quicker, if I swam. *More fool me.* Moonlight pushes through the clouds, throws shades of bronze and onyx on the water.

The recruits would have worn shoes when they climbed the rocks, and they would have worked together to scale the uneven footholds—like axe strokes—in the four vertical poles. If they were here now, I would have stood back and supervised as they climbed the poles again. But as it is …

My feet ghostly white in the gloom, I grit my teeth as I climb notches in the first pole, wrap an arm around it and untie the knots. When I move to the next pole and do the same, the banner falls to the ground in a heap. Untying the ropes at the base of the second banner is simple enough, but the knots at the top are too tight to unfasten. I grasp the banner and yank, freeing the banner but leaving ribbons of fabric and circles of rope. Repositioning my foot on the notch, I reach up again.

'Oh!'

When my foot slips from the notch, pain shoots through my arch. My eyes water as, using my heel, I find the notch again and slowly descend, hopping on my good foot when I reach the ground. I gingerly touch my instep and, through the stickiness of blood, feel the end of a spike.

Sitting on the bitumen, I bring my foot up on my knee, wipe away blood and find the splinter again. It's almost flush with the skin but, wincing and clenching my teeth, I manage to grasp it between the tips of my fingers and pull. 'Ouch.' I hold the fragment out, four centimetres long and as thick as a matchstick. Using one foot and the ball of my other foot, I limp to the banners and clumsily roll them up. Clasping them to my chest, I move crab-like down the boulders, wedging the banners into a crevice on the way. When I reach the rockpools and the farthest point of the break, I dive back into the sea, swimming freestyle until I'm close enough to the jetty to make out the silvery streaks on the barnacles. I duck dive, swimming underwater until my fingertips scrape the sand.

Foamy streams of whitewash curl around my ankles as I stand and test my foot. I can't feel anything poking out, and the wound must be clean. Extending my leg, I point my toe, smoothing the water by sweeping my foot back and forth.

Like my sisters and I smoothed the water in the river at Warrandale. Phoebe, Prim and I would play Pooh sticks, dropping twigs upstream and following their trail to the deep dark pools near the river red gums. I was a teenager when I'd visit the Halstead's farm in Horseshoe Hill. Hugo and I would sit on the sun-baked dirt at the riverbank with our feet in the shallows. In the dry, the water was sleepy and languid. After rain, it gambolled and cartwheeled.

Hugo asked when I was coming home.

Rivers and streams, small country towns. Golden wheat, woolly sheep, horses, cows and gum leaves.

I've left them all behind me.

CHAPTER 3

My quarters at HMAS Creswell are on the ground floor, but the ocean glimmers brightly through a mosaic of leaves. ABBA's 'Knowing Me, Knowing You' blares from my ear pods as I finalise notes on my files. As I've been forcibly relieved from my divisional officer duties, I could neglect to update whoever takes over my work, but that would hurt them and the recruits, not Ruddock. As threatened, he's detailed a string of accusations. But as none of them warrant incarceration, he's been forced to assign alternative duties—starting tomorrow.

It's only two in the afternoon when I save the updated files to the share drive. I sit back in my chair and stretch my arms over my head.

'Well, Commander Ruddock, what do I do now?'

My mother, her image captured in one of two framed photographs I keep on the shelf above my desk, smiles sweetly. She was only in her forties when she had a stroke that almost killed her. Prim, my youngest sister, was seven, I was ten, and Phoebe was twelve. Mum had been a successful academic, but the stroke robbed her of the vast majority of her medium- and long-term memory, and severely impaired her short-term memory. She *mostly* remembered she had children but couldn't remember their names.

She still can't.

Mum leads a good life in New Zealand with her sisters. It wasn't her fault she left us behind with our father.

Professor Cartwright. When he was conscripted to Vietnam, he was a prodigiously talented university student. His war experiences resulted in untreated PTSD, but that could never be an excuse for the way he treated his daughters. Phoebe was terrified that if people found out what it was like at home—our father's intolerance to noise, his outbursts, his neglect—we'd be taken away, separated, and put into care. She tried to keep us safe.

If only we could have done the same for her.

I was naturally good at maths and I had a temper, so our father mostly left me alone. Prim was young and had a speech difficulty—he barely acknowledged her. Phoebe was only twelve when she started looking after us. But the more she tried to please Dad by taking charge of me and Prim and the house, the crueller he became. It was just before Christmas when he locked Phoebe in the cupboard in the hall. Afterwards, she developed a paralysing fear of the dark. All our father had to do to bring us into line was to threaten to turn out the lights.

A bully.

My ear pods are still in my ears, so I feel rather than hear the pounding on the door. 'Patience!' I turn down the music. 'Open up!'

Sub Lieutenant Kat Stevens is a few years older than me, but we've been friends since, on my first posting, we shared a cabin.

She's a hundred and eighty centimetres tall and thin as a whippet, with a shock of bright red hair and a frenzy of freckles.

'The word is,' she says as she hugs me, 'you've been up to no good.'

When Kat finally lets me go, I lean against the desk and she sits on my bed. 'I should have got out there earlier.'

Reaching to my side table, she picks up my phone, checks the screen and rolls her eyes. 'ABBA was your Mum's favourite group. Are you still using that excuse?'

'I was brainwashed in the womb.' When I hold out my hands, she throws the phone. 'Happy music makes me feel better.'

'Were you dancing?'

'I didn't feel *that* much better.'

'Playing invisible drums?'

I smile. 'You know too much.'

'Well, Fernando, sharing quarters will do that to you.' She picks up the second photograph on my shelf. Phoebe, Prim and me, with paddocks of gold and green behind us, are laughing into the camera. It was taken the day after Phoebe married Sinn, and she looks happy enough to bust. Phoebe and I have similar colouring, but she's taller and curvier, and her hair is straight. Prim also has blue eyes, but her hair, pulled over one shoulder in the photo, is dark brown and wavy. 'Maybe you could take leave, catch up with your family?'

'Phoebe and Sinn are still on their honeymoon in Europe, and Prim is going back to Darwin soon.'

Her gaze goes to my foot. 'Why's that taped up? What happened?'

'I got a splinter. No big deal.'

'What work has Ruddock found you?'

'According to him, I was so interested in the activities of the summit, I can stand sentry outside the meeting rooms for the next four days, starting tomorrow.'

'When the base is crawling with security already? You'll die of boredom.'

'Maybe that's the idea.' I force a smile. 'I'm worried this'll end badly, Kat.'

'I'd like to tell you it won't, but you've been landed from your ship, and you're on quarterly reports.'

I line up my pens in colours—red, blue and black. 'The navy isn't only my job, it's where I live. It's *how* I live. I could be discharged. What would I do?'

She whistles. 'Being a genius, I reckon you'd have one or two options.'

'I'm serious.'

'So am I. You've come top in every freaking exam you've ever done.'

Phoebe remembers me sorting tomato seeds into rows when I was in my highchair. When Mum worked out what I was up to, she gave me a set of Cuisenaire rods, small rectangular shapes marked into units of ten, so my calculations could be distinguished from my food. Equations, calculations, predictions, computations … Numbers and patterns come easily to me.

I look out of the window at the cloudless summer sky. A seaman, an oxygen tank strapped to his back, sits on the bow of a dive boat.

'Patience?' When I turn, Kat smiles encouragingly. 'There are other jobs out there.'

'An academic? A financial analyst? An actuary? I don't want to sit in an office all day. I like the job I have.'

'You've always stuck up for the underdog, but you used to be better at biting your tongue. In the past couple of years, you've taken risks. There's a bureaucracy here like everywhere, you've got to go through the hoops. Those idiot recruits,' she rolls her eyes, 'could've been left to fight their own battles.'

'Ruddock insisted on knowing who was involved. Moussa has no hope of getting the transfer he wanted.'

'You got the banners down before the media cottoned on to them, otherwise he and the others could've been charged.' She grins. 'Meaning the junior officers love you even more than they did.'

'That's not why I did it.'

'Which is why they respect you.' She shoulder bumps me. 'Any word from Captain McCarthy? Reckon he'll have the final call on whether you're charged or not.'

'I'm waiting for my summons.'

She crosses two fingers and holds them up. 'What about the guy who was at the beach with you and Ruddock. Heard from him yet?'

'Hugo? How did you know he was there?'

'He was waiting on the parade ground for you to get back. Ruddock all but ordered him onto the hotel bus.'

'I didn't know that.'

'You wouldn't, would you, swimming back from the breakwater? Halstead was angsty about seeing you. You two got history?'

'Kind of.'

She whistles. 'Spill the beans.'

I glance at the photo of my sisters and me. 'Hugo is closer to Phoebe's age, but we swam together as kids, and then we were friends. His parents and brothers were good to me.'

'That face and body?' She fans her face. 'Jesus, he's hot.'

I dredge up a smile. 'Please don't.'

'Sorry, mate.' She crosses the room, drapes an arm across my shoulders. 'He didn't break your heart, did he?'

'We've both moved on.'

'You reckon? When was your last relationship?'

I walk past her to the door, opening it wide. 'Forget about Hugo.'

Grinning, she points to the window, the sparkling strip of water. 'Plenty more fish in the sea.'

Another forced smile. 'You'd better get back to your ship. I wish I could come.'

She mock punches my arm. 'No more running away.'

When I step back from the door, my instep pulls. 'Where would I go?'

CHAPTER 4

It's Friday, the last day of the summit and my final day of supposed guard duty. Many of the delegates have completed their sessions and gone home, but some of the most senior of the politicians, bureaucrats and scientists remain. Most of them are in the lecture room, nursing cups of coffee and tea or bottles of water. Professor Tedeschi, a university academic and highly regarded scientist, looks up from the podium.

'Lieutenant Cartwright!' He whips off his glasses and stands back. 'Thank you for bailing us out yet again.'

As the computer equipment isn't what many of the delegates are used to, and as a lot of them are accustomed to having research assistants to sort out their tech—including putting their data into a form that experts in *other* fields can make sense of—I've been helping them out.

'Any time.' As the professor polishes his glasses, I flick through the settings on his laptop, locating the documents and images he'd lost, and minimising them so he can find them later. I check his laptop is connected to the audio and screen equipment he'll need, and the microphones are set up in the way he prefers. 'It's good to stretch my legs.'

His thick grey hair falls over his brows. 'Why in the devil's name are you standing in the corridor anyway?'

'I have to follow orders, and I've been ordered to stand outside.'

'Where your talents are thoroughly wasted.' The professor smiles. 'The name "Cartwright" is well known in mathematics circles.'

I smile politely as I step away from the podium. 'Is that right?'

'Your father was a marvellous mathematician. As was your mother.'

I force a shrug. 'I'm better at numbers than words.'

'You won the University Medal in pure mathematics. Academia didn't appeal?'

'No way.' I smile. 'I like the *practical* side of maths.'

'As a navigator on a ship, you use these skills, I appreciate that. But …' he waves a hand towards the door, 'I'm at a loss to understand why you're stuck out there. Which is exactly what I said to your captain last night.'

'Captain McCarthy?'

He winks. 'I had the honour of being seated at his table at dinner, which gave me an opportunity to communicate my thoughts.'

'I've been abandoning my post all week. I hope he didn't mind.'

He winces. 'Crusty old curmudgeon, isn't he? Even though,' he smiles, 'he's a great deal younger than me. One of the few benefits of age, lieutenant, is the ability to speak your mind when the opportunity—'

We both look up when Hugo, the youngest delegate by a decade at least, and dressed casually in jeans, well-worn boots and a creased linen shirt, appears in the open door. In addition to clambering over rocks in rivers and streams and swamps to get to his frogs and snakes and lizards, he must work out at a gym. And I suppose he still works on the farm. Even though, unlike his brothers, he never aspired to make a living from the land, he seemed to enjoy the physical demands—baling hay, sinking fence posts, rounding up cattle on horseback. Does he still have a bump on the ridge of his collarbone?

He must.

On Tuesday morning, two days after we parted at the beach, he saw me outside a breakout room and asked me what had happened with Ruddock. I muttered something about everything being settled, and then I walked away. Since then, we've stayed clear of one other.

He has an overnight bag slung over his shoulder. 'See you next week, professor,' he says.

As the only biologist here, Hugo seems to work across all the different groups. When delegates turn and acknowledge him, his smile is open and generous. Shining green eyes, crinkling at the sides.

Sociable. Affable. Smart.

'Thank you for coming on such short notice,' the professor says. 'Your contributions were invaluable and I'm looking forward to working together again. Our next assignment will double your workload, young man.'

I feel Hugo's gaze on the top of my head as I studiously tap at the keyboard.

We held hands. A means to an end that was never achievable. It's over.

Pressing delete, I harden my heart.

Professor Tedeschi clears his throat. 'Lieutenant?'

The delegates, almost all of them looking at me, are waiting for the session to start. Hugo, leaning against the door frame with his arms crossed, lifts a brow. I force a smile in the professor's direction as I step away from the podium. 'Call out if you need anything else.'

Hugo straightens as I approach, leaning into the room to shut the door after I walk through. His three-day growth is darker than his hair.

I nod stiffly. 'Did you want something?'

'You said things were settled.' He indicates my chair. 'Is this your punishment?'

'Part of it.'

'What happens next?'

'Captain McCarthy decides. I haven't seen him yet.'

'According to Ruddock, you were already in trouble.'

Small. Barefoot. Trouble. I look around Hugo, to the security men standing either side of the exit. 'I'd better get to work.'

'Going back to sea …' He holds out a hand but drops it again. 'That's what you want?' His eyes are on my mouth. Mine go to his. My stomach flips. A traitorous tingling circles my heart. 'Imp?'

'When I'm at sea …' I shrug as if it's nothing, when for the past eight years it's been *everything*. 'I have responsibilities. I have colleagues and friends. It's a career, Hugo, like your career.'

'I get that.' He rubs around the back of his neck.

'Do you still get migraines?' When he blinks, I step back. 'Sorry. I shouldn't have—'

'Occasionally.'

I make sure the straight-backed chair is *exactly* parallel to the wall. 'How often do you go home? To Horseshoe Hill?'

'I bought a property just out of town, the old brewery across the river from the park. I get back when I can.'

'I recall a letterbox keg at the gate. Is there a house there?'

'It was abandoned decades ago. I'm fixing it up.'

'Next time you go back, can you say hello to your parents?'

He picks up his bag, drapes it over his shoulder. 'Down at the beach, Imp. I didn't mean to make things worse.'

I plant my feet a little apart, put my hands behind my back. 'Vindictive doesn't fit your profile. I appreciate that.'

He frowns. 'Do you believe it?'

Our eyes clash. 'Does that matter?'

'After all these years?' His eyes go to my mouth again. 'I wish to hell it didn't.'

CHAPTER 5

Three days after the summit has ended, I receive a message: *Report to Captain McCarthy immediately.* I drop the last of the packages in the quartermaster's store, smooth down my shirt and respond: *ETA 16:00 hrs.*

Even though HMAS Creswell is on land, the naval hierarchy operates here just as it does on a ship. Captain McCarthy is the most senior officer, but instead of a cabin he has a suite of rooms on the far side of the parade ground. I walk quickly over the short springy grass, taking deep breaths in an attempt to slow my heart rate. The sky is pastel blue, the sea a darker shade.

My cap is pressed firmly under my arm as I wait in the anteroom. Commander Ruddock has alleged that I've been negligent in the performance of my duty, and insubordinate. I'm an officer. I'm clearly in the wrong, so …

Do not tell the most powerful man on the base to fuck off. Repeat. Do not tell—

'Lieutenant Cartwright.' The captain's assistant smiles sympathetically as she opens the door and ushers me in. Tall, thin and sombre, Captain McCarthy faces the window that overlooks the bay and breakwater. Blue and white banners flap between the poles: *HMAS Creswell. Welcome to Jervis Bay.*

When he turns, my heels click to attention. 'Sir!'

His brow creases. 'At ease, lieutenant.'

Captain McCarthy, a stickler for rules and procedure, was a commander on one of my first postings, but his habit of learning junior officer's names, identifying their weaknesses and encouraging their strengths, garnered him particular respect. He set high standards, but he was fair.

'Commander Ruddock wants you out of the navy,' he says.

No chitchat. No preamble. 'Sir.'

'His documentation of recent events, and your apparent unwillingness to accept the chain of command, support his position.'

'The recruits deserved a second chance. They'll learn from this.'

'What if they hadn't been caught?'

'They'd learn from that too, sir. I would have—'

He holds up a hand. 'You failed to report the incident to your superiors, and you were insubordinate. Commander Ruddock wants me to support a notice to show cause why your appointment as an officer shouldn't be terminated.'

'That's—' I bite my lip, repress a retort. 'Sir.'

'Given past conduct, it would end your career in the navy.'

I swallow hard. Swallow again. 'I shouldn't have done what I did.'

'Because it was wrong, or because you got caught?'

My instep aches. 'Both, sir.'

Walking to his desk, he picks up a sheaf of papers from the dark mahogany surface. Dropping most of them next to a stack of folders, he flicks through the remainder.

'What do you have to say for yourself?'

'I take responsibility, sir, for the men and women who serve under me.'

'Good leaders take more than their fair share of responsibility, and less than their fair share of credit.' He runs a knuckle down the binding of a folder before looking up again. 'Was this your reasoning?'

'Yes, sir.'

'Discipline and good order come first!' He slaps the papers on the desk. 'You have a duty to respect and support your superiors!'

'Sir.'

'Poor performance and lack of leadership. I could have you out on your ear by the end of the month.'

'*Could*, sir?'

He looks at me critically. 'You might be too clever for your own good, lieutenant.'

'I value my career, sir.'

He glances at the papers. 'In which case, I have a proposal.'

'Sir?'

He walks towards the window before turning and facing me again. 'Hosting the summit was an opportunity to demonstrate our commitment to the environment, while acknowledging past mistakes. You'll be aware of what happened at Williamtown RAAF base?'

'The air force used fire retardants and other carcinogens in their operations. Surface and ground water, on and off the base, were contaminated.'

'The government put millions into cleaning up that site. The armed services contributed additional support.'

'As they should.'

'It was a precursor to the government's increased interest, through the military, in environmental issues.' He harrumphs. 'It's also politics, which is why I can't ignore it.'

'Sir.'

'The military supports environmental projects through funding, infrastructure and emergency response operations. They occasionally provide personnel on secondment.' He circles around me in the way Ruddock did last week. 'I have two choices. One, I accept Commander Ruddock's recommendation, which would end your career. Two, I send you away.'

'On secondment? You'll give me another chance?'

'I'm not confident you deserve it, but yes.' As I hold back from punching the air and bouncing up and down on the spot, he returns to his desk and rifles through more papers. 'A few months ago, a group of scientists and engineers known as the Macquarie team applied for a naval operative. Last month, in support of their objectives, the navy agreed to fund a position. It appears the scientists want a jack-of-all-trades candidate, a sailor with basic administrative, topography and map-reading skills, who knows their way around a boat—operation and maintenance.'

'I'm no engineer, but I'd manage the basics.'

'The candidate would have responsibility for dinghies, kayaks, outboards at best, so that should be sufficient. The scientists also expressed a strong preference for ...' he peers at a page, 'someone who can ride.'

'A motorbike? Sure, I can—'

'A horse.'

'No!' When he stiffens, I lower my voice. 'I don't ride, sir.'

He grunts. 'If you want this secondment, you'd better upskill.' Sitting behind this desk, he points to the chair opposite. 'Sit, lieutenant.'

I do as he asks.

'I've told you what the scientists want.' He picks up another folder, this one marked *Protected*. 'But now there's an additional requirement.' Opening a drawer, he takes out his glasses. 'This is highly confidential. It comes straight from,' he jerks a thumb over his shoulder, 'the government.'

'I'm listening.'

'The national water security project. What do you know of it?'

'The delegates have been discussing it all week. It's a ten-year plan, where States and Territories report on their water resources, and how these might be impacted by climate variation. The federal government wants to assess the infrastructure it has and what it might need—dams, desalination plants, underground reservoirs—in the future. Professor Tedeschi is lead scientist on the project.'

He sits back in his chair. 'I understood you were on guard duty.'

'I was, sir, but—'

He holds up a hand. 'Universities, scientists, consultants, support personnel. There are thousands of people and a number of specialist teams—including the Macquarie team—working on the project, and the government is throwing millions, billions of dollars at them, hoping it lands where it should. Which is where, Cartwright, you come in.'

I sit further forward on my chair. 'In what capacity?'

Opening the folder, he shoves loose pages to one side. 'I received this file a week ago. From my reading of it, the auditor-general's office has concerns about financial irregularities within the water security project. They believe people unnamed are cooking the books.'

'People in the scientific community?'

'Presumably.' He straightens a cuff. 'If the office had anything concrete, they'd send in an auditing team. As it is, they don't want to put noises out of joint by snooping around with mere suspicions. When they became aware the Macquarie team had requested an operative, they requested we select a candidate able and willing to assist them too.'

'In respect to irregularities?'

'The naval candidate will have a genuine reason for being on the project, so won't be under suspicion. However, given the circumstances, the auditor-general's office can't be too prescriptive. They've specified intelligence, IT competence and spreadsheet nous.'

'What would I be looking for?'

'Your guess, lieutenant, is as good as mine.' He drops the folder on the table. 'A scientist might be incompetent. He might be working elsewhere without disclosing it. He could be having Fridays off, or running a brothel. I suspect the auditor-general wants to set an example. If a problem is identified, it will serve as a warning to the thousands of others on the project's payroll.'

'It sounds underhanded.'

'It's sensitive.' He throws his pen on the folder. 'Dr Lipman, another academic, works closely with Professor Tedeschi. He also has access to the project's financial data.'

'If I'm a jack-of-all-trades at the river, how am I supposed to search accounts and—'

He cuts the air with a hand. 'You're nothing if not clever, lieutenant. Use your initiative.'

If it gets me back to sea ... 'I'll do my best, sir.'

'It was a happy coincidence that Professor Tedeschi and I met at dinner.' Yet another critical stare. 'He was aware that you were on report. Accordingly, even though you're simultaneously overqualified *and* underqualified for the role on the Macquarie team, he'll be inclined to believe we can do without you.'

'What if I find something?'

'The office will take over and investigate. You'd report to me monthly. Other than that, simply keep your eyes open and your mouth shut.'

'How long is the secondment?'

'A year, at most.'

I focus on the trees, a thousand shades of green. And beyond them the sea, a thousand shades of blue. 'If I agree to this, I won't be discharged? I'll get to leave the base, and then go back to sea?'

'Perform satisfactorily, lieutenant, and I'll consider it.'

'If I don't agree?'

'Your naval career is likely to come to a premature end.'

When he stands, I jump to my feet. 'I'll do it, sir.'

A lift of his brows. 'I'll nominate you as a candidate, but that doesn't guarantee your appointment. There'll be an interview. You'll have to convince the team leaders that you're suitable.'

'What's the team investigating?'

'Water, obviously.' He opens another folder, slimmer than the first one, and flicks through the pages. He reads. 'The operative will be appointed to a research team charged with identifying and cataloguing river and wetland species, including plants, insects, fish and amphibians in the Macquarie River region of NSW.'

Amphibians? I batten down unease. 'You said I'd be interviewed by the team leaders. Can you give me their names?'

He consults the folder again. 'In addition to Professor Tedeschi, the senior scientists are Dr Lipman, a botanist, Dr Lisa Stanhope, an environmental engineer, and ...' I follow his gaze to the beach, the creamy strip of sand fringed by blue and foaming white, 'Dr Hugo Halstead.'

CHAPTER 6

I lift my hair from my neck, sticky with sweat, as I walk down the hill to the beach. Twelve buoys form a semi-circle to the west of the jetty, curving past the breakwater to the ocean. The yellow buoys are vibrant with colour; the red ones have faded to pink.

How far to the furthest?

Phoebe's friend Sapphie made the groomsmen's buttonholes for Phoebe and Sinn's wedding. The leaves and gumnuts came from the river red gums in Warrandale, but Sapphie made peony buds from crepe she'd dyed herself, and the shades were identical those in the freshly picked flowers in Phoebe's bouquet.

Sapphie sees colours in her mind. I see how many strokes it'll take, given the swell and breeze, to swim to the furthest buoy.

Three hundred and twelve, give or take a couple.

Patterns, numbers, arithmetic. I was thirteen when a teacher pointed out that my wiring might be different from the other kids at school. And if I'd had my mother's wiring, I would have been happy with that. But even back then, I knew Mum's mathematical abilities were different to mine. *In this I'm like my father.*

The reflections on the water are blue tinged with gold. I dive into the waves, butterfly kicking until I break the surface and strike out in freestyle. Water trapped between the wetsuit and heat of my body slowly warms up. I carve a path through the swell, fingers long and arms outstretched, breathing to the side like Hugo taught me.

He asked whether going back to sea was what I wanted.

In addition to the reasons I specified—my career, colleagues and friends—I like the silence and the solitude. The rhythm of the waves, the promise of the tides. Sunrise and sunset. The taste of salt on my tongue.

I vowed I'd never go back to the country.

I flip onto my back, shading my eyes as the sun sinks into the clouds. Shadowy shapes appear in my peripheral vision. Two dive boats are moored to the jetty. Larger boats, a patrol boat and three survey boats, are anchored on the far side of the breakwater.

Will the scientists take me? When Commander Ruddock called me into his office an hour ago, he said there were no guarantees. While he can't do anything that would undermine the captain's recommendation, I doubt I'll get a glowing endorsement.

I complete the last few metres of the swim to the buoy, looping an arm around the bright yellow sphere and dipping my head into the water to clear hair from my face. Tomorrow morning at nine, I have an interview with Tedeschi and the others, an opportunity to convince them to give me the job. Their submission for naval support set out several requirements:

Map-reading skills. *Check.*

Administrative skills. *Check.*

Ability to identify and navigate rivers, streams, waterways and wetlands. *Check.*

Ability to manoeuvre dinghies, kayaks and outboards through shallow bodies of water. *Check.*

Experienced horse handler and competent rider. *No.*

Ability to carry scientific and other equipment (up to 40kg) for sustained periods. *Eighty per cent of my body weight? No.*

Craft maintenance including engine overhaul. *No.*

They wouldn't have been able to *specifically* request a man for this role, but I'm certain that's what they were looking for. Some women would be physically strong enough to lift an engine, but female mechanics are few and far between.

Hugo and other men in the team could share the heavy work, but they might not be available. According to images on Lisa Stanhope's professional profile, she's capable, tall and fit, so the floaty dresses and high heels on her Instagram page are likely restricted to her personal life. But Richard Lipman is in his forties and seems to have spent his whole life in a laboratory. At medium height and possibly underweight, I can't imagine him lifting a kayak over a sandbank or lugging an outboard through a bog.

I dive beneath the surface to the artificial reef near the breakwater. A pop-eyed fish, vibrant orange and as round as a dinner plate, darts through strips of seaweed. A shoal of minnows, spears of burnished copper, crowd in tight formation. I steer clear of a stingray and float on my back again, only turning for home when the sun dips towards the trees. I make out the grey gum at the top of the track.

Captain McCarthy said everyone is under suspicion—even Tedeschi. He doesn't behave like I'd imagine a criminal would. And Hugo would never rip anybody off. But the other men and women working on the project? *I have to keep my eyes open and my mouth shut.*

'Hey! Ma'am!'

The new recruits I babysat this morning, mostly young women fresh out of school, are laughing and talking, sprawled on the sand twenty metres away. When a cork pops from a bottle, they cheer.

'Come and have a drink!'

How much will they drink? Should I warn them? What would I say?

Watch out for bullies.

Take more care than I did.

A month before I was kicked off my ship, Lieutenant Commander Grantham invited me into his cabin. I suspected I smelled alcohol on his breath, but I couldn't be sure. For months he'd stood too close, touched my arm when we were on the bridge, leaned over my shoulder as I charted a course, brushed up against me as he weaved between the tables in the galley. He laughed too loud, he whispered sotto voce. Keeping my distance when I could, I hoped to bore him into disinterest. I didn't complain like I should have. Phoebe knew something was going on, but I didn't want to worry her. I told her I could handle it.

I thought I could.

He's a hundred and eighty centimetres with a thick neck and a rugby player's build. I entered the cabin, he offered me a drink. When I said no, he stepped in front of me and locked the door. I was trained in physical combat. I was capable and skilled.

I didn't react as quickly as I should have.

His hands were slippery on my skin. The scent of his flesh, his breath, the sounds he made, were nauseating. He touched my breast, fumbled with my belt, pushed me against a wall and pressed against me. When I turned my face away, his open mouth slid across my cheek. My stomach turned, I gagged.

He took my hand and put it on his crotch.

'No!' I lifted my knee and forced him back. I jammed an elbow into his throat and shoved him away. Wiping my face with my sleeve, I strode to the door and unlocked it before facing him again.

He'd tucked in his shirt and pushed back his hair. Rubbing his neck, he dredged up a smile.

'You've been sending mixed messages,' he said.

'I'll report you!'

He asked me to wait so that he could warn his wife. He pointed to the photograph on his desk, a smiling dark-haired woman with two adorable boys. Grantham often talked about them. *Samuel Paul. Timothy Patrick.*

We were in the Southern Ocean, midway through exercises with British and US warships. If I'd lodged a complaint immediately, Grantham and I would have been relieved of duty until the executive officer of the ship—responsible for morale and discipline—and the captain had considered the matter. I agreed to hold off until we'd finished the exercises, and until Grantham had warned his wife.

I felt sorry for her. *I know what can happen to families.*

On the final day of the exercises, Grantham set me up. Six ships. Months in the planning. But he didn't give coordinates in time, he changed his instructions. *He muddied the waters.* The officers involved in the exercises were publicly debriefed by the officers they reported to. Grantham catalogued, in detail, the mistakes I'd supposedly made. And afterwards, when I lodged my complaint about the assault, he accused me of fabricating the story to get back at him.

The executive officer appointed a commander engineer to conduct the initial investigation, the 'fact-find'. This officer was suspicious of my delay and took Grantham's side. When I swore at him and walked out, he informed the captain, who issued a formal warning that my behaviour was unacceptable, and ordered I be removed from the ship for poor performance. I was also warned that further misbehaviour could result in discharge from the service.

Welcome to HMAS Creswell.

Threading a hand through my hair to work out the tangles, I approach the women on the beach. A few hold out their glasses, telling the girl with the bottle to hurry up and pour. But as I get close, they quieten.

I wave away their messy salutes. 'You have an early start tomorrow, don't you?'

One of them groans. 'Six o'clock, ma'am.'

'Finish your drinks, return to your quarters.'

'Yes, ma'am.' One of the women carefully pours from the bottle. 'It's my birthday.'

I blow a kiss. 'Happy birthday.'

'Would you like some?'

'No, thanks.' I smile and point to the base. 'I have a meeting in Sydney tomorrow. I'll need a clear head.'

When I get to the top of the beach, I sit on the sand, burrowing in my bag for my sandals and strapping them on. I went back to the medic this morning. He prodded and poked my foot but couldn't find anything wrong. The hole has closed; there'll be no scar.

So when will the aching stop?

CHAPTER 7

It's barely seven when I leave the rush of commuters at Central Station, checking directions on my phone as I walk up Broadway to the university. A homeless man on the footpath strips off his sweater.

I offer a smile. 'It's going to be hot today.'

Shuffling backwards, he stuffs the sweater into a plastic shopping bag. 'Leave me alone.'

The interview will be held in a room on the top floor of a building in the quadrangle, but it's far too early to take the stairs to Professor Tedeschi's office, so I follow a path to a sandstone paved courtyard, deeply shaded by a peppercorn tree. A marble nymph, naked besides a patina of green, coyly peeks out from a tangle of vine.

'Do you mind if I hide here too?'

Sitting on a narrow bench, I finish my coffee and message my sisters, thanking them for calling and telling them I'll get back to them soon. My white shirt is creaseless and spotless. I brush imaginary lint from my pants, as uniformly black as my boots. Untying my lace relieves pressure on my foot—I massage my instep and retie the boot.

I glance at the nymph again. 'Now what will I do?'

The navy wants a competent and numerate sailor prepared to act as a sleuth. The scientists want a burly boat mechanic who happens to be an equestrian. To have any chance of getting this job I need …

I reach into the bag and pull out one of my books, turning to the index. In the past few days, I've learned more than I thought I'd ever know, or need to know, about—

'Imp.'

I hide the cover of the book as I close it and shove it to the bottom of my bag. I look up slowly.

Mossy stones, mottled ivy. Working boots, long legs and troubled green eyes. 'Hugo.'

'You've changed your number,' he says.

I nod briskly. 'How did you find me?'

'I figured you'd be close. I knew you'd be early.'

At five in the morning, I'd sit on the kerb outside the swim centre, waiting for the caretaker to open the gates. One day Greta, Hugo's mother, who drove the three-hour round-trip from Horseshoe Hill a few times a week, sat me down for a chat. She didn't like the idea of a ten year old sitting alone in the dark, and said she'd ask my father if she could collect me from home. When she wouldn't take no for an answer, I told her there was no need to talk to Dad—Greta could pick me up at the corner where he wouldn't be disturbed by the opening and closing of the car door. Hugo would be in the front of the car when Greta collected me, usually doing his homework. He offered to step in for his mum when he was seventeen and had a driver's licence, but by then I was fifteen. My father wasn't coping with the accounting work he did, so I had to help with that and do my schoolwork. I walked to swimming when I could.

'Why did you call?'

He shoves his hands in the pockets of his jeans. 'Happy birthday.'

'Oh ... Thanks.'

He frowns. 'Had you forgotten?'

Tightness in my chest. 'Why would you remember?'

When he crouches, elbows on his knees, we're much the same height. He hasn't shaved for a couple of days. His mouth is—

'We were friends.'

If I had the chance, I'd run out of the courtyard. And then I'd swim. The tempo, the beats, the counts. We're back at the pool in Dubbo, dripping towels, suntanned bodies, tangled sun-bleached hair. *Strokes through the water and the slap of the wash on the tiles.* Hugo liked to race, but I never cared about winning.

'Like every other girl,' I say, 'I was infatuated with you.'

'Why turn your back so completely?'

'Why ask that now?'

'We've never been alone. You haven't allowed it.'

The air between us crackles and snaps. 'It's in the past, Hugo. Forget it.'

He walks to the peppercorn tree and, with the side of his hand, he zigzags a line down the trunk. 'The work the Macquarie team is doing is important,' he finally says. 'Not only to the environment, but to my career, the things I believe in. Why did you apply for the secondment?'

'My name was put forward. I agreed.'

'You don't meet the criteria for the role.'

'Because I'm a woman?'

'You're not a mechanic.' His eyes narrow. 'You won't ride a horse.'

'How do you know that?'

'I was there when you fell.'

Dragged. Trampled. Broken. I push words through the images. 'I have other skills.'

He scans my face. He frowns. 'Breathe, Imp. You're white as a sheet.'

I exhale a shaky breath. 'I can be useful.'

'You said you'd never come back to the country. What's changed? Why are you doing this?'

'It's important work.' I mirror his words. 'It's important to my career. I've made up my mind.'

'I'm asking you to change it.'

I shake my head firmly. 'You don't want me. The others might.'

He turns away again, pulling up short when he sees the nymph. He walks to her slowly before lifting a hand and pushing aside her leafy green veil. He deliberately, meticulously, brushes dried leaves from her shoulders. He traces the rim of her ear and clears cobwebs from her eyes. He draws a line between her lips and—

I take a step back. 'Hugo?'

The pulse at his jaw, the firmness of his mouth, the creases on the outsides of his eyes. His shirt pulls across his chest when he breathes. His gaze is clear. Direct. 'What?'

Sunlight slips through the foliage above us. 'I haven't been interviewed yet. Give me a chance.'

He picks up his bag and puts it over his shoulder. 'It wouldn't work, you and me. It'd be impossible.'

We're approaching the entrance to the building where the interview will take place when a woman behind us calls out. 'Hugo! Wait up!'

Hugo and I turn in unison. Lisa Stanhope, the environmental engineer, is as tall and attractive as she appeared in my searches. Her hair is light brown and glossy. She pushes it back.

'I'm Lisa.' She holds out her hand. 'Lieutenant Cartwright?'

'Patience.'

She smiles. 'I thought we'd get a beefy bloke.'

'I'll do better in small spaces.'

'Let's go,' Hugo says.

'Hey!' Laughing, Lisa grasps his shoulder, swings him around and kisses him firmly on the mouth. 'You stood me up.'

'Nightclubs aren't my thing.' He shoots her a smile. 'But thanks for letting me stay last week.'

'You could've stayed longer.'

'It was a long drive back.'

'The Macquarie River will be closer to home for you.'

I'm like a clown at a carnival, head turning right and left. 'Do you often work together?'

'This is the third time,' Lisa says, 'not that we'll see much of each other. I do the day shift. Rick works early mornings and Hugo,' she touches his arm and lowers her voice, 'spends his nights in the swamps with the frogs.'

When Hugo holds out a hand, gesturing she precede him, she pokes him in the ribs. 'I found a replacement on the dance floor last night. Leo Abela.'

'If he can keep up with you …' Hugo whistles quietly. 'You're better with him than with me.'

Hugo always had close female friends—including ex-girlfriends. Or is Lisa a current girlfriend? The sun feels particularly hot as I push past him to the entrance, cool and welcoming dark. Gripping the rail, I walk up the stairs two at a time.

Professor Tedeschi greets me courteously, ushering me to a room with a solid timber table. I check my phone is on silent, flip open a pristine spiral notebook and sit back in my chair. The long and narrow leadlight window has diamond panes of glass.

Diamonds: a square with corners pulled tight. When did Mum teach me that? I must have been small, because I remember telling my kindergarten teacher what I'd learned *so far*. When her eyes grew wider and wider, I didn't know whether that was a good thing or not, so I kept on talking.

A diamond is a quadrilateral shape because it's two dimensional and flat, with four straight closed sides.

A diamond is a parallelogram because the opposite sides are parallel.

A diamond is a rhombus because the sides are the same length, and the opposite angles are equal.

Did I tell her how to calculate the angles? I suspect I would have. But …

It wasn't long before I worked out that *maths freak* made you different. I learned to keep my thoughts to myself.

When Tedeschi returns, Hugo and Lisa are with him. She smiles another welcome, but Hugo doesn't bother.

'Rick Lipman will dial in,' Tedeschi says. 'I've set aside an hour but,' he glances at Hugo, 'we're unlikely to take that long.'

I'm on one side of the table. Tedeschi is on my right and Hugo and Lisa sit opposite. When Hugo calls Dr Lipman on his phone, he refuses to be on speaker until Tedeschi, increasingly annoyed, insists. Tedeschi flicks through the pages in front of him before looking up again.

'Thank you, Lieutenant Cartwright, for joining us,' he says. 'As you're no doubt aware, I'm the lead scientist on the water security project. Many teams work under the project's umbrella, the Macquarie team being one of them. We've agreed that Lisa, as senior engineer on the team you'd be working with, will lead the interview.'

Lisa pulls her tablet closer. 'I suggest we go through the criteria one by one and—'

'The lieutenant is unsuitable,' Dr Lipman says.

Hugo leans back in his chair. 'You're on speaker, Rick. Lieutenant Cartwright can hear you.'

'I'm aware of that.'

Lisa shifts uncomfortably. 'It's Lisa, Rick. You'll require the successful candidate's assistance more than me or Hugo. Why don't you ask Lieutenant Cartwright questions before making your decision?'

'Hugo believes we're unlikely to be compatible.'

'Rick!' Hugo sits forward in his chair. 'Given Patience is sitting here, that was a little insensitive. Judge the applicant on her merits. How about asking a question?'

'I have nothing more to say.' When Rick disconnects, the screen goes blank. Lisa grabs the phone and pushes it to Hugo.

'I don't know how you put up with him,' she says.

'He's the best at what he does,' Hugo says.

Tedeschi turns to me. 'It's unfortunate Dr Lipman couldn't be with us in person. His communication style can be confronting.'

'My communication style might be different to Dr Lipman's, but that doesn't mean we'll be incompatible. We can work out how best to interact.'

'Yes, well …' Lisa props her tablet in front of her. 'How about we start again? Firstly, why apply for this role when you don't meet the criteria?'

Even before it was Phoebe, Prim and me; three children and an abusive father. Even before our mother was taken away and never came back. Even before I'd lost my front teeth.

I'd learned about survival.

If you're different, it's not easy to be liked. Approved of.

Understood.

This is the same.

I want this secondment.

It's a ticket to get back to sea.

Lisa leans forward with her forearms on the table. The professor's crossed arms rest on his paunch. Hugo sits back in his chair, his long legs extended. I sit with my hands linked in my lap. Shoulders back, chin up.

'I have a double science major in mathematics and physics, with first class honours and the University Medal. I'm a maritime warfare services officer in navigation and—'

The professor holds up a hand. 'Your academic and military credentials are incomparable. There's no disputing that. But these skills have little relevance to the position to be filled.'

I unlink my hands and put them, side by side, on the table. 'Hugo? Why did you tell Dr Lipman we wouldn't work well together?'

He takes a deep breath. 'I made an assessment.'

'Professor Tedeschi said Dr Lipman's communication style could be confronting. Is he neurodivergent, is that what this is about? So what?'

'That's not why—'

'Is he dangerous or abusive?'

Tedeschi sighs. 'Not at all, but he has idiosyncrasies. He resists deviation from set routines. He does field work before dawn and works long hours. He keeps to himself; he likes to work alone.'

'I'll work any hours he wants. I also prefer to do things on my own.'

Lisa looks up from her tablet. 'The physical requirements of this role. How will you manage them?'

'If water levels are low, I'll need assistance in manoeuvring the boats.'

'There's no guarantee you'll have it.' She looks up. 'Can you ride?'

I look out of the window, the deepening blue of the sky. 'Yes, but I haven't done so for a number of years.'

'Answer the question,' Hugo says quietly.

Bleeding face, broken bones. You held me on your lap. I put my hands back in my lap, press my nails into my palms. 'If I have to ride, I will.'

Lisa taps her screen. 'Engines,' she says without looking up. 'You're not a mechanic.'

'I can do basic maintenance.'

'That might not be enough.'

'The section of the river you'll all be working on is, at worst, two hundred kilometres from a reasonable sized town. If a motor blows up, I can get it fixed. I can arrange for its replacement.'

'I see.'

'What do you see?' I look from Lisa to Hugo and back to Lisa. 'You said Dr Lipman likes to work on his own, but from what I've been able to ascertain, both you and Hugo go into the field with teams of people—Indigenous leaders, scientists, landowners, parks officers, post-grad students. If neither of you will help me drag kayaks over mudflats or carry an engine back to camp, somebody else will. I'll work hard. I'll take direction. I'm also fully funded by the navy. I won't cost you a cent.'

The professor's smile is strained. 'Lieutenant,' he says, 'you're overqualified for this position. Why apply?'

'I'm on shore leave, which I hate. This is an opportunity. I'll make it work.'

'That would be your intention, of course.' He opens a file and flicks through pages. 'Do you have questions for us?'

'I have statements.'

He blinks 'What are they?'

'I'll be able to read and follow maps and nautical charts better than any mechanic—I can also draw them up. I'll be a better assistant to Dr Lipman.'

'In what respect?'

'He's a botanist and research scientist in environmental chemistry. He'll be collecting specimens from the river and wetlands, storing and testing them, and also comparing them to samples taken previously. I'm familiar with the processes of scientific research. I have skills in data analysis, comparative studies and modelling, all relevant to what he does.'

Lisa looks up from her iPad. 'Do you know what I do?'

'A little.'

'Tell me about it.'

'As part of the water security project, structural and civil engineers are required to consider dams and other large infrastructure solutions. As an environmental engineer, you'll work with ecologists to assess the feasibility of land restoration in areas previously drained for grazing, agriculture and plantations.'

'Why?'

'Natural floodplains and wetlands have been lost. This has serious implications for the environment because it threatens habitat and biodiversity. If there's less water in the future, or a larger population, you have to work out how to find alternative sources, while preserving the sources that are left.'

Lisa blinks. 'How does the Macquarie team, as a whole, fit in?'

'It has an environmental focus. Rivers, streams, estuaries, swamps and marshes all form part of a network. Within the parameters of the water security project, your team will survey what plant and other species were found in these places in the past, which ones are there now, and what could be reintroduced if the sites were rehabilitated.'

Hugo rubs around the back of his neck. 'You got it.'

Tedeschi's smile is apologetic. 'This knowledge, while impressive, is largely irrelevant to the secondment.'

'Knowing what Dr Lipman is trying to achieve in his research might encourage him to be more supportive.'

Lisa smiles. 'Possibly not, but let's hear it anyway.' She lifts her brows. 'In layman's terms, sum up his research.'

'If land is inundated, it changes the soil, and that means different plants will grow. He's working out what the soil is like now, what it was like previously, and what the impacts of a drier, or wetter, climate will be.'

Hugo sits back in his chair. 'You've been busy.'

'I went to the library. I read journal articles.'

'What are you up—'

'Wetlands are a habitat and refuge for native plants and animals.' I glance at my bag lying at my feet, praying I have this right. 'And frogs.'

'I don't—'

'In the Grampians, you've been studying the southern bell frog, which is also known as the growling grass frog and the golden bell frog.'

Lisa laughs. 'Let me guess. You know *a little* about frogs as well?'

'*Ranoidea raniformis* mates in August, and the females lay their eggs in October and November. Which is a problem if you don't have wetlands, because unless the ground is flooded in summer, the tadpoles won't survive.' My words trip over each other. 'Only sustained wetlands can support the southern bell frog, which is why it's listed as vulnerable. Diminishing frog populations have environmental ramifications in the Macquarie region as well.'

Lisa's lips are pressed tightly together, suppressing a smile. 'If Hugo won't ask, I will. How many species do you know a little about?'

'I borrowed some books.'

'This frog from the Grampians. Does it croak?'

'Short grunts, then a deep drone.'

'Hugo?' Lisa lifts a brow. 'Do you have any questions?'

He unlocks his jaw. 'Patience will know the distribution, habitat, dimensions, call and status of any frog I name.' He stands. 'No questions.'

'How are your admin and communication skills?' Lisa asks.

'Proficient.'

'We all,' she waves her hand around the table, 'have to write regular reports and document our progress. We also have to contribute to the water security project's social media profile. Dr Lipman is useless at it, and Hugo's not much better. Could you assist them? Put everything in simple terms like you just did?'

'If they outline what they're doing, sure, I could write it up.'

Lisa twists in her chair, puts her hand on Hugo's arm. 'What do you think?'

His face is set. 'I don't need help with social media.'

Lisa shuts her tablet with a click. 'Instead of focusing on what Patience can't do, perhaps you could all focus on what she—'

'Lieutenant.' Tedeschi nods formally. 'It was delightful to see you again, and I thank you for your application. You'll be informed of our decision in due course.'

I stand. 'Professor.'

'Thanks for coming in.' Lisa, still smiling, leans across the table to shake my hand. 'I hope we meet again soon.'

Hugo, muttering under his breath, pushes in his chair. 'I'll walk Patience out.'

CHAPTER 8

Hugo, turning sharply left when we reach the bottom of the stairs, strides along the path to the courtyard.

I run to catch up. 'I don't know about all the frogs, only the Grampians and NSW frogs. I should have confessed to that.'

He stops so suddenly I almost crash into him. 'You have a phenomenal memory. Don't apologise for it.'

'Where are we going?'

He sets off again. 'I don't want interruptions.'

The nymph watches on as we enter her courtyard. As I prop my bag against the seat, Hugo, arms crossed and face set, looks down on both of us.

'You shouldn't have applied,' he says.

He doesn't lie. *And I'm not very good at it.* 'I want to get off the base. The captain requested it.'

'You said you'd never come back to the country.'

'I said I'd never *move* back. Anyway, I won't be living in the towns; I'll be at the river.'

'Lisa wants you.'

'You and Dr Lipman don't, and I'm not sure about the professor. Will I get enough support?'

'If the professor is on side, you're in,' he says, as he walks to the nymph. He studies her closely, bends his knees to shift the vine from her plinth. Her legs, modestly crossed at the top of her thighs, are smooth and slender.

'I meant what I said, Hugo. I'll work hard.'

'For the first six weeks, you'd be assigned to Rick.'

'Do you hope I'll fail immediately?'

His mouth firms. 'So long as it's in the job description, you do what we want, when and how we want it. No questions or arguments. No trouble.'

Walking past him, eyes straight ahead, I face the nymph. *Like me, she locks her secrets in her heart.* I stand on my toes and, finding fresh threads of vine, I gather them together, concealing her body and most of her face.

'Imp? I want your agreement.'

'I have a term of my own.' Turning towards him, I put my hands behind my back. 'Treat me as you would anybody else.'

His eyes are unfathomable, deep as the sea. 'You trusted me once.'

'Now I know better.'

'You don't like me.' His eyes are darkest green. 'Why join the team?'

'It's not that I don't like you. It's …'

He pushes a hand through his hair. 'What?'

I loved you.

No matter how much training I did in the pool, I lacked the physique to be competitive other than in school and district competitions.

Hugo won at every level. When he was sixteen, he was offered a sports scholarship at an exclusive private school in the city, but by then he'd discovered biology and the importance of the rivers on his doorstep, so he turned it down. He cut down his swimming hours and raced less often. He studied harder at school and stopped asking me to do his maths homework. Even so, until he was twenty, in his third year of university, he was voted in as swim captain, meaning his parents hosted the club's social events at their farm. Start of season. Easter. Mid-season. Octoberfest. End of season. Christmas. I couldn't get to Horseshoe Hill without help—and I'd never ask for help—but Hugo invariably arranged for someone, often one of his succession of girlfriends, to pick me up from the corner of my street and drop me home.

He never acknowledged I was more important to him than any other member of the squad, but he didn't hide the fact that he looked out for me. When I didn't turn up for training. When I swam too many laps and threw up. When I swore at the coaches. After a while, I got used to it.

Did he care about me more than the others?

Breathing, tumbling.

I don't remember caring about whether he cared or not until my seventeenth birthday.

I fell off a horse called Jackpot.

I fell in love with Hugo.

If anyone had noticed, they wouldn't have thought anything of it.

Everybody loved Hugo.

When I finally matured, my body shape didn't change as much as I would have liked.

Waif. Foundling. Sprite.

Hugo was the only boy I wanted, and I dreamed he'd want me too. Our eyes met constantly. Smiling green on troubled blue. If I was quieter than usual at training, he'd call. If I was at a party, sitting in the shadows, he'd come and join me.

Sometimes he'd be cranky and then he'd apologise. He'd tell me to hurry up and finish school. I'd never said much about my parents, but one day I told him what Phoebe, Prim and I planned to do. I'd move out of home first, take a gap year and work full time so I could help support my sisters. Phoebe was training to be an occupational therapist, and her placements limited her ability to work. Prim needed speech therapy and braces and had three more years of school. Once she'd finished, we'd leave the Dubbo house.

We'd be free of my father.

After I'd finished school, and before my full-time tutoring job was due to start, Greta Halstead, for the third year running, asked me to work at the farm to help prepare meals for the itinerant workers. This solved another problem too—Hugo had quit swimming and we'd both had end-of-year exams. It was weeks since I'd seen him.

Greta was warm and welcoming, and Derek was gruff but kind. Hugo's brothers worked on the farm but came and went. They ribbed Hugo for preferring science books and horses to cattle, sheep and quad bikes, and me because I was even more of a nerd than Hugo. It was a *normal* family. I did my best to fit in.

At night, when I'd finished in the kitchen and Hugo was done with fencing or whatever other work he'd been assigned for the day, we'd sit on the day bed on the verandah, close without touching. We sat together at the dinner table too and after that we'd read, do jigsaw puzzles, play board games or watch television. He'd flop on the sofa when I called my sisters, waiting for me to finish before herding me to the kitchen for a snack.

'You need to fatten up.'

'Like a heifer?'

The day before I was due to go back to Dubbo, Hugo's family were in town for the evening. I must have known that Hugo would object to a picnic by the creek because otherwise I wouldn't have ambushed him, fresh from the shower with a towel around his waist, with a hamper.

'Hurry up,' I said, doing my best to keep my eyes on his face. 'I've packed all your favourites. Let's go to the river.'

When droplets of water fell from his hair and rolled down his face, he swiped them away. 'We can eat on the verandah.'

'We don't have to stay long.'

It was the year before the drought ended—the cracks in the paddock were centimetres wide and the grass was scrappy and pale. The water was sluggish over the rocks, barely a trickle. Hugo placed the hamper between the roots of a giant paperbark tree. Kicking off my boots and socks, I bunched up my dress, twisted it into a knot and tucked it in at the top of my thighs. Hugo was crouching by a log when I scooped up water and tossed it.

His hair was dark gold; he laughed as he pushed it back. 'Come here,' he said, holding out a hand.

I checked the skirt of my dress was secure before crouching next to him. 'Are you looking for tadpoles again?'

'Spotted grass frog.' When he pointed, our shoulders touched. 'See?'

I watched the tadpoles, svelte black bodies darting through the water, but every other sense was trained on him. My body warmed; my face flushed.

'They're called aquatic larvae, aren't they?'

When I looked up, he smiled into my eyes. 'You've been listening.'

'If I didn't listen, I wouldn't know that frogs are terrestrial adults.'

He was suddenly serious. 'Why do you think I call you Imp?'

'You said I was impatient,' I said.

His eyes were on my mouth. 'Things change, don't they?'

We stood at exactly the same time. I took a step up the incline, so our heights were more even. My heart banging hard against my ribs, I grasped his hands. And, after a tiny hesitation, he threaded his fingers, cold from the water, through each one of mine. He lifted our hands and ran his mouth across my knuckles.

'You're beautiful, Imp.'

His chest was hard against my breasts as I stood on my toes and wrapped my arms around his neck. His hands trailed over my shoulders, his fingers soft and then firm. He lowered his head and his mouth covered mine. The touch of his lips, the warmth of his kiss, weakened my legs, shot darts through my heart. His lips skittered and skipped, harsh and faint and sweet and rough.

'Beautiful.'

He cupped my face, stroked across my cheekbones with his thumbs. He traced my hairline, found a curl and played with it. He pulled the band from my hair and watched the ends unravel.

'It's like wheat,' he muttered.

He touched my mouth with a fingertip, pressing gentle and then hard, groaning a breath when I bit. When I leaned into his body, he took my bottom lip into his mouth and ran his tongue across my teeth.

'Oh!'

He lifted his head a fraction. 'Yes?'

'Yes.'

When I pushed back his fringe, he closed his eyes and we kissed again. His breathing was deeper than it was, but his body was rigid, immoveable. His scent was intoxicating. He kissed the corners of my lips, found the tip of my tongue, nudging and circling, tentative, careful.

'You taste of strawberries,' he whispered.

The heat in my veins, a shallow summer stream, pooled in my breasts and belly and thighs. His tongue slipped and searched, soothed, swept and slid. I wanted his hands on my body, searching and soothing, sweeping and sliding. I yanked at his T-shirt and found the warmth of his neck, the thick strong cords, the softness of skin. I inched back a little, freed my mouth a fraction.

'I love you,' I said.

He lifted his head, tucked hair behind my ear. 'You're too young to know that.'

'I'm not.'

There was passion and laughter in his eyes. 'I know more about love.'

'That's not—'

'Hugo! Patience!'

Derek, Hugo's father, shouted out from the other side of the river. Greta, wearing a floral dress and heeled red shoes, shouted out too. I'd never seen Greta on the quad bike before. *I should have sensed that something was wrong.*

'It is time to come home!' Greta called out.

Hugo held my hand as we walked back to the farm. An ant had bitten my ankle—I hadn't even noticed—but Greta sent me inside to find antiseptic and a plaster. I could only have been gone for ten minutes, but by the time I returned to the verandah, *everything had changed.*

Greta bustled past me, tugging Derek with her. 'Hugo will talk to you, liebchen,' she said. 'When you are older, you will agree. It is better like this.'

CHAPTER 9

'Why have you stopped rowing?' Rick asks.

I've been at the river with Richard Lipman, Professor Tedeschi's senior colleague and the botanist on the Macquarie team, for the past eight days. In his early forties, he has short brown hair parted neatly to the side and is always cleanly shaven. Underneath his life-jacket and waterproof, he wears corduroy trousers, a long-sleeved solid coloured shirt and matching socks.

'I'm admiring our surroundings.' I point to the goanna, mottled chocolate brown, lying on sandstone pockmarked with age. As if aware he's being looked at, he lifts his head and peers around. 'It's like he's waiting for a bus, isn't it?'

'I have work to complete, lieutenant.'

From three-thirty in the morning until we get back to the campsite four or five hours later, Rick collects water and plant samples from the river, checking and re-checking I've recorded exactly where they're from. In the dinghy, he sits on the bench seat to my left. He stands on my left, excruciatingly careful not to touch, in the makeshift office and lab he's set up in one of the caravans. Eating together at the picnic table, which only happens occasionally and always after hours, he's on my left or diagonally opposite.

The dinghy has a brand-new outboard, but Rick doesn't like the noise so dissuades me from using it. I enjoy the quiet too, but I'm rowing further and further each day to collect the samples he's after. It's drizzling again. I pull up my hood and reclaim the oars.

'You work hard to save the planet, Rick. It might be good to sit back and admire it from time to time.'

The glassy smooth river is dark before dawn but sparkles blue and green when the sun comes out. River red gums dip their toes into the water, and thousands of crickets turn on and off like taps. I'm manoeuvring around a log when our caravans appear through the trees.

'I examine the planet microscopically, Lieutenant Cartwright.'

I speak through a yawn. 'I wish you'd call me Patience.'

'You're here because of your naval credentials.'

'Yes, but—'

'Hugo calls you Imp.'

I slap the surface of the water with an oar, jarring my wrist. 'He doesn't do that in front of other people.'

'This is patently untrue.'

I laugh. 'Yes, Rick.'

'It's a shortening of impatience, isn't it? He also called you impossible. He didn't want you to be given this position.'

I'm dry and warm. So why do I shiver? As Rick has taken charge of the satellite phone, I have no idea whether he's reporting to Hugo or not.

'When were you last in touch with him?' I ask.

'By phone or in person?'

'Either.'

Rick purses his lips. 'Do you think me pedantic, lieutenant?'

'Often you're simply annoying. When did you last communicate with Hugo?'

The touch of a smile. 'I responded to his email.'

'How many emails has he sent since we've been here?'

'Four.'

'When was the most recent?'

'Last night.'

'What did he want?'

'He didn't want anything. He asked whether you were suitable for your role.'

I take a breath. 'How did you respond?'

'I wrote that he was incorrect in his assessment regarding our ability to work together. You are extremely intelligent and eminently suitable.'

I choke out a laugh. 'Thank you, Rick.'

He looks over my shoulder, the closest we ever get to eye contact. 'You and Hugo were friends when you were young.'

'That's right.' Splash. One two. Splash. One two. 'How did you and Hugo meet?'

'I was an examiner on his PhD thesis. Later, we worked on a project in Western Australia. He insisted on sitting next to me in the evenings.'

'You didn't want him to?'

'No, but he was persistent. I became accustomed to his company.'

'So now you're friends?'

'I respect his work ethic and loyalty. He says we are friends.'

'I think he'd be a good judge of that—he always had a lot of friends.'

'You and he aren't friends.'

'I …' As the boat glides onto a strip of sandy soil, our makeshift loading ramp, I secure the oars. 'We have little in common.'

'Eliza and I lived together for three years.'

'Was she a friend?'

'She was my de facto wife—an academic and also autistic. Hugo suggested we might not have suited because we had too much in common.'

I wave away a fly. 'Three years together is a long time.'

'Hugo should have told me what he thought earlier, instead of waiting until we'd grown apart.'

I hold back a smile. 'If he had told you, it could have hurt your feelings, or Eliza's.' I clamber over the containers to the bow. 'Leaving the decision to both of you was the right thing to do.'

'Hugo didn't approve of your decision, Lieutenant Cartwright.'

I sigh. 'Which decision in particular?'

'You ran away to sea.'

'I didn't run away.'

'You were forced to come back.'

My throat is suddenly tight. 'I was sexually harassed, and undermined, by a commanding officer.'

'You were unable to defend yourself?'

'I didn't take the steps I should have, and then I lost my temper.'

'The perpetrator was at fault.'

'Grantham was a sleaze and a bully, but he still got away with it.'

'You applied for this job because you were in trouble again.'

'Thanks for the reminder.' I hop out of the boat, take the rope and loop it around a tree. Holding the bow to steady it, I brace my foot against a rock. 'Ow!'

'You should see a doctor.'

'I already have. Can you get out of the dinghy, Rick, so I can unload? I'm starving.'

Rick stands with his feet apart to get his balance before holding onto the bow with both hands. As he swings a leg over the edge, I move to the side so he can be on my left.

CHAPTER
10

After three weeks of working with Rick, I've developed a number of practices that tie in with his. Following our early morning shift on the river, I eat breakfast at the picnic table before swimming lengths of the broad stretch of water adjacent to the campsite. In the outdoor shower, I wash my hair and check for leeches before dressing and tapping on the door of his work caravan. We label and store his specimens, and he tells me what he wants to achieve next time we go out. And, more and more regularly, he hands over his laptop. I create spreadsheets and enter details about the morning's activities, and because I type so much faster than he does he dictates responses to emails from colleagues and students at the university. I also draft his social media posts.

He's usually sitting or standing only a metre away as I work but is so intent on what he's doing that I have pockets of time to familiarise myself with his documents and share drives. *To spy.* And to make myself feel better about spying, I think about it as a way of ruling him out as a suspect.

Rick and Professor Tedeschi work independently in their specialist fields, but the professor's role as lead scientist in the water security project, and Rick's senior role, also require them to carry out administrative tasks. Hundreds of consultants, mostly engineers and scientists, are employed to work on the teams, and Rick and the professor have to approve invoices before they're paid.

As I can only access Rick's share drives after he's logged in and handed over his computer I have limited time to search, but over the past week I've found multiple documents relevant to the project's finances. One of the more comprehensive spreadsheets, produced monthly, names the project team, the contractors and consultants, a brief description of work undertaken, the number of hours charged, and total amounts claimed.

Rick has been looking through his microscope for an hour, occasionally making handwritten notes, while I build on the searches I did yesterday. As invoices are entered into the monthly spreadsheet in order of receipt from all the different teams, there are hundreds of entries. I use pivot tables to search, looking for possible anomalies in total and average consultant charges, total and average work hours charged per—

'Oh …'

Rick looks up from his microscope. 'Is there a problem, lieutenant?'

'No problem.' Leaning over the laptop screen, I lift my arms and stretch my shoulders. 'I'm a little stiff from rowing.'

As Rick returns to work, I consider the data again. The hours charged by consultants varies from month to month depending on the activities carried out, and number of staff employed. But by sorting the consultants by hours charged per month, I notice two of the consultants, working in two different teams, the Flinders and

Macquarie teams, have claimed *identical* hours of work for not only last month, but for the three previous months. After glancing at Rick, back at the manuscript with a hand at the small of his back, I sort for total invoice amounts for the two consultants.

The invoice amounts differ every month, but only by a few hundred dollars.

'Lieutenant?' Rick is standing next to me again, but is focused on the sheaf of handwritten notes on his side of the desk. 'It's one-forty. You break for lunch at one-thirty.'

I force a smile. 'Thanks, Rick. I'll just finish this.'

Next, I search the invoices on which the spreadsheet data is based, to find those for the two consultants. Each month's invoices record general details of work carried out, and total hours charged. The only difference in the *total* amounts of each invoice, is attributable to 'miscellaneous office disbursements' such as photocopying, stationery and postage.

A different total would make a duplication less likely to be detected.

Rick shuffles papers beside me, licking a finger to separate two pages.

My stomach rumbles. 'I think I'll have a toasted sandwich for lunch.' My words are stilted, but Rick doesn't appear to notice, snapping the papers on the desk to line up the edges.

I put the December invoices for the two consultants side by side on the screen. The dates are out by a few days, and the consultants have different names and bank account details, but they charge for the same hours, and the description of work performed is similar. Not only that, the pattern for the January, February and March invoices is the same. What is going—

'Lieutenant!'

'Oh!' I step sideways, put my hands behind my back. 'Yes?'

'What are you doing?'

'I was ...' The December invoices are still lined up on the screen. Consultant name, date and bank account details on the top right-hand side. Miscellaneous amounts at the bottom. Totals, hemmed in by one line at the top and two lines underneath, on the far right-hand side. Differences are minor. Similarities flash like neon lights.

'Financial information is confidential!' Movements jerky, Rick picks up the laptop and, screen still up, holds it to his chest.

'It didn't mean anything to me.' I line up my notebook with my pens. 'Why would it?'

Rick puts the laptop down but immediately picks it up again. 'Please leave, lieutenant.'

How could Rick do something wrong when he worries obsessively about doing everything right?

It's not the first time I've had that thought as, half an hour later, Rick, pale and shaky, steps out of his caravan.

'I made lunch for both of us.' I push a plate and sandwich to the other side of the picnic table and pick up my own, nibbling a corner. The toast is like cardboard on the outside, and soggy on the inside. The cheese is hard, the tomato cold.

'Why were you in the share drive?' Rick asks. 'Why look at the spreadsheets and invoices?'

I wish my story was better. 'You and your plants, Rick, it's a bit like me and numbers. I was updating your hourly charges for the team, like you'd asked me to do, and then I got curious about how many hours other people charged.'

'The invoices, lieutenant. They're almost identical.'

I take another bite, chew thoughtfully. 'I wondered about that too.'

'Each month, Professor Tedeschi reviews the contractor's invoices, to ensure claimed work has been completed, and I am charged with confirming that all is in order before payments are made.' He pushes the sandwich away. 'There is an expression, lieutenant, that you will be familiar with. Rubber stamping.'

'You didn't check what the professor had approved?'

He taps repeatedly on the table. 'The Macquarie team has never engaged the consultant named on the invoice.'

I pick up my sandwich, put it down again. 'There must have been a mix-up.'

Rick stands. Clicking his fingers repeatedly, he paces up and down in front of the caravan. 'I'll report this to the professor.'

'That sounds like a good idea.' I indicate the chair opposite. 'But you don't look well, Rick. Sit down first and eat your—'

The door of the caravan slams shut.

After his first call with Professor Tedeschi, Rick settles a little. He informs me that, as the professor gave strict instructions that he should keep this information to himself, he didn't tell the professor that I also knew about it.

'It was confidential, Rick, as you said.'

When the professor calls back, Rick takes the call in his caravan, but he's still sufficiently agitated to share most of the details afterwards. Professor Tedeschi reassured Rick that the circumstances are curious, but on a multi-billion-dollar project such as this, administrative errors are to be expected. He told Rick he'd spoken to someone familiar with financial matters and had been informed that, yes, mistakes might have been made, but these could be remedied. Which begs the question ...

Does Professor Tedeschi know more than he's letting on? Or am I overthinking this because I'm on the lookout for financial irregularities?

The day after I discover the invoices, I drive to the closest town. Sitting in the four-wheel drive outside the supermarket, I report my findings to Captain McCarthy.

'It warrants further investigation, sir. But I'm sure Dr Lipman isn't involved. Professor Tedeschi, I can't be sure about. On the bright side, Rick seems to accept that I stumbled on the information in error, and the professor doesn't know I'm aware of it.'

'I'll pass on your concerns to the auditor-general's office, but they're unlikely to act in haste. There might be nothing of substance. If there is, the office will want to investigate before alerting wrongdoers, lest they seek to cover their tracks.'

A semi-trailer loaded with sheep, their frightened faces pressed against the crates, rumbles past. 'What should I do now?'

'The same as before. Eyes open, mouth shut. As you appear to have Dr Lipman's confidence, see how this plays out between him and the professor.'

'I've lost access to Dr Lipman's files, sir.'

'As you were caught red-handed, lieutenant, what did you expect?'

On Wednesday, my twenty-fourth day at the river, I scrabble down the slope to the water and sit on the sand near the dinghy to take off my shoes and zip up my wetsuit. Sliding into the water, cautious of roots and debris, I strike out in freestyle. The fish, small, brown and gold, slice through the water like shadows. I duck dive and touch the sand before I surface again and float on my back. The tree canopy is thick, and the autumn sun is high and bright. Disco spangly lights burst through the foliage.

When my mother was in the hospital, my aunt played 'Dancing Queen'. Was that Mum's favourite—

'Lieutenant!'

'Oh!'

Rick, standing on the riverbank, has a phone in his hand. 'Greta Halstead called.'

I focus on the ripples on the water. 'You know her?'

'We met in Melbourne last year. She has asked me to lunch on Monday.'

I swim breaststroke towards him. *Hands together. Hands apart. Frog kick.*

'Greta is a wonderful cook.'

'It will take us two hours to get there.'

'Is that your way of asking for a lift?' I pull my hair to one side, squeezing it out as I walk up the bank. Wide strips of bark, like layers in a ballgown, gather round the trunks of the river red gums.

'Greta wants you to accompany me.'

CHAPTER 11

The main street of Horseshoe Hill has a large general store and two neat rows of terraced shops and offices. The Royal Hotel, a two-storeyed brick pub with stained-glass windows, wrought-iron fretwork and a balcony, sits proudly at the crossroads. The noticeboard of the small primary school, complete with an 1800s schoolhouse, is almost obscured by bottlebrush trees.

Sports carnival this Friday!

'How much further?' Rick shouts from the rear of the four-wheel drive.

I take out my ear pods. 'About fifteen minutes.'

He's sitting on the left of the seat, with papers and books spread out to his right. 'When you are anxious,' he says, 'you listen to ABBA.'

I meet his gaze in the rear-view mirror. 'We all have secrets.' As soon as the words are out, he stiffens. 'Rick. I didn't mean—'

'The invoices, lieutenant. You mustn't say anything to Hugo.'

'What would I say? I don't know anything.'

'The professor is continuing to investigate the matter.' With agitated movements, he stacks his books and papers. 'This is appropriate.'

'Which means you have nothing to worry about.'

He nods, but I can that see his heart isn't in it.

'Doing your admin kept me busy, and it lets you spend more time on research,' I say. 'I hope you let me do it again.'

'Do you give me your word that you won't talk to Hugo?'

'Why are you so adamant about that?'

'He would ask questions, of me and Professor Tedeschi. Hugo always asks questions.'

Slowing just before the T junction, I take a turn-off. To my right, buttercup yellow canola crops march up the hill.

'I won't say anything, so long as you keep your mouth shut about ABBA.'

His hands unclench, and he picks up his book. 'I agree.'

A stand of paperbark trees marks the entrance to the Halstead's farm. The letterbox, a large timber crate, has faded in the past nine years. *Bright crimson to pink.* Rick mutters complaints as I negotiate a dip in the roughly graded road and the car bounces over the cattle grid. A sheaf of his papers falls off the seat and onto the floor.

'Please pull over,' he says.

When I stop under the shade of a scribbly bark tree, low hanging leaves scatter shade on the bonnet. I open the window, close my eyes, and breathe in eucalyptus.

Long summer holidays in Warrandale. The Halstead farm at Horseshoe Hill. Sun-kissed skin, tangled hair and sunshine. The river and the creek and the dams.

I don't want to remember, but I can't forget.

Ignoring Rick's complaints as he sorts out his papers, I open the door, smooth the creases in my dress and turn sideways in the seat to stretch my legs. My sandals have laces that cross up my calves and I retie the bows. Crickets start up. When I'm at sea, I miss kookaburra laughs, cockatoo squarks and—

'We can proceed,' Rick says.

I put the car into gear. 'Maybe you should look around before we get to the house?' I point out the brown and white Poll Hereford cattle that gather under the trees at the side of the road and, near a milky brown dam, a pocket of land that's ploughed and ready for planting. 'Greta and Derek love this farm; they've worked for decades to make it what it is.'

'Greta spoke well of you. Do you like her?'

I liked her much too much. 'Yes, and Derek. I think you'll like him too. He doesn't say much, but he knows a lot, and he never stops working.'

Derek trained as a carpenter, so once he'd saved the money to buy this land he set about building a functional blonde brick house. New additions—bedrooms and a pool room to accommodate the three Halstead boys, and an enormous kitchen commissioned by Greta—were haphazardly tacked on to the original structure. At a few hundred hectares, the farm is comparatively small and has limited access to the river, but it's suitable for grazing and cropping and there are three or four large dams.

As we drive over the second cattle grid, Greta, wearing an apron over her blue and white dress and waving what looks to be a tea towel, appears at the top of the driveway.

'Patience!' she calls out, continuing to wave the tea towel as if we might not have spotted her. 'Dr Lipman!'

Not much taller than I am, Greta has a rounded figure and an abundance of thick grey hair that she ties back with a scarf. I've barely stepped out of the car when she grasps my arms, looking at me closely before hugging me tightly.

'Patience Cartwright,' she says, her words a little breathless, 'every time you are prettier.' Still holding my arms, she pushes me away to have another look, before pulling me into a second hug. 'And you wear a pretty dress. *Schöne mädchen*. You remember this?'

'Beautiful girl.' I smile. 'How could I forget?' I look around. 'Your house and garden, Greta, everything looks lovely.'

She lets me go and beams. 'You must see my geraniums!'

Hugo's paternal grandparents migrated from Austria to Australia after the Second World War, and Derek was raised in Tamworth. Greta was born in Austria but came here for a holiday in her early twenties. She was working as a fruit picker when she and Derek met at a dance. Horrified that he barely knew a word of the language of his forebears, she pledged to teach him. According to Derek, he tolerated the lessons but never learned a word—all he wanted to find out about was Greta.

'Thank you for your kind invitation.' Rick directs his words over Greta's shoulder.

'I said you must come if you were in the district,' Greta says, holding up a hand to shade her eyes. 'Derek will be here very soon.'

'Where is Hugo?' Rick asks.

'He cannot come.' Greta looks at me before quickly looking away. 'He is busy with other things.'

'We had matters to discuss,' Rick says.

Greta glances at me again. 'He lives not too far away, only twenty minutes, on the other side of the town. Perhaps ...'

On the rare occasions Greta and I have seen each other in the past nine years—the Warrandale fete, Gus's annual fundraiser, outside the church at Phoebe's wedding—she's gone out of her way to greet me. It was thoughtful to invite me to lunch, and she won't want to disappoint Rick.

I touch her arm. 'I could take Rick to Hugo's after lunch.'

Greta clasps her hands. 'Did Hugo tell you? He has bought the old brewery.' Her forehead furrows. 'I correct myself. Hugo and the bank have bought the old brewery. I do not know how the loan was approved, when the house is falling down.'

'Hugo wanted the land,' Rick says. 'He'll rehabilitate the creek.'

'That boy should have been born a fish,' Greta says, 'for the time he spends at the creek. And if not a fish, a horse. For his horses are more comfortable in the paddock than he is in the house. His father wanted him to demolish it and build a nice modern home, but Hugo would not listen.'

'He replaced the roof,' Rick says.

'If my dear mother,' she makes the sign of the cross on her chest, 'saw the state of Hugo's kitchen, she would turn in her grave.'

I smile. 'Your mother was a good cook, wasn't she? Like you are.'

'My mother was an excellent cook who enjoyed a simple life. Even so, she liked her bed to lie flat on the floor.' She holds out an arm and angles her hand. 'The rooms at the back of Hugo's house are sloped like this. He comes home often but what does he do? What does he do today? He digs at the creek!'

A tractor rounds the corner, with Derek in the cab and two kelpies perched beside him. Derek lifts his hat.

'Be with you in a jiffy,' he shouts.

One of the dogs jumps from the tractor, kicking up dust as he darts through the paddock and slips through the fence to the garden. At first, he greets Greta, but when I kneel, he dives at me, pushing me back on my heels.

'Soxy!' I rub his head and stroke his ears. 'How are you, lovely boy?' He licks my hands as he attempts to wriggle onto my lap. Now he's fourteen he has a greyish-white muzzle to match his four white paws, but his eyes are bright and his black coat is glossy. 'It's good to see you too.'

Greta smiles. 'He has a good memory, this old dog. You remember the drives to the swimming pool, yes? He wanted human company. He would not be left behind with the other dogs.'

'He snuck onto my lap in the back of the car.' I smile up at her. 'And into my bed when I stayed here.'

'This was against the rules.' She waves her tea towel at Soxy. 'While you wash your hands, Patience, I shall call Hugo and let him know to expect you.'

'If he's too busy to see us, we'll head back to the campsite.'

Rick speaks little at lunch. Derek, after asking after my mother and sisters, and updating me and Rick on his cattle and sheep and crops, dedicates himself to enjoying Greta's slow-cooked lamb and vegetables, and apple strudel with cream. After lunch, he offers to do the dishes and shoos Greta away. Rick, who keeps looking at his watch, declines to come with us when Greta takes my arm and announces we'll walk around the house so I can see her flowers.

The window boxes Derek built are even more numerous and substantial than I remember, all bursting with colourful geraniums. Greta snaps off a flower and hands it to me. 'It is a match for your dress.'

'Thank you, Greta.' I smile. 'And thank you for lunch.'

'You know all of my secrets, after working with me in the kitchen.'

'I'm not so sure about that.' When Soxy trots around the corner and sits at my feet, I stroke his head. 'All I did was chop vegetables and wash the dishes.'

As we move to the rear of the house, admiring the flowers in the window box outside the pool room, she pats my hand. 'Even after the accident, you came back.'

Three cows, all with calves close by, stand under the patchy shade of the stately gums in the home paddock.

'You don't have horses here now?'

'Hugo's brothers do not ride, and Hugo keeps his horses at the brewery. When he is away, the girls from the pony club care for them.'

Rick, pacing up and down in front of the four-wheel drive, points to his watch as we round the corner. When Greta titters a complaint, I smile. 'I'd better get going.'

She tightens her grip on my arm. 'It has been too many years,' she says. 'I knew you as a little girl, and as a young woman. I missed you, liebchen.'

'I missed you too, but ...' My throat is suddenly tight. 'I travel a lot. When I'm not on a ship, I live on a base.'

'But next time you see your sister, you will visit us? We are little more than an hour from Warrandale.'

I nod stiffly. 'I'll try.'

She sighs. 'You do not forgive Derek and me. This is true, yes?'

Derek's second kelpie lies on the balcony with his chin on his paw, waiting to get back to work. Three deep breaths. One. Two. Three.

'It was a long time ago.'

'I was afraid for you.'

'I'd made a mistake.'

'You have found another boy?'

I scrabble for keys in my bag. 'I've had boyfriends, if that's what you mean.'

'But no *particular* boyfriend?'

'I'm happy with my life as it is.'

'Yes, yes.' She smiles bravely. 'We are proud of you, working so hard for the nation.' She links her hands. 'An officer, a lieutenant. We are very proud. And what you do for Rick at the river, this is also important. Hugo says you will also help him and Lisa.' She looks down as she smooths her dress. 'You have met Lisa? Is she pretty?'

The car isn't locked, but I push the remote. 'She's intelligent and has a good career. But yes, she's also very attractive.'

'This Lisa, I believe she is Hugo's girlfriend.'

'I wasn't sure.' I force a smile. 'I'm sure you'll like her.'

'How will I know that? If Hugo will not talk about his girlfriends or bring them home to Horseshoe Hill.'

'Maybe he does bring them, but you don't know about it?'

She's genuinely surprised. 'You think he could smuggle in a girl without me, his father, or the town knowing of it?' She shakes her head. 'This is impossible.'

It's no dustier or hotter than it was, but suddenly the air is suffocating. I hurriedly kiss Greta before opening the door. Rick stands at the side of the car and leans over his seat, arranging books and papers. I place the flower on the dash and stare at it, not sure what to say next.

Greta touches my arm. 'Patience?'

I school my face before I turn. 'Rick wants to get back.'

'Are you still a swimmer?' she asks. 'You loved to swim. Always the first in the pool, and always the last to come out. Your mother was in New Zealand, she could not come. And your father, that man …' She looks at me, and then away. 'He never came. He never saw.'

'I swim when I can.' My voice wavers. 'And when I can't, I like to be close to the water.'

'You and Hugo were happy at the pool, yes? He took care of you. You cared for him.'

The geranium sits brightly on the dash, but it won't survive without water. Once I'm in the car, I open the glovebox and lay it on the logbook. Notwithstanding the dust, I keep my window down, breathing eucalyptus till we turn onto the highway.

Sunshine, shy smiles, sprints and steady strokes. Frog kicks, duck dives, tumble turns.

Deep breaths. Heartbeats.

Heartbreak.

Hugo and I were happy at the pool, just as Greta said.

We were happy till we kissed.

After Greta and Derek found us at the river, we agreed to return to the house. Hugo had the picnic basket in one hand, and my hand in the other. He said he'd never let it go, and as if to prove it, he dropped the basket but never my hand when we opened and shut the gates. As we approached the house, he talked about that day, and the next, and the days after that. How he'd keep hold of my hand.

When we finally got back, Greta and Derek were waiting on the verandah. I was sent to the bathroom where Greta kept her medicine box, to put antiseptic and a plaster on the bite on my ankle. I washed my hands, splashed water on my face and peered curiously into the mirror. I had no idea a kiss could be like that. *Surely* I'd look different.

Fair hair. Blue eyes. A scattering of freckles and a generous mouth. Beautiful? I couldn't see it. But …

He'd thought me beautiful.

Greta, tugging Derek's hand and telling me to go and talk to Hugo, rushed past me as I walked out of the house. Hugo was on the day bed on the verandah, forearms on his knees, looking across the paddocks.

He jumped to his feet. 'Imp.'

I touched his arm. 'What's the matter?'
I probably only took in half of what he said.
You're barely nineteen and have just finished school.
I grew up a long time ago.
Your homelife is a shambles.
I manage.
You've never had a boyfriend.
I only want you.
We can take it slowly.
I'm impatient.
You're vulnerable.
I am not!
How could you know about love?
Maybe I don't after all.

My mother had left me. I hated my father. I'd lied to teachers, social workers, my friends and their parents, so I could stay with my sisters. I'd been right to only trust them. I couldn't trust anybody else.

Especially not Hugo.

I called him an arrogant prick. I told him I never wanted to see him again.

And then I left him behind.

CHAPTER 12

Fifteen minutes after leaving the Halsteads' farm, I turn off the highway towards the town, take the tree-lined road adjacent to the park and follow the river to a single-laned bridge. A weathered post supports a sign. *Horseshoe Creek*. This is the point where water flowing from the densely treed Horseshoe range meets the river. A hundred metres further on, there's a left-hand turn down a pot-holed bitumen laneway.

'It can't be far now.'

Metre high drystone walls disappear into bushland either side of Hugo's driveway. The letterbox, a sun-bleached timber keg with metal bands around the middle, sits next a pillar. Two gates, wrought iron and black, lean haphazardly against the trunk of a red gum. The tree bark is smooth, the leaves long and slender.

All I can see of the house from here is two tall chimneys topped with terracotta pots. There's a paddock to the left, dotted with gums and fenced with posts, rails and wire. A large black horse and a much smaller pony with a silver-grey coat lift their heads when they see the four-wheel drive. The creek, narrow and with steeply sloping banks, carves a line to the right of the driveway. Either side of the creek are mounds of freshly dug earth and groupings of logs of varying length. Pots of saplings, shrubs and grasses are arranged in drifts and cross-hatched lines as if ready for planting. Seventeen rows of four, thirteen rows of seven, fifteen rows of eleven. Three hundred and twenty-four.

Turning back to the driveway, I'm blinded by sunlight. Blinking hard, I slow the car and pull down the visor and—

'Oh!' I slam my foot on the brake. 'Oh.'

Late afternoon sun casts a soft golden glow over the mottled yellow stones of the two-storey house. It's not a mansion, but far more substantial than a cottage. The verandah is broad; the roof tiles are slate, coloured charcoal grey. Four wide steps lead to the verandah and double front doors. The downpipes and gutters are new and grey like the roof. There are gaps on the top level, four tall rectangular spaces where windowpanes should be. From up there, there'll be views all the way to the river and park.

'The house was built in 1888,' Rick says. 'It belonged to the brewery owner.'

'No wonder Hugo is keeping it.'

'Repurposed materials and tradesmen are expensive,' Rick says. 'It would be far less costly to build a new house.'

'That could never be as beautiful.'

There's not even a hint of a garden, and the parking area is a wide strip of gravel close to the house. As I park next to another white four-wheel drive, presumably Hugo's, the horses, as if curious, walk across the paddock towards us. The tall one has a white star on his forehead and hangs his head over the timber railing, but the pony is too small to do that, and pushes his head between the wires lower down. His mane is shaggy and long; his forelock hangs halfway down his nose.

Rick is animated, stepping out of the car before I release my belt. When I jump down, he's waiting. He immediately points to the creek, the earthworks and hundreds of plants.

'The brewery cleared the land, changed the creek's flow and polluted the soil,' he says, as if answering questions. 'After the brewery closed, the land was used for grazing. Cattle destroyed what remained of the creek environment.'

The creek is like a channel, a canal. Besides weeds, the sides are bare. 'Greta said Hugo spends all his time down there.'

'Upstream, the habitat is diverse. Fallen trees and branches trap and collect water. They create shelter and micro-environments.' He points to the mounds of earth and logs. 'Until the trees grow, the logs will replicate this and—'

Hugo, an Akubra low over his forehead, is operating an excavator—like a tractor with a scoop on the front. His back is to us as he reverses the machine up from the creek, but when he spins it around and sees us, he jerks to a stop. Lifting the scoop high, he cuts the engine and jumps to the ground. He takes off his hat and pushes back his hair. He wipes his face with a sleeve.

Resisting the temptation to smooth down my dress, I lift a hand and wave. Rick is already ten metres away, rushing towards Hugo.

'I'll wait here,' I shout.

Rick walks quickly, meeting Hugo between the four-wheel drive and the creek. When Hugo holds out his hand, Rick briefly shakes it. They exchange a few words before Hugo walks to me. Given his pace, the uneven ground and the zig-zag trajectory through the rows of vegetation, we could close the gap with forty of his steps and forty-five of mine. Approximately. But then …

We'd be in the exact same space. My body and his.

His stomach is flat, his shoulders are broad. He pulls his shirt away from his skin but when he lets it go, it sticks right back again.

I tear my gaze away. 'Greta called, didn't she? Rick wanted to see you.' I slow down my speech. 'We can't stay long.'

He has dirt on his cheek and a tear in his shirt at the elbow. 'How was lunch?'

'Great. It was good to see your parents.' I search for something else to say. 'Soxy remembered me.' I take a step back. 'I like your house.'

He wipes his hands down his jeans. 'The kitchen's around the back. Help yourself to tea and coffee. There's juice and water in the fridge.'

Treat me as you would anybody else.

I fumble for my phone. 'I'm fine out here. I'll make a few calls.'

'Sure,' he says as he walks away.

I can't call Phoebe, because in Norway it's five in the morning. When I call Prim, her phone goes through to voicemail and I leave a message, letting her know it was nothing important. She texts right back. *About to castrate a bull. I'll call later.*

The men are deep in conversation as they walk through the rows of pots to the creek. Sometimes Hugo crouches, gesturing as if pointing things out. Five minutes pass, maybe ten, by which time they've walked so far along the creek that they're hidden behind the house. I retie the laces on my sandals and follow the path to the paddock and the horses, still waiting by the fence.

When we were still at school, Phoebe took Prim and me to the horses she cared for. Sometimes she'd saddle them up and lead us around the paddock, but being Phoebe, she was cautious, so unless the horse was exceptionally quiet, she'd keep hold of the lead rope. Even so, I learned the basics.

My job description for this secondment includes horse riding. Hugo made it clear it was important. And equally clear he thought I couldn't do it.

With good reason.

Once a year, the senior squad members, ranging in age from sixteen to twenty, spent an Octoberfest weekend at the Halstead's farm. Greta was welcoming but firm. No alcohol, pills or tobacco. One bedroom assigned to girls, another to boys. She'd cook schnitzels as big as our plates and make sauerkraut. Derek, who made vats of non-alcoholic cider, claimed he could smell Greta's pretzels—hand-baked bread shaped into knots and sprinkled with salt—from anywhere on the farm.

Angela was nineteen, the same age as Hugo, and made no secret of the fact that she liked him. He'd recently broken up with a girl from university, and Angela thought going horse riding with him would be a good opportunity to be noticed. On the basis that Hugo wouldn't abandon his other friends if only she were interested, she asked me to come along too.

'You hardly ever get to ride,' she said. 'You'll enjoy it.' I was aware she was using me, but she'd given me a lift to the farm and I needed one back. Anyway, I liked horses; I wanted to ride. Angela asked Andreas, Hugo's eldest brother, to choose three horses and saddle them. As Angela and Hugo were experienced riders, Andreas assumed that I was too.

I was playing pool with Hugo and the others when Angela walked into the room. 'Patience and I have a surprise for you,' she said.

Hugo looked from me to her. 'What?'

Angela took my arm, like we were co-conspirators. 'Come outside and you'll see.'

The curtains in the pool room were closed, but even in the gloom, Hugo's eyes were bright.

'What's going on, Patience?' he said. 'You're on my team.'

'Finish the game without her,' Angela snapped.

Three horses were tied to pieces of string hanging from the fence. One horse was Hugo's, a big grey thoroughbred. I thought Angela chose to ride the other gelding because the quarter horse mare, Jackpot, was slightly smaller, but afterwards I wasn't so sure. Jackpot was spirited. Did Angela want to look more competent than me? Was she jealous that Hugo had chosen me over her for his team?

We were in the home paddock, only a few hectares, and the land was relatively flat. Jackpot fidgeted when I shortened the stirrups and climbed the fence to mount. The paddock was at the back of the house, and I could hear the others hooting and shouting—the game must have ended. Angela cantered across the top of the paddock. She whistled. 'Hey guys! Out here!'

I *vaguely* remember seeing Hugo, his height and tawny hair. He didn't shout, but I had an inkling he wanted to. 'Patience. Get off that horse.'

Greta's giant brass cowbell hung on a hook outside the kitchen. When she wanted to get everyone's attention, she'd lean out of the window and hit it with a drum mallet—a drumstick with padding on the end. Breakfast, morning tea, lunch, afternoon tea, dinner, supper, Greta was *always* feeding guests. Jackpot must have heard the bell before—countless times—but as it rang out, she shied.

My foot slipped out of the stirrup. I should have regained my balance before I searched, but I leaned forward in the saddle and looked behind me, finding the stirrup a moment before she shied again. My other leg flew backwards, kicking her in the flank. For the second time, the bell rang out.

She bolted.

I stayed on her back long enough to see everybody running to the fence. Had Hugo climbed over it already? I don't recall. Angela was somewhere behind me, screaming my name. Reaching the fence at the end of the paddock, Jackpot turned sharply right. My sneaker pushed through the stirrup iron as I was thrown from the saddle. Only I wasn't *completely* thrown from the saddle.

My foot was caught in the stirrup and I was dragged along the ground.

A kaleidoscope of rocks and stones, grasses and weeds and dirt. Sharp black hooves, four, eight, sixteen, thirty-two. How far did I count? And how many hoof beats to a minute. Two minutes? Three? Blood in my mouth, thick and metallic. Ripped jeans. Stretched limbs. Suffocating dust. Bumping and scraping and kicking. I thought about Phoebe and Prim. They couldn't stand up to our father like I could. Who would protect them if I wasn't there?

Finally, no sounds, sights or smells. No counting.

Silence.

When I came to, the sun was an orange fuzzball, hidden in the clouds. Someone, Hugo's second brother Mateus I think, was telling Angela to stop screaming, and everyone else to stand back. Greta was there, wringing her hands. I couldn't see clearly until someone wiped my face. The cloth was cold and wet. I touched it with my tongue.

'She's awake.'

'More water.'

'Keep her still.'

'Where's the doctor?'

'Get her a drink.'

The words repeated one after the other like a relay. One swimmer gets to the end of the pool, the next swimmer dives. *Don't take off too early. Wait till I touch the wall.*

'Imp?'

Only Hugo called me that, so I wasn't too surprised to see his face. He was dabbing my mouth. His face was blurry. His *eyes* were blurry.

'Hugo?'

'The ambulance is coming,' he said.

I could see and hear. When I shifted my legs, my ankle hurt. 'Ow.' I opened and shut my fingers, tested my wrists and elbows.

'Don't let her move.' That was Derek, as white as a sheet, peering over Hugo's shoulder. 'Stay still, love, that's the way. The paramedics will be here in a jiffy. They'll patch you up.'

'I don't want …' It wasn't easy to talk, and there was a weird taste in my mouth. My saliva was thick and viscous like—

Hugo tried to keep me on my side when I choked, but when I fought against it, he helped me to sit. I coughed up so much blood it formed a puddle in the dirt.

'Your lip's cut, Imp. And—'

I took the cloth and held it to my lip. I spat into it, staining it red. When I ran my tongue along my teeth, I was relieved they all seemed to be there. Derek, holding a green and white pitcher of water, one of Greta's special ceramic jugs, knelt on my other side. We were in the paddock close to the fence, not far from where I'd started out.

'My face hurts.' I put a hand to my cheek, but it was too sore to touch. 'Is Jackpot all right?'

'She's okay,' Hugo said. 'She's fine.'

'She didn't mean it. Her hooves. She didn't know.' I could barely understand my own words, but Hugo made them out.

'Stop talking, Imp. Who do we call? Your father? Phoebe?'

I closed my eyes, but that felt even worse than when they were open. I pressed another cloth against my mouth. Hugo winced.

'Careful.'

I was dribbling and couldn't stop. It hurt to swallow. 'What's wrong with me.'

'Let me.' He took the cloth and laid it, tentatively, against my nose and mouth.

More blood.

'Don't call my father.' I tried to sit straighter, but my hip pinched and my leg wouldn't do what I wanted it to. 'I'll tell Phoebe if she asks.'

His green eyes were wet like mist on grass. 'She'll ask.' Each touch more careful than the last, he pulled strands of hair, sticky and red, from my face. He wiped my forehead. 'Fuck, Imp. *Fuck.*'

I was done with sitting up on my own. When I leaned against his chest, he stiffened and swore again.

'What?'

'Nothing.' He put his arm around my front. 'You stay there. Nothing.'

'Reckon you've buggered your collarbone, son.' Derek grimaced. 'We'll get the paramedics to check you out too.'

Hugo kissed the top of my head and I thought: he's never kissed me before. I was disoriented and confused. I ached all over. I had an English test on Monday. Phoebe would worry about me. Prim would fuss.

'I'll be okay tomorrow.'

Hugo made an odd noise, something between a laugh and a sob, but by the time I looked up, I could only see his profile. His lips were clenched tightly. His eyes blinked.

'Hugo?'

He did his best to smile. 'Impatient.' With blood-stained shaky fingers, he pushed back my hair. This time, he kissed my forehead. The hitch in my breath had nothing to do with the pain.

That's when I knew that I loved him.

CHAPTER

13

There's still no sign of Hugo or Rick by the time I reach the horses. When I hold out my hand, Hugo's black horse, his muzzle soft and velvety, sniffs and nudges. I think he's a thoroughbred, the breed of Phoebe's horse, but he's more solidly built than Camelot. And he's even taller.

Greta said: He took care of you. You cared for him.

That was true. *But it wasn't enough.*

The large horse backs up, moving away from the fence, but the pony stays where he is. His tail swishes and his ears are back. As I move closer, I see his problem—a ring on his halter is caught on a join in the wire.

I hold out my hand. 'Do you mind if I help?' The pony stands still as I attempt to lift the strap free of the buckle, but it's impossible to see what I'm doing from this side of the fence. Do I climb through? The black horse isn't far away, but he seems to be happily grazing.

I bunch up my dress and climb between the wires. But when the pony turns towards me, the strap pulls tight across his eye. Am I making things worse? I scan the creek but there's no sign of Hugo.

'If you let me undo the buckle,' I tell the pony, keeping my voice low, 'you can go eat grass with your friend.'

He's still again, his dark eyes wary as, using both hands, I release the fastening. Free of the halter, the pony pulls back, shaking his head and snorting before trotting to the middle of the paddock. I smile. 'No need to thank me.'

I'm prising open the wire by tugging at the halter when the other horse walks up behind me. Heart thumping hard, I drop the halter and turn. My sandals have thin soles; I have dust between my toes. His hooves are big and black like rocks and—

My throat clamps tight. I walk backwards, my hands extended to ward off the horse. When he follows, his dark eyes enormous, I glance at his hooves again. I don't want to see them. But it's better that I do, isn't it? To know exactly where they are.

When I reach the fence, I close my eyes and breathe deeply. I'm not lying at his feet, but standing on the ground. I only have to push against his chest or his shoulder, just like Phoebe explained, and he'll step away.

Ears pricked, he lowers his head. He wants me to pat him? Tentative at first, I straighten his forelock. But when he looks at me trustingly, I rub between his ears and stroke his cheek.

'You are a very handsome horse.' He lowers his head even further, as if in agreement. But when he lifts a rear leg before kicking it to the ground, I jump. The fence is at my back. If I turn away and slip through the wires—

He steps even closer, shoves his head against my stomach. The ground is uneven, hoofmarks carved in solid dry earth. I reach for the top railing and catch it but my foot slides down the slope and I fall awkwardly to my knees.

I know what to do—jump to my feet.

But I freeze.

I count.

Four black hooves. Eight, sixteen, thirty-two, sixty-four, a hundred and twenty-eight, two hundred and fifty-six. Chipped ankle, torn ligaments. Split lip, black eyes, fractured cheekbone and—

'Imp! Get up!'

Hugo leaps over the railing, landing on his feet and standing between me and the horse. He pushes the horse hard in the chest.

'Back, Arrow! Get back!'

Hemmed in by the fence, I scramble sideways like a crab. But when I try to speak, all I manage is a squeak. Hugo, a crease between his brows and a smear of dirt on his forehead, crouches next to me.

'Are you hurt?'

'No.' I bring up my knees and lean forward, putting my head between them. My dress has ridden up; I push it over my thighs. *Do not throw up on his boots. Do not throw up on his boots.*

'What happened?'

'He kicked his leg.'

'What?'

'He …' I force out words. 'Arrow stamped his foot.' As if the horse, picking at the grass ten metres away, is listening in, he stamps his foot again. 'Like that.'

Hugo frowns. 'He had a fly on his leg. That's how he gets them off.' He puffs out a breath. 'Why are you in the paddock?'

I glance at the halter, still attached to the fence. 'The pony was stuck.'

'Lavender?' One of his sleeves is up and the other is down. His boots are damp from the creek.

The lace of my sandal puddles around my foot. But when I lean forward to tighten it, I'm suddenly dizzy. Swallowing hard, I rest my head on my knees.

'With horses, wear boots,' he says as, muttering under his breath, he wraps his fingers around my ankle.

It would be *so easy* to give into his touch. But I bunch my hands into fists and yank my foot free. 'I'm fine.'

'You're not.'

I lean forward again and fumble for the lace. 'I might not have to ride when your team goes to the river. I could walk behind.'

'It'll be ten kilometres each way,' he says. 'Uneven ground, steep inclines. Twenty kilo pack.'

'I'm fit.'

'You'd have to run to keep up. No one's that fit.'

'I'll make it work.'

A hesitation. Then, 'Come to the house, Imp. I'll get you a drink, something to eat.'

'I have water in the car.'

'You've got a two-hour drive.' He searches my face. 'Does Rick help with the generator? Does he pump water? Change gas bottles?'

'Sometimes.'

'I don't believe you.'

'It's my job to do it.'

'He told me the hours you work.'

'I'm used to early starts. I have capabilities.'

'You think I don't know that?'

'I'm expected to work with all of you, I need to do the whole job.' I lift my chin. 'Anyway, you're meant to keep the personal out of this.'

He turns away abruptly. 'I know the theory.'

I point my toe and tighten the lace. 'Oh!' I have a new mark, a long angry graze, on the foot I hurt at the breakwater. I push my palm against it.

Hugo holds out a hand before pulling back. 'What's the matter?'

'Just a scratch,' I say as I stand. 'It's fine.'

He takes care to stay between me and the horses as we walk to the gate. As he opens it wide, our eyes meet.

Picnic baskets. Holding hands.

I tear my gaze away.

CHAPTER 14

I drag the windsurfing board and the sail onto a narrow strip of sand at Lake Burrendong. This section of the lake, which didn't exist until the river was dammed, is used for recreational activities—windsurfing, kayaking, paddle boarding and fishing. The early morning drizzle has cleared but, besides the staff in the hire shop and kiosk and two men fishing off the jetty, the place is deserted. Untangling hair from the zip of my wetsuit, I reach for the board again.

'Hey!' The man in charge of the hire shop, Jason, is about my age. He's slender but muscled. 'I'll see to that.'

Jason is leaning against the counter when, showered and changed, I leave the change rooms. I twist my hair, winding the plait into a coil.

'It was good to have the lake to myself. Thanks for the board.'

'It's one of mine.' He looks me up and down. 'To tell the truth, I didn't think you'd have the technique to handle it.'

'Then why let me have it?'

'You asked for it.' He grins. 'And don't get me wrong, it was good to be impressed. Not often I get clients like you. Where'd you learn?'

'All over the place. I'm in the navy.'

'No kidding?' He smiles as he reads my indemnity form. 'Patience, right? My shift ends in an hour. Can I meet you in the pub up the road, buy you a beer?'

'At eleven in the morning?' I pick up my bag. 'No thanks.'

He grimaces. 'How about a coffee?'

'I'm meeting my sister for lunch.'

'She can come too.'

I laugh. 'Perhaps another time.'

Phoebe often runs late, but Prim is generally punctual. I'm walking from the car park when she appears at the entrance to Dubbo's open plains zoo, her glossy dark ponytail swinging.

'Patience!'

Prim qualified as a veterinarian last year, but still volunteers at the zoo. Her uniform, a khaki cotton shirt with matching pants, complements not only her colouring but her shape—she's tall and slender with very long legs.

'It's s …' She stands back and smiles, deepening her dimples. 'It's good to … see you.'

Prim's speech hesitation became a full-on stutter when she was seven, after Mum had the stroke. She has numerous strategies to deal with it, but still finds many sounds difficult.

'I bought our lunch in Dubbo. Is it okay to eat it at the zoo?'

Her head tipped to the side, she reaches for my still damp plait and holds it up. 'You've been … swimming, haven't you? If we … sit near the Galapagos tortoises, do you promise not to go in their pond?'

When Prim talks to the woman at the gate, telling her we'll just be an hour, the woman looks from Prim to me.

'This is your sister? You don't look at all alike.'

Prim used to ask why she looked different from me, Phoebe and Mum. Most of all, she worried that her colouring came from our father. I once found her rifling through Mum's meticulously labelled photo albums—time capsules of how things were when Mum was well. There were very few photos of Dad, who we'd only ever known to have grey hair, but there were a lot of photos of aunts and uncles and cousins.

'Uncle Bob has brown hair like mine,' Prim said, as if that explained everything—even though Auntie Kate was our father's sister, so Uncle Bob was only related through marriage.

I searched for the kinds of words that Phoebe would have found. 'Me and Phoebe would love to have your dimples, and your long legs. Anyway, it doesn't matter what colour eyes or hair or skin you have. We're the three musketeers. It's what's inside that counts.'

There are four Galapagos tortoises in the pen near the entrance. They amble laboriously, as if dragging their giant shells is difficult. And they chew slowly, on long slender branches with glossy bright foliage.

'What are they eating?' I ask.

'Mulberry and hibiscus leaves.'

We choose a seat close to the tortoises, and I set salad rolls and bottles of water between us. Prim pulls a folder from her bag.

'It's not fair that you provide lunch as well as help with this,' she says.

'I'm off work for a couple of days.' I point to the folder. 'How did you go with the application for Darwin?'

'I've incorporated all your … suggestions.'

'Demonstrating you'll be in a position to analyse and disseminate results within a few months of getting the placement will strengthen your application.'

She smiles. 'It worked last time.'

Prim is doing post-grad studies in animal pain relief and relies on grants to pay the fees. For this application, I've helped her sort data into tables and graphs.

She checks her watch. 'Have you ... seen Dad yet?'

'I told the nursing home I'd be there at three.'

'It upsets you.' She attempts a smile. 'Don't do it.'

'You did it last month. Anyway, it's for Phoebe, not him.'

'You'll need all your strength.' She hands me a roll. 'Eat your lunch.'

'Give me the folder,' I say, as I peel back the wrapping paper. 'I can think while I eat. Have you got a pen?'

'How's the new job?' Head down, she searches in her bag. 'You must miss your ship.'

As I take a bite of roll, one of the tortoises, smaller than the others, wallows in the pond.

'The river is beautiful, especially in the mornings. The birds and wildlife are amazing, and I'm learning a lot from Rick.'

'W ... what about Hugo?'

Hugo never came to our house, but my sisters knew how much I liked him. Phoebe was cautious about it because I was still at school and he was at university, but after my accident she had many long phone calls with Greta, who reassured her that when I was ready to come back to the farm, she'd keep a close eye on me.

'I won't have much to do with him.'

Prim taps a long slender finger against her chin. 'I ... worried about you.'

Two tortoises reach for the last of the mulberry branches. The larger tortoise tugs and the other one lets go.

'You don't need to worry—or say anything to Phoebe. I'm on secondment, that's all there is to it.'

'You'd never choose to … work for Hugo Halstead.'

I summons a smile. 'Last week, I took one of the other scientists to Greta and Derek's for lunch.'

'You loved that family.' She picks a piece of tomato out of her roll. 'How are they?'

'The same.'

'Pity their … son was a shit.'

'Prim!' I choke.

She thumps me on the back. 'There's no delay with "sh" sounds.'

'Hugo felt differently than I did. End of story.'

'You … stuck your neck out,' she says. 'You trusted him and he let you down.'

'I don't know why it hurt so much.' I neatly fold my paper bag. And then I fold hers. 'What about you? Still specialising in one-night stands? You're careful, aren't you?'

She wipes her hands on her pants. Then she addresses the tortoises. 'I'm done with fooling around.'

'Phoebe found Sinn,' I say. 'They're perfect together.'

'Just like you thought you and Hugo … would be.'

'Everything is different now. For starters, he has a girlfriend.'

The largest tortoise ambles towards the pond. When he plonks himself down on the muddy banks and closes his eyes, I yawn in sympathy. I was only windsurfing for a couple of hours. Why do I feel so tired? I stretch out my foot, hiding a wince when it pings.

Prim smiles uncertainly, her dimples only hinted at. 'Are you sure you're okay?' she asks.

After Dad fell and fractured his hip, Phoebe finally agreed he should have full-time nursing care, and found him a room in a nursing home close to where he'd spent most of his life. He now walks with a stick but as he refuses to participate in any social activities, he spends most of his time alone. His room has a large window that overlooks well-kept gardens, and beyond them the highway into town. We were encouraged to furnish the room with personal items to make it more like 'home', but he was so angry about leaving his house that he refused to select anything. In the end, we bought him a bookcase and fitted in as many of his books as we could.

His thin white hair is almost translucent. The scars on his head—shrapnel wounds—are a constant reminder of Vietnam. He's elderly and unwell. He's paranoid and has dementia. I *should* feel sorry for him, but it's far easier to dislike him, just as I have for as long as I can remember.

He looks up from his notebook. 'You're here.' He slams down his pencil before reaching for his walking frame. 'Take me home.'

I put a bag of groceries in the kitchenette, near the small fridge. 'I've bought raspberries, and your favourite honey.'

'Take me home!'

'This is your home now, and they look after you well. I hope you don't yell at the carers and nurses like—'

'Where is your sister?'

I pretend not to know what he means. 'Prim?'

'The eldest! Tell her to come. Tell her to take me home!'

I line up tubs of yoghurt. 'She's away with Sinn—they won't be back for weeks.'

His fists clench. 'She gave her word she'd look after me!'

Phoebe insists that, so far as our father was capable of loving anyone, he loved Mum. And I suppose she must have felt *something* for him. But after she had the stroke, it played into Dad's paranoia. He blamed the doctors, the hospital, the government, and became even less rational than he'd been. Phoebe wouldn't have wanted to frighten us by telling us what would happen if the school or anyone else discovered what our father was like when no one was watching, but she had no choice.

We'd be separated.

A carer wheeling a tea trolley, cups and saucers rattling, pauses at the door. 'Would the professor like a cuppa, dear?'

'Dad? Would you like anything?'

'Take me home!'

We spent holidays with Auntie Kate and Uncle Bob in Warrandale. The river. Gum trees. Kookaburras. We also had the long-distance love of our New Zealand family. We became accustomed to our father's many rules. Don't enter my study. Don't raise your voice. Don't slam the door.

We were well behaved and largely compliant. We did well at school. Because I was good at maths, Dad gave me permission to swim. *Strong body, healthy mind.* He also let Prim keep her animals, her injured birds and lizards, appreciating the scientific nature of her passion. But Phoebe?

She was terrified of losing us. She was terrified of him. She tiptoed around him, and we mostly followed suit. Not to please him, but to keep our sister safe.

I unzip a duffle bag. 'One of the carers said you needed new pyjamas. I bought two pairs.'

He jerks the walker back and forth. 'They steal from me.'

'You should be grateful the laundry takes care of your washing.'

'Your sister should do it!' His hands clench, white and bony fists. 'Call her! Tell her to come!'

We had an outside laundry in the house we grew up in, semi-underground with a narrow door and small louvred window. The interior was sparse—a top loading washing machine and a concrete sink. One winter's day—years after he'd locked Phoebe in the hall cupboard—the washing machine unbalanced, shuddering so loudly that Dad heard the noise from his study. He could have turned off the machine, but he wouldn't get close enough to the noise to do that. Phoebe ran past Dad and pulled out the plug.

He switched off the light. He shut the laundry door and held it tight.

Screaming Phoebe's name loud enough to scare my father, but not so loud that the neighbours might hear, I pushed past Dad and opened the door. Phoebe was huddled on the ground, curled up like a ball. I stood on a box to open the machine, pulling out the clothes and throwing them in the basket before jumping to the ground again.

'If I give you the pegs,' I said to Phoebe, 'can you hang them up? I can't reach the line.'

'You're twelve years old.' Tears ran down her cheeks. 'You're so little.'

'Dad is a bully.' Standing on my toes, I hugged her, and to give her something else to think about, I swore. 'He's a *fucking* bully.'

CHAPTER 15

Rick darts between the caravans as I untie the dinghy. He checks and rechecks the gear he's left behind even though, in just a few days' time, most of it will follow him back to Melbourne. Late morning sun hides behind clouds as I look at my watch again.

'Rick! Are you ready?'

Hugo and his colleague, another biologist, are meeting us a few kilometres away. They'll consult with Rick at the place where the river widens, before deciding where to set up camp. After the meeting, Hugo will take Rick to the airport. Meanwhile, I'll spend one more night here, pack up the rest of the gear and arrange for the transfer of the dinghy and caravans.

'Rick! We're already late. And I want to be back before dark. Hurry up!'

It was almost a week ago that I slipped in the paddock. Within a couple of days, so long as I strapped my foot and wore boots, it barely troubled me. But when my alarm went off at four this morning, my foot was puffy and the pain had spread up my calf. Now? I'm tempted to untie my lace and, just as I did at dawn, slide my leg into the water to ease the throbbing.

I press my hand to my forehead. I took two paracetamol an hour ago, but I still feel hot and clammy.

'One,' I mutter to myself as Rick scrambles down the slope towards me, 'get Rick to Hugo. Two, load the four-wheel drive. Three, find a doctor.'

Rick's backpack and boxes take up most of the bow, so we're lower in the water than usual. And, given the meeting point is five kilometres away, I doubt I have the strength to row there. Rick sits on my left as I lay the oars on the floor of the boat and start the outboard motor. I ignore his complaints about the noise.

'Better duck your head.' Green and red parakeets squabble in the foliage as we motor to deeper water. Usually, I'd comment on the birds, but it's all I can do to steer the boat. My throat is parched, but whenever I drink from my water bottle, my stomach churns. I count slowly to ten as I wait for the nausea to pass.

'I'll return by the end of next week,' Rick says.

'While you're in Melbourne, make sure you take Eliza out to dinner.'

'Why?'

'She's been hinting about it all week. And no wonder.' For a moment I'm blinded, even though the sun can't possibly have moved. I blink and release the throttle. 'Reading three thousand words of your article must have been painful.'

'Her feedback was valuable,' Rick concedes. 'As was yours.'

'I get paid. Eliza helped because she cares about you. That's why I think it'd be nice to take her out.'

Rick taps his foot. 'What is Melbourne's most expensive restaurant?'

I manage a smile. 'How would I know that?'

He frowns. 'I'll ask Hugo.'

'You do that.' I push down another wave of nausea. 'In the meantime, if you want me to update your spreadsheets, let me know.'

'I'll email.'

The dinghy's frothy wake mirrors the clouds above us. When bile comes up my throat, I determinedly swallow it down.

'Even after you've finished your work, you pace in your caravan. No one can survive on two hours sleep a night. When you get back, we'll talk about the invoices again.'

'Professor Tedeschi is looking into the matter.' Rick's arms are tightly crossed. 'You gave your word not to talk to Hugo.'

I nod reluctantly. 'I did.'

We travel in silence for the rest of the trip. Hugo calls Rick twice to see where we are, and Hugo, standing on a log at the riverbank, is the first thing I see as we round the bend in the river. Broad shoulders, muscled arms. Tawny hair, gold like a lion. Last time I saw him, he was in Horseshoe. A degraded creek. A neglected but beautiful house. When I drove away, I looked in the rear-view mirror. Sandstone walls, yellow like butter. A charcoal-grey roof and a backdrop of gums. The sun slipped lower in a faded blue sky.

His world. *Not mine.*

I cut the engine and take an oar—dip, sweep, dip—guiding the boat to the shore. Hugo has stubble on his face, and creases in his shirt. His hat casts a shadow. Leaning one hand on the bow, he reaches for the rope with the other.

'Patience.'

Handing him the rope, my fingers brush his. It's only a momentary touch, but my heart skips a beat. 'Hugo.'

When I stand, my weight barely shifts, but all of a sudden the dinghy starts to spin. That doesn't make sense. And nor do the lights in my head.

'Lieutenant,' Rick says, grasping the seat either side of him. 'What is the matter?'

I sit again, hold on tightly.

Hugo tugs, bringing the boat alongside the log. 'What was the hold-up?'

When I open my mouth and nothing comes out, I fumble for my drink bottle. Wasn't it blue? Why is it white?

Sparkling like a unicorn.

I suspect Hugo is scowling, but his face is a blur. When the dinghy spins again, my stomach heaves.

'I was responsible for our delay,' Rick confesses.

Back at the campsite, we had clear flowing water. The river here is a murky shade of brown. The plants near the shore are decaying. Where are the fish? What about frogs?

Does it matter? The water will be cool. I'll feel better in the water. I lean forward, find the ends of my laces and tug on the bows. *Hugo said I should wear boots.*

'Imp!'

'Lieutenant!'

The dinghy stops spinning. Something digs into my back. Pain in my head. Yet ... I want to sleep. If only the sun weren't so bright. I lift an arm to shade my eyes. The shouting is close, but I can't decipher the words. The dinghy shifts as someone climbs into it.

A hand, blissfully cool, on my cheek.

His voice is loud and insistent. 'Imp.'

Green eyes deep as the ocean.

CHAPTER 16

This room is chock-full of unicorns.

There are lights above me and around me. Even through my eyelids they sparkle and flash.

'Patience.'

I blink into the brilliance.

Prim, shiny brown hair falling over her shoulder, holds my hand tightly. No dimples. She's crying.

'What's the matter?' I'm certain I say the words, but I don't think she can hear them. I lift my arm but can't bend it. I try again. Why can't …

A cannula. Two cannulas. In my wrist and in the back of my hand. Drip stands either side of me. A nurse dressed in blue.

Back to sleep.

Awake.

Asleep.

The blind is drawn over the window. Does that mean it's night-time? It's impossible to tell with so many lights. Lights in the ceiling are lined up in rows. Three, six, nine, twelve. Other lights flicker like traffic lights. Red. Amber. Green. The nurse's station is outside my door, a schema of lights on the desk.

An attractive doctor with clever dark eyes, a stethoscope around her neck and a clipboard in her hand, stands at the foot of my bed. Prim is here too, as is my favourite nurse. Chiara? She has a friendly smile and a tattoo of a tulip on her wrist.

Prim squeezes my hand. 'Hey.' Her smile is wobbly, but stronger than it's been. 'You have septicaemia, Patience, a serious infection. Do you remember Dr Lee? She's the ... surgeon ... who's been looking after you.'

I *vaguely* remember her visits. 'How long have I been here?'

The doctor points to the whiteboard at the end of my bed. 'This is day three.' She checks the lights on the machines. 'There's been a slight improvement.'

When I struggle to sit, the nurse adjusts my bed, pressing a button and raising the back. 'Why can I see unicorns?'

Day five. As well as the number of days I've been here, the actual date is written on the whiteboard. April 24. How many times have they taken my blood and asked for my date of birth?

I don't have to think as hard as I did.

There's someone close by, a shape in the doorway. Tall and thin. Hovering. Surely it can't be ...

No sitting up unaided like I used to, let alone standing to attention and saluting. When I fumble for the remote and push the button, the bed hums and rises. I can't have been asleep for long because remnants of breakfast are still on the tray. I reach for a cup and sip, swooshing water around before swallowing.

'Sir.'

Captain McCarthy's shirt is crisp and white, long sleeves buttoned at the cuffs. His epaulettes are black and gold. Four stripes, one looped. My bed has bars down the side and my gown has ties down the back. A catheter, drips and cannulas.

'Lieutenant Cartwright.' He nods sympathetically. 'I'm in Dubbo for an Anzac Day service.'

I look at the board again, do my best to concentrate. 'Tomorrow morning.'

He nods before looking around the room. The gerberas on the shelf near the window are from Phoebe and Prim. Yellow and red on long green stems, they pop from their box like fireworks. Sunflowers from Rick and Eliza. The roses on the shelf near the whiteboard, newly opened buds and multi-petalled blooms, are softest creamy pink, a gift from … my eyes drift shut. Did Prim tell me who sent them?

When McCarthy clears his throat, my eyes spring open. Walking to the formal arrangement of native flowers, too tall and wide to fit anywhere except on a chair near the door, he considers the card.

'I see they arrived.'

'Thank you,' I croak.

'From the base,' he says, as if I need to know the gift isn't inappropriately personal. 'We wish you a speedy recovery.'

'I won't be back to work …' My lips are dry and cracked. '… a few days.'

'Your sister said weeks.'

'Dr Lipman … Rick.' I swallow. 'The invoices.'

He moves to the side of the bed. 'There's nothing new, is there?'

What did I see? What did it mean? Burning heat, icy chills, pins and needles. 'Nothing new.'

His features are blurred, like I'm looking at him through a fish tank. Is it up to me to make conversation? 'I liked the river.'

'Would you prefer to convalesce at the base?'

'I want to …' When he rocks back on his heels, my stomach churns. But this important. I can't think why, but it is. There were frogs at the river. How is that relevant? I search for the words. 'I want to stay.'

His shoes squeak on the floor as he walks to the door and turns. 'Best wishes, Lieutenant Cartwright.'

The wheels of the trolleys. A kookaburra calling. Is the bird in a tree? Does she live in a nest with her family? Her sisters?

Where do I belong?

My eyes sting, I close them. My throat burns, I swallow. But slow steady tears stream down my face and plop, plop, plop onto the sheets. I sniff and shudder and shake.

I sleep.

'Hey.' A whisper.

Nurses chatter outside my room. One, two, three, four, five, six. It must be a change over, day shift to night shift. Even so, it'll only be late afternoon. I should be awake.

I'm holding someone's hand. Clenching someone's hand. So hard it hurts my fingers. A large hand, much bigger than Prim's. I shift my head on the pillow and …

The lights above Hugo turn his hair gold. 'Hey,' he says. He's frowning but not angry. *Concern.* Why would that be? I think for a while, and then I work it out.

'I saw a unicorn.' The words are consistent with my dream. 'On the boat, and when I got here.'

Sitting further forward, taking care of the cannula, he sandwiches my hand between his. 'What did it look like?'

'White. Sparkly.'

'Were you frightened?'

My head hurts when I shake it. 'I like unicorns.'

I lift a hand to wipe hair from my face. Swipe. I miss. Swipe. I miss.

'Let me.' He directs my hand to the coolness of the sheets before pushing back my hair. He rests the back of his hand against my face. 'I like unicorns too.'

'My eyes hurt.'

'Do they sting? You were crying.' He touches my shoulder. 'You're okay now.'

I think hard. 'Captain McCarthy was here.'

'Rest.' Another whisper. 'Get well.'

I search his eyes. Forest green. Moss green. *The green, green, grass of home.* 'I don't live here, do I?'

He hesitates. 'Not now.' When he lifts his hand from my shoulder, I miss his touch. 'You're hot, Imp.' He presses the buzzer. 'Better get the nurse.'

'She has a tulip.'

'Is that right?' He leans over me to loosen the sheet, pull it out where it's caught at my waist. I like his body. *Intimacy.* He knows things other people don't.

'Did you see the unicorn?'

'Not this time. Stay awake, Imp. Wait for the nurse.'

'What about the nymph in the courtyard?'

He picks up my hand, smooths out my fingers. 'She reminded me of you.'

My breaths are loud. Raspy. I want to close my mouth but can't. 'Hugo? You won't leave, will you?' There's something in my voice. Need? I shouldn't let him hear it. Why not? 'I can't remember.'

'I won't leave you, Imp.' He presses the buzzer again, looks up in relief. 'She's burning up.'

Rustling. Hurried footsteps. Trolley wheels. 'Not again.' My nice nurse, Chiara. She's in this dream too.

'Where is the unicorn?'

'Lie down, sweetheart.' Hugo again, pressing gently against my arms.

I look up at the lights. Blink and blink again. 'There he is. Look.' Hugo's hand is cool on my face. I lean into it, lean into him.

'I'll call Prim,' he says. 'Tell her to come early.'

My eyes are so heavy, I can't keep them open. But that makes sense.

I'm fast asleep.

This is a dream.

CHAPTER 17

Dr Lee is standing at the end of my bed again. I check the white board. *Day seven.*

'You're back on track,' the doctor says.

'Something happened, didn't it?'

Prim puts her hand on my shoulder. 'Your temp went through the roof the day before yesterday. Don't you remember?'

'I saw the unicorn again.' A shaky smile. 'Never a good sign.'

Dr Lee writes something on her clipboard. 'You're young and fit. With continued treatment and rest, you should make a full recovery.' She lifts the sheet and blanket, exposing my foot. *The initial puncture wound.* From my toes to my knee, my leg is swollen and there's a transparent dressing over a bloodied wound at the side of my foot.

'I thought it was healing okay.' I bend my knee and peer through the dressing. 'Yuck.'

'You had emergency surgery yesterday. Have you heard of Aeromonas?'

'Something to do with air?'

'It's a marine infection that's extremely difficult to eradicate. After additional laboratory tests and advice from an infectious diseases physician in Sydney, I conducted a surgical debridement.'

'That's the removal of the damaged tissue, and the foreign body that was causing the infection,' Prim explains.

'Without it,' Dr Lee says firmly, 'you could have developed gangrene and lost the limb.'

'Because of a splinter?'

'After your first injury, the bacteria lay dormant,' Dr Lee says. 'The second injury triggered the spread of the infection to deep layers of tissue.'

I consider my foot again. 'It looks a mess.'

'The wound will heal by secondary intention.'

Prim puts a hand on my shoulder. 'That means it won't be stitched. It'll be left open to heal by itself.'

'With time,' Dr Lee says, 'it will close naturally. In the meantime, you must rest, preferably with your leg elevated, and change the dressings regularly.'

I glance at my arms. 'How long do the drips stay in?'

'In addition to the infection you already have, which can only be treated with intravenous antibiotics, we have to guard against streptococci and staphylococci. Your white cell count is still extremely high, as are your inflammatory markers. You also require pain relief and fluids. You'll be here for another week, possibly longer, and then we'll arrange at-home nursing care.'

'Did you hear that?' Prim says. '*At home* nursing care. Which doesn't include a camping ground.'

'I refuse to move into a share house. Or kick you out of your bed. Anyway, you're not missing a term at the university in Darwin, or the placement that goes with it. You can't pass up that chance.'

'Your convalescence will be eight to twelve weeks, minimum,' the doctor says. 'Intravenous medications shouldn't be necessary for long, but you'll have other medications, and possibly physiotherapy. You won't need full-time care, but you will require assistance.' She raises her brows. 'I understand you're in the navy. Will your employer make arrangements?'

I turn to Prim. 'Captain McCarthy came, didn't he?'

'Early one morning. You remember that?'

'Vaguely.'

'Do you have any questions?' Dr Lee asks.

I talk through a yawn. 'Why do I fall asleep all the time?'

'You're still extremely unwell. I'll review your medications tomorrow.'

I check the whiteboard again. *Day ten.*

Everybody is talking about home. Nurses, tea ladies, doctors.

'It won't be long till you can go home.'

'Once you get home, you'll feel better.'

'I imagine you're looking forward to going home.'

I might not have a home, but I do have an income and savings. I can pay for an Airbnb until I'm back on my feet, or take a short-term lease, or …

As Prim constantly points out, accommodation like that doesn't come with personal staff, and the hospital is fussy about where I go because I'll need outpatient care for a week or two. After that, I *could* live at Phoebe's house—a converted church in Warrandale—but it's out of the town so I'd need to rent a car and I won't be able to drive for weeks and—

My phone rings. Phoebe.

'Did you sleep well?' she asks.

'Most of the night.'

'You had a terrible sleep, didn't you?'

'I woke up early, that's all.' I yawn. 'I'll sleep after my shower.'

Phoebe sniffs. 'I wish I were closer.'

'I hope you're not going to cry again. I'm fine, Phoebe, really.'

'I'm not.'

'What?'

'I'm having a baby.' Another sniff.

'What? That's wonderful! It's what you wanted, isn't it? Why are you crying?'

'It's ...' She clears her throat. 'It's the best. Sinn and I are very happy.'

'So why ...'

'Because you're sick! I wanted to come straight home, but then I started bleeding and had to rest until the test results came back and ...'

'What's wrong? Is it you? The baby?'

'We think everything is okay, but it's early days and the medical staff think we should stay for longer, just to make sure—'

'You have to stay!'

'Prim said you won't live with her in her share house.'

'You know how messy and disorganised she is, and—'

'Patience!'

I sigh. 'I want her to go to the Territory as she planned.'

'Warrandale is a long way from the hospital, but Sinn said we could get a private nurse to come and care for you.'

'A baby? A real baby? You'll be back before the birth, won't you?'

'Course I will.'

By the time Prim arrives, carrying two cups of freshly squeezed juice, I've said goodbye to Phoebe and shuffled to the side of the bed.

'Auntie Patience.'

'Auntie Prim.'

Prim wheels my drip alongside me as I walk the few steps to the chair and tray where my breakfast is laid out. We talk nonstop as I pick at cereal and an apple, pushing the coagulated eggs and bacon aside. Prim moves the tray away before sitting on the side of the bed. She unties her ponytail and reties it before smiling uncertainly.

'Prim? What's the matter?'

She stands. 'Greta Halstead called.' She flicks the ponytail over her shoulder as she stretches out her legs. 'She'd like to visit. Is that okay?'

'I like Greta.' I pluck a tissue from the box. 'It's just …'

'Hugo.' Prim fusses with the flowers, leaning the flagging gerbera heads against the upright ones and propping up wilting flannel flowers.

'I remember McCarthy's visit.' I lift myself higher in the bed, roll the tissue in my hand. 'Did I have other visitors that day?'

She sighs. 'Hugo thought you might have forgotten, so I didn't mention it.'

'I *kind* of remember.'

'It was action stations, apparently. The nurses, then the doctors. It was good of him to call me.' She puffs up her cheeks, lets out a breath. 'For the … second time.'

Prim fills me in on what happened the first time, telling me that Hugo was waiting on the banks of the river as I untied my bootlace, deliriously imagining a swim might refresh me. When I passed out,

Rick was understandably alarmed, as was Hugo, but he was far more practical.

When he called emergency services, they told him to drive me to the hospital. He refused, insisting I was in much worse shape than heatstroke or dehydration or a regular virus would explain. After he took off my boot and saw my foot was red and swollen, and I had streaks going up my leg, he explained he was a biologist, he knew about bacterial infections and cellulitis, and feared that's what I had. At that point, they said they'd send an ambulance, but he was adamant I be given an airlift to hospital, and thankfully they listened. Within twenty minutes, he and Rick had driven me to a clearing near a fire trail and I was picked up by helicopter.

Prim crosses her arms. 'Hugo … stayed in the … waiting room for hours after they bought you to the hospital, even though he knew I was the only one who'd be allowed to … see you. He calls every morning. He tells the nurses he doesn't want to disturb you, just wants to … see you're okay.'

I study the bruises on my hands. 'I'm on the Macquarie team. He'd think visiting is the right thing to do.'

'He also drove to the campsite and fetched your things.' She points. 'That's why you've got toiletries and underwear.'

I trace around the patch on the back of my hand. 'You've changed your mind, haven't you? You don't think he's a shit any more.'

'I can … see why people like him,' she says. 'And that reminds me. A woman, Lisa, called a couple of days ago. She'd … spoken to Hugo but wanted to find out first-hand how you were. There was something that made me think …' She shrugs. 'Her and Hugo. Are they together?'

'Greta assumes they are.' I pull the sheet higher over my legs, press down on the creases. 'I was grateful Lisa supported my appointment.' I smooth the tissue and bunch it up. 'If Hugo contacts you again, can you ask him to call me directly? I'm well enough to coordinate my own visits now.'

She grimaces. 'Prospectively or retrospectively?'

'He's already called?'

'You're only allowed one visitor at a time, which is … why they all call me. I can change the schedule I've drawn up to accommodate them, but—'

'I should thank him.' The tissue is a small hard ball; I pass it from one hand to another. 'When is he coming?'

'Late this afternoon.'

CHAPTER
18

He lives well over an hour away, but Hugo's hair is still damp. Was it dripping when he left his sandstone house in Horseshoe? He tucks his shirt into his jeans as he walks to my bed. His scent is fresh and clean.

'Hey,' he says.

My pyjama top has small buttons down the front, and I check them carefully. Five pink buttons. Five yellow sunflowers in the vase near the window. The pattern of seeds in the spiral of a sunflower are a Fibonacci sequence. Zero, one, one, two, three, five, eight, thirteen, twenty-one … Now my scattered heartbeat is under control, I find the remote and lift the bed higher.

'Prim told me what you did.' I cross my legs and pull a sheet over my lap. Careful of the lines, one in the back of my hand and one in the inside of my wrist, I sip water and place the cup on the tray. 'Thank you.'

He glances at the door. 'She said it was okay to visit.'

'Thank you for getting me here. And for fetching my clothes.'

'Forget it.'

'Sorry it happened.'

He carries a chair to the side of the bed. 'Not your fault.'

'Prim said Rick was upset and …' A pillow shifts and slips, and he catches it. As I shove it back into place, our eyes meet. 'Can you talk to Rick for me? Tell him I'm fine, and as soon as I'm out of hospital, I'll let him know when I can help him again.'

'Imp …' He sits forward in the chair. 'Don't rush this.'

'I was meant to be at the river with Rick next week.'

'I'll take him out in the dinghy.'

'You have your own work to do.'

'I'll sort it.'

I straighten the pillows again. 'I won't be back for a few weeks, but I can do admin and—'

'Months.' He runs fingers through his hair. 'Prim said it could be months.'

'It might not be.' The skin around the catheter on my hand is vibrant red. I tuck it under the sheet. 'They don't know yet.'

'Rick is concerned about you. And I think there's something else.' He pushes back his fringe. It's longer, scruffier than it was. 'We're ahead of schedule, but he's anxious, jittery. When I asked him what was going on, he said it was not only none of my business, but none of yours. Any idea what he was talking about?'

Am I a spy even though I'm on sick leave? I suppose I must be.

I bend my knees, adjust the sheet again. 'Has Rick done something wrong? Is that why he's anxious?'

Hugo frowns. 'Why would you think that?'

I have trouble selecting menu options for breakfast, lunch and dinner, and find it hard to draw a cross in a box. How could I possibly spy?

'Imp?'

'You said …' *Do not make things worse.* I focus on the gerberas, their sadly hanging heads. 'I didn't think anything.'

A fresh-faced student nurse hovers at the door. 'Since you're awake, can I do your obs?' Flushing as she apologises to Hugo, who walks to the window, the nurse draws a curtain around my bed. 'He looks like Chris Hemsworth,' she whispers.

I show her my hand. 'I think it's happened again.'

She sucks in a breath. 'I'll get Chiara.'

I focus on the tulip on Chiara's wrist as she leans over my left hand, eases off the translucent tape and takes out the needle. She picks up my right hand, examining it closely.

'This is the only way to get antibiotics into you, but it irritates the veins.'

'I think I'm running out of them.'

'This hand's even worse than the other one.' She goes back to my left hand, searches through the mottled bruises, prodding and poking. 'Sorry.'

My eyes water. 'That's okay.'

'You're not counting how long it takes today?'

'When I'm not delirious, I do it in my head.'

'How many seconds are we up to?'

'Inserting IV lines? When my temp went up, I was out of it and missed a day. It mucked up my cumulative total.'

She laughs. 'Estimate.'

'Two thousand, six hundred and eighty-three.' As she joins the new needle to the cannula, I unclench my toes.

'You're a brave pincushion.' She puts a hand on my shoulder as she lowers the back of the bed. 'And you're exhausted.'

My eyes want to close; I force them open. 'What time is it?'

'Almost bedtime—five o'clock.'

'Is Hugo still here?'

She silently whistles. 'Yes.'

As she pulls back the curtains and leads the other nurse out of the room, Hugo walks to the side of the bed. He glances at my hand, lying limp against the sheet.

'Get some sleep, Imp.'

I talk through a yawn. 'Prim said you came before.'

'You don't remember, do you?'

'Not much, but …' I stretch out my legs and raise the back of the bed again. 'I want to get back to work.'

'When you're out of here, we'll talk.'

'Why not now? Sit down.'

He sits in the chair, hands on his knees. Jaw tight. Mouth firm. 'Even before you were hurt, I didn't think things would work out.'

'I wasn't hurt. I started out with a problem that I didn't know I had. Rick's been happy with my work. I'll be fine to get back to it.'

'Phoebe isn't around to look after you. Is Prim going to be okay to stay?'

'I won't let her do that.'

'Do you have to do everything on your own?'

'What are you getting at?'

'When I swam,' he says, 'Greta laid out my clothes, cooked bacon and egg rolls and drove me to the pool. You walked in the dark and sat on the kerb with a towel around your shoulders. At best, you had an apple and a vegemite sandwich.'

'Greta drove me too. Sometimes.'

'You always said you had to pay your way. That's why you did my maths homework.'

'I did a lot of kids' homework.'

'They gave you second-hand goggles and swimmers. Hot chocolate in winter. You Cartwright girls …'

My fists clench. 'What about us?'

'Phoebe tried to protect you.'

'She still does.' I open my fingers, rub the cramp at the back of my leg.

'You were a fighter.'

'I wasn't as afraid of my father as my sisters were.'

'You're independent, successful, all three of you.' He stands and shoves his hands in his pockets. 'Did Greta ever tell you that she and your mother were friends?'

'What?' I blink. 'No.'

'Your father didn't want visitors, particularly people who'd known your mother. That's why Greta had to keep her distance.'

With a fingertip, I follow tiny little stitches in a hem of the sheet. Eight to a centimetre. 'I'm grateful to Greta. I learned a lot from your family.'

'You studied us so seriously.' He sits again, pushes the chair closer. 'Do you remember?'

'Derek was quiet and kind. Greta was bossy and generous. You and your brothers complained about school, got drunk, had girlfriends.' My lips are so dry and cracked that it hurts to smile, but I can't hold this one back. 'You were a family, like on TV. I was interested. I wanted to know more.'

'Impatience.' He slowly shakes his head. And then he puts his hand, tanned against the whiteness of the sheet, on the bed. 'Can I get you anything before I go?'

Besides the crimson and purple bruises, my hand is pale. I lift it off the bed, but then it flutters down again. The tips of our fingers are close.

Half-asleep. Half-sick. Half-afraid.

I don't want him to go.

After we held hands on the beach, I accused him of setting me up. Since then, besides him possibly saving my life, we've kept our distance. I can't meet his eyes because I don't know what he'll see in mine.

'Imp?' His voice is strained. His shirt cuff is blue with two white buttons. His nails are clean, but he has a callus on his index finger, three torn cuticles and a black half-moon at the base of his thumbnail.

My heart rate is up. Not because I'm unwell. Not because I'm swimming ...

In his final lap of the pool, he'd glide to the wall faster than anybody else. I'd study his technique, trying to work out how he could finish so well—time after time after time. I would have been twelve or thirteen when I asked about it—the precision of his strokes and how he measured them. When he shrugged, I did my best to explain why I needed to know.

'Your arm is like a single unit,' I said, 'divided into parts. The tips of your fingers, your first, second and third knuckles, your wrist, elbow and shoulder, are fractions of the whole.'

He smiled in the way he used to smile, crinkled eyes, generous mouth. 'It's not about counting, Imp. It just feels right.'

Having Hugo next to my bed *shouldn't* feel right because ...

As the dinner trolley rumbles down the corridor, I bend my knees and bring them up to my chest. I pull the sheet over my lap.

'When will you see Lisa again?'

'Tonight.'

He laughs with her. They shoulder bump. She takes him by the arm and kisses his mouth. No awkwardness or courteous concern. *No unhappy history.*

The dinner trolley stops at the nurses' station. Voices. Laughter. Clinking lids on mushy food.

I re-count the stitches in the sheet. 'Thank you for all you did.'

CHAPTER 19

Prim grabs the door frame and swings into the room. 'S … surprise.'

I laugh. 'Did you bring my clean washing back?'

'Whoops.'

At Prim's entreaty, Chiara finds two creased surgical gowns, blue with white ties. She supervises my shower before helping me into them—one tied at the back and one at the front.

She winks. 'To preserve your modesty.'

'I'll bring everything back tonight,' Prim says cheerfully. 'In the meantime, that colour is good with your eyes.'

I climb into bed and lean against the pillows. 'I'm feeling much better today.'

'Strong enough to face Hugo's mum?'

'Why wouldn't I be?'

She puffs out her cheeks. 'I was… sixteen. Your … sobbing made an impression.'

'I didn't sob.'

'You did it in your sleep.'

'I knew what I wanted. Hugo didn't. That's all there was to it.'

'His parents backed him up.'

'He obviously agreed with what they said.'

When I tighten the bow at the back of my neck, Prim moves behind me, untying and tying it again.

'You loved him.'

I smooth the gown over my legs. 'I thought I did.'

'It was just like *Persuasion*.'

'What?'

'Jane Austen's novel.'

'I know that, but—'

'Anne's godmother and family persuaded her not to marry Captain Wentworth, even though she loved him. He went away to sea to try to forget her.' She grins. 'Hugo is Anne. You are Captain Wentworth.'

'What the …'

'They were wrong.'

'Greta and Derek thought I needed time to grow up.' I place my hands primly in my lap. 'It's not fair to blame them.'

Prim tips her head to the side, stares into my face. 'You're … still so pale. What did Dr Lee say this morning?'

'The same thing she said yesterday. My blood count is all over the place and septicaemia, including getting over all the drugs they pumped into me, takes a while to recover from. That's why I'm so tired.' I yawn. 'It'll get better with time.'

'Which is why it's important you give yourself some,' Prim says firmly.

A tap on the door. 'Liebchen?' Greta Halstead's hair is tied back with a red and white scarf. When I smile, she puts an enormous wicker basket on the floor before rushing into the room. Frowning at my bruises, she gently pats my fingers.

'I would have visited sooner,' she declares, 'but Hugo does not tell me when he comes. He does not collect me.'

'Maybe he came straight after work.'

She purses her lips. 'His work is at the river near my house.'

Prim jumps in. 'Don't you drive, Greta?'

'Not on the left side of the road,' she says, as she takes Prim by the shoulders. 'You are a pretty girl, Primrose, just like your sisters. You are also clever.'

'Oh.' Prim's dimple dips. 'Thank you.'

Greta releases Prim and reaches for her basket. 'I have bought flowers from my garden.' She lifts one side of the basket lid and takes out roses, already arranged in a jar.

'They're lovely, Greta. Thank you.'

She looks curiously at the roses already on the shelf. Some of the heads are drooping, but the colours, the soft creams and pinks, are as lovely as they were a week ago.

'These are from Hugo, yes?'

'I don't remember him bringing them in.'

'I, liebchen, do not remember him harvesting them.'

'Are they from your garden?'

Prim grins. 'He stole them, didn't—'

'Did Derek drive you here?' I ask. 'Where is he?'

Greta takes scissors, a plastic jug and a roll of paper towel from the basket. 'Men do not belong in a hospital.'

I croak a laugh. 'Please thank him for driving you all the way here.'

She examines my shelves. 'I will fix your other flowers, yes?'

Prim points to the gerberas. 'Those are past saving.'

'Find clean vases, Primrose.' Greta holds out the jug. 'And water.'

I rest against the pillows as Greta and Prim laugh and fuss with the flowers. 'I was not a scholar like you girls,' Greta says. 'But I am an adventuress. I am also a mother, a grandmother, and the wife of a farmer. These things I am proud of.'

'You came to Australia alone?' Prim asks.

'I was twenty-one and worked on the farms. This is how I met Derek.' Greta takes containers out of the basket—fresh strawberries, stewed apples, a bean salad and sufficient homemade biscuits to feed four shifts of nurses. After she's stacked them on the tray, she tentatively lifts the plastic lid from my breakfast.

She shudders. 'This is not good, but you must eat it.'

'I spend most of the day sleeping.'

'You are thin and pale like Tinkerbell, Hugo warned me of this.'

Prim looks at her watch. 'I'd better get to work. We'll discuss everything tonight, Patience. I'll get your washing done and find you an apartment, I promise.'

'What apartment is this?' Greta asks.

'Somewhere for Patience to live when she gets out of hospital.'

'And who will care for her there?'

'I'll take time off.'

'You're flying to Darwin on Monday,' I say firmly. 'I'll get nursing help if and when I need it.'

Prim looks doubtful. 'Like I said, we'll talk about it tonight.'

Greta places the rearranged flowers on the shelf. When she turns, her gaze passes deliberately from me to Prim.

'Your sister will come to me,' she declares.

'Greta!' I lower my voice. 'I couldn't possibly—'

'I have a house with many rooms, and a garden with many flowers,' she says. 'It is decided.'

'I'll be perfectly fine on my—'

'You are a private person; I know this. And that is why the granny flat will be best.' She crosses herself. 'Since my dear mother went to heaven, there has been no granny.'

I try again. 'You're very kind, Greta, but—'

She beams. 'When will you come?'

'I don't think—'

'You worry about my sons?'

'I don't want—'

'Andreas brings his boys two nights a week, and sometimes on the weekends. Mateus is busy with his own farm and comes rarely. Hugo?' She throws up her hands. 'He helps his father with the farm. But visit his poor mother? We would as likely see snow at Christmas.'

'Greta …' I take a deep breath. 'Hugo and I …' Another breath. 'It's awkward. I couldn't stay with you.'

'I am in charge at my house.' She purses her lips. 'This is old-fashioned, yes, but my husband and sons must do as I say. You will convalesce, undisturbed, in the granny flat. This is my promise.'

'It's very kind of you to offer, Greta.'

'I will care for you until you are well again. After that …' she smiles and lifts her hands. 'Pouf! I will disappear like edelweiss in summer.'

Prim looks at me hopefully. 'Dr Gupta has his surgery in Horseshoe Hill. His nurse could do the house calls you'll need, and you can go to the surgery when you're well enough. And if I go to the Territory like you want me to …' Her dimple appears as she smiles. 'I could visit when I get leave.'

Greta walks to the side of the bed and smooths a crease in my gown. 'I will cook for you, Patience, and also for your sister when she visits. I will wash and iron. This is my pleasure.'

'Patience?' When Prim tips her head to the side, her dimple nudges her cheek. 'You insist you'll be better in a couple of weeks. What do you think?'

With Phoebe away, Prim won't leave me by myself. Any more than I would leave her. My eyes sting. My heart hurts.

'I'll think about it.'

Greta's gaze softens as she kisses my cheek. 'When you are unwell, it is better to rest than to think. There will be no argument. You will come home to me.'

CHAPTER 20

There are no baths in student accommodation, or on ships, or in the shared facilities I'm accustomed to. There was no bath in the house I grew up in. Did Mum wash me in a plastic baby bath? She must have.

'This bath ...' I say quietly as I sit on the edge of the enamelled cast-iron tub in Greta's bathroom, 'I'll never forget.' I test the water before turning off the taps and, lifting my good leg over the side, lower myself into the water. I prop my other foot on the rim. It's already mid-May, and this is my second week staying at the Halstead's, but as the nurses and doctors predicted, the wound on my foot is still tender and vibrantly red. When bubbles gather round my breasts and dance on my stomach, I swish with a sponge and make shapes.

Southern ocean waves. Snow-capped mountain peaks. Dandelion seedpods in summer.

He loves me.

He loves me not.

Were things ever so simple with Hugo?

I've seen him twice in the past ten days. Even then, we were so far away that lifting a hand was enough. The granny flat is at the back of the house, separated by a strip of verandah. It's self-contained—a bedroom with two single beds, a kitchenette, a tiny bathroom with a cubicle shower, and a living room with a view of the Horseshoe range. As Greta promised, I convalesce in privacy.

For the first few days, when I wasn't in bed I spent my time in an armchair. And in the following days, legs propped up and half-asleep, I lay on the day bed on the verandah outside Greta's kitchen window. In the evenings, I'd eat whatever Greta put on my tray, before showering and collapsing into bed.

Yesterday, feeling better than I had for weeks, I carried my breakfast tray to the kitchen. But Greta, frowning fiercely, linked her arm through mine and marched me slowly but firmly back to the verandah. Derek was sitting on the steps, a mug of tea in his hand and pastry crumbs on his chin. Soxy sat on the day bed as if waiting. As I lay back against the cushions and stroked his soft black ears, Greta nodded approvingly.

'You must rest, liebchen, for today you have your bath.'

Derek smiled. 'You going to put Patience in that bathing room of yours?'

Greta huffed. 'It is the perfect place.'

'So how come you never go in there yourself?'

'Every week, I clean it.' Greta pursed her lips. 'It is spick and span.'

'It might smell like a perfumery, but you never get into that tub.' He winked. 'It would've been better to keep it for my bull.'

When he still worked as a carpenter, and before he'd met Greta, Derek intercepted an oversized bathtub destined for the scrap merchant and kept it at his parent's house. Years later, Greta spotted the bath, now used as a water trough, in a paddock. She asked Derek to build yet another extension to their house—a bathing room to remind her of Bad Ischl, her birthplace and a spa town.

'I'd love to have a bath,' I said to Greta. 'But only if you have enough water in the tanks.'

She delicately put a second pastry on Derek's plate. 'Now you can see my sense,' she said haughtily. 'The bathing room is useful.'

Having a bath doesn't equate to a swim, but it's the closest I'm likely to get to a body of water for at least the next few weeks. I look through my fingers, fringed with tiny bubbles. The bathing room is the size of a large bedroom, and the walls are painted a soft shade of pink. White timber shelves are stacked with fluffy white towels, embroidered face washers, sponges, bubble baths and salts.

Many of the unopened bottles have gift tags. Attached to a bright pink bottle is a handmade tag, the size of a large envelope, with upright rounded letters in smudged and faded pencil. *Dear Mummy. This is for your birthday from me for your bath. I got it at a shop. I got money from Daddy for feeding Bertha. Love from Hugo*

Another is penned in ink, the writing sloped neatly to the right. *Dear Mum. I found these salts at a spa town near Salzburg. Happy Mother's Day. Love, Hugo*

Sunlight streams through the window—too high for anybody on the verandah to see through, but low enough that when lying in the bath, I can make out the tops of the gums and an ocean of sky.

Now it's almost winter, it's cool in the mornings, but the old-style radiator and heated towel rails take away the chill. Inside the tub, the enamel is smooth like silk. I make another shape in the bubbles. A boat's wake. I close my eyes and inhale the scent. *Mountain Mist. Bergamot and pine.* Holding my breath, I tip back my head.

Besides my leg, I'm submerged.

Weightless.

Waterfall.

Warmth.

How long until I'm back at the river? The nurse from Dr Gupta's surgery will make house calls for another week at least. She checks my temperature, takes a blood sample and prods and pokes my wound. I sleep twelve hours a night, I eat more than Derek and Soxy combined, and when Greta's not looking I walk painfully slow laps of the verandah.

Surfacing, I push back my hair and wipe bubbles from my face. I stretch out my hands and fingers, let the water hold me up.

'Patience?' A tap on the door. 'You are well?'

'Yes, Greta. I'm fine.'

'I will go to the kitchen. You will ring the bell if you need help, yes?'

A brass bell with a handle, like an old-fashioned school bell, sits at the foot of the tub near the taps. Greta made me promise to use it in an emergency.

'I also have my phone,' I call out.

'Phooey your phone. A bell is waterproof. It has no need of a battery or reception.'

'Yes, but—'

'This morning, Andreas comes to work with his father, and Hugo arrives later. I tell you this because of my promise. There is no need for concern. You will rest. You will have peace in the granny flat.'

It's almost five o'clock and the bright orange sun burns low in the sky. I'm lying on my side on the day bed when my phone buzzes.

'Rick.' I hold in a yawn as I position cushions against the solid timber arm and lean back. 'Hello.'

'Eliza has purchased an appropriate gift,' Rick says. 'I'll send it care of Greta.'

'You've already sent flowers, but thank you. Please thank Eliza too.'

'I'll reimburse her.'

'Yes, but …' Bending my knees, I pull the throw over them. 'Have you received my messages?'

'I'm pleased to hear of your recovery. As is Eliza.'

I slip my fingers through the fringe of the throw. The bruises on the backs of my hands are less purple than they were.

'I'm sorry I've been useless, but you can send me things to do now. How did you go in Melbourne? Did you get all the data you wanted from the river? What are you working on now?'

My back is to verandah stairs when I hear footsteps. The screen door opens and closes as someone, without knocking or calling out, walks into the house. Derek's tread is slow and deliberate. One, two. One, two. One, two. Andy's tread is similar, but heavier.

This is someone else, possibly Hugo, but I don't dare turn around to find out.

'Rick? Is everything okay?'

'No.'

'Can you be more specific?' I rest my chin on my knees. 'When Hugo visited me in the hospital, he said you were anxious about something. Is it to do with the invoices? Has Professor Tedeschi told you what's going on? Has he fixed the problem?'

When Soxy jumps on the day bed, sitting close to my leg but with his head over the edge, I rearrange the throw to cover him.

'You mustn't talk to Hugo,' Rick says.

'I don't—'

'I don't want to talk on the phone. When can we meet?'

'Can you come here?'

'No.'

I lean against the cushions and close my eyes. 'I can't drive for another week, maybe two, and aren't you back at the river on Monday?'

'Hugo was afraid you would die.'

'Yes ... well.' Greta is in the kitchen. Her voice is raised and she's scolding. 'I'm okay now.'

'When can we meet?'

'Realistically ...' I count days. 'Four weeks?'

A shadow appears on the boards as Hugo, hands in his pockets, closes the gap between us. I clear my throat. 'I have to go. See you soon.'

Hugo leans against the verandah railing and stretches out his legs. His eyes are shades of green. *Gum leaves, streams, the golden haze of summer.*

'Hugo.'

'Imp.' His shirt and pants are creased but clean. He's freshly shaven. 'How are you feeling?'

I'm wearing trackpants and a faded T-shirt. I smooth the throw over my knees. 'Much better, thank you.'

He nods towards my phone. 'Making plans?'

I have no idea what Rick wants to talk about. Invoices? Misappropriation? But whatever it is, he doesn't want Hugo to know about it. Anyway, my job requires me to keep my mouth shut.

'It was my sister.'

'In Norway?' He looks at his watch. 'What time is it there?'

I force a smile. 'Prim.'

His eyes narrow. 'She said you should call in the morning.'

'What?'

'When she couldn't get through to you just now, she called Greta.'

I hold onto the arm of the day bed as I stand. *Cling onto the arm.* 'Did you want me for something?'

'Why so many secrets?'

I smile stiffly. 'Anything else?'

His hair is longer, the sun-tipped ends are bright. 'Lisa said you'd emailed, asking for work.'

'Until I can join Rick again, I'll have to work remotely.' When Soxy jumps from the day bed, I fold the throw and line up the cushions. 'I have skills. I want to use them.'

He slowly shakes his head. 'It's too early.'

'Rick asked me to set up social media platforms for the team, and I've been posting for him. What about your frogs? I could write about them too.'

'Memorise and recite?'

'You think that's all I'm good for?'

'I didn't mean—'

'You did!'

He lifts a hand and drops it. 'Why contact Lisa? Why not me?'

'Because you underestimate me.'

'That's not true.'

'Rick makes an effort to engage with people online. I'm helping Lisa with materials for environmental science students. Why won't you do anything like that?'

'I have better things to do with my time.'

'People must look you up, ordinary people. They'll be interested in your work.'

'I have a profile.'

'One photograph, and links to scientific papers with hundreds of footnotes. A lot of your work is funded by the government and universities. You must have to report on outcomes, and the impacts of your work in the community. Blog posts, Instagram, they might help with that.'

'You sound like Sapphie.'

'As she's on Horseshoe's Environment Committee, she'd know what I'm talking about. You have to engage with people to get the message out, and to maximise funding.'

He frowns. 'I talk to people constantly.'

'Colleagues at conferences and mates at the pub. Those people are already aware of you and your work. It's important to reach out to others in the community.'

He smiles stiffly. 'Do blog posts if you want.'

'One a week?'

'Sure.'

I nod politely. 'I also want to ride again.'

His mouth firms. He walks to the railing and grasps it with both hands. His back to me, he looks over his shoulder. 'A unicorn?'

My chest tightens. My breath catches. The frame of the day bed is hard against the backs of my thighs. But then I push off and—

He spins and blocks my path. 'I shouldn't have said that.'

'But you did!'

He closes his eyes for a moment. He lifts a hand and drops it. 'It's not easy, Imp, seeing you here.'

'Do you want me to go?'

He slowly shakes his head. 'That'd be even worse.'

'Then let me do what I'm paid for.' My voice is scratchy; I clear my throat. 'I'll be well enough to go back to the river soon. After the secondment, I'll leave.'

'Back to your ship.'

'That's where I belong.'

Greta calls out from the kitchen. 'Hugo!'

The Frog Blog
I'm a lieutenant in the navy, but currently on secondment to a team of scientists researching river and wetland environments. Part of this research relates to frogs and their habitats, which is where this blog comes in. Dr Hugo Halstead, a biologist and herpetologist (an expert in reptiles and amphibians), is one of the members of the team. When he's not in the field, knee deep in ponds, creeks, rivers, wetlands and bogs as he searches for tadpoles and frogs, he'll also hop on the blog ...

CHAPTER 21

When she makes pastry, Greta cools her hands by soaking them in water. She kneads flour, egg and olive oil into a dough, resting it at room temperature for at least four hours before stretching it onto a lightly floured tablecloth until it's as thin as parchment paper. To make the filling, she sprinkles the dough with toasted spiced breadcrumbs, freshly sliced apples, lemon rind and a tablespoon of sugar, rolls it up and brushes it with butter. The strudel is baked until the top is golden brown.

She calls me into the kitchen and serves me a slice from the baking tray. I lick flaky crumbs from my fingers. 'Delicious.'

'You must eat more,' she says, holding out the tray again.

'Your grandsons will want some too.' As if on cue, a car door slams, and then another.

'Children are always hungry after school.'

I'm sure Mum would have given us something nice to eat when we got home from school, but just like the bath, I can't remember.

Phoebe made us vegemite sandwiches. When I was older, even in summer, I warmed milk in a saucepan and made her hot chocolate.

'Patience! Patience!'

Remy is five, in his first year of primary school. Ryan is fourteen, in his second year of high school. According to Greta, Andreas and Maria had a second child in the hope of saving their marriage, but things didn't work out anyway.

As the boys wanted to stay in Horseshoe and Maria's new partner lives in Dubbo, Maria mostly sees her sons in the holidays, and often on the weekends. The rest of the time they live with Andy, who has a farm close by.

Remy, who has curly brown hair like his father and a rounded cherub face, trots into the kitchen and sniffs the air. He has his arms out in front with his hands down, as if he has four legs. He whinnies and tosses his head.

'Apfelstrudel! Yum!'

I laugh. 'It's lucky horses like apples, isn't it?'

Ryan is a taller and ganglier version of his brother. 'Thanks, Oma.'

'I hope you were good boys for your teachers,' Greta says, joining Remy at the kitchen table and pouring a glass of milk. 'Drink, liebchen. This will make you a strong, wise horse.'

Remy tips his bag onto the table and forages for a library book. 'Look, Oma!'

Ryan, grumbling under his breath, takes a seat next to me at the bench. 'What's the big deal about books?'

'Do you have a lot of homework?' I ask. 'You know I'd be happy to help, right?'

He kicks his bag so hard it shoots across the floor and hits a cupboard. 'Dad says you're a mega brain.'

'I like maths.'

'I hate it.'

'Andy said you're getting help at school.'

'Yeah,' he mutters. 'I'm at the bottom of the remedial class.'

'If you want to ask me anything,' I say, collecting the last of the crumbs from my plate, 'I'll be on the day bed.'

I've only been on the verandah for five minutes when Ryan, schoolbag over his shoulder, clumps along the boards. He drops his bag at his feet and kneels to stroke Soxy, lying next to me with his head on a cushion.

I close my laptop. 'I'm looking up facts on frogs.'

'Uncle Hugo knows heaps. Ask him.'

'He's a specialist. I want the basics. Did you know that every frog's pattern, like a fingerprint, is unique?'

'Why do you care about frogs when you're in the navy?'

'Because I'm working with Hugo's team at the river.'

'Do you need maths to navigate? Can't you use a sat nav?'

'Radar and satellites are useful, but weather patterns, ocean currents and territorial boundaries have to be factored in. Even the moon and stars.'

'You get to live on a ship. That'd be ace.'

At Greta's insistence, her window boxes are always freshly painted—pastel pink, wedding-dress white and fire-engine red. Half curtains, cream and lacy, hang from most of the windows.

'Greta's home is nice too.' When Ryan opens his bag and pulls out his books, I gesture that he sit next to me. 'Show me what you're doing.'

'Failing.'

'I've heard you're talented at art, and design and technology. Maths can be useful for those subjects too. You'll be able to specialise in what you enjoy in your final years of school.'

'If I ever get there.'

I stack the books in a pile between us. 'You might have to tackle things differently, that's all.'

'Hugo doesn't understand how I don't get it.' He looks at me dubiously. 'You're a genius, you'll be even worse.'

'People look at words and numbers—they process information—in different ways. That might be your problem.' The verandah frames the cows and calves, gathered near the water trough. 'That fence,' I say as I point, 'what do you see when you look at it?'

'It's a fence.'

'Sure it is. But how would you describe it?'

He rolls his eyes. 'The posts are driven into holes. The railings are fixed to the posts by C brackets. The wire in between is six-gauge galvanised steel.'

'What type of timber is it?'

He squints. 'Tight grain and no knots. Old ironbark, I reckon.'

'Now you've told me about those things, I can see them too. But they'd never be the first things that come into my head.'

He looks at the fence again, and then back at me. 'What can you see?'

'Assuming the paddock is 650 metres by 700 metres, which looks about right, and the posts are an average of two metres apart, there'll be 1,350 horizontal rails and, assuming two strands, 5,400 metres of wire.'

His mouth drops open. 'When did you work that out?'

'Just then.' I shrug. 'I often see things in numbers, but I've learned to push it aside when I have to.'

'You always count stuff?'

'It's my default, but not very practical for everyday life. In the navy, I have to write reports that make sense to others—I learned the basics of that at school. I've also got to take orders, lead by example, and boss people around. That involves people skills.'

'Do you have friends?'

I laugh. 'Yes, I have friends. I also have my sisters, and my family in New Zealand.'

'Oma said you've still got a swimming record at the pool.'

'Really?' I put a cushion behind me and lean back. 'That'll be because I trained longer and harder than any other moderately talented kid.'

'You didn't grow big enough to win much, did you?' Ryan pulls out a textbook from the pile. *Year Nine Mathematics*. 'Not like Uncle Hugo.'

Taking the book, I study the chapter headings. 'I didn't need to win. I liked to count the laps.'

'No joke? That's why you stuck at it?'

'Like I said, we all see things differently. Anyone who watched me swim would think I was committed to the squad and determined to improve, but mostly I swam to calm down. Instead of drawing attention to myself by blurting out numbers, I could count in my head. Swimming let me process what was happening at home and at school.'

'You can't swim on a ship.'

'No, but I can go on deck and see the ocean, smell the salt, feel and hear the movement of the water. That's calming too.'

One of Soxy's ears has flopped over and Ryan puts it right. 'Did you get picked on at school?'

'Kids laughed at me, like they probably laugh at you. I was teased mercilessly.'

'Same.'

'That's bullying, Ryan. Do you need help? Have you told your dad? Your teachers?'

'Yeah.' He nods jerkily.

'Improving in maths isn't the way to fix bullies.'

'I get that, but ...' He pulls Soxy's ears straight up. 'Who do you reckon Soxy looks like?'

I consider the question. 'Batman?'

'He was a genius too.'

'I liked The Puzzler.'

He grins as he smooths Soxy's ears again. 'You reckon you can help?'

'If you really are failing ...' I flick through the pages of the book, look up and smile. 'You've got nothing to lose.'

An hour and a half later, Ryan's homework is finished, and he and Remy are down at the shed with Derek, loading bales of hay onto the trailer. I'm sitting on the steps of the verandah, yawning as I will myself to walk the few metres to the granny flat, so I can get ready for bed.

Andy, a mug of coffee in his hand, sits next to me on the steps. 'Greta reckons you've been chipping away at Ryan all week. Thanks for helping him out tonight.'

'You know about the other problem?'

'The bullying? It's better this year than last.'

'Is that why Hugo teaches him how to fight?'

'Just to make him feel better about himself.' He slaps his bicep. 'Build him up a bit.'

'He's agreed to sit down with me again.'

'The teachers try their best, but they aren't having much luck. His attitude sucks.'

'He has gaps in his knowledge. If we fill those gaps, he's bound to improve. I wrote out explanations for the concepts he's struggling with, gave him examples of solutions, and set exercises for him to do on his own. If he works at the exercises and succeeds, it should help his confidence.'

'Makes sense to me.'

'I told him we could do more of the same tomorrow, if that's okay with you. Regular sessions are important.'

When Andy stands, I hold out my hands and he pulls me up. 'Greta says she's keeping tabs on Hugo, making sure you get peace and quiet in the granny flat.'

'She's also feeding me up.'

'Did I ever apologise for getting you all but killed on that horse?'

'Only about a million times. It wasn't your fault.'

'Don't suppose you get to ride these days.'

Hugo suggested I ride a unicorn. My throat tight, I shake my head. 'It's on my list of things to do.'

CHAPTER 22

My hair is still wet from my bath when I walk to Greta's rose garden—a paved area with a slatted timber pergola—midway between the house and the home paddock. The mother cows doze in the shade of the gum trees, their calves standing closely by their sides. Sitting on the wide timber bench and putting in my ear pods, I search my phone for a soundtrack and—

'Imp!'

I take a deep breath as I roll up the sleeves of my shirt. Greta found it while cleaning out her cupboards and claimed it would not only supplement my wardrobe but flatter my colouring, so I didn't have the heart to refuse it. The front panels hang below my thighs, so I've tied them in a knot at my waist. My denim shorts are faded and frayed.

Daisy Duke, eat your heart out.

'Imp!'

The wind chime above me tinkles in the breeze. 'Down here!'

Four solid posts support the climbing roses, but now it's early winter, the flowers are sparse and the leaves are pale and spotted.

A rosemary hedge, low but dense with spiky green leaves, marches from post to post.

Hat in one hand, Hugo jumps from the verandah and strides through the garden, stopping short at the edge of the paving. Mud sticks to his boots and there's dirt on the knees of his pants. He combs through his hair with his fingers.

'Greta said you'd be on the day bed.'

'As Greta is at a CWA meeting, Derek is on the tractor and Andy is drenching sheep,' I aim for a nonchalant shrug, 'no one will know.'

'What if you fell?'

'Off the bench?'

The hint of a smile. 'Your blog posts are good.'

'Frogs have webbed, unwebbed and elongated feet,' I count on my fingers, 'depending how they've adapted. Some jump through grasslands, others climb trees or burrow underground.'

A definite smile. 'Tell me about desert spadefoot toads.'

'They burrow into the ground, wrap themselves in a waterproof cocoon made from layers of their own shed skin, and won't come out, sometimes for months or years, until it rains. They wait until conditions are right.'

A brief pause. 'Like us?'

My words trip over each other. 'Tree frogs have waxy skins, also known as secretions, to keep their skin moist and help with their breathing, and adhesive pads on their toes, like suction cups, so they can climb.'

He sits next to me on the bench, an elbow on the backrest. 'What's going on with Rick, Imp? Why won't you tell me?'

I check my pockets for a hair band. Nothing. I push stray ends behind my ears. 'You let him do what he wants, don't you? Sit on the left and get up early in the mornings? Make sure he drinks even when he refuses to eat? That all helps.'

He tips back his head. 'Not enough.'

'I don't know any more than I did.'

'And you won't even tell me that.' His gaze slips to my feet, finally coming to rest on the dressing that covers my instep. 'At least get rid of those sandals.'

'I won't go near the livestock.'

'What about snakes?'

Bending my knees, I bring my feet onto the bench. 'I'll wear sneakers next time.'

He opens his mouth and shuts it again. Then, his hand moving slowly but deliberately, stopping just short of touching, he points to the shirt.

'I got that for my sixteenth birthday.'

'What!' My hands flutter. 'Greta couldn't remember where it came from.'

'Blue checked flannelette with metallic silver threads? Who would own up to it?'

I touch the fabric, trace a seam. 'I would never have …' I untie the knot, smooth out the creases. 'I'll put it in a charity bin.'

When he turns on the seat to face me side-on, I smell his shampoo. 'Don't,' he says quietly.

'Why not?'

He flicks the collar. 'I like it on you.'

My skin warms. My heart jumps. And then I remember. *No, no, no, no, no.* I scrabble to my feet.

He stands much more slowly. 'Imp?' He frowns. 'What's—'

'You can't …' I wipe my hands down the shirt.

'Can't what?'

Squeezing my eyes shut, I recall a shard of a memory. 'At the hospital, you held my hand, didn't you?'

He rubs around the back of his neck. 'I wouldn't have, Imp, but you reached out. You wouldn't let mine go.'

'I …' I nod stiffly. 'I was sick and—'

'The nurse with the tulip tatt, she was with you when I got there. She told me you'd been crying in your sleep, and said you needed company.'

I tug at the shirt collar. 'I might have overreacted.'

'Why? What prompted it?'

A deep breath. *Long strokes and tumble turns.* 'You shouldn't have said anything about the shirt.'

'Because it was personal?'

I tie a knot in the shirt again. 'What would Lisa think?'

'Why would she care?'

'You're right.' I nod even *more* stiffly. 'You and Lisa are none of my business.'

He opens his mouth, shuts it. Then, 'Fuck.'

'Greta wouldn't approve of you swearing in her garden.'

His eyes narrow. 'Don't change the subject.'

'I have to go back to—'

'Do you think Lisa and I are together?'

'Greta thought …'

He mutters under his breath. 'Like I'd tell her anything.'

'Lisa said something to Prim, who also thought …'

'We dated two years ago. For six weeks, maybe seven. Now we're friends.'

'She might want more. Have you asked her about that?'

He blinks. 'You're giving me advice on communication?'

I scuff my sandals in the dust. Then I scan the path, as if on the lookout for snakes. 'I'd better get back to the house.'

'Can we finish this conversation first?'

After picking a lavender flower, I'm not sure what to do with it. Hugo takes it and puts it on the seat next to his hat.

'I like the shirt on you,' he says quietly. 'And I like you.'

I open my mouth, but all I can find is one single word. 'Oh.'

'How do you feel about me liking you?'

My head aches. My heart skips and dances. 'Last time we spoke, you said you didn't like seeing me here.'

'I said it was hard to see you here. That's different.'

'We were friends.'

'There was more.'

'We have history.' I lift my chin, meet his gaze. 'We're possibly attracted to each other.'

He turns towards the paddocks, scans the horizon, shoves his hands into his pockets. 'There's more.'

'When I was here last,' I shake my head, 'you didn't want me.'

'You didn't stay long enough to find out what I wanted.'

Two bees fly around the rosemary, hovering, buzzing. 'I started again.'

'I tried to forget.'

'Why did you come down here?'

'Maybe I'm like Ryan and Remy.' His green eyes are shadowed. 'Maybe I can't keep away.'

'Please don't.'

'What? Pretend this doesn't happen? That there's nothing between us?'

One of the bees hovers over a sprig of rosemary. Where is the other bee? 'I don't trust you, Hugo. I can't.'

'You started this on the beach. You asked for my hands.'

'I didn't—'

'I did what you wanted.'

'We were pretending. It didn't mean anything.'

'Then this won't mean anything either.' He holds out his hands. 'Take them.'

Lightheaded and wobbly, I do as he asks. His hold is firm. His hands are cool. He brushes my knuckles with his thumb.

'I didn't want to go back to how we were,' he says quietly. 'You forced me to.'

'What we had is over.'

'Prove it.' He searches my face. 'Kiss me.'

We can't go back. *We can't*, but …

I lean in close, rest my hands on his chest and stand on my toes. I touch the side of his face, find the pulse at his temple. The rhythm, the beats, the …

Gentle waves in sheltered bays. Ripples on a river in the sunshine. The push and pull of the ocean. A meandering creek, a trickling stream.

When our lips touch, I sigh against his mouth. I search the contours, the fullness, the texture. Our tongues meet carefully, a gentle exploration. The warmth of his body. The thumps of his heart.

'Imp.' He murmurs the word, a plea, an entreaty, as he kisses a trail from my mouth to my cheek to my neck to my throat. He follows the line of my cleavage as far as the buttons allow. He draws in a breath as his hands cup my breasts. I lean in close and press into his caress.

'Hugo?' When I find his mouth again, he mutters against my lips—complaints, endearments, frustrations. He lifts his head and studies my face. Then, as if he can't help himself, he kisses my mouth again.

'I missed you,' he whispers.

He kisses me hard and soft and then in-between. Passionate, potent, persuasive. His hands scoop my hips, slide up my sides. He finds the skin at my waist, groans low in his throat. His fingers clench and release. I want to climb onto his lap. *Into* his body.

I tug his shirt free of his pants and pull at the buttons. His skin is smooth, his muscles hard. He groans against my mouth.

'Remember the jigsaws?'

I answer on his lips. 'One thousand, two thousand or three thousand?'

'I missed you like the piece of a puzzle.'

His scent, his words, the caress of his lips. The rhythm of it, the tempo, the beats.

We're hours from the sea but he tastes of the ocean. North, south, east and west. I make circles round his tongue, push it back, draw it in.

Radius. Diameter. Circumference.

Circumference over diameter equals pi multiplied by *3.14159265*.

Area equals pi multiplied by radius squared.

He groans and pulls me closer. 'Imp.'

'Mmm.'

'You're counting.'

'I'm …'

He touches my neck, finds my pulse. 'You were always counting.' His eyes are green like springtime grass.

'I hide it now.'

'Don't hide it from me.'

How easy would it be to fall in love again?

Far too easy.

Far too hard.

I swallow down the sadness and push against his chest. I look around him to the house. Three thousand, two thousand, one thousand.

'I promised Greta I'd be on the day bed.'

His brows crease, his mouth firms. 'Imp?' He waits for me to meet his gaze. 'Tell me what you want.' He takes my hands, touches where the bruises were. He kisses them gently.

Possessively.

His lips are damp.

My heart might want him. But my head ... I pull my hands free, inch away. I fasten a button, bite the inside of my lip to still the trembling.

'Imp?' His breaths are as unsteady as mine. 'Are you all right?'

'I can't ...' The lump in my throat is so big it aches.

'We can—'

'No.' The lump explodes in a rush. I can't hold back the tears that run down my cheeks. 'We can't.'

'Oh fuck.'

'I've been sick.' The rosemary stems are a blur, but I don't need to see them to know what they look like. *Slender yet strong.* I wipe my nose on the arm of the shirt. *His shirt.* More tears. I sniff and wipe my nose again. 'Sleepy.' I press the palms of my hands against my eyes. 'Emotional.'

'It's okay, Imp.' He lifts a hand, drops it. 'I'm not going to rush you. I can wait.'

A car beeps twice as it sweeps down the driveway—Greta's friend Hendrika is dropping her home. Derek's tractor, a flash of blue, appears over the rise near the dam. A dog's excited bark. I push out words.

'I have to get back.'

Andy's quad bike scoots around the tractor in an arc. Years ago, he rode a horse. There were a lot of horses, kept in the paddock where I fell.

'I want to learn to ride.'

'What does that have to do with—'

'It's important to me.'

'Patience!' Greta is leaning over the verandah railing. 'Why are you down there? Hugo! Your father wants you to come. At once! Quickly!'

Hugo walks as slowly as I do to the house. Halfway there, I stop and turn towards him. 'Are my eyes red?'

He considers me closely. 'A bit.'

As we continue to walk, our little fingers touch. Once. Twice. 'I'll have to hide from Greta.'

'You know Douglas, the biologist on the Flinders team? His wife is unwell, and I've said I'll relieve him at the end of next week so he can get home. I'll be away for eight days, maybe longer.'

'She has diabetes, doesn't she? I hope she's all right.'

'I didn't plan to—'

'It was me. I did it.'

Greta, both hands on the verandah railing, is watching every step. 'Liebchen?' When we're a few metres away, she runs down the steps and puts an arm around me. Then, glaring at Hugo, she shepherds me onto the day bed. 'What is the matter with Patience, Hugo? You must tell me.'

Hugo, mouth tight, shakes his head.

'I make a promise to her sisters,' Greta admonishes. 'Patience shall rest. She will have peace in the granny flat. You believe I make a promise willy-nilly?' She crosses herself. 'On my mother's grave, I do not do such a thing.'

CHAPTER 23

Hugo said: *Tell me what you want.*

'I might not know what I want, but I know what I *don't* want,' I tell the hens bustling around at my feet as I throw kitchen scraps from a bucket into the chook pen. The big black hen pecks at a watermelon shell and the fluffy feathered white hen excitedly flaps her wings. Caramel brown hens with floppy red crests squabble over peanut shells. Greta's yellow gumboots are three sizes too big and I curl my toes to keep them on as I walk to the series of boxes where the hens lay their eggs.

'How could I trust him?' One of the hens, feathers puffed, runs between my legs. 'How could we go back?'

Over a week has passed since we kissed.

That kiss.

Eight nights of tossing and turning and waking up too early. He believes I ran away. *From him.*

I didn't run just anywhere. I ran *to* something. A degree. A career. I'm independent, financially secure. I'm older and wiser.

Greta knows something is wrong, but as neither Hugo nor I have informed her what it is, she respects my wish to avoid him. I've seen Hugo twice—he came to help Derek with the ploughing, and to see Ryan and Remy. I pretended I had calls to make and Rick's administration to sort out. I was ready for an afternoon nap, and an early night.

But now he's in Western Australia, I miss him. More than I should. More than my heart can afford to.

In the rose garden, he told me he remembered how we used to be, that he missed me. *The piece of a puzzle.* On the phone, he's courteous and reserved. *You're doing great with Ryan. Rick said you should call at six.*

Within a month, I hope to be well enough to move out of the granny flat and live in whatever accommodation the navy has budgeted for. Maybe I'll be back at my caravan with Rick? The personal, living at Hugo's childhood home, will be over. If I can ride, I can finish the secondment and go back to sea.

If I can ride …

There are other reasons too. Phoebe has horses. She doesn't say anything when I stay on the other side of the fence, far away from their hooves, but it's clear that she worries. Terrors. Anxieties. I've never ever faced them.

'Since I'm in the country, maybe it's time I did,' I tell the black hen who pecks the ground beside me. I place the last of the eggs, six white and two brown, into the basket and fluff up the bedding before turning the bucket upside down and tapping the base to free the last of the scraps. Carefully stepping around the hens, I rinse the bucket and lather my hands in the outside tub.

Greta calls out as I walk to Derek's ute. 'Patience!' Holding a cardboard box, she rushes down the steps. 'I have biscuits for Mandy.' She looks worriedly at the keys in my hand. 'Are you certain you can drive?'

'It's about time I did. And I'll be careful, I promise.'

The sky is blue, dotted with white scattered clouds, as I drive to Mandy Flanagan's property on the outskirts of Warrandale. She has twenty hectares of neatly fenced paddocks running either side of a poplar-lined bitumen driveway. *So many fence posts.* Sturdy vertical posts and two horizontal rails, all painted white. The neat but simple house, white with dark blue doors and window frames, sits at the top of the driveway. A much larger structure, a brick stable block, stands behind a number of post-and-rail yards.

Mandy's ponies aren't as small and thickset as Hugo's Shetland pony Lavender, but would be too small for most adults to ride. I can't see much of the ponies in the paddock and yards because they're wearing smart cotton rugs and matching hoods, but they seem to be either black or grey. There's only one large horse, wearing a faded red rug and grazing on the far side of a paddock.

I'm parking the ute when Mandy walks from the stables with a bucket in each hand. She's in her early sixties but, wearing close-fitting jodhpurs and a white collared sports shirt, she looks much younger. I hadn't seen her since school—she was a counsellor and psychologist there—but we met again at Phoebe's wedding.

She smiles warmly as I step out of the car. 'Good to see you're out and about. Quite a stir you caused with the airlift.'

I reach into the back seat for the biscuits. 'Does everybody know?'

'Everybody who knows Phoebe but,' she smiles again, 'in a small town like Warrandale, that's everybody. How're things going at the Halsteads? Don't suppose you can go too wrong with Greta's hospitality.'

I hold out the box. 'These are from her.'

Mandy laughs. 'Perfect timing. I've just put the kettle on. We'll talk about a possible solution to your problem over coffee.' She prises open the lid and peeks in. 'What are they?'

'Spekulatius. Cinnamon. Delicious.'

When I called Mandy last week, she told me she'd don her equestrian *and* psychologist hats in order to consider my riding options. I admire her thick hair, salt-and-pepper brown with a distinctive silver streak, as we walk along the path to the stable block. Only two horses' heads peek over the stable doors. One is a little grey mare, heavily pregnant. The other is Fitzwilliam, one of Mandy's black stallions. He's a handsome pony with bright dark eyes, a long forelock and mane, and a tail that sweeps his woodchip bedding.

When I hold out a hand, he sniffs it. 'He's lovely.'

She looks from the pony to me. 'Because there's a three-inch half-door between you?'

I grimace. 'You got it.'

She gestures to the end of the block. 'Coffee awaits.' When Mandy walks briskly down the path, I follow, but pull up short at the threshold to the kitchen.

The space is large, with a high ceiling and exposed beams. Wide repurposed boards stretch across the floor and stainless-steel sinks and appliances glisten along one wall. Brass pendant lights hang low over a speckled granite benchtop.

'Wow.'

'Since I spend most of my time at the stables,' Mandy says, 'I might as well make myself comfortable.' She waves me to a chair at the long timber table. 'Take a seat.'

Phoebe made it clear that it was Ms Flanagan who, a number of times, saved me from being expelled. I was argumentative in the classroom. I also had a habit of walking out of the school grounds whenever I felt like it. But what brought me back—in addition to having nowhere to go and a dread of being kicked out of the swim team because I wouldn't be able to compete for the school—was a fear of hurting Phoebe, who always blamed herself whenever something went wrong with me or Prim.

'Let's get down to business,' Mandy says, placing two mugs of coffee on the table. 'Give me a recap.'

'I'd like to ride again, but I didn't appreciate how difficult that would be until recently,' I say. 'When I was in the paddock with Arrow, Hugo's horse, just seeing those hooves …' Suddenly cold, I rub my arms. 'It freaked me out.'

'A profound fear of horses, any phobia, has the potential to do that.' She sips her coffee. 'Not facing up to your fears makes things worse—there's a lot to be said for getting straight back on the horse.'

My coffee is halfway to my mouth when I carefully put it down again. 'I had a fractured cheekbone.'

She winks as she holds out the biscuits. 'There was that.'

'Have you ever been scared?'

'As a three-day event and show jumping competitor?' She sits back in her chair. 'I would've been a fool if I hadn't been. But you, Patience Cartwright, are hardly a straightforward case.'

'Because of my fall?'

'Not only that.' She pushes the biscuits across the table again. 'There's your childhood to consider.' She lifts her brows. 'How is the old bastard? I was hoping he'd die before Phoebe went away so she had one less thing to worry about.'

I circle my mug with both hands. 'Dad is unhappy with the nursing home.'

'What about your mother? How are you getting on there?'

'I suspect you know the answer to that.' The table has a coarse grain and a series of knots. I circle a figure eight around two of them. 'The stroke was a tragedy.' I puff out a breath. 'I feel guilty that I find it so hard to talk to her.'

'You were a child. Distraught that you'd lost her, angry that she'd left you.'

'Phoebe remembers her better than me. By the time I started high school, I could hardly recall what she'd been like.'

'That's not surprising.'

'I love my aunts and uncles in New Zealand, and of course I love Mum. She must have protected us when we were little, even though I don't remember much of that.'

'She loved you, Patience. Until, through no fault of her own, she was forced to abandon you to the care of a father incapable of satisfying the emotional needs of a child.'

'I had Phoebe,' I say quietly. 'She was enough for me and Prim.'

'Only she wasn't.' Mandy considers me closely over the rim of her cup. 'She was the eldest, and she did her best, but you supported her just as she supported you. It was you who looked after her when your father was cruel. You fought back on her behalf.'

'It ...' My eyes sting. 'I would have done anything for her.'

Mandy takes my arm, her grip reassuring. 'The musketeers. You've done remarkably well, all three of you.'

I summons a smile. 'Is this relevant?'

She sweeps crumbs from the table into her hand. 'If you'd had a stable home, or counselling after your fall, you *might* have come good in terms of your fear of horses. As it was, you went back to doing what you've always done—you put your fears aside.' She sits back in her chair again, considers me closely. 'How are you getting on with Hugo? I was surprised to hear you were working together.'

Forget the kiss. Forget the kiss. 'It's just work.'

'You were close once, weren't you?'

I take another biscuit. 'I can't see how *this* would be relevant.'

'Maybe, maybe not.' She pyramids her fingers. 'Turning away from fear, avoiding it, can be responsible for feeding it. Your mother inadvertently let you down. Your father did it with malice. Consequently, you don't trust easily. Did Hugo dump you or the other way around?'

I swallow my mouthful of biscuit, have another sip of coffee. 'I wanted more than he did.'

'In other words, he let you down. All this adds up, Patience. Fear of relying on people, trust issues. This other fear, of horses, has elements of that.'

'I need to ride for the secondment I'm doing, but …' I wipe my hands down my jeans. 'It's become more important than that. I don't want to be scared.'

She brushes more crumbs from the table. 'An excellent start.'

'So, what do I do about it?'

'To overcome a fear, you have to face it. Well before you get back on the horse—literally or figuratively—you must be ready, willing and able to do the groundwork.'

'Do you mean therapy?'

'Not in the way you imagine.' She drains her cup. 'To begin with, learn how to communicate with a horse. Feed him, lead him around, groom him. In that way you build confidence, and an ability to predict his behaviour and ultimately trust him. There'll be no place for fear.'

'The groundwork is literally on the ground?'

'Clever girl.' Pushing back her chair, she links her hands on the table and leans forward. 'I'll be able to help to an extent, but …' She winces and rubs her shoulder. 'In a couple of weeks I'm booked in for a shoulder reconstruction.'

'Oh no!'

She smiles. 'Nothing to do with the horses, I'm happy to report. But the trouble is I won't be the one to get you back on the horse.'

'You don't have to do anything, Mandy. Look after your own—'

'My proposal,' she holds up a hand, 'involves very little input from me. In fact, all I need to do is set you up at the Halstead's. Greta and Derek are eminently suitable to supervise.'

'They don't have horses any more.'

'We'll get to that later. But first …' she flips her plait over her shoulder, 'do you avoid other hoofed animals?'

'Like cows? Sure I do. Even sheep …' I slump in my chair. 'It's pathetic, isn't it?'

'You didn't merely witness a horrific event, you experienced it.' She firmly closes the box when I decline another biscuit. 'There's nothing pathetic about that.'

It's like I'm back at school, sitting on the worn fabric chair in Mandy's office. A photograph, Mandy and a chestnut horse sailing over a water jump, was propped up on the bookcase. I was on the cusp of being expelled for swearing at a maths teacher because he'd made a fool of Amy. Kind and painfully shy, she was in love with Justin Bieber. I can't remember exactly what I said to him, but *you're a fucking bully* was in there somewhere.

'What happened to Mr McNab?' I ask. 'He left, didn't he?'

She purses his lips. 'He was offered a retirement dinner with a Scottish piper, or a formal complaint from the school's psychologist. It wasn't a difficult decision.'

'I didn't appreciate all you did. Or thank you properly.'

She waves her hand dismissively. 'I was doing my job.'

When we reach Fitzwilliam's stable, Mandy opens the half-door and pushes the pony back. She pulls a carrot from her pocket.

'Would you like to give it to him?'

I'm not sure what she sees on my face, but as I take a tentative step into the stable, she withdraws the carrot and gives it to him herself.

'Good lad,' she says, patting him firmly on the neck. 'That's from Patience.'

'I could have done it.'

'With your eyes shut?' she says brusquely. 'You might have lost a finger.'

We leave Fitzwilliam securely locked in his stable, skirt around the yards and walk to the paddock furthest away from the house. Galahs with pink chests and grey wings gather between two poplars, flying away when we pass.

'When you called,' she says, 'you said you had to be riding confidently in just a few months.'

I follow her through the railings. 'I have an October deadline I'd like to meet.'

'Less than four months away?' She swipes moisture from the leg of her boot. 'There's very little chance you'll succeed within that time frame.'

I look over her shoulder, to the horse with the faded red rug. He has four black hooves, wet from the grass. Dragging my eyes away, I search for other things. His blaze is white against the brown of his coat. He walks determinedly towards us.

'I'll do what you suggest,' I say firmly. 'I'll start on the ground.'

She follows my gaze to the horse. 'Which is where this handsome lad comes in. Say hello to Minstrel.'

CHAPTER 24

On Saturday morning, I lie back in the bath and take a deep breath. *Jasmine and sandalwood*. Other than tiring easily, I feel well. The bath is now a luxury, an extravagance. I shouldn't need it any more. I *don't* need it any more. But when I close my eyes, I imagine I'm swimming.

Strokes through the water. Counting. Control. Contentment.

Sunlight streams through the window and shines on the round-faced cherubs, wings at their shoulders, that perch around the frame of the mirror. Cockatoos squark outside and cockatiels squabble. After my bath, I'll email Rick about next month's schedule, prepare feeds in the shed, and draft another post for the frog blog. I could write about the moss froglet, which lives in mountains in south-western Tasmania and lays eggs that take twelve months to develop, or—

Boot steps on the verandah outside the window. 'What the fuck is that horse doing there?'

Besides calls about work, it's been three weeks since I've spoken to Hugo. *Or kissed him.* When I sit up in the bath, a wave of water slops over the edge in a rush. The shade of the bathmat darkens to crimson.

'Hugo!' Greta hisses. 'You do not use this language at my house!'

A muttered curse. 'Why is that horse here?'

'Minstrel is a peaceful and very friendly fellow,' Greta says calmly. 'Mandy finds him for Patience.'

Their voices fade. Silence. I remind myself …

I'm afraid of relying on others, of trusting them. And I have good reasons for that. I'm attracted to Hugo and I like him. *He let me down.*

Hands clumsy, I condition my hair and rinse it under the tap. I study the wrinkles on the pads of my fingers.

Footsteps again. 'Sixteen fucking hands.' Hugo again. 'Solid as a double brick shithouse.'

'Keep it down, son,' Derek speaks slowly but firmly. 'You'll upset your mother.'

My limbs are light and warm, but my chest and throat are tight. Placing my hands on the rim of the bath, I push myself upright and stand. Lacklustre bubbles curl around my knees.

'Minstrel is none of Hugo's business,' I remind myself.

I was dressed in a towel when I walked from the granny flat to the bathing room, so that's all I have when I walk back again. Large and white, the towel is tucked over my breasts and falls past my knees. I pull my hair over my shoulder and squeeze it out. I'll change quickly and then—

Hugo leans, one long leg in front of the other, against a verandah post at the top of the steps. Green eyes bright, he straightens when he sees me.

'Imp.' He hasn't shaved in a while. He's far more tanned than he was. T-shirt black and tight, blue jeans worn and faded.

Don't think about the kiss. Do *not* think about the kiss.

I focus on the window box outside Greta's bedroom window. Maybe she couldn't decide which colour geraniums to choose, and that's why she planted a variety. Red, white, light and dark pink. Six plants. Nineteen blooms. Twenty-two buds.

'Hugo.' I nod formally. 'Are you waiting for me?'

His eyes narrow. 'The horse.'

'His name is Minstrel. That's his paddock name. He has a much longer name on his registration papers.' I recheck the overlap on the towel. 'He's a warmblood.'

Hugo mutters a curse. 'He's big.'

'Mandy said I could keep him at her stud, but she's recently had shoulder surgery and I didn't want to burden her. Anyway, it takes an hour to get to Warrandale.' I link my hands, slow my speech. 'Greta and Derek invited him to stay here.'

'Invited?' He rubs the back of his neck. 'They shouldn't have.'

'This has nothing to do with you.'

His lips tighten. 'You want to ride because of me.'

'It's not only because of the team. And I've initiated it on my own, so you're not responsible for anything that might happen.'

'Why do this, Imp? Why—'

'It's important to me.'

'Yeah, and it's important to me that you don't break your neck.'

'Can I get past?' Cutting the corner to the steps, my arm brushes his. It's barely a touch, but my heartbeats scatter. One, three, two. Three, two, one. Two, one, three. I put my hand on his arm and rub.

'I've wet you.' His muscles are hard; his body is warm.

'Imp,' he growls, putting his hand over mine. 'What the fuck?'

Our eyes lock. 'Why do you keep swearing?'

His gaze slips to my mouth. 'Why do you think?'

No, no, no, no, no. I free my hand, take a jerky step back. 'I have to change.'

'Patience! Patience!' Remy, brown curls bouncing, canters towards us. He does an exaggerated skip to change his lead leg. 'Did you see me? Do you remember what that's called so you can do it on Minstrel?'

'A flying change.' I summons a smile from somewhere. 'You're early today.'

'Dad said Ryan has to do his homework or he can't go to the football and Ryan cried even though he said he didn't.'

I crouch. 'Don't tease him, Remy. It's unkind.'

He glances at Hugo. His lip wobbles. 'Sorry.'

'I'm sure you won't do it again.' I take his hands and squeeze. 'Did Ryan bring his maths books? Tell him I'll meet him at the day bed in five minutes and we'll get to work so he can go to the football.'

Remy makes a face. 'Why can't we do my homework?'

'Bring it tomorrow, as much as you want. And after it's done, we'll play horse shows again.'

'Oi,' Hugo says. 'Get over here.' When Remy, grinning, grasps Hugo's hands, Hugo spins him upside down before setting him on his feet again.

Remy jumps up and down on the spot. 'Can I ride Lavender?'

'You're going to the football.'

'I want to ride Lavender instead. *Please,* Uncle Hugo.'

'If it's okay with Andy, I'll think about it.' He jerks his head towards the front of the house. 'Tell Ryan that Patience will be waiting. Talk to your dad about Lavender. Then get back to your stable.'

As Remy, neighing loudly, gallops away, Hugo's gaze stays firmly on my face. 'Did you buy the horse?'

'Yes.' When a droplet of water slides down my neck, I swipe it away. 'Mandy said she'll take him when I go.'

'Uncle Hugo!' Remy yells out. 'Oma wants you! Oma wants you now!'

Ryan and I, sitting on the day bed, work our way through the exercises. It's almost one when Greta puts a heaped plate of sandwiches next to the textbook.

'Thanks, Oma.' When Ryan reaches for a sandwich, opening his mouth wide to accommodate the fillings, Greta smiles.

'It is important to learn mathematics. This is why you are excused from joining your father and uncle at the table.'

There's only one sandwich left when, with the end of my pencil, I tap the final diagram.

'This is where we bring a whole lot of principles together. Farmer Jenny has to calculate how many sunflower seeds she needs to plant in her field. Where do we start?'

Ryan chews as he talks. 'Work out the area.'

'Which will give us the square metreage. Good. Because we're told there are twelve seeds per square metre.'

'That's not enough seeds.'

'Isn't it?'

'You don't care about the seeds.' He takes another bite of his sandwich. 'You'd only want to know about the posts.' He grins. 'How many would she need to fence the paddock?'

'I don't *only* count fence posts.'

'Do you count...' He glances around. 'Close your eyes.'

I do as he asks.

'How many boards on the verandah?'

'Horizontally between here and the railing? Fifteen.' When he laughs, I open my eyes and tap his book again. '*If* you were asked about fence posts, it would be a different calculation, wouldn't it? How would you approach it?'

For a moment he frowns, but then his brow clears. 'Work out the perimeter.'

'Excellent.' I tie my hair, almost dry, into a plait. 'And how would you go about that?'

'Length and width, then multiply by two.'

When I hold up my hand, he slaps it. 'We'd have to sort out the shapes first though, wouldn't we? So, let's do that for the area, before applying it to the perimeter.'

'Farmer Jenny's an idiot. No field looks like this one.'

'Jenny does her best.' I take my pencil and divide up the drawing. 'Can you recognise the shapes?'

'Triangle, rectangle, trapezoid.'

'We have to calculate the area of each of them, and then we'll add them up. What kind of crop do you think Jenny could sow with twelve seeds per metre?'

'I dunno.' He laughs. 'Anyway, you just said that's irrelevant.'

'Now I'm curious.' Soxy jumps on the day bed, looking with interest at the crumbs. 'Tell me the calculations.'

'The triangle is base over height, divided by two. The rectangle is length by width.'

'And the trapezoid?' I go back a couple of pages. 'We looked at that shape on Wednesday. Do you remember what we did?'

He stuffs the last of the sandwich into his mouth and picks up his pencil. 'Calculate base one and base two and multiply by the height.'

'That's a great start. Write it down and apply it. What happens next?'

'Divide by two.' He carefully writes numbers in his workbook, setting them out like I've shown him, so it will be easier to pick up a mistake should he make one. No mistakes this time.

'That's great, Ryan.' We slap hands again. 'The area is sorted.' So now we work out the quantity of seeds, and then the perimeter.'

'I can't believe I gave myself more work.'

After Ryan has finished the exercise, we consider the work he'll be assigned in class next week, so instead of assuming it's new and he doesn't have the knowledge to tackle it, he'll be able to work through the steps. He makes notes in the margins.

'Well done,' I say. 'Have fun at the football.'

Another slap of hands. 'Thanks.'

When Hugo walks towards us, Ryan drops his books and raises his fists. Laughing and feinting, they jab and dodge and fool around. Scrabbling off the day bed, I group the cushions. One, two. One, two, three. One, two.

'Imp?' By the time I turn, Hugo has the shadow of a smile on his lips. His hair is tousled and he runs a hand through it. When my gaze runs down his body and up again, he catches me staring.

My skin warms. 'You always let Ryan hit you.'

He winces as he rubs a spot on his ribs. 'Not for much longer.'

'Does Greta need help with something?'

When he crosses his arms, his T-shirt pulls tight across his chest. 'She said you have to rest.'

'I was going to post on the blog.'

'I'll be back tonight. We'll talk about the horse.'

CHAPTER 25

A little before four o'clock, I hurriedly push my feet into boots. *Please, Hugo, don't come back early.* Minstrel's feed and other things are stored in one of the sheds. The nights are getting colder, and he doesn't have the stable he had at his old home, so I bought him a new winter rug—waterproof canvas with a tail flap and thick cotton lining. His leather halter with smart brass fittings hangs from a hook next to his saddle and bridle.

His bridle has a stainless-steel bit.

His saddle has stainless-steel stirrup irons.

I'm not ready to ride quite yet.

Breathing deeply, I lift the halter from the hook and clip on the lead rope, an even brighter shade of red than the rug. I loop the grooming bucket, brimming with brushes and other paraphernalia, over my arm with the rug and halter. In my back pocket I have three large carrots, cut into pieces, from Greta's vegetable patch.

'Minstrel!'

I don't know whether he looks up from the grass because he hears his name, or because he sees me, but he sets off at a trot, nickering a greeting as he nears the fence. I ignore the thumps of his hooves on the dirt, focusing instead on his pricked ears and dark inquisitive eyes. I hang the rug on the fence far enough away that, even if there was a breeze, it wouldn't flap and spook him. He helpfully hangs his head over the railing as I slip the halter over his nose, but as I thread a strap through the buckle, I fumble. The strap slaps him in the nose. He blinks in surprise.

I give his nose a rub before starting again. 'Thank goodness you're not only peaceful and friendly, but tolerant too.' As soon as my hand goes to my pocket, he dips his head and nudges my hip. His mouth soft on my palm, he takes a piece of carrot. 'I'm relatively brave from this side of the fence, aren't I?'

I stroke under his mane and feel the thickness of his glossy winter coat. He's mostly dark brown, but below his knees and hocks his legs are black, as are his forelock, mane and tail. *My horse's colour is bay.* I push his forelock to one side to reveal the top of his blaze. His tail hangs down past his fetlocks, almost to the ground.

Hugo said Minstrel had big feet, but Mandy focused on his placid temperament and excellent schooling. For many years he was a successful dressage horse, but after his owner had a baby she only rode him occasionally. When she bought another horse, she searched for a home where Minstrel, now sixteen, would be cared for not only in the next few years, but into his retirement. Which is why it was a condition of the sale that Mandy take him from me when I leave.

You'll leave him behind.

Leaning over the fence, I tie the lead rope to the piece of string that's threaded around a post. 'Mandy's horses are loved in the same way children should be—and she knows what she's doing. You'll have a nice home with her.'

The fence is designed for cattle and difficult to climb through, so I enter the paddock through the gate. Minstrel munches contentedly on another piece of carrot as, standing close to his body, I run a stiff bristled brush down his shoulder.

He's a solidly built horse, much more so than most stock horses and thoroughbreds. Has he gained weight in only two weeks? It's tempting to feed him because he always seems to be hungry, but I don't want to make him unhealthy. When he stamps a back leg, I jump. 'He has a fly on his belly,' I reassure myself.

I count strokes as I brush, first his neck, then shoulder, body and rump. With a soft bendy brush, I also groom his legs. Sometimes he thinks I want to lift his hoof—he takes the weight off his leg when I bend over his fetlock—but Andy said I could defer checking for stones until he gets shod.

'I've arranged for the farrier to come next week,' I tell him. 'Mike will trim your feet and put nice new shoes on.'

I'm learning how to communicate with Minstrel. Build my confidence. Predict his behaviour. Trust him. *There'll be no place for fear.*

Minstrel occasionally looks around—to the cattle in the paddock that leads to the creek, to Greta as she sweeps the verandah, to Derek as he parks the tractor in the shed—but only in a curious way. Before I go back to the house, I'll give him a hay net and he'll pull long strands of lucerne through the gaps. Sometimes he shakes the bag around, gets dust up his nose and snorts.

I glance at my watch. It's not yet five. I'll lead him around the paddock before settling him for the night. As I have the rope, I'll be in charge.

I have to be in charge to feel safe.

I won't look at his hooves.

He walks calmly by my side as we follow the well-worn track along the fence. 'It might surprise you to know I can navigate a warship with a displacement of 27,500 tonnes.' My hands are steady on the lead rope, one near the halter, the other halfway down. 'Displacement is the mass of water the hull displaces.' His ears move, as if he's interested in hearing more. 'I don't need a computer to navigate—the stars and a compass are enough.' Clip-clop. Clip-clop. 'Before I was put on quarterly reports for swearing at the commander investigating my harassment complaint, I was down in the Southern Ocean.' When he snorts, his halter jangles. 'Robert Falcon Scott, an early explorer, took ponies to Antarctica to pull the sleds. Were you aware of that?'

Greta is at the washing line, spinning the hills hoist she's used for decades—nappies, school uniforms and man-sized shirts. *A checked blue shirt with metallic silver threads.* Derek, holding a basket as he follows along behind her, lifts a hand in salute. I take one hand from the rope and wave back.

'When I finish this secondment,' Minstrel walks calmly by my side, 'I'll go back to sea again. Hopefully it'll be my old ship, so I can monitor said offending officer. Next time, he'll be the one kicked off the ship.'

I usually eat at the house on Sunday evenings, because Greta goes to a lot of trouble with her roast. Andy, Ryan and Remy are often there, and others come too, generally neighbours or people new to the district who Greta believes could do with some company. Andy and his boys won't be at the table tonight, but Hugo will be. Do I care?

It'd be easier if I didn't.

At the end of the paddock, the land slopes downhill and the ground is dry, pockmarked with cattle hooves. We skirt around a bore tap and a large concrete laundry sink. How long has it been used as a water trough? Twenty years? Thirty? I don't know that there's anything too valuable in the paddocks, sheds or even the house, but the memories here are a beautiful tapestry. Even the gardens, tangles of roses and other shrubs that Greta has collected, have their own histories. A lone Norfolk pine—Derek refuses to accommodate another one—in one of the paddocks adjoining the road was purchased as a Christmas tree in the year that Mateus was born.

'Time to turn around, Minstrel.'

The upright corner post is weathered and grey, thicker and higher than the other posts. On the house side of the post there are three metal steps. Have I climbed them before? I think I have. A line, thick and black as charcoal, creeps up the post. That's familiar too.

I pull up short and stare. Tension claws my chest.

This is where I fell.

Hooves thundering. Angela screaming. Hugo running. When I was thrown from the saddle, my foot was in the stirrup and my head was on the ground. Dragged and bruised and scarred.

Broken.

A wave of nausea sneaks up my throat. Head down, stomach churning, I press the heel of my hand against my mouth. When my knees start to wobble, I grasp the top rail. I can't fall down because if I'm in the dirt all I'll see is …

Minstrel stretches his neck and reaches for tufts of grass peeking under the fence. He lifts his head again, chews noisily, looks back the way we came.

Releasing a shuddering breath, I put my hand on his neck. My stomach settles, my heart rate slows. I'm not on his back or under his feet or—

'Patience!' Derek calls from somewhere near the house. 'Need a hand over there?'

After clearing my throat, I shout. 'Maybe.'

I manage to keep breathing until he arrives, but not much else. Leaning over the fence, he peers silently into my face.

'What's going on, love?'

'He didn't do anything,' I croak.

'Why're you stuck out here?'

'I just …' I take another deep breath. 'I fell here, didn't I?'

Derek climbs the steps of the corner post, swings a leg over the railing and drops to the ground.

'Give me the horse.'

My fingers are stiff when I open my hand to relinquish the rope. My palm stings. 'Ow'

'What's up?'

Two neat crescents mark my palm; one of them is bleeding. 'My nails dug in.'

Giving Minstrel a solid pat on the neck, Derek leads him away. He unclips the rope, clicks his tongue and pats Minstrel's rump.

'Off you go, mate. Supper won't be long.'

'I'm sorry, Derek.'

'Unhappy memories,' he says. 'That's what Hugo would say.'

My tears come out of nowhere. Stinging eyes, wet cheeks. But not for long. I wipe my face with my sleeve. I sniff again.

'I feel so useless.'

Derek takes off his hat. 'Take a minute and catch your breath.'

'I might have rushed things.' I look towards Minstrel, waiting patiently at the gate. 'I'm okay.'

'When you were a kid,' Derek says, 'you darted around like a mosquito. That nickname Hugo gave you wasn't bad. Imp for impatient.'

I do my best to smile back. 'Yes.'

'With horses there's no rushing. They take the time they need to get their heads around things, and we've got to take our time too.' He holds the brim of his hat, turning it around. 'That's new to you, Patience, because you like to keep moving. You like to run at things.'

I sniff. 'It's better than running away.'

'Nothing wrong with running when you've got a good reason.' He frowns as he turns his hat again. 'What's the expression? With your military training, you'd know it for sure.'

'A tactical retreat?'

'That's the one. Reckon that's what happened when you left. You had your father and sisters to worry about. Not to mention my youngest son, and all that went with that. You wanted to sort yourself out before coming back.'

'But I'm not coming back. My career is in the navy.'

His eyes disappear into creases when he smiles. 'Even so, here's Patience Cartwright, standing right in front of me.'

'For now.'

'Like I said to Greta when we met, there's nothing wrong with stopping a while.'

'You've both been so good to me.'

'Yet the minute you're out of your sickbed, you rush off again, setting yourself a challenge. Hugo says he can work up north without you. Greta likes having you round the place. Why not—'

'I'm supposed to support the team on this project. It's my job.'

'And you always do your job?'

'If I'm capable of it, yes.'

'And there's the rub.' He puts his hat back on. 'Because Hugo doesn't want you breaking your neck.'

When I push off the fence post and walk towards the gate, Derek walks beside me. I clip the rope to Minstrel's halter, running my fingers through his mane before tying him to the string. Derek fetches the hay net from the shed as I lay the rug across Minstrel's back, securing the chest and leg straps. I strap the hay net to the fence and Minstrel pulls stalks through the gaps.

'Sleep well.' I push aside his forelock and stroke his blaze. 'I'll see you in the morning.'

Car lights curl up the driveway. Hugo's four-wheel drive. Doors slam.

'Are you having dinner with us tonight?' Derek asks. 'Gus hitched a lift with Hugo. He's got real friendly with Phoebe and Sinn in the past year or two. Reckon he's missing them.'

The verandah lights flicker on. 'Thank you, Derek. I haven't seen Gus in ages.'

'You sure about this riding caper?'

'I hate being scared. I want to do something about it.'

'In that case …' He glances at Minstrel. 'I'll have a word to Gus. Between the two of us, I reckon we can get you sorted.'

The moon casts a silvery glow as I walk up the steps to the verandah at the front of the house. Hugo, standing at the railing, looks at my face as if searching. Red eyes? Tear tracks? I thought I'd washed them away. Gus Mumford, an elderly farmer with a shock of white hair and grey bushy eyebrows, leans back in his chair and nurses a beer. Derek, sitting next to Gus, puts his beer on the table.

'Can I get you a drink, Patience?'

'I'll just check whether Greta needs help—'

'She's pissed off,' Hugo says gruffly. 'Best to keep clear.'

'Greta is upset,' Derek corrects, glancing at his son, 'on account of Hugo not staying to dinner.'

I've been compiling reasons for *not* wanting to face Hugo across the dinner table, but an ache of disappointment sits deep in my chest. I turn my back in case he sees it, and adjust the cushions in the old tatty armchair that no one except me ever sits in. As soon as my legs curl to the side, Soxy jumps up and snuggles in the gap.

Gus sits back and smiles, a little misty eyed. 'My Maggie was like Greta. She liked all the kids lined up like ducks. She was a good cook too.'

'Greta cooked Maggie's lamington recipe last week,' I say.

'Your sister does that one too.' Gus smiles. 'How's she getting on? Heard there's a bub on the way. I bet she and Sinn can't wait to get home …'

When the conversation turns from Phoebe to sheep, I must close my eyes. Because, by the time I open them again, Hugo is sitting at the end of the table. He glances at me and then away. When I sit straighter in my chair, Soxy looks up.

I smother a yawn and scratch his chest. 'Have I been neglecting you?'

Gus smiles. 'Derek reckons you didn't nap as long today.'

I tug burrs from Soxy's tail. 'I don't sleep every day.'

Derek clears his throat. 'Patience was with Minstrel this afternoon, weren't you, love?'

'He's a good-looking horse,' Gus says. 'Trouble is, Patience is knee-high to a grasshopper.'

'Minstrel has a fine temperament.' Derek wipes his mouth with the back of his hand. 'You can't discount that.'

'When I was younger,' Gus says, turning to me, 'I rode some damn fine horses myself. I met my Maggie on the rodeo circuit, as a matter of fact.'

Derek clears his throat again. 'I told Hugo how good you were doing with your groundwork, Patience. And d'you know what? Gus offered to help with what comes after.'

'I grew up on a horse,' Gus says proudly. 'And if not for my dodgy eyesight, I'd still be saddling up.'

'You'll be all right on the ground though, won't you, Gus?' Derek says. 'Leading and lunging, things like that. It's how Mandy wants Patience to start.'

'With a well-mannered horse, I don't see why not,' Gus says. 'I'm only eighty-two after all.'

I stroke Soxy's ears again. 'That's kind of you, Gus. I'll let you know when I'm feeling more confident.'

'I know a fair bit about horses myself,' Derek says.

'Andy wasn't the best of horsemen,' Gus says. 'Looked like a sack of spuds on a horse, from what I recall, but he'd lend a hand if we were desperate.'

'Greta can fill a nice hot bath in the bathing room,' Derek says, 'should Patience get sore or take a tumble.'

'Dad!' Hugo's glass clunks on the table. 'What the hell are you up to?'

'Now, now, Hugo,' Gus says. 'There's a lady present. Mind your language.'

Hugo opens his mouth and slams it shut. He turns to his father. 'How can Patience ride here, given what you said before?'

I look from Hugo to Derek. 'What did you say?'

Derek shifts uncomfortably. 'Leading Minstrel around stirred up memories, no shame in that.'

Hugo leans forward. 'Show me your hand, Imp. You hurt it, didn't you?'

I bunch it into a fist. 'I'm going to do this!'

'Don't see why not,' Derek continues conversationally, 'but you've got to acknowledge that Hugo's got a point. We only have one paddock that's suitable for what you need—not too big, only a handful of trees, and a nice level surface. Trouble is, that's the paddock where you had your fall.'

'In a few weeks, Minstrel can move to Mandy's stud,' I say. 'She has suitable paddocks.'

Hugo unclenches his jaw. 'Mandy has an arm in a sling.'

'Which brings us back to the start,' Gus says, winking at Derek. 'I'm happy to give it a go if you—'

Hugo stands. 'No.'

'You got a better solution, son?' Derek asks. 'Being it's you who's so opposed to this caper?'

'Caper? Last time Patience rode, it could have killed her.'

I uncurl my legs. 'But it didn't.'

Hugo talks between his teeth. 'You can't ride here.'

'Maggie always said girls can do anything boys can do.' Gus drains his beer. 'Patience has guts.'

'Her sex is irrelevant.' Hugo says, glaring at me. 'As are her capabilities.'

'Talking of that,' Gus says, 'the marsupial frog is an interesting critter. After the female lays eggs, the male dives into the jelly mass around them. Did you read Patience's blog?'

Derek hides a smile. 'Reckon Hugo might've.'

'After the eggs hatch,' Gus continues, 'tadpoles wriggle into flaps of skin, like pockets, at the bloke's groin. And guess what happens next?' He slaps his thigh. 'Frogs come out!'

Hugo mutters under his breath, but Derek nods politely. He turns to me again. 'Riding is important to you, isn't it, love? That's what you told me.'

'I'm determined to do it.'

'Dad!' Hugo jabs a finger. 'Get that horse out of that paddock.'

'And where do you suggest we put him?' Derek says. 'Where do we find a nice safe alternative? A place where Patience can ride, under supervision, when she's ready?'

'If we don't do it here,' Gus says dubiously, 'it's got to be at Mandy's place.'

'We're going in circles,' Derek says. 'Mandy couldn't give Patience a leg-up with only one arm, not on a big horse like Minstrel. And how's Mandy supposed to hold him steady if he shies and jumps around? And you and me can't be going back and forth to Mandy's in Warrandale, Gus. Not with all the work that needs doing around here.'

Hugo curses. 'Send him to me.'

'What's that?' Gus says, holding his hand to his ear.

'I'll take the horse.'

'You'll have him at the brewery, is that what you mean? Patience can ride there?'

'If she agrees to do what I say.'

My socks are fluffy and striped—pink, white and yellow. I feel Hugo's gaze as I pull them up. Our eyes meet. Blue on stormy green.

'Why would you help me?' I ask.

He walks to my chair and crouches, his arms on his thighs. He's tired and rattled and his eyes are bright with annoyance. The temptation to touch him, to smooth out the creases between his brows and kiss his cranky mouth is—

'I don't want you hurt,' he says quietly. 'And I don't pretend.'

CHAPTER 26

I don't pretend. If Derek and Gus heard what Hugo said, and I'm not sure that they did, they would have thought he was referring to my accident, how he couldn't pretend it hadn't happened. I could have turned his offer down. I could have …

I recall how he looked on a horse. No fear. No whip.

He'll do his best to teach me. I'll do my best to do as I am told.

But I'll keep my distance.

Keep my heart to myself where it's safe.

Weeks have passed since Rick requested that we talk in person. At first, I couldn't drive. And then he was away. Last night he told me he'd arranged a lift to Dubbo and asked me to meet him at the park.

I pull over outside Dubbo's oldest pub. The thick timber doors, firmly closed at eight in the morning, are neatly framed by green and cream tiles. A quick calculation. Six hundred and forty-eight. I'm almost at the kerb when I turn and check the tiles again. This time taking more care, I count the lines and multiply.

A sigh of relief. 'Six hundred and forty-eight.'

No more tears, no more slip ups. *I'm finally thinking straight.*

Pushing my hands into my sleeves to warm them, I stop by the cenotaph and Anzac Day wreaths. The artificial flowers have held onto their colours, but the fresh flowers and foliage are faded and dry. Rose and chrysanthemum, viburnum, rosemary and sasanqua. Would my father have been different if he hadn't gone to war? *Lest we forget.* A lorikeet swoops into the clearing, red feathers bright against the plinth.

Rick, the collar of his customary shirt peeking out of a round-necked sweater, sits on a bench that faces the lake. He's on the far left of the seat; a bulging folder and two scientific journals are on his right.

'Good morning, Rick. It's good to see you again.'

'You're late, lieutenant.'

I check my watch. 'Twenty-two seconds. Can you make room for me, please?'

He gathers up his things. 'How are you feeling today?'

'Have you been practising that line?'

He barks a laugh as he holds up his phone. 'Eliza reminded me.'

'Thank you for the gifts.'

'I was told they were appropriate.'

'There was also a get-well card, ostensibly signed by you. Did you see it?'

'Eliza sent an image.'

'It's nice that you're still friends.'

Rick files his folder and journals in his bag before looking up. 'We have a matter to discuss.'

Leaning back on the seat, I cross my feet at the ankles. As if I'm not concerned. *As if I'm not a spy.* 'I'm glad you wanted to meet. Hugo's been asking what's worrying you and I haven't known how I should respond.'

'You claimed the invoices meant nothing to you. This was untrue.'

Interrogation was a compulsory unit in training—I spent weeks poring over the literature and was fine at the theory, but not so good at the practice. *Avoid awkward questions.* Tick. *Tell a lie.* Cross.

'The December invoices from the two different consultants had identical chargeable hours—that's how I noticed them. And when I looked at later months, January, February and March, a pattern emerged. It was you who told me the invoice relating to the Macquarie team shouldn't have been paid because the work had never been done.'

'Why were you interested in chargeable hours?'

'Like I said back then, you work too many hours to be able to claim them all. I was curious about the practices of others who work on the project.'

The wind picks up, stirring the grasses adjacent to the lake. Rick puts one hand on his leg and taps it with the other. One, two, three, four, five. 'I find this stressful, lieutenant.'

I turn on the bench, facing him side on. 'You spoke to Professor Tedeschi about what we saw, and he told you not to worry. Has anything changed?'

He stands and paces on the grass. Back and forth. Forth and back. 'No.'

I move to the very edge of the bench. 'Have you told him I know about the invoices?'

'I have not.'

'The professor hasn't explained, has he?'

He stops mid-stride, turns abruptly and sits. 'It was my responsibility to check the invoices.'

'When you found out there was a possible duplication, you reported it to the professor.'

Tap, tap, tap. 'I considered my role was an administrative inconvenience.' He taps again, five sets of five. 'Four invoices were issued for services that weren't carried out. Professor Tedeschi is aware of this.'

'Do you know if they were paid?'

'I do not.'

'What's the professor doing about it?'

Rick looks around but, besides a family of ducks, two adults and three ducklings, we're alone. 'He assures me the administrative errors will be corrected.' He crosses his hands in his lap before tapping again. 'You mustn't repeat what I've told you.'

'Why would you leave this to Tedeschi?'

Rick jumps to his feet and paces again. 'I was careless. If this was made public, I would be disciplined by my university. More importantly, it would threaten Hugo, Lisa and others on the Macquarie team.'

'They wouldn't want you to die of stress over it.'

As a siren blares in the distance, Rick reaches into his sweater, pulls his phone out of his breast pocket and scrolls.

'I'll wait until the end of the month for Professor Tedeschi's explanation.'

'That's three weeks away.' The sun is warm on my back, but my hands are stiff with cold. I rub them together and slip them into the sleeves of my coat. The adult ducks dive, their tails and back legs waggling. 'Will you bring your laptop next time I see you? I might be able to find out more.'

'Why is that necessary?'

'You trust the professor so completely?'

'He's an honest man, lieutenant. I've known him for many years.'

'That doesn't mean you can trust him. If there was an administrative error, you could ask Tedeschi to explain exactly what it was, how it happened.'

Rick taps again. Five plus five plus five. 'I will do this.'

My head hurts. The cold? I untie a lace and refasten it. 'Do you have anything in writing from the professor?'

'We speak on the phone.'

'Please, Rick. Tell him you're not approving invoices any more. Let him take responsibility for it.'

'You mustn't tell anyone.'

Two black and cream birds wade into the water. Their legs are like stilts, their beaks long and curved.

'When you hear from the professor, let me know.'

He stands, puts his backpack over his shoulders and secures the straps. He peers over my shoulder.

'Did you like the get-well gift?'

'I've never seen a scarf like it.'

'The water lilies were appropriate.'

'I love the crystal embroidery. They're real stones, like turquoise and lapis lazuli. Did you know that?'

'It was very expensive.'

I hold back a smile. 'I don't have many clothes. It was a perfect gift.'

After I stand, we both stare at the lake. No more long-beaked birds. No ducks. 'Hugo will be waiting,' Rick says.

My breath hitches. 'You didn't tell me he was here.'

'I don't drive.'

'But …' I take a deep breath. 'Does he know you're with me?'

'I refused to confirm it.'

When I scoop up a stone and throw it, it bounces across the water. One, two, three, four, five skips. I follow its progress and then ...

Hugo walks along the path towards us, stride long and purposeful. He's had a haircut, and he's cleanly shaven. Pale blue linen shirt with sleeves rolled up, buff coloured pants, leather boots with thin laces.

Urban Hugo.

He's not surprised that I'm here. 'Patience.'

The duck family swims towards us, silvery ripples spreading out behind them. 'Hugo.'

He puts his hands in his pockets, looks from Rick to me. 'What's going on?'

'This is a private matter,' Rick says.

Crossing his arms, Hugo faces Rick. 'We're way ahead of schedule, but you continue to hassle me, Lisa and the rest of the team. I can't keep making excuses if you won't tell me what's eating at you.'

Rick looks determinedly straight ahead. 'I'll modify my behaviour.' He adjusts a strap on his backpack. 'I'm ready to go.'

'I'm not,' Hugo says, handing him a bunch of keys. 'The car is where I dropped you off.'

Greta wants me to buy cinnamon sticks and paprika. Derek's hardware order is in. I have things to do. Yet ...

'Imp?' Hugo frowns. 'I'm concerned about him.'

'I can't say anything, but ...' I sigh. 'I'm watching out for him.'

He opens his mouth as if to argue, but slams it shut again. Then, 'This can't go on.'

Nodding stiffly, I turn to face the lake. A duck family appears through the reeds, hops onto the bank and waddles to the grass a few metres away. The adult ducks have smart brown feathers; the ducklings' fluffy feathers are mottled brown and white.

When the mother duck shakes water from her wings, sunlight catches the droplets. The ducklings, on their tiny spindly legs, shake too.

Hugo's lips tilt. They soften. 'A duck has built a nest at the creek.'

'At the brewery? Is that okay?'

'Why wouldn't it be?'

'Won't the ducks eat the tadpoles?'

Definitely a smile. 'Biodiversity, Imp.'

My heart flips. I steady it. 'When should Derek float Minstrel to you?'

'Handling one horse won't be enough.'

'How many do I need?' I walk closer to the seat, rest a hand on the backrest. 'There must be commonalities.'

'There's no hurry.' His eyes are unreadable. 'Greta said you don't wake up until ten and —'

'I look after Minstrel on my own. I'm ready to start swimming again.'

'Are you eating enough?'

What does he see when he stares? Flat chest. Bruised eyes. I gather my coat more closely around me. 'It takes time to gain weight.'

'I wasn't—'

'Yes, you were!'

He rubs around the back of his neck. 'You're beautiful, Imp. That'll never change.'

The mother duck leads her family to the reeds. One of the ducklings, smaller than the rest, pushes her way to the front of the queue. The sun breaks through the trees and throws beams across the lake.

'I cry for stupid reasons.' I clear my throat. 'I'm scared of horses. I'm worried about my job.'

'And whatever it is you and Rick won't tell me about.'

I can't see the ducks any more, just movement in the rushes. 'I started the secondment, and I want to finish it. Then I'll go back to sea.'

'You need time.'

I take a step back. 'When can I start riding?'

'Handle Arrow first,' he finally says. 'Groom him, pick up his feet, get used to him.'

'When do I do that?'

He pulls out his phone, frowns at the screen. 'We can start Wednesday week. After that, I'm back in Victoria.'

'Wednesday week is good.'

He searches my face. 'You're pale, Imp. You should sit down.'

I could sit down. *Or I could lean against him.* Another step back, but smaller than the last. 'If I can manage Arrow, what will happen then?'

'I'll bring Minstrel home.'

CHAPTER 27

I'll bring Minstrel home.

Hugo's home has a grey roof, wide verandahs and butter yellow sandstone blocks. He'll put glass in the upstairs windows and rehabilitate the creek. He'll welcome the ducks and frogs, the echidnas and the wallabies. When he gets around to it, he'll create a garden. What will he plant? Bottlebrush and grevillea trees, kangaroo paw and native orchids.

He comes from a loving family. He knows where he belongs. He knows about home.

Home is where I lay my hat. When I said it on the beach, I almost believed it. But now …

If I trusted him, what would that look like?

As I turn off the loop road into Horseshoe Hill, a call from a landline comes through. I pull over next to the line of bottlebrush trees outside the primary school. When I wind down my window, crisp winter air blows into the four-wheel drive.

'Patience Cartwright.'

'It's Emma, Captain McCarthy's EA, returning your call. I'll put you through to him now.'

'Lieutenant.'

'Sir.'

'How are you?'

Sapphie Brown's baby must be due very soon, but she crosses the playground with long graceful steps, dipping her head as she talks to the little girl next to her. A wiggly line of girls and boys walk and skip behind.

'I'm fine, but I didn't report in last month, or the month before that. I thought I'd better get in touch.'

'I couldn't make much sense of what you said at the hospital.'

I was half dead, sir. 'Have you heard back from the auditor-general's office?'

'Briefly.' A rustle of paper. 'The engineering company that issued the invoices doesn't exist. The auditor-general is looking into it.'

'I spoke to Dr Lipman yesterday. He told me that Professor Tedeschi is still insisting the errors were only administrative, and they'll be corrected.'

McCarthy snorts. 'If the company has been paid, how might that be achieved?'

'Have the invoices been paid? Does the auditor-general's office want—'

'The ball is in their court, lieutenant. If they have further questions, they'll ask them.'

'I've encouraged Dr Lipman to ask Professor Tedeschi to explain what's going on, but I can't push too hard in case he, or the professor, get suspicious.'

'Tedeschi is still in the dark about what you know?'

'So far as I'm aware, yes.'

'Keep it that way.'

'Professor Tedeschi *and* Dr Lipman are tied up in this, even though Dr Lipman's done nothing wrong.'

'He had a duty to oversee payments.'

'He's not dishonest, sir. I'm sure of it.' A magpie flies over the schoolhouse and sits on the school fence. 'And I'm concerned about the implications for the Macquarie team.'

'You shouldn't be.' Another rustle of paper. 'Get well, finish the secondment, return to the base.'

When the phone disconnects, I drop it into my lap and rest my head on the steering wheel. I've taken an oath to do as I'm asked, but …

The auditor-general won't care about Rick or the team any more than Captain McCarthy does. And Rick trusts me. How would he react if he found out I'd been spying?

Hugo?

I told him at the start that I was here to do the job set out in the secondment criterion. *A candidate with basic administrative, topography and map-reading skills and a knowledge of boats, their operation and maintenance.*

I put the car into gear. 'As well as horse riding,' I mutter to myself. 'Don't forget that.'

I'm certain Hugo wouldn't want to be associated with fraud or dishonesty any more than Rick would, but I denied I had another agenda. I've denied I'm keeping secrets.

Sapphie, dark hair neatly coiled in a bun, holds out her arms and herds the children into their classroom. She was in her late teens when she moved to Horseshoe, and I didn't know her well, but she and Hugo were good friends at school. They're still good friends.

Sapphie, Lisa, and others. He has a lot of good friends. Friends he can trust.

Putting my head on the steering wheel, I count backwards from ten.

Friendship with Hugo.

That could never be enough.

I flick through back issues of *National Geographic* in Dr Gupta's waiting room. There's a piece on Galapagos turtles. And critically endangered corroboree frogs. I jump when the doctor, in his sixties with thick dark hair and permanent smile lines at his mouth and eyes, opens the door to his surgery.

'Sorry to keep you.' He stands back. 'Please come in.'

I hold up two magazines. 'Can I borrow these? I'll bring them back next time.'

He laughs. 'Certainly!'

I lie on the paper sheet on the narrow bed as he checks me over, finishing up with a thorough examination of the wound on my foot.

'It's feeling much better.' I wince when he presses against my instep.

'There is improvement.'

As I climb off the bed, he puts a kidney-shaped plastic bowl on his desk, plucks out a syringe and takes my fortnightly blood sample. I press a plaster to the spot on the inside of my arm.

'The pathology lab must be sick of me.'

'It's important to monitor your white cell count.'

'That's been way better too.' I roll down my sleeve. 'Can I go back to work?'

'Subject to satisfactory pathology results, deskwork is possible.'

'I'm supposed to be at the river.'

Moving around his desk and sitting in his chair, he consults the forms in front of him. 'You were hospitalised for an extended period after a particularly nasty infection, and emergency surgery. The antibiotics alone would have been sufficient to decondition you.'

'But—'

'This is not what you wish to hear, Patience, but the naval medical criterion,' he holds up a form, 'is most particular. You are demonstrably unfit for active duty.'

'I'm swimming at the pool in Dubbo, and I help Greta around the house when she lets me. I'm hoping to ride again soon.'

He lays his pen firmly on the desk. 'Is this wise?'

'Under supervision.'

His brows lift. 'Do you rest in the afternoons? Sleep ten to twelve hours at night?'

I sigh. 'Mostly. And yes.'

'Your blood pressure is low.' He makes notes in my file. 'Come back in two weeks. We shall reassess.'

By the time I drive home, Greta is back from her CWA meeting. She takes grocery bags out of my hands and shoos me to a stool at the bench.

'Sit down, liebchen,' she says, putting a basket of eggs, a fork and a bowl in front of me. 'You can help with this.'

'How many eggs should I crack?'

'Six.' She lays slices of beef on her chopping board. 'Dr Gupta is happy with your progress?'

'Not as happy as I'd like him to be. I have to go back in two weeks.'

'Two more months of rest—this is what I tell Dr Gupta.'

I crack three eggs into the bowl. 'Does he tell you about patient confidentiality?'

'He does not talk to me at all,' she says with a smile. 'It is the other way around.'

'I can move out, Greta. You and Derek have been so generous already and—'

Greta pounds the beef with a mallet. 'You help with the cooking,' she finally says, 'and you are the tutor for Ryan. You are happy here.'

'I'm grateful for everything you've done, but—'

'You like the granny flat, yes?' She pounds the meat again. 'You are not bothered by Hugo. You are kept in peace as I promised.'

Kisses in the rose garden. Pleasantries on the verandah. Watching him work on the farm. The scent of his skin, the taste of his mouth. The tilt of his head, the smile in his eyes. The shape of his body, the length of his stride. *Other than those things, I'm kept in peace.*

'I could pay board.'

Her eyes widen. 'You are a guest! You must not throw your money away!'

'Greta …' I crack two more eggs. 'I was nineteen when I joined the navy. It paid my student debt, and it continues to pay me now. I invested the money Auntie Kate left me. I have savings.'

'You must keep them in the bank. There they are safe.' She wipes her hands on her apron. 'No more talk of this, or I will have the headache.'

'Two more weeks, Greta, then we'll—'

'This meal we make,' she interrupts. 'It will be good for your blood.'

Defeated, I crack the final egg. 'They're very large slices.'

'I do not use veal—newborn calves should be left with their mothers to suckle. This fellow,' she slams another piece of meat on the board, 'he has grown strong in the paddock. He has had a good life.'

'Until he was sent to market.'

'My dear mother,' she crosses herself, 'in the war, she almost starved to death.'

'Yes, but—'

'We are fortunate. We are farmers. It is our duty to eat.'

Piece by piece, Greta dips the meat in flour, swishes it in egg and rolls it in breadcrumbs—fragments of homemade bread and freshly chopped herbs.

'After I swim tomorrow afternoon, I'm going straight to Hugo's. He wants to introduce me to Arrow.'

Greta nods encouragingly. 'This will be a test of your horsemanship.'

I lay the crumbed pieces between sheets of greaseproof paper. 'Let's hope I pass.'

CHAPTER 28

Long straight arms and scissor kicks.

Twenty-eight freestyle strokes for every fifty metres. At the end of each lap, I duck my head, tumbling and twisting before kicking off again. Arms stretched out, hands together, I break the surface. Stroke twenty-eight. Stroke twenty-seven. Stroke twenty-six. Head to the side and breathe. Stroke twenty-five …

Dr Gupta's words ring in my ears. *A moderate swim is sufficient to improve your fitness and clear your mind.* Meeting Hugo at four o'clock has been fogging my mind all day. Fear of my feelings for him or fear of his horse?

Both.

When my arms ache and kicks slow, I pull off my goggles, wrap them round my wrist and flip onto my back. The sun is setting. Swimming lazy laps of backstroke, I close my eyes against the glare and—

Treading water, I check the clock. 'Oh!' I swim freestyle to the side of the pool and haul myself out. There's no time to shower and rinse chorine from my skin, or shampoo and condition my hair. I run to the change room, tug on underwear, jeans and a shirt before racing to my car where I throw socks, boots and a toiletries bag onto the seat. *This will be a test of your horsemanship.*

I never fail tests.

I'm never late.

The sun is low in the sky, lengthening the shadows thrown by the red gum, when I turn into Hugo's driveway. To the right is the creek and the newly planted grasses and saplings. The house, even without sunshine, is beautiful.

Golden sandstone blocks and a grey slate roof. A broad verandah with weathered boards and tall timber posts.

The horses, the black thoroughbred and grey Shetland pony, stand at the fence to my left. Arrow has an athletic build—long in the neck and back, with powerful hindquarters. Lavender is even smaller than I remembered, his forelock so long and thick I can't think how he sees through it.

My gaze goes back to the driveway. I brake.

The four-wheel drive parked by the house doesn't belong to Hugo. And it looks very similar to the four-wheel drive I've been issued—a late model but slightly battered Landcruiser. Two people, a tall slender woman and a man with thick grey hair, walk through the plants near the creek. Their backs are to me, and the woman's hood is up, so I'm not sure at first, but—

Lisa Stanhope and Professor Tedeschi.

Thinking about the horses makes me tense. Refusing to think about Hugo makes me tense. *And now I have this.* Lisa turns, as does

Tedeschi. He shields his eyes, leaning forward to peer through the windscreen of my car. Lisa waves.

'Patience!'

By the time I've parked the four-wheel drive, Tedeschi is walking in my direction. Lisa, her red calf-length coat cinched at the waist, pushes back her hood. Hands in her pockets, she shouts again.

'Hugo's running late, but I have a key. Want a coffee?'

When I took Rick to the Halsteads' for lunch, Greta complained that Hugo didn't bring his girlfriends to Horseshoe. Was she wrong about that? I glance at my phone. Hugo must know that Lisa and Tedeschi are here. Why didn't he tell me not to come?

My hair is still damp. I untangle it with my fingers as I walk on tiptoes to the other side of the car. As I pull on socks and boots, I tell myself over and over. *Forget Lisa.* But what about Tedeschi? Is this an opportunity to talk to him?

McCarthy has told me to finish the secondment and come back to the base. But it might be helpful to the team if I can work out whether Tedeschi can be trusted or—

'Lieutenant!' Dressed in pants with lots of pockets, sturdy black walking shoes and a thick padded jacket, Professor Tedeschi, hand outstretched, crosses the distance between us. 'What a delightful surprise. I understood you wouldn't be back on board for some time yet. Not rushing things, I hope. How are you bearing up?'

'Please call me Patience.' We shake hands. 'I'm much better, thank you. I'm not officially back at work, but,' I point to the horses, 'Hugo has offered to help me ride.'

'Working with Hugo's team will be a different experience than working with Rick. Having said that, you and Rick appeared to get on well.' He stamps his feet, scuffs the soles on the gravel. 'Mind you, I only have Rick's perspective.'

'Rick taught me a lot, and I didn't mind the early morning starts.'

'Hugo is concerned about Rick.' Tedeschi steps back as we negotiate a puddle at the bottom of the steps. 'Do you have any idea what's going on there?'

Is this a trick question? I shrug, hopefully convincingly. 'Rick is always uptight about something. I've never worked with anybody who pushes themselves so hard.'

'Assisting him during your convalescence is above and beyond the call of duty.'

We walk side by side up the long shallow steps to the verandah. 'Until I get a clear medical, I can't be of use at the river, but I want to pull my weight.' When a breeze blows in, tossing my hair around, I push it under my collar. 'Anyway, I'm interested in what Rick does, and I don't mind helping with his admin.'

'Does that include his IT?' He smiles. 'I found your assistance at the conference invaluable, Patience.'

'You weren't so bad.' Yet … he *was* bad. If he's the person behind the false claims, he'd need help to cover his tracks. Rick isn't involved, so who is? I aim for a neutral expression. 'It can be confusing if you don't deal with it all the time.'

'I prefer to focus on my scientific work.'

'I liked being out on the river.'

'Field work and scientific rigour can go hand in hand. Hugo is a fine example of that.'

'For Hugo …' I indicate the four-wheel drives lined up in the place where the garden should be. 'The creek comes first.'

'His tertiary studies were very much a means to an end, he's made that clear enough. And, unlike many in his field, his path isn't via academia.' His brows lift. 'An approach which, after forty years of university politics, I'm increasingly sympathetic to.'

'Do you enjoy your work on the water security project?'

'It's a tremendous amount of work,' he says, wiping imaginary sweat from his brow. 'But thankfully it's only an interim role. I retire at the end of the year.'

I school my features to neutral. 'What will you do?'

'I'm passionate about the environment and its preservation,' he says brightly. 'I'd like to use my profile to push back against further exploitation of our natural environment. I might not be around to see the long-term benefits, but future generations will.' He looks beyond me, out towards the creek. 'According to my son, we have to get the message out any way we can.'

'Is he a scientist too?'

'Charles has no formal qualifications,' Tedeschi says, 'but he's extraordinarily committed to the environment. I couldn't be prouder of him.'

Rick is concerned about the invoices. Tedeschi clearly isn't. Other than a confirmation of that, I've learned nothing.

Lavender nickers when he spots Hugo's four-wheel drive, and trots to the fence adjacent to the driveway. Lisa's boots are loud on the boards as she walks to the front of the house. She grasps a post and swings around it.

'There's such a lot to do!' She laughs. 'I can't believe Hugo is still sleeping upstairs. It's *freezing* up there!'

Statistics: the analysis of events covered by probability. *Hugo has brought at least one of his girlfriends home to Horseshoe Hill.*

'What do you think, Patience?' Lisa says. 'Could you live here?'

I force a smile. 'I'm only here to see the horses.'

'Hugo is giving you lessons, isn't he? Sorry to barge in, but we were close by. I was keen to see the house again, and the professor was curious about the creek.'

The professor purses his lips. 'Quite a bit of work to do there, as well.'

'Are you still at the Halsteads' farm?' Lisa asks. 'What's it like there?'

Brightly painted window boxes with colourful geraniums. Weathered timber crates stuffed with mismatched boots. A day bed with throws and hand-embroidered cushions. A rose garden hedged with lavender and rosemary.

'The house is very different from this one.'

'It was good to see you, Patience,' Tedeschi says as he glances at his phone, 'I'll say hello to Hugo, then I'd better respond to this email. I'll see you at the car, Lisa.'

Hugo, hair damp and shirt open at the neck, wipes his hands on his jeans before greeting the professor.

'Patience?' Lisa looks at me curiously, as if it's not the first time she's said my name. She runs a hand through her glossy straight hair, and it slips right back into place. 'When do you think you'll be back at work?'

'I shouldn't be off for too much longer.'

Hugo tucks in his shirt and rolls up his sleeves as he walks towards us. He stops at the bottom of the steps.

'Lisa.'

Grinning, she runs down the steps, delicately jumps over a puddle and puts her hands on his shoulders. She kisses both cheeks before picking a leaf from his hair and touching a smudge on his chin.

'Been getting down and dirty in the swamps, Dr Halstead?'

He glances at me. Nods formally. 'Patience.'

'I have a few more ideas for your house,' Lisa says, as she links her arm through Hugo's.

'I can't afford your ideas.'

'C'mon.' She laughs. 'It won't take long.'

Hugo said it was over between Lisa and him. He wouldn't lie about that. He *especially* wouldn't lie about that just before we kissed in Greta's rose garden. But ...

They look good together. They laugh together. They have history—but not the kind of history that Hugo and I have. Hugo mightn't want to be with Lisa now, but he could want that in the future. Could Lisa be a piece of his puzzle?

I shove the thought aside as I walk towards the horses. *This is what I'm here for.* I think about what Mandy has told me, and what I've studied since.

Trust overcomes fear.

I'm fearful because I fell from a horse. And since that happened, I've collected tidbits of information that reinforce that fear. Last month in Melbourne, a horse fell on a jockey and crushed his pelvis. Camelot, Phoebe's horse, panicked and knocked her over.

I have to reframe my fear, to acknowledge and accept that, just as in real life, accidents happen. On a ship, I navigate around reefs and cyclones. On the way here, I slowed before crossing the bridge. 'I follow the rules and rely on others to do the same.'

To overcome my fear, I have to predict what a horse might do and respond appropriately. I trust the horse; the horse trusts me.

Lavender is dry under his forelock, but the white star on Arrow's forehead is damp. I trace the whorl as he reaches over the fence. 'Hugo won't be long,' I say, as I look over my shoulder.

Lisa and Hugo are standing side by side at one of the upstairs windows. I imagine Lisa laughing, complaining about the cold. *His upstairs bedroom is freezing.* Hugo *was* my friend, but then I fell in love. *What did I want?* For him to love me back. A happy family. A home.

Lavender wanders away, but Arrow seems happy to hang at the fence. Hugo rubbed the base of his ears the last time we were here, and I do the same. He lowers his head even further, presses his nose against my stomach. Car doors slam, goodbye calls ring out. I lift a hand when Lisa drives past. Professor Tedeschi, in the passenger seat, waves back.

Did I respond to his questions appropriately? He seemed friendly and open, not a care in the world. Because he's not hiding anything? If that was the case, why is he evasive with Rick? *Is* he evasive? Is there a straightforward explanation for whatever's going on with the invoices?

Captain McCarthy would tell me to leave everything to the auditor-general's office.

Rick wants me to give the professor more time. I have no choice but to agree to that, but as soon as the month is over, I'll pin Rick down and—

'Imp.'

When I jump, Arrow lifts his head. 'Oh!' I take a step back and stumble into Hugo. His hands are firm on my shoulders. His body is warm on my back.

CHAPTER 29

Unlike Lisa, I can't kiss Hugo casually, or joke about the dirt on his chin. Twisting out of his hold, I turn and face him. The sun is going down, but his eyes are bright. There's a halter slung over his shoulder.

'You could have cancelled.'

'Sorry to start late.'

'I've been practising with Minstrel, catching him in the paddock instead of over the fence.' My words tumble over each other. 'I told him he could only come for a holiday with your horses if he cooperated.'

I think he laughs, but as he's walking behind me I'm not sure. When we pass through the gate, my grooming bucket clenched tightly in my hand, he steps closer, not touching but within reach.

'Breathe, Imp.'

We're five metres from Arrow, and he's looking towards us. He *turns* towards us. One hoof, two hooves, three hooves, four. I look up, suck in more air.

Trust overcomes fear. Arrow is black; his star is white. After I greeted him, I rubbed around his ears. If he senses my fear, he'll wonder what's wrong. He'll be tense and jumpy and …

'I've been talking to Mandy and reading about fear. The theory …' *I'm good at the theory.* 'Horses sense fear.'

'And they're unpredictable. Tell me about that.'

I open my mouth, but no words come out.

'You want to learn about Arrow, don't you?' His touch on my arm is light, encouraging. 'How he shies at gusts of wind, unexpected movement, things that only he can see and hear. When we're with horses, we have to expect that, anticipate it. Minstrel is placid, Arrow isn't. We have to work around that.'

'I need to know my own horse, while keeping an eye on the others. I have to try to predict what they'll do.' I keep close to the fence. 'I have to be prepared.'

'A horse is less likely to act unexpectedly if he feels safe. Arrow will feel safe through you.'

I blink. 'Are you serious?'

'With you, Imp,' his lip lifts, 'always.'

After firmly patting Arrow's neck, Hugo slips on his halter, clips on the lead rope and loops it through a piece of string hanging from a post.

'Introduce yourself.'

Arrow's coat isn't as thick as Minstrel's. Because he's a thoroughbred? I ask him about that as I stroke his neck. I tell him he's a handsome horse, and I like his name. He doesn't turn his head towards me, but his ears twitch as he listens. He stands quietly, but I've been warned.

If something unexpected happens—a cockatoo's squawk or airbrakes on a truck or a wombat's grunt or …

A cowbell hit with a drum mallet.

Jackpot shied. I lost a stirrup. I bounced on the ground, bloodied and broken.

'Imp?' Hugo, frowning, holds out his hand. 'Take it.'

'I …' I shake my head. 'No.'

His eyes narrow. 'You agreed to do what you were told.'

My hand is smooth, small and cold. His is rough, large and warm. He grasps my fingers firmly, pulling me close to his side. Our forearms line up wrist to wrist, but I ignore my jittery heart. This is a means to an end. He won't have to worry about me breaking my neck if I can ride. If I can do my job. *If I can finish my job.* This has nothing to do with friendship. Or love.

My hair smells of chorine; I push it back. 'What do I do first?'

'Have you handled Minstrel's feet?'

'I've brushed his legs. When Mike came to put on his shoes …' I look down at Arrow's feet and quickly up again. 'I held him.'

He mutters under his breath. Then, so quickly that I barely keep my balance, he releases my hand and pulls me against his body. My back is flat against his front, his arm is a band across my stomach.

'Is this okay?' He searches for my hand again. He opens his fingers to find a path through mine.

The first time we held hands, I told him I loved him.

'Yes, but … Hugo? What are you doing?'

'Do you feel safe?' When his body shifts, he takes me with him. All Arrow's feet are on the ground. His hooves, like the rest of him, are black.

'Yes. And no.'

He lowers his head and I feel the heat of him. 'You're shaking.'

When Arrow turns his head, we're reflected in his eyes. 'I don't know what I'm supposed to do.'

'Breathing is a start.'

I take deep breaths. 'How's that?'

'Better.' He squeezes my hand. 'Like you said, horses sense fear. Arrow would want to know why you're afraid—what's out there that's dangerous.'

'I'm only afraid of him.'

He laughs, a rumble against my back. 'Have you heard of chemosignals? Through scent, horses can read human emotional states. They have physiological responses to fear. They react to it.'

'Did you do research too?'

His chest lifts and falls. 'An interspecies transfer of emotion. It's interesting.'

'So …' I shut my eyes, focus on his words. 'I have to control my fear. Not only on the ground, but when I'm on a horse.'

'You weren't experienced when you rode, but you had a good seat, light hands. You rode without fear.'

'That was a mistake.'

'It was understandable. Remy has no fear, most children don't.'

'I was old enough to know better.' His thumb stills. He breathes deeply. He must smell the chlorine in my hair, on my skin. 'I don't have PTSD or anything like that. I'm only afraid when I'm with a horse.'

'How do you feel now?'

'You're not afraid,' I say quietly. 'And you wouldn't let me be hurt.'

'If you feel safe, so will Arrow. It's the same,' his arm tightens, 'as this.'

My heart thumps slowly. 'You're sending messages of confidence to me.' My body softens. 'You're the human.' I breathe him in. 'I'm the horse.'

'You got it.'

'What if I was frightened by something? What if I shied and knocked you down?'

'I'd deal with your response,' he says, releasing my hand and putting his other arm across my front as well. 'I'd take control, communicate that I'm not afraid. You'd sense how I feel and respect it.'

'I wouldn't be afraid any more.'

He breathes deeply. Then, 'Imp? It'll be dark soon.'

I stiffen, pull away. 'What do I do first?'

As I unfasten the leg straps of Arrow's rug, I stay close to his hindquarters. And when all of the straps are undone, I fold the rug like Derek showed me, before pulling it off and laying it over the fence. With Arrow, I go through the same routine I have with Minstrel, removing the loose hair and dust, scraping the dirt from his belly and legs, untangling his mane and tail.

'You're doing well, Imp.'

I hold out a shaky hand. 'You reckon.'

Hugo comes closer, stands at Arrow's shoulder. 'Remember how early you got to the pool? A scrawny little kid, sitting on the kerb at five in the morning, waiting for a bad-tempered pool attendant to unlock the gate.'

'Why are you …'

He gestures to Arrow. 'Think about something else.'

'I …' I release my breath. 'I was always up early.'

'How long was that walk? A kilometre and a half? Two?'

For a ten year old, four thousand two hundred and seventy-two steps. When I was eleven it was … I shake my head clear of the numbers. 'Something like that. But I didn't always do it. Greta picked me up.'

'She warned me about your father,' he says quietly. 'If we said anything about you waiting alone, or talked about him, he might stop you coming.' I feel his gaze as I brush Arrow's rump. 'We'd lose you.'

'I was happy in the pool. At swimming.'

'How often are you swimming now?'

'Three times a week.' *Fifty-nine strokes per lap. Fifty-two laps. Three thousand and sixty-eight strokes.*

I glance at the bucket. 'I should clean out his hooves.'

'We can do it next time.'

'If I can operate a compass, sextant, barometer and chronometer, I *should* be able to manage a hoof pick.'

His lip lifts. 'Handle him right, and he'll do the work.' He takes Arrow's halter, strokes his neck. 'Stand close to his shoulder. Run your hand down his leg to his fetlock, lean against him if you need to. He'll shift his balance and lift his foot.'

I grip Arrow's leg as firmly as I can. My heart races double time as I run my hand down his leg.

His hoof lifts, a glint of metal shoe. 'Oh!' When I jump back, he stamps his foot on the ground again.

Hugo springs forward, grasps my arm. 'It's okay, Imp.'

'I asked him to do it and he did.' My voice is much too high. 'I should have hung onto it.'

'Don't overthink it. Look at him, read the signals. He doesn't care that you didn't want his foot this time, but he's trained to think you'll want it next time. Also …'

My eyes go to his. 'What?'

His lip lifts again. 'Breathe.'

Arrow *doesn't* look too concerned. I walk closer, holding his halter as Hugo bends and runs his hand down Arrow's leg. When Arrow lifts his hoof, Hugo rests it on his knee and gives me the pick.

'Take out the dirt and stones, anything that might bruise his sole.'

We stand close, our shoulders and arms lined up, as I run the pick, a thick piece of metal with a blunt hook on the end, around the inside of Arrow's foot. His shoe is like a fence, defining the parameters. I work my way around the fleshy but tough triangle in the middle of his sole.

'That's called the frog, isn't it?'

'You got it.' I feel his gaze on the side of my face. 'You want to do the others together too?'

By the time we get to Arrow's last leg, his offside rear, the shadows are long. 'I can try this one by myself.' I run my hand down his rump and over his hock to his fetlock, keeping close to his leg in case he kicks out. He lifts his foot but adjusts his weight afterwards. 'Oh!' When I let the hoof go, Hugo, his body hard up against mine, catches it before it hits the ground.

'He's getting his balance, Imp, that's all.' He holds out the pick but, glancing at my hands, he frowns and withdraws it again, cleaning Arrow's foot himself.

'I could have done it.'

'Your fingers are white.'

I blow on my hands. 'Just cold.'

'We started late.'

Because Tedeschi and Lisa turned up. I take a jerky step backwards. I pick up the bucket and put it back down again. 'We shouldn't have done this. You should have cancelled. I have to go.'

'Imp.' His voice is a growl. 'What's going on?'

I don't like the idea of Lisa in your bedroom.

I don't like the idea that I don't like the idea of Lisa in your bedroom …

How do I explain that?

'You've been working all day, and Greta's expecting me, and Lisa and—'

'Imp!' His eyes narrow a little. 'You were with Lisa when I got here. Is that what this is about?'

'She said your bedroom was freezing.'

Tight-lipped, Hugo yanks the rug from the fence, throws it over Arrow's back and fastens the straps. Slipping off the thoroughbred's halter, he slings it over his shoulder.

And then he takes my hand.

CHAPTER 30

If Hugo's hold was too tight. If he tugged too hard. If my heart wasn't jumping about like a jack-in-the-box …

I'd make him let me go.

But as it is …

'Are you marching?'

'What?' he snaps.

'A regular and deliberate measured tread. That's marching.'

'Do you want to come into the house?'

'I should've been back at the farm twenty minutes ago.'

He doesn't release me until we reach the four-wheel drive. 'Wait here. I've got something for you.'

I touch his arm. 'I'm sorry about before.'

'Lisa and me.' He unlocks his jaw. 'I wouldn't lie about something like that.'

'No.'

'She's been here once before. After we dropped off gear, I showed her through the house.'

'I wasn't expecting them.'

He nods stiffly. 'I won't be long.'

After stomping up the verandah steps, Hugo turns on the lights, illuminating the house in a soft golden glow.

I pull out my phone and text Greta. *Leaving Hugo's now.*

His footsteps are loud on the floorboards. Silence. Footsteps again. I'm sitting sideways in the seat, my eyes on the open front door, when he appears. After taking the steps two at a time, he closes the distance between us.

He puts a large paper bag with sturdy rope handles on my lap. 'Here.'

'What is it?'

When he rests a foot on the running board, lifts my boot and examines it, my long thick laces dangle on his knee.

'Where did you get these?'

'They're navy boots. Reinforced toes.'

He indicates the bag. 'Wear these instead.'

'But I already—'

'They're riding boots.'

'Oh.' I pull the box, shiny green with a gold-leaf logo, from the bag. 'I'll pay you back.'

'They're a gift.'

The boots are a well-known brand. *Expensive.* Brown leather with elastic sides. I turn the box and check the size. 'Did Greta brief you?'

'I can exchange them.'

'I'll try them on now.' One of my laces is already half undone so it's easy to untie—the second lace takes longer. I remove both boots, throwing them into the well in front of the passenger seat. 'Why don't you like the boots I have?'

He holds up one of the new boots. 'These have smooth soles. No laces.'

'When I fell from Jackpot …' I clear my throat, 'I wore sneakers.'

He gives me the boot. 'It wasn't anything you did.'

'Or Jackpot or Andy or Angela did.' Head down, I pull on the left boot. When he hands me the right, our hands touch. Warmth, sudden and sweet, flows though my veins. Avoiding his gaze, I pull on the boot and, stretching my legs to one side of him, point my toes. 'They fit.'

He stands back. 'Go for a walk.'

Jumping to the ground, I salute. 'Yes, sir.'

I keep to the weeds that push through the gravel, worried about marking the boots. The leather shines softly. Unmarked. *Perfect.*

Like Hugo and I once were.

Like we could be again?

I pull up short, grasp the verandah post near the stairs.

A perfect number is a positive integer that's equal to the sum of its proper divisors. Six is a perfect number, because it can be divided by one, two and three. God created everything in six days. Twenty-eight is a perfect number. One, two, four, seven, fourteen. The moon has a twenty-eight-day cycle around the earth.

I put my hands against my cheeks, warm against my palms.

'Imp? You okay?'

He steps aside when I climb back onto the seat. I sit sideways again, place my hands on my knees, focus on the boots. 'Thank you. I like them.'

'No problem.'

'And thank you for before.' I wave a hand. 'With Arrow. What you said, the way you took my mind off things.'

His brow creases as he looks towards the horses. He still has dirt on his chin. 'We'll do more when I get back.' The overhead light in the car times out. We're both in the shadows, but neither of us move. When we were on the beach, I imagined the colour of his eyes. Clear and bright. Shades of the ocean.

Does he lean in? Do I lean out? His stomach, rock hard, presses against my knees. He reaches for my hands, clenched in my lap.

'Imp?' He squeezes. 'What's in your head?'

Our hands are a sphere within a sphere. A circle in a three-dimensional place is a sphere. Volume equals four over three, times pi, times the radius to the power of three.

'You don't want to know.'

'I do,' he growls.

He doesn't smell of swamp. Or chlorine. His scent is fresh. 'The value of pi.'

When he lifts our hands, his breath is warm on my fingers. 'Three point one four one five … something.'

'There are a lot of decimal places.'

'You'll know them.'

'I stop at a hundred.'

He kisses the base of my thumb. 'No one is smarter than you.'

'A lot of what I know …' My forehead against his, I whisper. '*It's not useful.*'

'Imp?' A request? A plea?

Shuffling to the edge of the seat, I wrap a leg around him. And when I stroke the bristles on his jaw, run my hand along the nape of his neck, he burrows under my coat and grasps my waist, his fingers opening and closing. He mutters low in his throat, kisses the inside of my wrist.

'Your hair is darker.' My voice is light, breathy. 'It's different.'

'We've changed, Imp.'

'You still call me that.'

'It's mine. Yours.'

Trust overcomes fear. I want to trust him. So much so it hurts.

Our mouths touch like butterflies. And when our tongues meet, I sigh in relief. He advances, retreats, circles and strokes. I thread my arms around his neck, press my breasts against his chest. There are layers of clothing between us. Shirts and sweaters and jackets. But I find the soft skin at his throat, his face and neck and hands.

He mutters under his breath. His gaze slips to our hands. He releases them to follow a path from my hips, along the outsides of my legs. A traitorous tingling starts in my thighs and pools in my stomach. As if he knows it, he eases my legs apart and slides into the gap.

Promise. Yearning.

He wraps my plait around his wrist. He breathes into my mouth as I breathe into his. Giving and taking. This is what I want. *I don't want to leave.*

When I stiffen, so does he. 'Imp?' He lifts his head, frowns again. 'Sweetheart? What is it?' He touches my lip with his thumb. 'Tell me.'

'I'll try to do better.'

He pulls back a little. He stares into my eyes. 'I won't hurt you again.'

When I give him my hands, he bunches them between his. Spheres. Back to where we started ...

Better than when we started.

CHAPTER 31

The passengers disembark and walk across the tarmac, but I only have eyes for my sister. Prim is taller than most of the other women and her gait, long and lithe like a tiger, is distinctive. Her long dark hair, tied in a ponytail, swings in time to her steps.

'It's … so good to see you,' she says as she hugs me.

'Four days won't be enough.' My voice is muffled.

She laughs as she stands back. 'Am I hugging too tight?'

'Never.'

'You look …' She tips her head to the side as she holds me at arm's length. 'You don't look as good as I was hoping.'

I thread my arm through hers as we walk to the car park. 'As you're between share houses, Greta insists the farm is your home.'

Working dogs, lapdogs, cats and other domesticated animals fall in love with Prim. Wild animals, the broken birds and lizards she brought to the house in Dubbo, the injured joeys, wombats and possums she smuggles into her share houses, appear to trust her too.

Phoebe mothered us. I fought for us. Prim? We didn't consciously do it, but we tried to live our childhood, the innocence of what a childhood should be, through her. We did our best to protect her. From our father. And from other things.

Soxy sitting at her feet, Prim picks up one of Greta's baskets and loops it through one arm. 'By the weight of this, we can picnic for a month.'

I throw a blanket over my shoulder. 'You can always stay longer.'

Grinning, Prim tips her Akubra to the back of her head. 'W … which way to the river? Greta … said it's not too far for you to walk.'

I had too many memories to brave it earlier. Now?

It's a piece of the puzzle of Hugo and me.

Prim swaps the basket to her other arm as we walk towards the gums. The level of the water in the dam, less murky and brown than before, has risen since the rain, and a gentle breeze ripples through the grass. When I take the track to the river, Prim falls in behind. Either side of us are old-growth trees, red gums mostly, but there are also smaller trees, shrubs and native grasses. The river widens, forming shallow pools. Prim squats on the broad sandy bank and runs her hand through the water.

'This is amazing.'

'In the last drought, Derek said there was barely a drop of water anywhere, but now …' Sunlight, filtered by the trees and gossamer thin clouds, throws dapples on the water, sparkling blues and greens.

'Did you ever come here with Hugo?'

Deep breath. 'Sometimes.'

She perches on a rock and peers into the water. 'He must love the habitat.'

'I hope he can do the same for the creek where he lives now.'

'Greta ... said the house is a mess.'

I think it's beautiful. 'I haven't been inside.'

I pull off my boots and socks and sit on a rock. Then, rolling up my jeans, I put my feet in the shallows. The water ripples and swirls, ebbs and flows, finds a path around my ankles. 'I wish I had a wetsuit.'

She laughs. 'No!'

I peer into the shallows. 'The water's not deep enough to swim in, so I couldn't stay warm without one.'

'If you get ... so much as your knees wet, Greta will kill me.' She lays the blanket on the sand and opens the basket. 'Come and ... sit down before you do ... something ... stupid.'

'Your speech, Prim.' I tip my head to the side, smile encouragingly. 'You're struggling again, aren't you?'

She forages in the basket. 'My ... speech is shit.'

'It's lucky you don't have a problem with "sh" words.' I smile encouragingly. 'What about more speech therapy?'

'Remember when I removed all "s" words from my vocabulary?' She smiles, but her dimple barely shows.

'You could do a refresher course, to remind you of things. That's worked before.'

She pulls out apples and sandwiches. 'I'll think about it.'

'I'd be happy to pay if that would—'

When she tosses an apple, I catch it. 'I already owe you for flights.'

'I can afford to help. This is important.'

She sticks out her tongue and points to it. 'You'd think I'd be old enough to remember ... whether to put it in front or behind my teeth.' Her hair shields her face as she takes out more food—berries and biscuits. She selects another container and holds it out. 'W ... what are these?'

'Knödel, dumplings.'

When she unwraps foil and puts a knödel on her plate, it rolls around the perimeter. 'It's heavy.'

'There are apricots inside in summer, plums in winter. Careful, the fruit will still be hot.'

She takes a bite. 'Yum.'

'The dough is made from steamed and grated potatoes, flour and egg. Greta wraps it around the fruit, boils the knödel in water and rolls them in toasted breadcrumbs.' I rummage in the basket and find a small container of brown sugar. 'You dip them in that.'

'Delicious.' Plum juice dribbles down Prim's chin and she wipes it with the back of her hand. 'Aren't you going to have one?'

'I had bacon and eggs for breakfast.'

'Greta put four eggs in my omelette, then added mushrooms, capsicum, tomatoes and at least half a kilo of cheese.'

'That's the price you pay for vegetarianism.'

'She treats it like a peanut allergy. I have a dedicated chopping board.'

I'm not sure where the tears come from, but it's hard to blink them back. 'She's been so good to me.'

Prim, dimple disappearing, hands me a sandwich. 'We're both … worried about you going back to work. You'll … stay here until you're fit, right?'

'Being here …' I take a bite of the sandwich. 'It's like living at the Hotel California.'

Prim smiles again. 'Checking out but never leaving would be heavenly.' Lying down, she tips her hat over her face. 'I love being in Horseshoe.'

'Phoebe would be relatively close.' A trail of tiny ants march in a line past my hand. 'So would the zoo.'

She sighs dreamily. 'I'm like the northern corroboree frog from the Brindabella and Fiery ranges.'

'What?'

'Or the Baw Baw frog from the Baw Baw Plateau in Victoria.'

'Are you making fun of my blog?'

'Never! It's how I know those frogs have specific range and habitat requirements. That's me too.'

Prim knows where she belongs.

I aim for a smile. 'I'll visit you here whenever I can.'

She swipes at a fly. 'I've liked having you in just one place. So has Phoebe.'

When I open a thermos, ribbons of steam curl round my hand. I pour water into a metal cup and jiggle a teabag.

Hugo *also* knows about home. Could I ever—

Crashes in the undergrowth. Grunting and mooing. Closer and closer and …

Nine steers behind us, only metres away. I jump to my feet.

Prim sits and smiles, tips her hat to the back of her head. 'Want me to get rid of them?'

I have bare feet. They have hooves. Thirty-six hooves. Cattle have split hooves. Seventy-two. The steers at the back are restless, pushing against the steers in front.

'Prim!' When I drop the cup, it clunks over the rocks to the sand. 'Get up!'

She stands and puts a hand on my arm. 'Patience?' She peers into my face; her grip tightens. Keeping between me and the steers, she pulls me back towards the water. 'Stay here, all right? Don't move.'

Prim forages for a branch, discarding two before she finds one the size of a hockey stick. Holding her hands out wide, she hits low rocks, bushes and trees as she walks towards the steers. 'Off you go, boys!'

The first steer, head down, stands his ground. But when Prim bashes her stick on the ground in front of him, he steps back. Trampling bushes as he goes, he pushes past the others and breaks into a trot. The remaining steers, suddenly alarmed, follow suit, crashing after the leader until …

Birdcalls. Water gurgling gently.

My lips are dry. My fists are clenched. I open my hands, hold them out and study them. The raised weal between my thumb and index finger is long and fiery red.

'I burned it.'

'What?' Prim takes my arm, tugging so hard that I stumble. But when we reach the water, she tugs again. I drop to my knees. The water is cold. The stinging stops. My breathing steadies.

Prim, crouching next to me, puts a hand on my shoulder. 'You're … still … so … scared?' She's shocked, disbelieving.

I look up, smile bravely. 'It's lucky I'm not in the cavalry.'

She croaks a laugh, sits back and bends her knees. 'I knew you kept away from Phoebe's horses, but …'

'Until I came here, I didn't realise how bad things had got.' I swish my hand through the water, open my fingers and close them. 'I don't know how I've got away with it for so long. If the navy had *any* idea …'

She grimaces. 'You've done peacekeeping tours in Asia.'

'I stayed clear of the buffalo.'

'What about the Middle East?'

'Same with the donkeys. Anyway, I was mostly on the ship.' The pink of the burn is stark against the whiteness of my fingers. I sit more comfortably, legs crossed. 'It's about time I confronted it.'

'I must've been fourteen when you fell.' She balances her hat on her knee. 'After you came home from hospital, you stayed with our next-door neighbour for a couple of nights, then you came home.'

'I couldn't wait.'

'You could hardly open your eyes. You drank ... soup from a ... straw.' She straightens the rim of her hat. 'Dad ... sent visitors away.'

'We were okay on our own.'

'I was at school, Phoebe was at university. Who looked after you?'

'I stayed at home for the term. After the holidays, I was well enough to go back.'

'As if nothing had happened?' Prim finds a bottle of juice in the basket and pours it into two plastic cups. Yellow for her and blue for me. 'You're white as a sheet. Come and ... sit down.'

After straightening out the picnic rug, I sit cross-legged again. Careful of my hand, I unwrap the remaining half of my sandwich.

'The next time I went to the Halsteads' was October,' I say. 'Greta and Derek made sure I stayed clear of the animals.'

Prim hands me a wet tea towel and I wrap it around my hand. 'You're doing well with Minstrel,' she says.

'I wasn't expecting the steers. I didn't have time to prepare myself.'

'It doesn't make much sense, relying on Hugo when he has to go away all the time.' She lies down next to me, her hat over her face again. 'Are you sure he's the best person to help? I could do it when we ... see each other at Christmas.'

'Thanks, but ... You like him now, don't you?'

She tips her head to the side. 'Far more importantly, do *you* like him now?'

A lizard with brown striped skin and spines along his back shoots across the clearing. He crawls his way up the trunk and then he stills.

'Yes.'

'Can you trust him?'

'Please, Prim.' I straighten my legs. 'I don't want to say anything else, not yet.'

'You're even worse than Phoebe, the way you clam up.'

One handed, I put lids on containers. 'Please don't tell Greta or Derek.'

'You think they'll object again? Greta adores you and—'

'I have to get used to the idea.'

'I'll kill him if he hurts you. Tell him that from me.'

Prim is down at the shed with Derek while I lie on the day bed, my head propped up on two cushions. My phone rings.

'Hugo.'

'Hey.'

'How's your hand?'

I sigh. 'What did Greta say?'

'You walked to the river. It was too far.'

'I wanted to go there.'

'I want to go there too, but—'

'Derek will float Minstrel to the brewery tomorrow.'

A grumble. 'Give him a few days to settle.'

'I'll see you next weekend, won't I?'

'I miss you.'

'I miss you too.'

CHAPTER 32

I curl my legs to the side on the day bed and lean back against the cushions. The home paddock looks empty without Minstrel. I can't ride him until he's settled at Hugo's, but next time I go there I'll wear my new boots.

Smooth soles. No laces.

Greta, holding a tray, smiles as she approaches. 'You must eat.'

'I've only just had lunch.'

'You do not like these biscuits? They are as light as a feather.'

The glass is brimming with milk; I take it carefully. 'Like everything you bake, the biscuits are delicious.'

'After you eat, you must rest.'

I smile. 'I don't think—'

Sitting next to me on the day bed, she indicates the plaster on my hand. 'Maybe tomorrow is too early for the horses.'

'You've seen the blister.' I pinch my fingers together. 'It's this big.'

She frowns at the laptop. 'You are always so busy. Primrose was the same—busy, busy, busy. It is no wonder you Cartwright girls do not cook. You are not in the kitchen long enough to warm the oven.'

'Thank you for all you did for Prim.'

'With her it is all cows and sheep. She was helpful to Derek. Always helpful. You will miss your sister, both of your sisters.'

I lean back against the cushions. 'We have a group chat, and we talk on the phone. You wouldn't have had those options with your family.'

She smiles. 'At twenty-one and all alone, I travel across the world. Like my mother, I liked to cook, and I liked to keep the house clean and tidy. It was not expected that I go on an adventure.'

'Why did you do it?'

Greta smooths her apron over her legs. 'Many years ago, Derek told me of an expression.' She smiles in reminiscence. 'I did not know the meaning at the time, but now that I do, I believe that is when I decided to marry him.'

I laugh. 'What did he say?'

'*Defy expectations*. It means, liebchen, to do what is not expected.' She pats my hand. 'In this, I have Derek's admiration. I am an adventuress.'

'You must have missed your family.'

'On Sundays, very early, I would go to the phone box and call my mother.' She crosses herself. 'I am the only child. Always, I did this.'

'It was good that she came here to live.'

'I was sorry she had lost my stepfather, a very good man, but yes, I was happy. And after he builds the granny flat, Derek is happy too.'

'Only then?'

'My mother was a fine woman, but also one with opinions.'

'Hugo said …' I drink again, place the glass on the arm of the day bed. 'He told me you and my mother were friends.'

'We met often at the kindergarten.' She smiles. 'Hugo and Phoebe were close in age.'

'Mum was happy, wasn't she?'

Greta turns her biscuit in her hand. *Like Derek turned his hat.* 'As Mateus and Andreas were older, Hugo was my baby. Your mother, she has two little girls after Phoebe. She loved her daughters. She was proud of her work at the university.'

'I asked you whether she was happy. Can you tell me?'

Greta smooths her apron on her lap. 'You are a woman now, liebchen, you will understand. Sometimes we sense unhappiness. Your mother didn't talk often of your father, but he didn't come to the kindergarten or community events. At first, she made excuses, but then she did not. I believe she would have been happier alone.'

'After Mum left for New Zealand, our father's behaviour got worse, but Phoebe remembers earlier times. He shut himself away, we were never allowed to shout.'

Greta nibbles the biscuit distractedly. 'Phoebe and Hugo were at different schools, but Barbara and I would talk on the phone. One year, I met Barbara and you and your sisters at the Warrandale fete.'

'How old were we? I don't remember.'

'Primrose had started school that year.'

'If she was five, I must've been seven or eight. Phoebe was ten.'

'You girls were holidaying with your Aunt Kate and Uncle Bob. Your mother was anxious to see me alone and she came to the farm. This is when I made my promise.'

'Another promise?'

Greta nods. 'You stayed with your aunt and uncle in the holidays, but they were older now, and it was not easy to care for three little girls. Barbara was worried for Phoebe, responsible for you and your sister, and for you because you would not bow down to your father. Primrose, she was not more than a baby.'

'Mum was afraid?'

'Only for her daughters. When you were not at school, your father was intolerant. And it was important for your mother to keep her job.'

'Was she going to leave him?"

'This I do not know, liebchen. Only that she needed a safe place for the holidays.'

'What did you promise?'

'I promised that when your aunt and uncle could not look after you, you could come to the farm. That here you would be safe. As I had no daughters of my own, I made this promise.'

'But we didn't come, did we?'

'Your mother had the stroke. And when she was at the hospital, I called your father. I said I would take you and your sisters in the holidays, or any time, but your father would not agree. We thought he grieved, liebchen. We did not know of his cruelty.'

'He was clever.'

'I did not look hard enough.'

'We hid the abuse. We had to stay together.'

'Yes, yes. This was the way. But always, liebchen, I have this promise to Barbara in my mind. I will care for her daughters.' Her lips are unsteady. 'But it was not Phoebe, or Primrose.'

My throat tightens. 'It was me.'

'When I saw you at the pool …' She crosses herself. 'It was a sign.'

'That's why you picked me up, looked after me?'

'You were independent, even at ten years old, but this was my chance. Your father approved of exercise, and he liked you to swim early in the mornings as it did not affect your schooling. He let me take you to the pool, to the swimming competitions. Later, you came to the farm.'

'I was happy here.' My voice catches.

'If they need me, I will care for her children like daughters. This is the promise I made to your mother. They will be safe with me always.'

'I was safe.'

'You had a terrible accident with the horse. I swore to myself, to Derek, you would not be hurt here again. But then there was Hugo. He was a handsome boy, clever and popular, you know this.'

'I don't think—'

'Every week …' Greta looks down as she twists her hands together. 'Sometimes twice in a week, Hugo has a new girlfriend. But one day, when he is twenty-one, he goes with you on a picnic. Straight away, he makes a declaration. He tells me he will no longer wait. He wants one girl only. And who is this girl?' She looks up, her eyes bright with tears. 'It is the girl entrusted to me. What do I think, liebchen? I think this is not safe.'

'Oh.' I take a shaky breath. 'Oh.'

'Only Derek knows of this promise to your mother, and it is Derek who makes an impression with his son.' When Greta's cheeks flush pink, she waves her hands in front of her face. 'Derek speaks to Hugo of his girlfriends. When he is eighteen, nineteen, twenty, they have come to our home, and they have shared his bed.'

'Oh, Greta.'

'Derek tells Hugo that if you are different, then he must wait. You are young, you have had sadness, you do not even know that you are pretty. There must be forbearance and restraint.'

Was I a nymph? A sombre-eyed nymph with a delicate heart? Did I hide among the vines knowing nothing of the world?

'I was too damaged. Is that what you thought?'

'No, liebchen.' She slowly shakes her head. 'We thought you are clever and brave. First you must have adventure, and then you can decide. This would be safe. This is what we believed.'

Greta, as if nothing much at all has been said, stands and brushes crumbs from the day bed. 'Another biscuit?'

'I have one already.'

'You have biscuits, peace and quiet. This will make you well.'

'Another promise?'

'This promise I make to your sisters.'

'I'll call them tomorrow and tell them it's working.'

'Your mother, liebchen, my friend from long ago, you do not speak to her as you speak to them?'

I consider the biscuit, the tiny flecks of cinnamon. 'Mum's lost so much of her memory, and I don't remember her like Phoebe does. I find it hard to talk to her.'

'Phoebe telephones?'

'Every Sunday at midday. I haven't had an excuse *not* to call in the past few months, but …'

'Of course!' Greta unties the bow at her back and flicks off her apron. 'It is I who should speak with my old friend. We will talk of our children, my boys and her girls, as we always did.' She shakes a finger. 'You will call your mother, Patience. We will have a Zoom.'

Greta and I are sitting at the kitchen bench, my laptop between us, when Debra, Mum's sister, connects. She has curly greying hair and blue eyes. The collar of her thick oilskin jacket is turned up.

'Patience!' She smiles. 'What a lovely surprise! I was checking off orders in the office when your email came through. How lucky was that? And even better, Barbara is here. She's been helping in the dairy all day.' She stands and beckons. 'What did I tell you, Barbara? Patience is here to say hello.'

Mum, also warmly wrapped up, is in her mid-sixties, but has very few lines on her face. Her hair is straight like Phoebe's and cut in a bob. She smiles uncertainly into the screen.

'Hello, darling.'

'Hi, Mum. How are you? It's Patience.'

'Patience? Yes, Patience. Where are your sisters?'

'Prim's been here for the week, but now she's back in the Territory, and Phoebe is still in Norway. It's exciting about the baby, isn't it? We can't wait to be aunties.'

Mum turns to Debra. 'What baby?'

'Phoebe's baby, dear,' Debra says. 'I'm busy knitting a layette, aren't I? Every night in front of the television. You've been such a help choosing the colours.'

When the silence extends, Greta leans into the screen. 'Hello, Barbara. It is very nice to see you again. We met many years ago, when our little ones were babies.'

'Do you remember Greta, Mum? I've been staying with the Halsteads since I came out of the hospital.'

Mum turns to Debra. 'Why was she sick?'

'She had a nasty infection,' Debra says. 'How are you now, dear? Phoebe tried not to worry us too much, but she was so relieved, as were we, that you had a lovely family to care for you.'

'I'm well.'

'Not so well,' Greta pipes up.

'I'm a lot better than I was.'

Debra smiles at Mum. 'Patience was always so independent, wasn't she, Barbara? After you came to live with us, we worried about Phoebe and Primrose, but Patience …' she smiles through the screen. 'You were such a tiny little girl, but always so fierce.'

Greta blinks. 'Fierce, I do not see so much. Determined, yes.'

'And she was clever, just like her mother.'

'Her cooking also,' Greta says. 'It is getting better.'

'With her grades, she could have done anything, she could have gone to Oxford or Harvard like Barbara, but she had her heart set on the navy. And we're as proud as punch about that. It was so brave to go off on her own to fight for her country.'

Mum fiddles with her cuff. When she looks up, she frowns politely, as if wondering who I am again.

My throat is suddenly tight. 'I'll be back at sea soon.'

'We couldn't imagine anything else,' Debra says.

Greta and Debra talk about their farms and families, bringing Mum into the conversation when they can. But when even Greta runs out of things to say, I check the battery on the laptop, adjust the brightness.

'We'd better let you get back to the dairy. I'll try to get over there next year.'

'You and your sisters are always welcome. We're so glad you called. Isn't that right, Barbara?'

Mum, eyes the same shade as mine, smiles kindly. She has a good life on the farm she grew up on. She has loving sisters like I do. But sometimes I wish … My eyes sting. My throat tightens. When Debra disconnects, the screen goes blank. My hand hovers over the keyboard as if …

I can bring her back.

A memory, distorted like water on glass, plays out in my mind. It's dark, so dark I can barely see my hand in front of my face. I can't be in the bedroom I shared with Phoebe and Prim, because Phoebe was afraid of the dark. I was …

Before she had the stroke, Mum created a pond at the bottom of the garden. It was made from a plastic shell, sunk into the ground behind the jacaranda tree. Mum filled it with water and submerged three pots of lilies, one for each of her daughters. For most of the year, lily pads covered the surface, and occasionally there were flowers. We imagined that's where the fairies lived. And when we lost a tooth, we'd throw it into the pond and make a wish.

That's where I am in the memory, back at the pond. It's late at night and everyone else, Phoebe and Prim and our father, are asleep. My hand is in the water and my eyes are tightly shut. I'm making a wish.

I can bring her back.

'Liebchen?'

Kitchen drawers opening and closing. Greta's arm around my shoulders, pulling me close. The tears are relentless, wetting my cheeks and dripping from my chin. Greta presses something into my hands. The apron, threadbare and faded, smells like lemons. I open it up before folding it again. There's a recipe on the pocket, printed in German. Did Greta, twenty-one and all alone, carry it from Austria in her backpack? Or is it even older? Did it belong to Greta's mother?

The apron is soft against my face. How many times has it been washed? A hundred? A thousand? How often has Greta tied the bow at the back and wiped her hands on the front?

My body shakes and shudders. Did I cry like this when I was a toddler? When I fell on the pavement and skinned my knees?

I cried like this when I sat by the pond in the middle of the night and wished for my mother.

I sniff and hiccup as Greta rubs my back. I swipe at my eyes and blow my nose. 'The promise you made about keeping me safe, and talking to Mum. I think it's worn me out.'

'You are tired, liebchen. I am sorry.'

I scrunch the apron in my hands. 'How old is this?'

'It was mine as a girl.' She counts on her fingers. 'Forty-five years? Fifty?'

'You must have washed it a lot.'

'Many times.'

I fold and refold the apron. 'I don't know that I'm brave any more.'

'You will ride a horse, liebchen.' She pushes hair from my shoulder and strokes it down my back. 'You will find a place to be happy.'

I offer a watery smile. 'I'm not sure those things are brave.'

'You face what you are afraid of,' she says, as she reclaims the apron and dabs at my cheeks. 'This is how you are brave.'

CHAPTER 33

By the time Greta herds me into the bathing room, the sun is low in the sky. She selects a tall, slender bottle of body wash.

'For relaxation and rejuvenation,' she says approvingly. As I undress, she turns on the taps and squeezes a generous portion of liquid into the rapidly filling tub. She pats my cheek. 'Whatever you do in your life, your mother is proud. I am certain.' After checking the heater is switched to high, she closes the door quietly behind her.

Light filters softly through the stained-glass window. The bubbles hold me up and unravel the knot in my chest. My eyes sting less than they did, and my nose has stopped running. Through the steam, I read the ingredients. *Frangipani. Lemon blossom. Bergamot.* A note, scrawled on a scrappy piece of cardboard, is attached to the bottle with baling string. *Thanks, Mum. Love Hugo.*

I hold my breath as I sink beneath the surface.

Mermaid hair. Warm skin. Soft limbs.

Echoes of things that might have been.

The promise of things to come.

Not long after six o'clock, I sit at the kitchen bench and eat two bowls of slow-cooked pea and ham soup. When I take the dishes to the sink, Greta stacks them and waves me away.

'You must have an early night, liebchen. It is time to go to bed.'

Within twenty minutes of shutting the blinds in the granny flat, I've changed my clothes and cleaned my teeth, and I'm curled up in an armchair. ABBA plays from my phone, and a book is propped up on the mohair throw in my lap.

A knock on the door.

Persuading Derek to wish me goodnight would be a good way for Greta to check up on me. I lean over the arm of the chair and turn down 'Waterloo', then pull my shirt down over my thighs to cover my underpants. I pull up my socks, blue like my shirt.

'Come in!'

'Imp.'

Hugo's hair is damp. His boots, clean and shiny brown, match his belt. His jeans are black, and his shirt is pale blue linen.

The shirt I'm wearing, the shirt I said I'd toss in the charity bin, is checked flannelette. My book is open and face down on my lap. *Frog families of Australia—Bufonidae, Hylidae, Limnodynastidae, Microhylidae, Myobatrachidae and Ranidae.*

His eyes, cautious and green, stay firmly on my face. 'Imp,' he repeats.

'You said next weekend.' Snapping the book closed, I push it down the side of the chair cushion. I pull the throw high over my knees and tuck it in. 'When did you get back?'

'Just then.' He glances at my phone. *The Winner Takes It All.*

I reach over the arm of the chair and turn off the music. 'How did you get here?'

'Professor Tedeschi roped me into a meeting later tonight, and got me on a flight. I hitched here from the airport.'

'Where is your meeting? How will you get there?'

'The meeting's in Dubbo. Derek said he'll take me back. I fly out again tomorrow.'

'Oh.' I nod. 'Yes.' I nod again.

The door is ajar. He firmly clicks it shut before walking to the chair. He searches my face. Red eyes. Puffy lids. 'Greta said you were a mess.'

'I talked to Greta. And then I talked to Mum. There was a lot to take in.'

He bends his knees and crouches, his forearms on his thighs. 'Want to talk to me about it?' Lamplight softens his features, lightens his hair.

I swallow. 'Not tonight.'

He lifts a hand, withdraws it. 'Can I do anything?'

I shudder a breath, shake my head.

'Imp?' He reaches out again. He touches the side of my face. And when I lean into him, he strokes my lip with his thumb. His moan or mine? I'm not even sure. 'What are you thinking?'

A tingling ache seeps through my body. 'I can't think.' Tears blur my vision. My voice wobbles. 'That's the trouble.'

'I missed you.' When he kneels, I take his hand. I run my lips over his knuckles. I kiss his thumb.

'I missed you too.'

'I only want you,' he whispers. 'I'm done with pretending I don't.'

'I'm not ...' I wipe my eyes with the back of my hand. 'I'm not as communicative as I could be.'

'No kidding?' He puts his hand under my chin and lifts. He kisses my mouth. Soft lips, searching. His eyes go to the V of the shirt. He flicks the collar. 'Didn't I tell you this is mine?'

'You threw it away.'

He kisses me again. Persuasive, possessive. His hands move slowly up my sides. He stills. He glances at the door.

'Greta will bust the door down any minute.'

'Or she'll send Derek.'

'Fuck.' His face against my neck, breath warm on my skin. He pushes hair from my face, looks into my eyes. 'Do you think you could like me again?'

'I like your shirt.'

He kisses my temple, feels for my pulse with his lips.

'And I like your frogs.' When the book digs into my hip, I lift it from under the cushions.

He groans a laugh as he takes it, glancing at the cover before throwing it onto the floor. He cups my face, kisses the corner of my mouth. He kisses down my neck to the top button of the shirt.

'My shirt and my frogs.' He mumbles against my skin. 'For now, that'll do.'

I'm warm from the bath and the soup. It's warm in the room. His chest is warm. And hard. His heart thumps steadily. Eighty beats a minute. Eighty-five. How many hundreds or thousands of beats can I hang onto before it all comes crashing—

'Imp?' His hands slip under my shirt. *His shirt*. 'Are you counting?'

I wriggle to the end of the chair and wrap my legs around his hips. I tug at his shirt, pull it out of his pants, open the buttons. He sucks in a breath as my hands slide up his chest. I rest my hand over his heart.

He unfastens my top button. Hesitates. 'Is this okay?'

I put my hand over his. 'I don't ...'

He frowns, lifts my hand and kisses it. 'Tell me.'

'My body. It wasn't ever …' I shrug. 'And I've lost weight.'

'You know what I think?' He goes back to the button and twists it. 'You have a perfect body.'

'It's not—'

He cups my breasts over the shirt, feathers his thumbs across my nipples. And then he looks up, green eyes heated, skin flushed. He kisses my mouth, tangles our tongues. And when I lean against him, he grasps my hips and rolls backwards, taking me with him.

'Oh!' I laugh as I fall on his chest.

He rolls us onto our sides, comes up on an elbow. Serious and sombre, he touches my mouth with a fingertip. 'I like it when you laugh.'

'I like your shirt, your frogs *and* your body.' I run my hands over his skin, muscles, the line of hair from his navel to the button of his pants. He watches me, touches my hair, strokes my arm, draws lines across my shoulders.

'Imp?' When he lowers his head and nudges my breast with his nose, lust shoots straight to my toes. 'Can I kiss you here?' He looks up, eyes hot. 'It's okay to say no.'

I bring my leg over his thigh. 'Yes.'

With muttered endearments, he undoes the buttons. He caresses my breasts; he kisses and plays.

'Hugo.' My voice is needy, hoarse.

He kisses my mouth with warm wet lips. Eyes closed, he trails his hand down my side and over my hip. When he traces the lace around my underpants, I press against him.

'Can I touch here?'

'Yes.'

His fingers find the place that I want him most. Stroke, slide, advance and retreat. The warmth of the currents, the tug of the tides, the depths and the shallows, the darkness and light. I'm crying again, salty and wet on my face.

He stills. 'What the ...'

I press against his hand. 'Don't stop.'

He rolls me onto my back and brushes hair from my face. He runs his lips over my cheeks and lashes. He kisses my mouth, softly, sweetly.

'I wouldn't hurt you.'

This time, he kisses my breasts as he strokes. He sets up a rhythm. Like swimming. Like a race. Until I'm wound so tight, I'm frantic. Another kiss on my lips. A different rhythm.

Echoes, waves and ripples. Sunshine on water. Lapping shallows, crashing waves. Pulsing, throbbing, pounding. One after the other after the other. Finally, when the tremors subside, I climb back onto his chest, warm and strong and—

'Safe.'

'Sweetheart?' He kisses my neck. 'What did you say?'

I sigh, shake my head. 'Nothing.'

Scooping me into his arms, he kneels and then stands, walking backwards to the chair. When he settles me on his lap, I move his shirt to one side and rest my cheek against his skin.

'That was nice.'

'Why did you cry?'

'Which time?'

His heart thumps against my ear. 'Both times.'

I take his hand. 'The first time, with Greta, I remembered something I did when I was a child. We had a backyard pond with lilies, and ...' I shrug. 'It was where the tooth fairy came to visit.'

He links our fingers together, kisses the top of my head. 'I'm sorry it upset you.'

'The second time ...' I yawn and press closer. 'I'm not sure.'

He strokes my breast with the back of his hand. He mumbles under his breath. He kisses my mouth, softly, briefly. *Too softly. Too briefly.* The tingling warmth starts up again. His erection is long and hard. I change positions, glance towards the bedroom.

'Do you want to—'

'No.' He runs his thumb under my eye. 'No.' As if to convince himself.

'I haven't done much of this.'

He lifts my hair, kisses my neck. 'I wondered.' Hands a little unsteady, he fastens the buttons of my shirt. 'Why not?'

'I didn't enjoy it much.'

'I won't be back till the weekend.'

'You've got the whole team there, haven't you? I understand.'

He pulls me even closer. 'I want to be with you tonight.'

'You said no.'

'Sleep. Not sex. You can barely keep your eyes open.'

'What about your meeting?'

'This is more important.'

The front door slams. 'Hugo!' Greta's voice.

He closes his eyes. 'Fuck. Fuck. Fuck.' He wriggles out from under me and sits on the edge of the chair. He kisses my nose and straightens my collar. 'We can't stay here.'

'No, but …' When my eyes sting, I press the palms of my hands against them. 'Sorry.'

He links his hands around my back. 'Come home with me.'

'Hugo Halstead!'

His shirt is still open. I count the buttons: one, two, three, four, five. And the buttonholes: one, two, three, four, five. And his abdominal muscles: one, two, three—

'Imp?'

'I don't …'

'You don't want to come home?'

'I do, but ...' More tears threaten. 'Greta won't approve and ...'

His eyes are solemn, concerned. 'We can wait.'

Swallowing hard, I take his hand. 'Greta told me what happened—how Derek told you to wait.'

He closes his eyes for a moment. He opens them again. *Pain.* 'If I'd known how far you'd run, I'd never have agreed. But what Derek said ...' He squeezes my hand. 'You were different for me, I had to prove that, to show I'd give you a chance to work out what you wanted.'

I lift his hand, press my lips against his skin. 'We both had to work that out.'

'Hugo! Hugo Wilhelm Halstead!'

CHAPTER 34

The sun is barely up when I kick off Greta's gumboots and take the basket of eggs, white, brown and speckled, to the kitchen. Derek, who makes breakfast for Greta every Saturday morning, whistles tunelessly.

'Good morning,' I say. 'That bacon smells good.'

His hair is unruly and the neck of his favourite sweater is frayed. 'Sleep well?'

My smile is forced as I put the basket on the draining board. 'The hens laid well last night.'

'We getting any joy from that big black chook?'

'As the matriarch of the coop, I'm sure she encourages the other hens to lay.'

'Might encourage them more to see her head on the chopping block.'

'You say that every Saturday.'

Grinning, he puts the kettle on the stove. 'Greta might let me get away with it today, seeing as Hugo's the one in the bad books.'

Rinsing eggs under the tap, I store them in a carton. 'I'd prefer not to talk about that.'

'He should've buttoned up his shirt.'

My face warms. 'Is Greta still upset?'

'Reckoned she'd let you down, that's all.' He cracks an egg into the frying pan. 'You didn't get the peace and quiet she'd promised.'

'I've never seen her angry before.'

'Not the first time Hugo's had strips torn off him, and won't be the last.' He nods his thanks as I put two slices of bread in the toaster.

'I tried to explain he didn't do anything wrong.'

'That boy's the apple of his mother's eye. She'll get over it soon enough.'

'I don't think she has a favourite.'

He smiles. 'Royal Gala, Jonathon, Golden Delicious. All the boys are different varieties. And Hugo's had a particularly easy run of it. He was a sportsman, and he went to university. He's too fine-looking and cocky for everybody's good, including his own. Greta has to take him down a peg or two sometimes.'

'She seems to be tougher on him than his brothers.'

'He doesn't need her as much as Andy and Matty.' Turning his back, he cracks another egg into the pan. 'She doesn't want him to get a big head.'

'I don't think he does.'

'And he won't, not with the way she got out her wooden spoon last night.' He chuckles. '"No hanky-panky in the granny flat." Don't reckon we'll forget that line in a hurry.'

'Please don't repeat it.'

'Hugo couldn't see the funny side any more than you. He wasn't good company when I drove him to his meeting last night.'

'His plane left at seven?'

'He didn't seem too happy about that.'

'I sent him a message, asking if it was okay to visit Minstrel while he's away. He hasn't got back to me yet.'

'He'll be waiting for me to get back to him first,' Derek says. 'Asked me to go with you, to supervise.'

'I don't think you—'

'Even before you fell, he had a soft spot for you.'

'He worries.'

Derek flips the bacon again. 'Like I said to Greta last night, you're a good girl, but you've had it tough. And Hugo? He's got worries too. He's flat out with his work at the river, and he's got land with a hefty mortgage attached.'

'Greta said he'd borrowed a fortune.'

'Fifty hectares on the town's doorstep was never going to come cheap, even without competition. But old Bill Riley was after access to the creek, a tree changer planned to knock down the house and build a mansion, and another city bloke fancied a vineyard. What a joke.'

'Hugo also wanted the creek.'

'It's what he cares about. And without labour costs, and with low-cost materials, working there is cheap. Unlike bringing in tiles, timbers and contractors for a kitchen or staircase.'

'A garden wouldn't be too expensive.'

'It's not on Hugo's list.'

I scoop leaves into a teapot as Derek folds a fuchsia pink napkin, adding it to the tray with the salt and pepper shakers. He plucks two rosebuds from the posy in the vase on the windowsill and places them next to the knife and fork.

He winks. 'Bonus points for presentation.'

'You bought this land before you met Greta, didn't you? Did you imagine you'd have a rose garden?'

'Soon as I found Greta, I figured I'd have to. She deserves whatever I can give her.'

'I think she feels the same about you.'

'Going by that blog of yours, it's up to the female to choose which frog she'll take. Lucky for me, Greta liked my croak.' He smiles. 'I promised Remy I'd get him to Lavender after lunch. Want to tag along?'

'To pacify Hugo? Even though I'm only doing groundwork?'

'When it comes to you, that boy's yolk is all mixed up with his white. Past time you both got that into your heads.'

The sky is an ocean of blue, but in the paddock where I fell, mist hovers softly on the grass. When the toast pops up, I spread it with butter.

Last night, Hugo said, *I'm done with pretending.* Is he showing me a way to be brave?

Hugo calls late in the afternoon, long after I've swapped riding boots for gumboots. My hands aren't quite steady as I pull off my glove. 'Hello.'

'Hey.'

My heart skips around. 'I'm sorry about last night.'

Silence, then, 'I'm not.'

'I'm in the rose garden. With Greta.'

Greta straightens. 'This is Hugo, yes?' She purses her lips. 'You will give him a message, liebchen, that I am like this religious frog you write of in your blog.'

'The crucifix frog?'

'This fellow with a cross warns others not to eat him. And I warn Hugo too. He will respect the promise I made to you and your sisters—peace and quiet in the granny flat.'

'Yes, but …' Two magpies hop onto the bench and cock their heads.

'Hugo?' She raises her voice. 'Patience will have relaxation and rejuvenation! This is the message on the bubble bath!'

When Hugo starts to swear, I talk over him. 'You won't be back till next Friday, will you?' Kneeling again, I push the trowel into the soil and pull out an onion weed, careful to collect all the bulbs. 'Can I come over on Saturday?'

I'm in bed but not quite asleep when my phone vibrates. An unknown number. I yawn. 'Hello.'

'Lieutenant Cartwright. It's Albert Tedeschi.'

'Oh.' I struggle to sit. 'Is everything okay?'

'I spoke to Rick five minutes ago.' His voice is high pitched. 'He confessed you know something about this.'

'Can you explain what you mean?'

'I didn't take Rick seriously. I was a fool. A fool!' He lowers his voice. 'We have to resolve this. For all of our sakes.'

'Why are you so upset, professor?' I bend my knees and wrap an arm around them.

'I'm nothing, lieutenant, without my reputation. And I have so much work to do yet. But this, the implications of it, they're frightening.'

'You're going off at tangents. Can you slow down? Tell me what you mean.'

'Technology isn't my strength, as you well know. Errors were made with payments, but they can be resolved. Charles is still adamant about that.'

'Charles?'

'My son.' I hear a voice in the background, but I can't make out the words. 'We can't settle this on the phone.'

'In person, then,' I say calmly. 'When?'

'Charles will act as my delegate. He will explain.'

'Explain what?'

Silence. Then, 'The invoices, Patience. Have you spoken to anyone?'

Only a naval captain, who's spoken to the auditor-general. 'I've been waiting for you to explain everything to Rick.' A thump on the roof. A scampering possum. 'When do I meet Charles? Where?'

'The Halsteads' farm is out of the question. Hugo can't find out.'

I sit back against the pillows, draw the doona over my legs. 'Why keep this from Hugo? Why the secrecy?'

'He won't—' He cuts himself off. 'This matter could have serious implications for me, and for Rick. You mustn't tell Hugo.'

Rick said Hugo would demand explanations. 'Will Charles tell me what's going on?'

'Give me your word you'll say nothing until you've spoken to Charles.'

Tedeschi is frightened about something. I want to protect Rick. My *original* brief was eyes open, mouth shut. Meeting with Charles is consistent with that so …

'I'll be in Dubbo on Friday morning. We can meet there.'

CHAPTER
35

When I saw Professor Tedeschi at Hugo's property, he said of his environmentalist son, *I couldn't be prouder of him*. I presume the man sitting in the tiered stand in the indoor aquatic centre is Charles Tedeschi. He'd be in his early thirties, with dark hair pulled back in a bun. Was he the protesting university student with dreadlocks I found on Google images?

How long has he been here? And why so early? He stands as I climb from the pool. My swimmers are black, one piece with a high neck and a thick-toothed zip up the back. His eyes travel up my legs to my breasts as I pull off my cap.

'Patience?' He smiles as he holds out a hand. 'Charlie Tedeschi. It's great to meet you.'

Charlie, not Charles? An American accent. I wipe my hands on my swimmers before we shake. 'Sorry to keep you waiting.'

'No problem at all.' Tanned skin. Artificially white teeth. 'How many laps was that? What are you? An Olympian?'

'Hardly.' I look around him to the cafe near the entrance. 'I thought we were meeting for a coffee.'

'Just wanted to check I had the right place.' He's dressed casually but expensively. Patagonia hiking pants. Arc'teryx jacket. Scarpa leather boots.

'I'd better change.'

Another appreciative look. 'That's a shame.'

I gather my thoughts as I wash the chlorine from my hair and squirt on conditioner. When I called Rick early on Sunday morning, the day after I'd got the call from Professor Tedeschi, Rick told me he'd finally worked up the courage to confront the professor. And when Professor Tedeschi had prevaricated, Rick blurted out that he had a responsibility to answer to both of us. A few hours later the professor, clearly upset, called Rick back, telling him he now appreciated the seriousness of the matter, and he'd contact me directly.

It wasn't easy to calm Rick down, to reassure him that I'd find out what was happening.

After I've met with Charles, I'll have to call Captain McCarthy. I shut my eyes against the three hundred and twenty-three tiles in the shower cubicle and rinse my hair.

When I walk into the cafe, Charles is leaning against the counter near the coffee machine. 'My shout,' he says. 'What'll you have?'

'A cappuccino would be great.'

I'm sitting on a black plastic chair at a white plastic table when, carrying two cups and saucers, he joins me. He has a slight limp. Not a knee or ankle. Maybe a hip?

'Thanks.' I zip my hoodie and warm my hands around the cup. 'Do you prefer Charles or Charlie?'

'Fathers, right?' He takes the chair opposite. 'Only my dad calls me Charles.'

'You work as an environmental lobbyist, don't you?'

'That can be a dirty word in the country.' He looks around and smiles. 'Better keep your voice down.'

If his son is concerned about what Professor Tedeschi is hiding, he's doing a good job of disguising it.

'All the farmers I know care a lot for the environment. They have to.'

'Overstocking and methane gas? Land clearing and carcinogenic fertilisers? Soil degradation?' He jiggles his tea bag. 'Your farmers have a weird way of showing it.'

Change the subject. 'You've always done environmental work?'

'When I was younger, I was on the frontline.'

'Of the environmental movement?'

He winks. 'I put my body on the line all over the world—in the States, South America, Europe. I thought the louder I shouted, the better I'd be heard. I work smarter now.'

'You run your business from here?'

'I represent people who care about the planet, and help them get their message out.'

'I met your father at a climate summit. He's highly respected.'

'Academics have their place,' he says. 'I guess you tilt that way too. You studied science, didn't you?'

'Not in the way your father and Dr Lipman did.'

'Lipman?' He laughs. 'That guy drives Dad nuts.'

'Rick works hard. He's passionate about what he does.'

'He's on the spectrum, isn't he?' Charles sits further forward in his chair. 'Is that why you're backing him up?'

'I support Rick because I respect him, both professionally and personally.'

'I didn't mean—'

'My father has a personality disorder, and PTSD from Vietnam.'

He sits back in his chair. 'Patience, seriously...' He puts his hands palms up on the table. 'I put *both* feet in my mouth. You're bound to have a position on this.'

I bring my coffee closer. 'Not the position you might expect.'

'You don't have to explain.'

'In addition to being smart, Rick is kind and generous. He cares about people. I thought your father was a colleague as well as a friend. I thought he supported Rick too.'

'He is.' He holds up his hands again, lowers his voice. 'He does.'

I sit back in my chair. Take a deep breath. 'What's going on, Charlie?' I wave a hand around. 'Why did your father set us up like this?'

'Like a date?' He smiles. 'I wish it were.'

I look at him over my cup. 'So, answer me.'

'This whole thing,' he puts his elbows on the table, 'is an administrative hiccup. Nothing more.'

'Rick has nothing to worry about?'

'Just like Dad's been telling him.'

'Your father sounded like he had something to worry about last weekend. What's changed? Why hasn't Professor Tedeschi explained what's going on?' I turn my cup 360 degrees. 'Rick needs reassurance.'

'And you?'

I meet his gaze, honestly, sincerely. 'I want to do the job I've been assigned to do.'

'Because you got kicked off your ship.'

'Is that what your father told you?'

'Is it true?'

'The secondment gets me off the base and gives me something useful to focus on. Part of that is working with Rick. As this is an administrative error, fix it and give Rick the details.'

'You'd leave it at that?'

I swirl chocolate through the froth on my coffee. I tap the spoon on the cup. 'It makes no difference to me.'

He considers his own coffee. 'We might have more in common than you think.' He sips slowly, places his cup on the saucer. 'A consultant invoiced the wrong team. You and Rick worked that out.'

I scoop up froth and take it from the spoon. 'Are you the consultant?'

'I'm not going to answer that.' He sits back in his chair, stretches out both legs. He winces and rubs his thigh.

'You favour your right leg.'

His smile is tight. 'I was twenty-two when I was run down. That's why I work behind the scenes.'

'Tell me about this consultant.'

'A company received payment before it'd done the work it was contracted to do, nothing more. The money will be repaid.' His smile is stiff. 'You have my word on that.'

I stretch my legs too, careful to stay clear of his. 'The professor said you were better placed to explain than he was. How come?'

'Excel? IT? My father is another generation, so I help him out. I punch in numbers.'

'You assist with his paperwork like I help with Rick's?'

'Bingo.'

I sip as he watches. *Like he watched me in the pool.* Are we agreeing to disagree? He's admitted payments were made. He's told me they'll be repaid and asked me not to pursue it.

'If the professor is prepared to fix the problem ...' I speak with as much confidence as I can muster. 'If it won't happen again, I think Rick will be satisfied.'

He nods. 'Can't ask more than that.'

'Has your father appointed you to handle me?'

'As you're not only stunning but smart,' he looks me up and down, 'I wouldn't have a problem with that.'

Two small children with wet hair and bare feet walk into the coffee shop with their heavily pregnant mother. After they scrabble onto chairs, she pushes them closer to the table.

'I'll talk to Rick. I'll tell him not to worry. But I have a condition.'

He fakes a smile. 'Shoot.'

'Can the professor find someone else to check future invoices? It'd free Rick up for the work he wants to do.'

He taps the side of his head. 'Makes sense to me.'

We're outside the aquatic centre when I push hair, still damp, from my face. I hold out my hand. Charles's hand, smooth and well-manicured, meets it firmly.

'Where do you live?' I ask.

'Dad has a house in Mudgee. I'm working from there.'

A car reverses, and we're forced to move out of the way. Pulling my hand free, I manage a smile. 'Thanks for coming all the way out here.'

'Being set up with you has its advantages. Are you dating anyone?'

I *might* be in love with Hugo, but that doesn't mean we're dating. In any case, I have a job to do, and not offending Charles is part of it.

'I rarely date. I'm usually on a ship.'

'Not now you're not.' He winks. 'Mind if I call and arrange something?'

'I'll be working up north again soon, but …' I shrug. 'Sure.'

When he opens his arms, I briefly return his hug. But as he walks to his car, I take my time rifling through my bag as if searching for keys. A few minutes after he's pulled onto the road, Captain McCarthy's assistant transfers my call.

'Lieutenant,' the captain says. 'What's the urgency?'

'Professor Tedeschi called me last weekend. He set up a meeting between me and his son, Charles.'

'I understood Tedeschi didn't know you were involved.'

'Dr Lipman let the cat out of the bag.'

'When is the meeting?'

'Charles has just left it, sir. He told me he helps with the professor's paperwork. He knows about the invoices.'

'Why wasn't I informed of this meeting?'

'I thought there might be nothing in it. Rick told the professor I hadn't spoken to anyone, and I agreed to everything Charles suggested, so he didn't suspect I was onto—'

'Hold on.' There's a delay as he calls out for a file. And another delay as he sorts through papers. Then,

'Are you still on leave?'

'Technically yes. But I'm back again on Monday, working remotely for the Macquarie team.'

'I have a request.'

'A what?'

He barks a laugh. 'I can hardly give orders to an ailing officer. It's important, lieutenant. How long would it take you to get here?'

'Six hours, sir.' I release the handbrake. 'If I leave immediately.'

CHAPTER
36

I'm walking across the parade ground to Captain McCarthy's office when I call Rick, reassuring him I'm looking into what happened with the invoices, and he can leave the worrying to me. I'm about to disconnect when he tells me Hugo wants to speak with me.

Since he left the granny flat five days ago, Hugo and I have spoken three times. But he can only call late at night, reception has been scratchy, and as he's camping with his team, he's never on his own.

I want to hear his voice. But …

I want to protect Rick, the team, and, after meeting his smarmy son, possibly Professor Tedeschi. I also want to finish the job I set out to do.

Captain McCarthy's assistant waves me into the anteroom of the captain's office. 'Rick?' I say hurriedly. 'Tell Hugo that I'll call him back.'

'He wants to talk to you now.'

'Yes, but—'

'Imp.' My heart skips around. 'You're at Jervis Bay?'

'I was called to a meeting.'

'In person? When you're on leave? Couldn't they come to you?'

'It doesn't work like that.' I lower my voice. 'And before you ask, Rick won't tell you why I called.'

'Can you?'

I stare at the screen of my phone. And then I close my eyes. One, two, three. Every second, a thousand millisecond pass. Three thousand milliseconds. If I were on the farm, I'd count chickens and eggs. White, black, caramel chickens. Brown, beige, speckled eggs. Three, two, one. 'I'll see you tomorrow.'

When the desk phone buzzes, Captain McCarthy's assistant looks up. 'Go straight in.'

I drop my phone into my bag, straighten my hoodie and knock on the door. Why so quietly? *That's how my father trained me.* A pain, sharp as a knife, stabs through my chest.

I knock again, so hard it hurts my knuckles.

'Come in!'

The last time I saw Captain McCarthy, he stood uncomfortably at the end of my hospital bed. I stand to attention between the door and his desk, snapping my heels as he lifts his head

'Sir!'

'At ease, lieutenant.' He indicates the chair opposite. 'Please sit down.' He glances at his screen, hits a few keys. 'This secondment of yours is becoming rather interesting.'

I sit on the edge of the seat. 'Sir?'

'The auditor-general's office has called in the federal police.'

'Because of Charles Tedeschi? What's going on with him?'

'As you've met him, I'd welcome your view.'

'He was confident and opinionated. He fancied himself.'

'What do you know of his background?'

'Most of what I have is from Google.'

He types at his keypad, keeping his eyes on the monitor. 'Go on.'

'Before he dropped out of university, he was involved in student protests, everything from old-growth forests to animal rights—he referred to that when we met. In the past few years, he's kept a much lower profile. His most recent LinkedIn role is as a lobbyist for environmental organisations, and that's how he described himself.'

'LinkedIn lacks a category for environmental terrorism.'

'What?'

'How would you describe it?'

I shrug. 'Violence committed in the name of the environment?'

'The organisations behind it believe the means justifies the ends,' McCarthy says. 'That the greater good, their version of it, trumps the rule of law. There's been little of it in Australia, but it's a growing problem in the US and Europe. It appears Charles has links to US organisations.'

'Environmental terrorists trespass, don't they?'

He grunts. 'At best. At worst it's a form of anarchy, involving the destruction of farm machinery and buildings, industrial espionage and infiltration, incendiary devices and IT terrorism. It's sabotage, ecotage.'

I sit back in my chair. 'Charles is involved in that?'

'In its funding, yes. But the authorities have never got close to pinning him down. When Professor Tedeschi became a person of interest, the auditor-general's office made the link to Charles. They communicated with others, including foreign affairs and the police.'

'Where does that leave the auditor-general's office?'

'It's been asked to step back.'

'I told you about the invoices months ago. Does this explain why nothing has happened so far?'

'There's a fear of alerting Charles that they're onto him.'

'I can't see Professor Tedeschi backing anarchists.'

'Allowing Charles to play fast and loose with government money could get him tied up with them.'

'The professor relied on Charles to fix the so-called administrative errors. When he worked out that might be more difficult than Charles had told him it would be, and I was aware of that, he freaked out. That's how I got to meet Charles.'

'You should have told me this earlier.'

'Like you should have told me that Charles was a terrorist?'

He frowns. 'Would you care to rephrase that, lieutenant?'

I look past him to a photograph mounted in a frame—the captain saluting Queen Elizabeth on the bridge of a warship. 'I wasn't aware that Charles was a terrorist, sir.'

He grunts. 'I'll pass on what you've told me.'

'What's my role now?'

'You don't have one, lieutenant.' He looks over the top of his glasses. 'And to be frank, my primary reason for bringing you here was to make that perfectly plain.'

'You haven't heard everything I have to say.'

The captain looks at his watch. 'Put it in your statement.'

I speak a little louder. 'It's important you hear it in person, sir.'

He sighs, sits back in his chair. 'At the commencement of this secondment, lieutenant. you were on the lookout for sloppy accounting, and scientists clocking off early. This goes beyond that.'

'Will the police arrest Charles?'

'He looks after funding, while minions do the dirty work. They'll be anxious to gain access to his phones and computers. By all reports, he's a slippery character, so I don't imagine they'll wait long.'

'Professor Tedeschi is retiring soon. This will be a terrible end to his career.'

'That's not your problem.' He sits forward again, links his hands on the desk. 'Don't talk to anyone. Sit tight until the authorities move in.'

'The Macquarie team thinks I'm on a simple secondment.'

'As of now, even before now, you are.'

'What about Dr Lipman? They won't arrest him too, will they?'

'That's their business.'

'That's not fair.' When he looks at me sharply, I lift my chin. 'I want to be involved.'

'Drop this.' He shuts the folder with a snap. 'That's an order, lieutenant.'

To the left of the photograph is a clock. Five forty-five. The shadows of the building have lengthened. If I was back in Horseshoe, I'd be outside with Derek, or in the kitchen with Greta. I could be on the day bed doing homework with Ryan or—

'Lieutenant. Do you follow?' When McCarthy turns on the lamp, a circle of light spills onto the desk. 'You're not to contact Charles Tedeschi.'

'Sir.'

'Finish the secondment and I'll send you back to sea.' He leans over the desk and shuts down screens. 'In the meantime, find a bed for the night.'

I have a bed in Horseshoe.

Standing alone on the parade ground, I pull up my hood and tuck my hands into my pockets. The moon is a pewter disk; the golden stars shine brightly. Waves, frothy pearl ribbons, drift haphazardly onto the shore. Near the breakwater, three anchored boats roll on the swell.

If I were on the ocean, I could search the stars to navigate. I'd know where to look for the lights.

How do I navigate now?

A group of sailors, dressed to go out, move off the path as I walk to the car park. The salty breeze is familiar, but not in the way it once was.

When the lines on the sides of the highway begin to blur, I wind down the windows and turn up the music. 'Why Did It Have To Be Me?' I'm wide awake by the time I pull into a truck stop, parking on the far side of three semi-trailers, but my hands are like ice blocks and my feet ache with cold. I walk laps of the bitumen in the hope of warming up.

'Hey there!' One of the drivers leans out of his window. 'Where'd you serve?'

Reggie, a sixty-year-old ex-army sergeant from Queensland, tells me he knew I was military because of my turns. When he invites me into his cab, I climb the steps, clamping my teeth to keep them still. After sifting through a box, he pours a mug of milky tea from a thermos. I'm sipping it gratefully when he throws a rolled-up downy swag on my lap.

'It's a cold one tonight. You'd better take this.'

'Are you sure you can you spare it?'

He cranes his neck to peer down at my car. 'Don't look like you've got much else.'

'I have a damp towel.'

'Are you absent without leave?'

'Thankfully, no.' I press my hands against the mug, blissfully warm. 'I'm on my way back to Horseshoe.'

'Nice little place from what I remember. You got family there?'

'I'll be staying with friends for the next few weeks.' I sip the tea. 'If you're ever close by and need a break, ask for directions to the Halsteads' farm. If I'm not there, Greta or Derek will be.' When I swallow again, my throat tightens. 'It's like the Hotel California.'

He laughs as he pours more tea. 'Glad you've got somewhere to go.'

In February I wanted to get back to sea. *Now I want more.*

I send Hugo a text at midnight. *I'm a few hours out of Horseshoe. See you mid-morning. Patience*

He gets back to me immediately *Drive carefully, Imp.*

I'm curled up on the back seat of my car when the rumble of Reggie's truck wakes me. It's only three o'clock, but after another mug of milky tea, I return his swag and follow him onto the road, flashing my lights in thanks as I take the loop road towards Horseshoe.

CHAPTER 37

At six-thirty, hair damp from my shower, I walk into Greta's kitchen with a basket of eggs. Derek looks up from filling the kettle.

'Welcome home.'

When I put the basket on the bench and hug him, he blinks in consternation. 'What's this then?'

'Thank you.'

He smiles and shrugs. 'No worries.'

'I hope I found all the eggs.'

'Miracle you got any in the dark.'

'It was too late to go to bed.' When Derek turns on the gas, blue and yellow flames dance circles round the hob. 'I'll stay with Minstrel until Hugo is ready.'

'You getting back on the horse, then?'

Extending my leg, I point the toe of my riding boot. I speak with more confidence than I feel. 'Not long now.'

Arrow and Lavender, pulling hay from their nets, look up as I park next to Hugo's mud splattered four-wheel drive. The roof racks are stacked high with camping equipment, and there are mountains of bags, boxes, and other gear inside.

We both had a long way to travel to get back.

Minstrel, also eating hay, is in his paddock at the rear of the house, but he nickers a greeting when he sees me, and trots to the gate.

'Hello, boy.'

The door to the shed is open, and Hugo's excavator is parked at the entrance. The shed is large with a hardwood frame, broad-planked timber walls and a corrugated iron roof.

'Imp!' Hugo rolls his shoulders as he walks around the excavator. Last time I saw him, we were in the granny flat. Even talking on the phone about field work and the weather doubles my heart rate. Seeing him like this ...

How does he feel? Where to from here?

I'm wearing a sweater and jacket. He's in a shirt. Tight across the shoulders, sleeves rolled up, muscular forearms. He drops tools on the excavator seat, wipes his hands on a rag and throws it on top of the tools. The morning light is behind him as he walks towards me.

He kisses my mouth, moaning low in his throat when I wrap my arms around his neck. But then, as a pulsing aching need coils through my body, he lifts his head.

'Derek said you got in early.'

'I had a few hours' sleep.'

'You go for a swim, then drive hundreds of kilometres for a meeting.' He stands back, keeping hold of the tops of my arms. 'Aren't you on secondment? Aren't you working with me and the others?'

Every time I think about Rick, I feel uneasy. I'd like to warn him that the federal police might turn up at his door, but there's a risk he'd pass it on. Anyway, I've been ordered not to. And the possible impact on Professor Tedeschi and the team? I worry about that too.

'Yes, but …'

He tips up my chin, kisses me briefly. 'I wish you could trust me.'

You have good reasons not to trust me. I stand back a little, take his hands. His hair skims his collar; he needs a haircut.

'I don't want to hurt you.'

He searches my face. *He searches for the truth.* 'You're here,' he finally says. He kisses my mouth again, tender, possessive. 'We take our time.'

I lay my hands on his chest, feel the beats of his heart. 'I'm not sure I deserve you.'

'What?' His eyes crinkle with his smile. 'When you've always been smarter than me.'

'I memorise facts and regurgitate them. Numbers jump around in my head.'

He takes my hand, kisses my palm. 'Smart. And beautiful.'

My chest tightens. 'Sometimes I worry …' I shake my head. 'I don't know.'

'Imp? One step at a time, okay?'

When he tugs, I follow him into the shed. Much of the space is taken up by bales of hay, work benches and tools, but he's built new shelving on the eastern wall. One set of brackets and hooks, low enough for Remy to reach, holds Lavender's saddle and other gear. The others are for Minstrel and Arrow. Minstrel's smart leather halter hangs from one hook, and his bridle with the black and tan headband hangs from another. Under his saddle is a sheepskin blanket I haven't seen before. The saddle's stirrup leathers and irons, glowing silver in the gloom, are folded neatly over the seat. Willing nausea away, I touch the cold metal surfaces and run my hand inside the rims.

Even before he puts his arm around me, I feel his warmth. 'Imp.'

'Should I ride today?'

He turns me around to face him. He holds out a hand and tilts it back and forth. 'We take our time there too.'

'Maybe tomorrow?'

'Otherwise next weekend.'

'Are you going away again?'

'Monday to Friday.'

Minstrel nickers when, the grooming bucket swinging between us, we reach the gate. Hugo stands back as I walk through, watching closely as I fasten Minstrel's halter, unbuckle the straps of his rug and slide it off. With the pick, I lift his hooves and scrape out dirt. I speak over my shoulder.

'You're not still angry with Greta, are you?'

'I wish she'd shut up about hanky-panky.'

'What's the problem with your excavator?'

'It's old. The gearbox is fucked.'

'Pistons, tubes, internal combustion? Do excavator gearboxes work like other engines?'

'Yes, but this one can't be fixed.'

'Greta would say—'

He swears. 'Please don't.'

'She'd tell you the broken gearbox is a sign from your granny. You should spend less time at the creek, and work on your kitchen.'

I forage in the bucket for the stiff-bristled brush, showing it to Minstrel before smoothing his coat. The rug keeps his body clean, but he has mud on his belly and legs. Hugo stands at Minstrel's head, rubs under his chin.

Over ten years have passed since my accident. I can confidently handle a horse on the ground, even pick up hooves. Surely—

Hugo leans over my shoulder and brushes a kiss on my neck. 'You okay?'

'Yes,' I croak.

Besides occasionally looking around as if wondering why this is taking so long, Minstrel, resting a leg, stands at ease. Hugo pats his neck, runs a hand down his shoulder.

'Whatever you paid, he's worth double.'

'I paid a lot.' I glance up at the house. 'Probably more than windows, or a staircase.'

He smiles. 'Still worth double.'

'You said he was too tall, and his feet were too big.'

'He is and they are, but he's still a good horse. I wouldn't let you on him otherwise.'

I try to smile. 'Trust overcomes fear.'

He takes my hand and puts it on his chest. 'Match my heart rate.'

I open my fingers and count. 'Yours is almost non-existent.'

'In that case …' He burrows under the cuff of my sweater to find the pulse at my wrist. 'Our average is good.'

I glance at Minstrel's feet. 'I don't want to let him down.'

Hugo ties Minstrel to the fence. 'He doesn't plan on trampling you.'

I shudder. 'No.'

He grumbles under his breath. 'Come with me.'

We walk to the corner of the paddock closest to the house, where Hugo finds a relatively dry patch of grass. When he sits, I bend my knees to join him but …

'Uh-uh,' he says. 'You stay on your feet.'

'Why are you down there?'

He looks from Minstrel to me. 'You were anchored to Jackpot, and he couldn't get free. That's why you were trampled.'

'No.' My voice wavers. 'Yes.'

'You equate riding with the worst that can happen.'

'Falling isn't always so bad. I understand that.'

'Do you?' He lies on his back, shades his eyes with an arm. 'Start at my feet and walk up my body.'

'Hugo …' The lump in my throat gets bigger. 'I couldn't do that.'

'It wouldn't feel right, would it?'

'I'd hurt you.'

'A panicked horse wouldn't think like that, but he wouldn't want to trample you anyway.'

Two blue-chested sparrows sit on a railing near the gate. One bird swoops to the ground and picks up a piece of hay. When he flies away, the other bird follows. Are they making a nest? How many wing beats per second? Four? Five? Two birds, in only a minute, would flap their wings hundreds of—

Hugo comes up on an elbow. 'Imp? What would a horse do?'

'Try to avoid me.'

'Stepping on someone …' He sits and drapes his arms over his knees. 'It'd feel uneven and unsafe. Unpredictable. Jackpot couldn't get free of you—that's why you were trampled.'

I nod and back away.

He holds out a hand. 'Come here before you faint.'

I do as he asks, bend my legs and wrap my arms around them. He loops an arm around my shoulders, dips his head. 'A rider generally falls clear, and to the side of a horse. If a horse stumbles, or stops suddenly, a rider can fall over his head.'

I glance at Minstrel, reaching delicately under the fence for new shoots of grass. 'Stirrups are triggering. What if I rode without them?'

'If he shies or misbehaves, it'll be harder to stay on.'

'If I fell, I'd fall clear. Maybe I'd break a limb. I could handle that.'

He runs a finger down my cheek, puts hair behind my ear. 'I don't know that I could.'

'If I can ride, I can help at the river.' My hands are sweaty; I wipe them on my jeans. 'I can help with your frogs.'

The crease between his brows is back. 'You're not riding today.'

The buzzing in my ears is like a chorus of cicadas. I'm hot and then cold. Lightheaded and jittery and—

'We can get Minstrel ready *as if* I were going to ride. I'll lead him around the paddock.'

As we bridle and saddle Minstrel, Hugo keeps close to my side. On my left, behind me, on my right, in front of me. I lean against him as Minstrel opens his mouth and takes the bit. Our hands tangle up as we tighten the girth. We estimate the length of the stirrups. Hugo's touch is competent, assured, deliberate.

'Do you think he minds having a bit in his mouth?'

'He's used to it.' Hugo pushes the stirrup irons up the leather straps, securing them close to the saddle so they don't bump Minstrel's sides. 'A ten-minute walk, Imp. Quit while you're ahead.'

'Imp doesn't only stand for impatience, does it?'

'No.'

'When I was about thirteen, I looked it up.'

'What?'

'In the *Macquarie Dictionary*, there were a hundred and sixty-three words that started with "imp". I can list them alphabetically.'

'Why doesn't that surprise me?' He checks Minstrel's girth 'Tell me six.'

'Alphabetical order?'

He laughs. 'Sure.'

'Impenitent, impertinent, impetuous, impossible, imprudent, impulsive.'

He tips up my chin, kisses my nose. 'You've walked him a lot with a halter. The bridle's the same.'

I glance at the stirrups, then away. 'I'm imagining myself up there. He's tall like you said.'

'Stand at his shoulder.'

'One hand on the rein near the bit, the rest of the rein in my other hand.'

'You've done it before, like riding a bike or driving a car.'

'I can pilot a warship.'

He pushes Minstrel backwards, turns him so we're facing away from the house. 'That too.'

'Southern Ocean. Gulf Sea. Pacific.'

'Breathe, Imp.'

'I can't stop talking.'

'That's okay, but …' He searches my face. *Green eyes like gum trees.* 'If you can manage it, focus on Minstrel.'

Minstrel's mane mostly falls to the right. Near his whither it's on the left. Keeping the rein in my hand, I stroke his neck.

'Good boy.' His ears move, just a fraction. 'Are you ready?'

'Let him know you're in charge.'

'I'm going to circumnavigate the paddock, Minstrel. Would you like to come too?'

'It's not an invitation.'

I search for words. 'Please come with me.'

Hugo swears under his breath. 'Keep him to a walk. No more.'

When I take a step, Minstrel follows suit, and we walk towards the trees near the creek. How many trees? Four. Minstrel has four hooves. Four black hooves. One, two, three, four. I was tangled up in Jackpot's hooves. Fractured cheekbone, torn ligaments, stitches, bruises—

Focus on Minstrel. He's well educated and eager to please. He likes carrots and trots to the gate when he sees me. Mandy said he's bombproof. Hugo said he's worth *double* the cost of windows and a staircase. His ears aren't pricked but they're not pinned back. They're firmly in the middle, as if he's undecided.

Waiting to see what will happen.

I have cicadas in my head again, but they're not quite as strident as they were. When a flock of cockatoos flies over the trees, Minstrel ignores them. The ground is uneven near the fence, but that doesn't worry him either.

The paddock is roughly rectangular, with scores of fence posts two metres apart. On first glance, around 50,000 square metres. Minstrel picks up speed. The grey gums are tall—long green leaves, broad trunks and strips of bark like aprons.

Aprons like Greta's. I glance at Hugo, pacing near the gate.

Minstrel's hooves pound softly on the ground. 'Knowing Me, Knowing You'. One, two, three, four. Four, three, two, one. He walks across leaves, muffling the beats. He steps on twigs. Snap. Snap. Snap. Snap.

As we turn back towards Hugo, Minstrel picks up speed. I pull him back, make him stop, remind myself that I'm in control. The stirrup iron on the near side has slipped down the leather. As I resecure it, Minstrel stays perfectly still.

A car door slams. Another door. A high-pitched shout. Remy? He often rides Lavender on Saturdays. He's fearless like I used to be.

Is this too easy? Do I need more of a challenge? 'Should we trot, do you think?' I ask Minstrel. As I run, he matches my speed.

'Imp!' Hugo isn't pacing any more. Facing me, his arms are stiff by his sides. 'Walk!'

I pull up too quickly and stumble. 'Oh!' Four black hooves, but …

I'm safe. I gather the reins again.

When we reach Hugo, he grasps Minstrel's bridle. 'Why did you do that?'

'I wanted to see—'

'You think I enjoy this?' He's white around the mouth. His jaw is tight. 'You think I want to re-live what happened?'

'But you said …'

'You had to do as I say!' He glares 'You agreed to that.'

My back to him, I take off my helmet. I fumble with the chin-strap of Minstrel's bridle. I study my boots. *The boots he gave me.* I feel his gaze on the top of my head.

One pathetic tear, and then another. I swipe with my sleeve, blink and swallow and blink. I hiccup as I unbuckle Minstrel's girth and pull off his saddle and blanket, laying them on the ground near the fence. I sniff as Hugo slips off Minstrel's bridle, puts on his halter and ties him up. And then I hiccup again.

His fists are clenched when he turns. 'Why are you—'

'Shut up!' I take a giant step. I clamp my hand over his mouth. 'I never cried!' Tears roll down my cheeks. 'Never!' I grasp his shirt and wipe my face on his shoulder. 'Not till you!'

Swearing under his breath, he puts a hand on the side of my face. 'You don't get it, do you?'

I hiccup. 'I thought you'd be happy.'

He wipes under my eye with his thumb. 'You're killing me.'

I open my hands, feel the strength of his body. I look into his eyes, see the honesty there. Standing on the toes of my boots, I press against him. I kiss his mouth.

He stills. And growls. 'I don't want to lose you again.'

Our tongues slide and search, lips wet and salty, breaths light and soft. I run my hands over his chest and burrow under his shirt, searching for his skin. His erection, long and thick through his jeans, presses against my stomach. He buries his face in my hair, razes my neck with his teeth.

'Imp,' he mutters, kissing a trail to my lips.

'Uncle Hugo! Uncle Hugo!'

When I take a step back, Hugo's arms tighten. He groans against my cheek. 'Stay.'

Pulling back, I rest shaky fingers on his mouth. 'Ryan will be waiting. He needs help with his homework.'

'Fuck.' He takes my arm and kisses my wrist, finds my pulse with his tongue. 'Fuck.'

'Greta has a book club meeting tonight and I promised to help her prepare. She won't want you in the granny flat, but I could come to you.'

He lifts his head. Sighs. 'How much sleep did you get?'

I hold in a yawn. 'Reggie warned me it'd be cold.'

'Who's Reggie?'

'One of the truckies. He gave me a swag.'

He swears again. 'Tomorrow, after we're back from the horses, I'll show you the house. We can talk.'

I soften against him, wrap my arms around his neck. I kiss him sweetly, warm and tender. I talk against his mouth. 'I'll be back in the morning.'

CHAPTER 38

Greta adds sugar to the butter, holds the bowl on her hip and beats with a wooden spoon. 'It is good that you keep me company.'

Ryan, sitting on the stool next to mine but slumped so low over his books that he's almost lying down, pulls a plate of biscuits, small, crescent shaped and dusted with powdered sugar, between us.

He takes two. 'Ace vanillekipferl, Oma.'

I tap his textbook with a pencil. 'Next question.'

He sits up long enough to turn the page. 'Farmer Jenny. She's killing me.'

'This is Hugo's expression,' Greta says. 'It is not a good example to follow.'

Hugo said *you're killing me* when I ran instead of walked. *I cried for that?* I tap the textbook again.

'What is Jenny up to this week?'

'She's got to have her water tank filled,' Ryan says. 'And buy petrol so she can take her cattle to the markets.'

'Where does Jenny live?' Greta asks.

Ryan laughs. 'How would I know that?'

'I am afraid there is a drought,' Greta says, 'and this is why Jenny cannot feed her stock. It is hard, yes, but it is best that she sells. Otherwise ...' She puts the bowl, half full of creamed butter and sugar, on the bench. 'She will have too much debt.'

I hold in a smile as I read through the questions. 'You have to calculate capacity for the water tank. For the trip to the market, you need to determine petrol consumption.'

'This is very useful work,' Greta says. 'Ryan will be a mathematician farmer.'

Ryan grins. 'Living the dream.'

'The water tank is a cylindrical shape,' I say. 'Where do we start?'

'Work out the radius of the top or bottom of the tank,' Ryan says. 'And use that to find the area. It's pi x r^2.'

'Excellent. After that, you multiply by the height.'

As Ryan and I work through the components of the question, I grease a spring-form pan and line the base with paper. When Greta pushes a chopping board and pile of almonds across the bench, I take a knife from the block.

'Oma?' Ryan asks. 'Why don't you buy chopped nuts?'

Greta blinks. 'How would I know they are fresh? No, no, no, we must do this ourselves.'

'You should get a ThermoMix. Mum's got one.'

'Your mother's bolognaise sauce, it is delicious,' Greta says, nodding reluctantly. 'But beaten too much, nuts will be oily. A knife, it is better.'

I hold the point of the blade with one hand and the handle with the other, chopping through the nuts. 'How many linzer torte are you making?'

'One each for Andreas and Hugo, and two for my book club.'

'Why does Uncle Hugo get one to himself?' Ryan slips from the stool and forages in his schoolbag. 'Not fair.'

Greta breaks two eggs, putting the yolks and egg whites in different cups. 'Hugo has no kitchen.' Looking up from the bowl, she purses her lips. 'If he has a guest, that guest must be fed. This is important.'

'Only one guest?' Ryan says. 'That's half a linzer torte each. Still unfair.'

I cut through the nuts again. 'It's good you're thinking mathematically, Ryan, but we looked at fractions last week. Let's move on to petrol consumption.'

He considers the knife. 'You can fight, right?'

'I know about heavy weaponry, like the guns used on warships.'

'What about hand-to-hand combat?'

'I'd be reluctant to use it.' I point to his book. 'Get back to work, Ryan.'

He holds up his fists. 'Uncle Hugo teaches me.'

When Greta sieves flour into a bowl, motes puff into the air. 'Your uncle does not fight in real life,' she says sternly. 'He works hard, and mostly he listens to his elders. As you should listen to Patience.'

Greta adds the egg whites and half the yolks to the bowl before claiming her wooden spoon again. I'm reminded of what Derek said—that he feared she'd use it on Hugo—but I press bravely on.

'I might be back late tomorrow. Has Hugo told you that already?'

'He warns me it is not my business,' she says quietly.

'You don't mind though, do you?'

'I wish for happiness, liebchen, for you and my son.' Glancing at Ryan, she lowers her voice even further. 'Your dear mother, she has the same wish; of this I am certain.'

The numbers on the textbook blur and jump around. 'Thank you.'

'No way!' Ryan slams his pencil on the bench. 'You're Uncle Hugo's guest! You get the other half of the linzer torte!'

I choke out a laugh. 'Are these nuts chopped small enough?'

Greta inspects them. 'A little more.'

Ryan looks nothing like his uncle, but when he narrows his eyes, I'm vaguely reminded of Hugo. 'How tall are you?' he asks.

'A hundred and fifty-two centimetres.'

'What were those frogs you had on the blog? The shortest ones?'

'Most frogs under thirty millimetres are known as froglets. The javelin froglet is only sixteen millimetres long.'

'I bet *he* doesn't get half a linzer torte.'

Greta hides a smile. 'Patience also writes of a giant fellow.'

'The white lipped tree frog,' I say, 'can grow to a hundred and forty millimetres.'

'Big or small, a guest must be fed,' Greta says firmly. 'It is the law.'

'Ryan?' I drum the table. 'Do you need any more help with your homework?'

He rolls his eyes. 'Who cares if the market is on the other side of the mountain?'

I take a fresh pencil and make notes. 'You need to work out not only the distance the truck has to travel, but factor in the route—whether it involves driving slowly up hills, or a level straight road. You also have to think about how heavily the truck is laden. These elements will determine how far Jenny can drive per litre.'

'Where's she going? Mars? She should fill up on the way.'

'There's another factor too. Look at all the information provided in the question. Pretend it's a test.'

He flips to the back of his textbook, pulls out a booklet, then hides it again. 'I got my exam back.'

'You're working hard and improving every week,' I say encouragingly. 'A raw mark in a test doesn't necessarily reflect that.'

This time, he presents the booklet with a flourish. 'Sixty-eight per cent.'

'Ryan!' I take the paper and scan the pages. 'That's fantastic!'

'I thought tests didn't matter.'

'They don't, but …' I can't hide my smile. 'It's a good result.'

Greta beams. 'Such a clever and hard-working boy.' She snatches the booklet. 'I will look at it and give it back tomorrow.'

Ryan grimaces. 'Don't show it to anyone, Oma.'

Pursing her lips, she puts the booklet in a drawer. 'I will *inform* my friends of this achievement. It is not bragging.'

I hand Ryan a ruler. 'We're finding factors that will affect fuel consumption. Have another look at the question.'

Placing the ruler on the page one line at a time, he reads again. 'The weather?'

'It might be worth thinking about.' When I hold up my hand, he slaps it. 'Jenny has a full truck. She's driving up a mountain and down the other side. There's a gale force wind outside, the roads are wet.'

'Rain at last,' Greta says, crossing herself. 'Farmer Jenny's prayers have been answered.'

Ryan laughs. 'Too late, Oma, she's taking the cattle to market.'

Within a few minutes, we've split the question into manageable sections. 'See how you go on your own.'

Greta measures vanilla, ground cloves and cinnamon into the bowl. After I tip in the almonds, she adds flour before holding the bowl on her hip again and combining the ingredients.

'If petrol's so expensive,' Ryan mutters, 'Jenny should get herself an electric truck.'

After flouring a large timber board, Greta spoons out the contents of the bowl and kneads with both hands.

'What will the miners do for a living,' she says, 'with so much electric and solar power?'

'Didn't you read the rest of Patience's post?' Ryan asks. 'If there's too much pollution and development through mining, tadpoles and frogs lose their habitats. That's a problem for them, and for their predators.'

When Ryan lifts his hand, I slap it. 'It's also a problem for agriculture because frogs not only eat invertebrates but keep algae to manageable levels.'

'Frogs eat mosquitos, flies and ...' Greta shudders, 'cockroaches. But we all have bills to settle, Hugo more than he should.' She rolls out the dough. 'If not for this job with Professor Tedeschi, he does not pay his mortgage.'

'Uncle Hugo's always got work,' Ryan says.

'He does work for environment committees like Sapphie's, all as poor as church mice, and he does research to know more about frogs. In his spare time, he digs his own and his neighbour's land.' She cuts a circle of dough around the pan, lifts it with a spatula and presses it into the base. 'He could work at a university, which would be a good and regular income.'

'That'd suck,' Ryan says. 'Like being at school forever.'

'It is a good job,' Greta says firmly, as she gathers the remaining dough and kneads and pounds. 'But does Hugo want it? No, he does not. He says there is too much teaching. It does not let him get his hands dirty.' She holds up her hands, covered in flour. 'How dirty does he want them to be? The debtor's prison is dirty. This is what I say to him.' She pounds again. 'And what does he do? He buys potions for my bathing room, and Remy a pony.'

He also bought me boots, and Minstrel a saddle blanket. What are the implications for his team if Professor Tedeschi has done something wrong?

'If this job didn't work out,' I say hopefully, 'he'd get work elsewhere.'

'Where is this other job?' Greta rolls out the remaining dough, making another circle and cutting it into ten narrow strips. 'In Perth? Darwin? Thousands of kilometres away? Last year, he was six months in Victoria. To work close to home is best.'

'You live on a ship, don't you?' Ryan takes another biscuit. 'Where's your home?'

When Hugo asked me that question on the beach, I said 'wherever I lay my hat'. I hugged Derek this morning when he said 'welcome home'. I'm hot, yet cold. My hand isn't as steady as it should be as I spread homemade raspberry jam onto the dough in the pan.

'A home is a shelter, where you are safe and loved,' Greta says, answering for me. 'This is all.' She takes five strips of dough and lays them over the jam, before crossing the lines diagonally with four more strips, creating a lattice pattern. With the final strip, she makes a circular border, pressing against it with a fork. She brushes the remaining yolk over the dough.

'I remember you baking linzer torte for the swim squad Christmas party.'

She looks up as she rinses the bowl. 'When the others played pool and watched television, you were here in the kitchen.' She passes the pan and a plate of almonds, cut in half lengthwise, across the bench.

'Finished!' Ryan, having checked the answers in the back of the book, grins as he takes another biscuit. 'I'm done.'

'Almost.' I open his second textbook. 'We'll have a quick look at next week's work. That way, you won't have any surprises.'

He groans. 'Algebra?'

'When you get used to it, it's fun, like solving puzzles.'

'Only you would say that.' He bends the spine of the book to keep it flat. 'What's an abundant number?'

I press the almonds into the dough, making a frame around the edge. 'How many nuts am I using?'

He counts. 'Twenty-four.'

'Weihnachten,' Greta says. 'This is Christmas Eve.'

Ryan laughs. 'Oma!'

'Twenty-four is an abundant number,' I say. 'What are the divisors?'

'One, two, three, four ...' Ryan writes in the margin of his book. 'Six, eight and twelve.'

'Excellent. When you add those numbers together, you get thirty-six, which is the sum.' I press each of the almonds again, making sure they're firmly attached. 'If the sum is more than the number, twenty-four in this case, the number will be abundant.'

'Thirty-six is bigger than twenty-four. That's it?'

When my phone vibrates, he peers over the books. 'You want to pick up?'

Charles Tedeschi.

Captain McCarthy said *You're not to contact Charles Tedeschi*. But technically, he's contacted me. It's a phone call. There's no harm in talking to him.

I pick up the call. 'Hang on a sec.'

Signalling to Ryan and Greta that I'll be back soon, I leave the warmth of the kitchen and step outside. Turning my back to the wind, I sit on the verandah steps.

'Sorry, Charlie. I can talk now.'

'Where are you?'

'Horseshoe Hill. At the Halsteads.'

'That's a long way from the pool.' There's a smile in his voice. 'Meet me for a drink tonight? How about Denman? Or Dubbo.'

Derek, Soxy at his heels, lifts a hand as he closes the gate near the shed. 'I'm busy at the farm this afternoon, so I don't think that will work. Maybe—'

'I'm tied up for the next few days, but how about Wednesday? You're working from home, aren't you? We could meet for an early lunch. Twelve o'clock? I have a mate who runs a hotel in Dubbo. The food is sensational.'

Soxy charges ahead of Derek, disappearing into the shadows when he opens the shed. The icy wind threads through my clothes.

'Wednesday should work.'

He laughs. 'You don't sound too excited.'

Hugo needs his job. Rick deserves protection. Pushing McCarthy's directives to the back of my mind, together with the likelihood that Charles is not only a sleaze but an eco-terrorist, I lighten my tone. 'It'll be good to meet up.'

'What we talked about at the pool. That's behind us, right?'

Screws hold the boards to the frame; I trace circles around the heads. 'I reassured Rick that your father was on top of everything.'

'Dad went through it all, worked it out. He's cool with it. The only thing that worries him is sorting out his retirement. Next year, he plans to put his feet up, go on a cruise.'

The professor didn't say anything about a cruise when I spoke to him at Hugo's house.

Charles is lying.

But I'll listen to what he has to say. Because finding out more might garner additional evidence against him. It could protect Rick's reputation and save Hugo's job. After I see Charles, I'll own up to Captain McCarthy. But what about Hugo? How would I explain lunch with Charles Tedeschi?

Well, Hugo, Professor Tedeschi's environmental terrorist son took a shine to me when we met at the pool. That prompted me to take off to Jervis Bay and …

A tonne of guilt lodged firmly in my chest, I march up and down the steps, wiggling my toes to warm them. 'Text me a link to the hotel.'

'We got ourselves a date.'

I'm sitting on the armchair in the granny flat, my laptop on a cushion on my lap, as I contemplate another blog post. The curtains are shut against the cold and the heater clunks softly in the corner of the room. One of Greta's hot water bottles, dressed warmly in a handknitted red and white sweater, is under my feet. There's a tap on the door.

'Come in!'

Mandy Flanagan, svelte in black stovepipe pants and a fitted yellow crewneck, is a member of Greta's book club. Her hair is up in a bun, and she has a glass of red wine in her hand.

'Not joining us, Patience?'

'I didn't get much sleep last night, and I'm going to Minstrel early in the morning.' I yawn. 'Anyway, I doubt I'd be able to keep up.'

She raises the glass. 'I suspect I'll be staying the night.'

'There's enough food and drink to stay for the week.'

She laughs. 'How's it going with Minstrel?'

'Today I saddled and bridled him, and led him around the paddock. If I don't use stirrups, I think I'll be able to ride.'

'Avoid what you're most afraid of?' She puts her glass on the table and crosses her arms. 'We can do better than that.'

I would have been eighteen the last time I saw Mandy in her office at school. She was sitting at her desk and had some type of report—like Ryan's test paper—on her lap.

'Bloody hell,' she said.

Surprised she'd swear in front of a student, I leaned forward in my chair, crossing my legs at the ankles.

'What's the matter, Ms Flanagan?'

'They want to expel you again.' She folded the report in half and dropped it on the desk.

I could barely draw breath. 'I have final exams next week.'

'Tell me what happened.'

'It was Mr McNab, wasn't it? I told him he was …'

Her brows lift. 'A fucking bully.'

'If I don't finish school, it'll be hard to get a job, a decent one. Phoebe can't work and support us when she's got compulsory terms at the hospital, and—'

'You'll go to university, surely?'

'Not until the year after next. It's my turn to work.'

She sat back in her chair. 'Why did you swear at Mr McNab?'

'He bullies Amy. He humiliates her. He shouldn't—'

When she stood, I flinched. And she sat again immediately. 'You've denied it before, Patience, which is why I haven't reported it, but I need to know the truth. Does your father hit you? Sexually abuse you?'

'No.' I shook my head. 'And he's not as manipulative as he was, as controlling.'

'Phoebe is safe? And Prim? How old is she now? Fifteen?'

'We look out for each other, Ms Flanagan.' I sat back in my chair. 'What should I do about Mr McNab? Do I have to apologise?'

'This isn't the first time he's made a fool of Amy, is it?'

'She's in love with Justin Bieber, Ms Flanagan, but that's none of his business, is it?'

Mandy pushed a blank piece of paper across the desk. 'Write down what you know.'

'I don't have to grovel?'

'We can do better than that.'

'Patience?' Picking up her glass, Mandy flicks the rim with a fingernail. 'Your fear revolves around stirrups. It's important you use them. I'd be happy to supervise.'

I want Hugo to myself tomorrow, but …

He wants me to trust him. *I want him to trust me.* He's already suspicious about the secondment, and I don't want to lie about something else. *Especially* a date. A date that, until the police have arrested Charles, I could never hope to explain.

I thread my hands together, swallow down regret. 'What about your shoulder?'

She rotates it, only wincing a little. 'Improving every hour.'

I lift my feet from the hot water bottle and pull up my socks. 'As you're already in Horseshoe, I'd be grateful for your help.'

She lifts her glass in a toast. 'And you shall have it!'

If I don't protect Rick, who will? Not Captain McCarthy, or the auditor-general's office. The federal police won't care. If I meet Charles, I might find out more. I might be able to help.

Doing my best to push Hugo from my mind, I carefully consider my socks. 'We'll start at ten-thirty.'

CHAPTER 39

It's just before ten when I drive over the cattle grid to Hugo's property. Three kookaburras, two adults and a youngster, swoop over my car to the solitary red gum. Arrow and Lavender are both at the fence, looking towards the house. The sun shines brightly, bouncing off the bonnets of—

Mandy's four-wheel drive is parked next to Hugo's, and Mandy is standing on the verandah with her hands on the railing. I could have called Hugo to warn him she'd be here, but I thought I should do it in person. *She wanted to help. I couldn't say no.* By the time I'd greeted Greta in the kitchen, Mandy had already left.

I'm fastening press-studs on my coat as I walk up the steps of the verandah, but stop in surprise when I see Gus. Holding a steaming mug in each hand, he smiles broadly as he hands one to Mandy.

'I made the coffee good and strong like you have it at the pub,' he says.

'Leon's double shot of beans is a very different beast to Hugo's instant coffee,' Mandy laughs. 'But thank you.'

He turns to me and winks. 'G'day, Patience. Fancy a cuppa?'

The tea and toast I had for breakfast sits uneasily in my stomach. 'Thanks, Gus, but I've just had one.'

Mandy, wearing her customary jodhpurs and boots and last night's sweater, leans a hip on the railing. 'I hope our book club shenanigans didn't keep you awake.'

'Greta had a lovely time.' I try not to look for Hugo *too* obviously. 'You left early this morning.'

She sips the coffee and winces. 'I picked Gus up on the way.'

'Being it was me and Derek who set you up with Hugo,' Gus says, 'I was keen to see how you were getting on.'

'There's not much to see yet.'

'I can't wait to get riding again,' Mandy says. 'With this new shoulder, I have a whole new lease on life. Isn't that right, Gus?'

'As my Maggie used to say, you can't keep a good woman down.'

'And you can't underestimate one either.' Mandy looks at me over the rim of her mug. 'You'll be riding with stirrups by lunchtime.'

I aim for a smile. 'I'd better get Minstrel ready.'

'Hugo's done that already,' Gus says, shading his eyes as he peers into the sun. 'Thought he'd be back by now.'

'He's riding Minstrel?'

Gus winks at Mandy. 'He reckoned your big bloke might like to stretch his legs.'

As if on cue, from somewhere behind the house Minstrel neighs. In response, Arrow spins away from the fence. Tail and head high, nostrils flaring, he canters to the far corner of his paddock where he can see a corner of Minstrel's.

With a stiff smile for Gus and Mandy, I follow the verandah to the side of the house. Hugo leans low in the saddle as he closes the gate that leads to the farm behind his property. Tall and well-built like my horse, holding the reins in one hand, he sits easily in the saddle. I jump from the verandah, half-running, half-walking to meet him.

Minstrel's neck and flanks are dark with sweat. Eyes bright, ears pricked, flared nostrils. Hugo loosens the reins and pats Minstrel's neck. He takes off his Akubra and wipes an arm across his brow.

'Imp.' He's very serious.

'Hey.'

He lifts a leg over Minstrel's whither, facing me and sitting sideways in the saddle, before sliding to the ground and landing on both feet. He secures one stirrup iron through the leather and walks to the other side of Minstrel to fix the second one. Then he comes back.

Eyes smoky green, he searches my face. 'Did you sleep?'

'Course I did.'

He kisses me briefly, a brush on the lips. 'Mandy and Gus are waiting.'

I remind myself of the facts: *Less time alone means less chance of lying—about Charles Tedeschi or anything else.* When Hugo turns his back to loosen the girth, I go to Minstrel's head, holding his noseband between my hands. 'It's a lovely morning, Minstrel, don't you think? Wasn't it kind of Mandy to offer to help? Did you have an exciting adventure with Hugo?'

Hugo mutters under his breath. 'Don't, Imp.'

A cranky lion. I walk to him, put my hands on his chest. His sweater is old and soft. I trace the V at the neck. 'I'm sorry.'

'You should've warned me.' He pulls me close. He kisses my neck, grumbles as he nuzzles in my hair.

'Mandy knows what she's doing.'

'Yeah, yeah, I know.'

'Gus likes to help.'

'If he asks you to the dance on Saturday, tell him you're going with me.'

'I'm helping Greta with the pretzels.'

Narrowing his eyes a little, he points to Minstrel. 'Take off his bridle and put on his halter. I'll get him a drink.'

'What about his saddle?'

'You'll be riding soon.'

'Doesn't he need to rest?'

A half-smile. 'I rode him to wear him out.'

When Hugo returns from the shed carrying a bucket of water, he's doused his face, and his hair is damp and pushed back. Lifting a knee, he balances the bucket on his thigh as Minstrel drinks.

He glances sideways. 'What?'

'When we swam, you looked like you do now.'

He puts the bucket on the ground where Minstrel can reach it, then takes my face in his hands.

'You, Patience Cartwright, always get more beautiful.' He kisses my forehead, but when I lift my face, he kisses my mouth. It's a light but lingering kiss. Desire, sweet and aching, threads through my veins. A drip rolls down his jaw and I catch it with a fingertip.

'Thank you.'

Another kiss, swift and hard. 'Get your helmet,' he says. 'I'll let them know we're ready.'

Minstrel, his bridle on again, nudges my pocket as I fumble with the strap of my helmet. After it clicks into place, I stroke the downy softness of his muzzle.

Gus is on the other side of the fence, Mandy is at Minstrel's head, and Hugo is standing next to me. He rests a hand on my hip. 'I'll give you a leg-up.'

When I put my hands on the seat of the saddle and lift a leg, bent at the knee, Hugo links his hands at my shin. If I leaned back, he'd keep me safe. *I could stay on the ground.*

I shift my weight. Force out words. 'I'm ready.'

He lifts and I spring, swinging my leg over the saddle and clinging to the pommel with both hands. Nausea claws at my stomach. Minstrel sidesteps.

'Oh!'

Hugo's arm is firm around the small of my back. His weight pins my leg to the saddle. 'Imp,' he says calmly. 'Open your eyes.'

I speak through stiff lips. 'Why did he move?'

'I leaned against your leg. He thought you'd signalled.'

'He feels my fear, doesn't he?'

'It's okay that you're scared.'

'I feel sick.'

'You've prepared for this. You know what to do.' He stands back a little, untwists Minstrel's rein. He runs his hands down my arm before loosening my fingers and threading them through the reins. 'You hold your hands like this. Remember?'

'Low and close together, thumbs on the top.'

'That's right.'

'Elbows, hips and feet lined up. Heels down.'

'Yes.' He slides his hand down my leg to my foot. 'Good.'

I sit in the saddle as stiff as a statue, the stirrup leathers and irons hanging directly in front of my legs. Hugo's forearm is rigid at the small of my back.

'I'd be better without stirrups.' My voice is high and shaky.

Mandy huffs. 'You'll be familiar with the facts. What can go wrong, why you were dragged.'

Hugo whistles a breath. 'You don't—'

'You've done well with the groundwork, Hugo,' Mandy says firmly. 'But having seen the accident, you lack objectivity.'

He speaks between his teeth. 'I don't want her hurt.'

'And she won't be,' Mandy says calmly. 'The theory, Patience. What is it?'

'You can be trapped in the stirrup iron if you use it to get on the horse. If you slip, your bodyweight is lower than your foot.'

'That is why, when a leg-up isn't available, it's safest to use a mounting block. And take both feet from the stirrups before you dismount.'

'If you fall from the saddle, or if you're thrown, you can also get trapped.'

'In the unlikely event your foot slips through the iron, downward pressure, your weight, keeps you tied to the horse.' When Minstrel rubs his head against her side, Mandy scratches between his ears. 'However, there are steps you can take. Preventative steps. What are they?'

When nausea hits, I look up from the stirrup irons. 'They can't be too wide or too narrow.' I glance at Hugo. 'You should wear smooth-soled riding boots with heels.'

Hugo's hand is firm around my ankle. 'You got it.'

'Not lace-ups, but elastic sides so if you do get dragged your boot will fall off. The irons should be weighty.'

Mandy moves Hugo aside when she lifts the iron. 'Other irons have catches and releases, but they aren't infallible either. You're strong and fit, with excellent balance and good core strength. Your horse is exceptionally well-schooled.'

'There are no guarantees,' Hugo says.

'Granted, he might spook or stumble. But if Patience falls, it's likely to be attributable to something else.'

'Human error,' I croak.

Mandy turns to Hugo again. 'If it makes you feel better, take the friskiness out of Minstrel before Patience rides, as you did this morning. But you know as well as I do that, even if she did fall, he's unlikely to carry on without her.' Mandy places my foot in the iron and forcibly pushes down my heel. She does the same on the other side.

'You know Jet Kincaid, don't you, Patience?' Gus takes off his hat and smooths his thick white hair. 'Her mother was killed when she fell off a horse. A jumping competition it was, and Jet was there. Saw her mum take her last breath, as a matter of fact.' He turns his hat in his hands. 'Poor girl hasn't ridden since.'

Hugo mutters under his breath. 'This isn't the—'

'Hear me out.' Gus tugs at his ear. 'Jet has no fear of horses. How could she, with her being a blacksmith? But she doesn't want to ride on account of what happened to her mum, and that's a decision she's sticking to.' He puts his hat back on, shading his face. 'She was a fine equestrian, Jet's mother, God bless her soul.'

I'd wipe my hands on my jeans, but my hold on the pommel is too tight. I look straight ahead, focusing on the darker hair that outlines Minstrel's ears.

Mandy clears her throat. 'Gus, I don't know that this is helping.'

'What I'm getting at is this,' Gus says. 'Patience here, with a lot of hard work, has learned how to handle a horse. She should be feeling as proud as punch about that.'

Mandy nods. 'That's a good point.'

'And there's nothing to suggest that riding will be different. If Patience puts her mind to something, she goes ahead and does it.' When Gus bangs his hands on the railing, Minstrel pricks his ears. His body tenses, he shifts his feet and—

'Patience.' Hugo's voice is quiet but firm. 'Open your eyes.'

There are three pairs of eyes staring back. Gus is smiling. Mandy is frowning. Hugo's expression is a somewhere between annoyance and concern.

The stirrup iron is firm on the ball of my foot. I release the pommel and collect the reins. 'I think I'll go round the paddock.'

Mandy checks my position in the saddle. 'Drop your shoulders, lift your chin,' she says, before joining Gus at the fence again.

Hugo puts his hands on mine. 'Keep to a walk,' he says quietly.

'I can't let Minstrel feel my fear.'

His hand slips to my leg. 'That's a big ask.'

'I have to think about something else.' My voice is shaky. 'What?'

Frowning, he looks around. 'You were in this paddock yesterday. Did you calculate dimensions?'

'I had to skirt around the trees at the creek. It was only an estimate.'

'That'll do.'

'There are two hundred metres to the north, and two hundred and twenty-five metres on the western boundary. Two hundred and five metres along the creek. Which means, with the additional fifty metres on the eastern boundary, the paddock is fifty thousand square metres.'

'Five hectares. You got it.' He runs a hand down my calf and pulls my heel down further. He shifts the ball of my foot to the very end of the iron. When he puts his hand on my thigh, my skin warms. My toes curl up.

'Hugo?' The pitch of my voice is much too high. 'I need something else to think about.'

His hair, now dry, falls onto his forehead. 'How many steps does Minstrel take around the perimeter.'

'Eighteen hundred and twelve.' The words tumble out. 'The diagonal is …' I bite my lip. 'Sorry.'

His lip lifts. 'Quit apologising.'

Quit making me love you more than I should.

CHAPTER 40

Although I keep Minstrel to a walk, I challenge myself in other ways. An extended walk. A slow walk. Halts and turns and backing up. By the time we turn at the creek, the sweat on Minstrel's neck has dried, my thighs are sore from squeezing his sides, and the backs of my calves are stiff from pushing down my heels. I loosen the reins as we head towards the gate. I stretch out my fingers.

Mandy and Gus are on the other side of the fence. Hugo, watching and pacing, is still in the paddock. When I free my feet from the stirrups and jump to the ground, he grasps my waist and spins me around.

'You did it!'

I laugh in relief. 'Me and Minstrel.'

He's suddenly serious. 'Never a doubt.'

When Gus proclaims loudly that his tummy is rumbling, and Mandy laments the lack of a hat and the need for a decent coffee,

Hugo takes a very deep breath before telling me they'll see me at the house. It takes half an hour to brush the dried sweat from Minstrel's coat, feed him morning tea and settle him into the paddock, so it's almost twelve by the time I follow the verandah to the back of the house and the kitchen. A microwave, an old-fashioned electric stovetop, and a concrete sink and floor. I think this room must have been the original house's mud room or laundry. No cupboards, just a weathered pine bookcase holding cutlery, crockery, tinned goods and containers of cereal, pasta and rice. A fridge is squeezed into one corner. *No wonder Greta is horrified.*

Gus and Mandy sit at a dining room table. It's old like the rest of the furniture, but well-made and large. The timber is dark brown, a similar colour to Minstrel. Hugo, smiling a welcome, leans against the sink.

'Take a seat.'

The linzer torte has been divided into eighths, and there are only three pieces left. Moving the coffee plunger aside, Mandy puts a slice onto a plate and pushes it across the table. 'You did well.'

'I chopped the nuts and spread the raspberry jam.'

She laughs. 'That too.'

The kettle pings. 'Imp?'

A nickname. A diminutive.

An endearment.

When I look up, it's into his eyes, the green and gold and grey. 'Hugo?'

His brows lift. 'Coffee or tea?'

'Tea please.'

When he leans over my shoulder to place the teapot and mug by my plate, I'm tempted to lean back and press my head against his stomach. I want to look up and smile. But …

I have too many secrets.

A feather-light touch to my neck. My skin prickles, my face warms, a traitorous tingling travels down my spine.

Gus clunks his mug on the table. 'This riding caper ...' He looks pointedly at Hugo before turning to me. 'You know what my Maggie would say? You don't cook a sponge and a fruit cake together.'

'Well ... I guess not.'

'Same goes with riding. Mandy here didn't swim with you when you were a mite, or see the accident, which is how she got you riding with stirrups. Same with me. I'll give you a leg-up any time you want.'

My mug has three chips in the rim, but I work around them. 'Thank you, Gus, for all you've done.'

He beams. And then he slaps the table. 'You know about the Horseshoe dance, don't you?'

'It's on Saturday.'

'I generally go with Sapphie,' he says, 'but little Amélie's only a couple of weeks old, and Sapphie shouldn't be overdoing things. Jet is in the family way again, throwing up like there's no tomorrow. Which is why I asked Phoebe—Sinn not being a barn dancing kind of bloke—if she would be my partner.'

'She's sorry to miss it.'

'To sign up for the barn dances, you've got to have a partner.' Gus puts one calloused hand over the other. 'Greta tells me you'll be there.'

'We're selling pretzels.'

'Get to the point, Gus,' Mandy says. 'It's time to go home.'

'My Maggie used to say I danced like I was roping a bull. Not sure your shoulder would stand up to that, would it now, Mandy?'

'It certainly wouldn't, which is why I turned you down.'

'Greta told me you like a tune, Patience, and Phoebe confirmed it. So, what do you say? The pretzels always sell out early. Will you be my date for the dance?'

'Imp?' Hugo crosses his arms. 'Aren't you going with me?'

'Give the lady a chance to decide.'

One step at a time.

My nails dig into my palms. 'Thank you, Gus. I'll be your partner.'

When Gus emits a hoot, Mandy pushes back her chair. 'Come along, Gus,' she says, brushing crumbs from her jodhpurs. 'We don't want to outstay our welcome.'

Gus picks up his mug. 'Better get this down quick smart.'

'I can drop you home.' I collect crumbs with my thumb. 'I'm leaving soon.'

'Much appreciated, Patience,' Gus says, 'if it's not too much trouble.'

'Patience?' Hugo says quietly. 'I thought you were staying.'

'I'd better get back.'

Mandy looks curiously from Hugo to me. 'I'll let myself out,' she says briskly.

When I brush past Hugo to stack my plate and mug next to the sink, his smile goes nowhere near his eyes.

'Would you like to see the house before you go?' he says.

Gus, already pulling a *National Geographic* magazine across the table, looks up. 'No need to hurry on my account.'

I pass through the narrow doorway of the makeshift kitchen and—

'Oh!'

Towering ceilings. Broad timber floorboards, skirting boards and picture rails. Intricate fretwork. The walls are plastered, most of them patched and roughly sanded. Two ladders lean against arched double doors that separate the hallway from the dining room. Paint splattered groundsheets heaped on the floor lead to an entrance space, large enough to be a room all on its own, and beyond that, the double front doors. To the left of the doors is a winding timber staircase that leads to the upper floor. Many of the treads and major support posts have been replaced with newer timbers, but there are yawning gaps in the railings. Strips of red and white striped tape, like sticks of candy cane, mark the places struts should be.

'Can you use the stairs?' I ask.

'My bedroom and office are up there. Three more bedrooms.'

'Is there a bathroom?'

I follow him to another hallway, and he opens a door. The room is small but has tall timber windows that look out to the creek. On one side of the windows are a toilet and ancient porcelain sink, and on the other side a shower with a curtain. Electrical fittings jut out of untiled walls.

I clear my throat. 'I should explain.'

He nods. 'That'd be good.'

Our footsteps echo on the floor as we walk into the lounge room. The fireplace has a timber mantelpiece and surround, a cast-iron grate, and a thick black granite hearth. A wicker basket, overflowing with kindling, sits next to a half barrel keg filled with logs. Besides the sofa and coffee table that face the fire, and two standard lamps, the enormous room is bare.

'It's beautiful, Hugo.' The windows, facing the front of the house, have windowsills broad enough to sit on. I consider the ornate cornices. 'The ceiling is new, isn't it?'

'The original couldn't be saved.'

The weathered parquetry, laid out in squares and diagonals, is golden like honey. 'You saved the floor.'

He's standing much closer now. 'You said you'd explain.'

Taking two steps back, I grasp the mantelpiece. Out of reach. Out of temptation.

'I got a call yesterday afternoon, something to do with work. It made me realise ...' Feet apart, I release the mantelpiece and put my hands behind my back. *At ease.* 'I don't want to lie to you. I don't want to hurt you.'

'Like you're not hurting me already?'

'I'm trying to do the right thing.'

'Is this something to do with Jervis Bay? I spoke to Rick yesterday.'

'What did he say?'

'Nothing, that's the problem.'

When does Hugo fix the holes in the walls? In the weekday evenings? On the weekends when he's not digging at the creek, helping Derek, supervising Remy, looking after Minstrel?

'You want information, Hugo. I can't give it to you.'

His jaw locks, unlocks. 'I said I wouldn't rush you, but you've got to be fair. Trust and honesty, it goes both ways. You've got to give me something.'

When I don't answer, he walks away, long determined steps towards the window. One, two, three, four, five, six. *Long fair plaits. Two missing teeth. Kindergarten. Six is a perfect number, Mrs Latimer. Explain what you mean, Patience. A perfect number is positive integer equal to the sum of its positive divisors. 1 + 2 + 3 = 6. Do you want me to explain about—*

When Hugo prises open the window, a breeze rushes in. Suddenly cold, I picture my coat, hanging on the back of the chair in the kitchen.

'Imp?' Slow and quiet, like we're with Minstrel. 'Look at me.'

He's framed by the window. Behind him, the gum trees. His lips are slightly apart. His chest lifts and falls.

I do as he asks, but no words come out.

'Tell me what you want,' he says.

When I was a child and sat at the pond and wished for my mother, I knew what I wanted. *When I was nineteen and told you I loved you, I knew what I wanted.* Now?

Nothing has changed. Everything is different.

The floorboards creak as I walk towards him. I stand on my toes, hold onto his shoulders and press my cheek against his. I breathe him in. And then I let him go.

'I'll see you at the dance on Saturday.'

CHAPTER
41

Greta insists I must be exhausted, even though all I've been doing is sitting on the day bed with my laptop—posting on the blog and sorting through Rick's data.

'For three days, you have been busy from dawn until dusk,' she says. 'You are with the spreadsheets, teaching Ryan mathematics and fixing Derek's tax returns. You will have peace and quiet in the bathing room. I promise.'

'I have to be in Dubbo by one.'

'This school friend, you should meet him in Horseshoe.'

I don't like lying to Greta, but I suspect anything I say will make its way back to Hugo. Greta didn't ask why I was home so early on Sunday, but nudged Derek at the dinner table, encouraging him to ask questions about not only my riding lesson, but Hugo.

'My friend knows the chef at the hotel,' I say. 'It won't take me too long to get there.'

'You do not get your afternoon nap.'

'I stopped having naps two weeks—'

'You will leave the granny flat soon,' she says, herding me down the hallway. 'We do not see you again.'

'Rick needs my help, but I'll visit on the weekends when I can. I've already scheduled lessons with Ryan.'

After carefully considering her shelves, Greta selects a pale green bottle. A garland of off-white paper flowers, small and delicate with long pointed petals, is draped around the neck.

'This elixir is "Auf Wiedersehen". You know the meaning?'

'Goodbye. But please don't open it for me.'

'Phooey,' she says, unscrewing the top with a flourish. 'It was to celebrate our thirty-year wedding anniversary.'

'Did you and Derek go away?'

'Hugo paid for a trip to Tasmania, a cabin with a spa bath. I prayed we could go but …' She crosses herself. 'It was the drought.'

'This bubble bath was also from Hugo, wasn't it?'

'Of course.' Turning away, she sorts through the towels. 'You know Hugo is kind, yes?'

I sit in the white wicker chair. 'Yes.'

She faces me again, a towel hugged tightly to her chest. 'When Derek and I said you were too young to decide, you believed we were afraid for Hugo. But now you know, liebchen, we were also afraid for you.'

'You'd made a promise to my mother.'

She opens the towel before folding it again. 'You remember how I told you of Derek's talk with Hugo? How he must have forbearance and restraint. After you left, Hugo does not bring girlfriends to Horseshoe.'

'Never?'

'This is when it stopped.'

'Oh ...' I pull off my socks. 'Oh.'

Greta pours a generous amount of bubble bath into the water. 'Sapphie would want you to enjoy this, but we must not get the paper flowers wet.' Unravelling the string, she pulls the garland free. 'The perfume is geranium.'

'Like the flowers in your window box.'

Greta puts the garland in the pocket of her apron. 'The edelweiss is for beauty and purity. It has no need of perfume.' With one last smile, she closes the door behind her.

On a large ship, unless you're on deck, the engines drown out the sounds of the ocean. In the bath, the water laps gently like a kiss. I secured my hair in a bun but curls escape, clinging to my cheeks and neck. I close my eyes.

Do not cry again.

'You smell amazing!'

I don't want Charles to put his arms around me, but it's impossible to avoid him in the crowded hotel entrance. Smiling politely, I pull back from his embrace and follow his lead as we walk up the stairs to the restaurant. Like Charles, most of the patrons are wearing long pants and smart shirts, so I'm relieved I wore a dress, short but floaty, with my sandals. Charles's chef friend, a lanky American, greets us as we're shown to our table.

'Welcome!'

The room has high ceilings and dark timber floorboards. Hanging from the picture rails are photographs of vineyards, and thoroughbred horses like Arrow. We're shown to a table next to a window that looks down on the street. A waiter, dressed in dark pants and a white buttoned tunic, brings oversized menus and a carafe of iced water.

I lay my napkin neatly over my lap. 'Nice place.'

Charles considers a wine list. 'What would you like to drink?'

'Water will do for me,' I say as I fill our glasses from the carafe, 'but you go ahead.'

'You don't drink?'

'Toasts at weddings.'

He sits back in his chair. 'Like I said to Dad, you're an enigma. You do your own thing. You've got spirit.'

I do my best to shrug naturally. 'Why were you talking about me?'

'You care what he thinks?'

'He has overall responsibility for the team I'm working on.'

'Fair point.' It takes a few seconds, but then he smiles again. 'I like you, Patience. I like you a lot.'

I study the menu. 'You've been here before. What do you recommend?'

We discuss the government's environmental policies, but he won't be drawn on what he's currently working on, and when I raise the water security project, he immediately shuts me down.

The day-to-day operation of warships is neutral territory, so I move onto that. After we've finished our main courses, an ancient grains salad for him and a fancy halloumi burger for me, I indicate his black and silver watch.

'It's a Rolex, isn't it? With titanium casing. Do you dive? What's the underwater pressure limit?'

He laughs. 'As it only gets wet in the shower, you tell me.' When he reaches across the table and slides his hand over mine, I grit my teeth and tolerate it. I count backwards as I consider the specifications.

'Up to three thousand metres. Not bad.'

'Patience!' Lisa, standing a few metres away, says something to the woman she's with and, as I pull my hand free, walks confidently to the table. Her fitted red dress has a low V neck.

'Hello.' Even to my ears, my voice is stilted.

'Good to know I'm not the only one having a long lunch.'

I link my hands in my lap. 'I'll be going back soon.'

She laughs. 'I wasn't having a go at you.'

I force a smile. 'I thought you were in Narromine.'

'I got delayed in Sydney.' She smiles at Charles. 'I'm sure I know you from somewhere.'

He stands and holds out a hand. 'Charlie Tedeschi. Lisa, right? You work with my father.'

'Of course!' Her gaze comes back to me. 'Sorry to interrupt, but I've only seen you once in the past few months, and that was at Hugo's. It's nice that you're out and about.' She glances under the table. 'No issues with your foot?'

I extend my leg and point my toe. 'All good now.'

'Back at the pool,' Charles says, 'you were kicking like an Olympian.'

'Which reminds me,' Lisa says. 'Hugo thought you might be swimming later today. Did he get on to you?'

'Oh, I …' I smooth out my napkin. 'I'll call him after lunch.'

Draining his third glass of wine, Charles watches Lisa weave between the tables and sit opposite her friend. 'Small world,' he says.

I study the menu. 'Are you having coffee?'

Charles orders black coffee and a liqueur, and I order a cappuccino. As he leans back in his chair, he winces.

'Does your hip stiffen up? Would you prefer not to stay?'

'How did you know it was my hip?'

'The way you walk. Is there anything you can do about the pain?'

'I could ask the man who smashed it to stick it together again.'

'I'm sorry. I didn't mean to—'

'You can ring Halstead now if you like.' He gestures to my bag.

'It won't be anything urgent. Do you know Hugo too?'

'He was at the party where I met Lisa. Dad thinks a lot of him.' He nods when the waiter brings the drinks. 'You know him well, do you? Is that why you're living with his parents in Horseshoe?'

'We were in the same swimming squad when we were kids.'

Charles drinks half his liqueur in a gulp. 'You told me you weren't dating anyone.'

'I'm not.'

'Could have fooled me.' He looks over his shoulder as he searches for Lisa. 'You jumped a mile when she came along. You shut her down when she asked about Halstead.'

'Did I?'

'How did he know about the swim?'

'I presume Greta, Hugo's mother, told him.'

'Did you tell her about lunch?'

'She knew I was meeting a friend.'

'Did you mention my name?'

'She didn't ask. Would there have been a problem if I had?'

When he picks up his glass and swirls, amber liquid clings to the side. 'Why so secretive if nothing is going on?'

I could ask the same of you. Ignoring his hands, fisted on the table, I speak calmly. 'I'm not dating anyone.'

His gaze travels from my face to my breasts. His lips twist. And then, one hand supporting his hip, he stands.

'Ready to go?'

I've barely touched my coffee, but I stand too. Charles waves me away when I offer to pay half the bill, then insists on walking me to the car park. I do my best to speak naturally about the river, the weather and the town, but he answers in monosyllables. My four-wheel drive is parked in an outdoor space near the supermarket. I unlock it, open the door and put the key in the ignition.

'Thank you for lunch. Give my regards to the professor.'

'Why would I do that?'

'Given you live in his house, I presume you see him regularly.'

'You, Patience ...' He rests a hand on the open door, trapping me. 'You got a face and body as sweet as apple pie, but I reckon my dad is right about you. You're as sharp as a tack, and you've got answers to everything.'

I throw my bag over the centre console to the passenger seat before facing him again. 'You don't hold back, do you?'

'I'm a little disappointed, is all,' he says, as he steps closer. 'Remember our chat at the pool? You said you'd keep things to yourself. Dad was adamant you hadn't talked to the others about the invoices, but now I have my doubts.'

I'm not supposed to be here. I don't want to say anything I shouldn't. But I have to say something. *Stick to the truth, to what he already knows.*

'Hugo was never aware there was a problem, and neither was Lisa, so I didn't talk to them. As agreed, I reassured Rick that the professor would correct the mistakes, nothing else.'

'Even before Lisa rocked up, you were edgy, so why agree to a date?' His breath, aioli and alcohol, turns my stomach. 'What's your agenda?'

I'll report that you have something to hide. I'll take a step back.

'Can you get out of the way?'

'What's the rush? You got another date at the pool?'

Dipping under his arm and grasping the door frame, I step up to the running board before pulling myself onto the seat. I swing my leg—

He slams the door on my foot. A flash of blinding pain. A wave of nausea. My eyes water. I whimper.

He opens the door. 'How about that wind?' he says, licking a finger and holding it up.

I suck air through my teeth as I drag my foot into the car. I clasp my leg with both hands.

'Not having a lot of luck with that dainty little foot of yours, are you, Patience?' He steps back, angles his head and peers into my face. 'You gotta take more care.'

Determined not to look down, I tentatively move my toes. I bend my ankle and put my foot on the brake. There's stickiness between the sole of my foot and my sandal. With a shaking hand, I grasp the key in the ignition.

'Stay away from me.'

'Let's not fall out.'

I underestimated his nastiness. His malice and intent. *What he has to lose.* I pull the door towards me, but he won't let it go.

'I like you, Patience,' he says. 'Another time, another place, we could've made this work.' His gaze travels from my legs to my feet. 'So how about we make a deal? Keep your mouth shut, and we don't second date.'

If I kicked the door open, it would throw him off balance. I could grab him by the throat, knee him in the groin and punch him in the hip. But then what? My word against his. He could claim I'd attacked him without cause.

I could get arrested. Or possibly even worse, since I'm not supposed to be here, *he* could get arrested.

Not only that, but his suspicions would be confirmed: someone I'm in league with is onto him.

CHAPTER 42

I buy a bottle of water and ask for a cup of ice at a fast-food drive-through in Dubbo, before driving to a truck stop and parking under the shade of a grey gum. Taking off my sandal and washing away the blood, I inspect the damage. The swelling isn't too bad, and the cut isn't deep, but an angry blue line crosses the top my foot. After angling it to examine my instep—still pink from the surgery but otherwise okay—I stuff ice into a shopping bag, wrap my foot, push back my seat and wind down the window.

I rehearse what I'll say to McCarthy. Charles Tedeschi asked me on a date. It might have looked suspicious if I *hadn't* gone. I hoped he'd give me more information than he did. Unfortunately, I have nothing new to report except …

Tell the federal police to hurry up!

I pull out my phone. I touch the screen, the photo of Minstrel. I search my contacts and—

When the phone rings, I jump a mile. 'Patience speaking.'

'Cartwright!'

'Commander Ruddock?'

'I'm here with Captain McCarthy.' After blasting me for meeting Charles Tedeschi, Ruddock tells me the police have been tapping his phone for weeks. They weren't too interested in our date until, just a few hours ago, someone put two and two together, worked out I was on secondment to the water security project, and contacted the base.

'You had no authority to meet him,' Ruddock says for at least the tenth time.

'Why haven't they arrested him? He's dangerous.'

'How do you—'

'He shut my foot in the door!'

After I've detailed my conversations with Charles, and the assault, Captain McCarthy pipes up. 'Given past form, lieutenant, I appreciate your restraint in not retaliating. Do you require medical assistance? I'd prefer not to see you at death's door again.'

'I'm okay.'

'Did Charles Tedeschi mention your naval credentials?'

'He knows I was on report and used the secondment as an excuse to get off the base. He doesn't trust me because I know about the invoices, but I don't think he connects me to a formal investigation.'

'Do you want to return to the base?'

I've agreed to partner Gus at the Horseshoe dance. Greta needs my help with the pretzel stall. I promised Sapphie I'll take care of her newborn baby, Amélie. Rick will need my help at the river. And then there's Hugo …

'No, sir.'

'I'll pass on what you've said. In the meantime, stay clear of Charles Tedeschi.'

'What about Professor Tedeschi? He has to live with him.'

'The professor might be involved,' McCarthy says.

'He wouldn't harm the project, or those that work on it.'

'That's not for us to judge.'

'What's being done to protect Dr Lipman? He's relying on the professor to fix an administrative error. If he works out there's no such thing, he'll hound him. Say Charles finds out and—'

'Cartwright!' Ruddock again. 'This is out of our hands.'

'The police already know about Charles. They've had all week to arrest him.'

'I'll pass on your concerns,' McCarthy says.

'I've worked closely with people on this project. It doesn't feel right to hide the facts from them.'

'You've been ordered to do so!' Ruddock snaps.

'Their safety and livelihoods are at stake!'

'Your options are mutually exclusive,' McCarthy says. 'One, lay low. Two, withdraw from the secondment and return to the base.'

Derek, eating afternoon tea, is sitting on the top step of the verandah as I climb out of the four-wheel drive. Freeing my foot from the bag of ice, I walk barefoot over the gravel, trying not to limp too obviously.

He stands. 'You haven't been with Minstrel, have you?'

'I went to Dubbo.'

He looks at me dubiously. 'What's going on?'

'It's only a bruise and a scrape.'

'How'd you do it?'

'I tripped over a kerb on my way to the car park.'

'You want a lift to Dr Gupta?'

'It's nothing, Derek, really, but …' I cross my fingers. 'Is Greta out?'

'Decorating the hall for Saturday.'

'I'd prefer to explain this to her when I'm wearing shoes.'

Hugo arranged with two girls from the pony club to look after the horses from tonight until Saturday. When I told him I'd be visiting Minstrel every day and I could do it instead, he refused my offer, claiming the girls relied on the pocket money. Millie Honey, on P-plates, is at the end of Hugo's driveway as I indicate to turn left. Her younger sister Mary is sitting in the back and winds down her window.

'We told them you'd give them their carrots!' she shouts.

Hugo calls as I open the door to the shed. Leaning against a bale of lucerne hay, I take the weight off my foot.

'Hey.'

'Imp.'

I burrow in the bag for carrots. Two for each horse. Three horses. Six. 'I should have called back. I'm sorry.'

A brief hesitation. 'How was lunch?'

Has he spoken to Lisa? If so, I hope she hasn't let on about Charles. Did she see his hand, resting over mine? I cross my fingers for the second time tonight. 'The food was great.'

'Did you swim afterwards?'

'I wanted to get back.' When I walk outside, the shadows are long and deep. 'Rick sent an email. Your fieldwork has been delayed, hasn't it? You won't be home until Monday or Tuesday. I'll miss you at the dance.'

'Less competition for Gus.'

I gather the carrots together and shove them in my pockets. 'I won't ride till you get back.'

'Derek said you've hurt your foot.'

'It's fine.'

'What happened?'

'I'm sure Derek told you.'

'He didn't believe you'd tripped over a kerb.'

Minstrel is waiting at the gate; I comb through his mane with my fingers. 'I don't want to lie to you.'

'Okay …' I imagine him, mouth tight, pushing back his hair. 'Is whatever happened likely to happen again?'

I pat Minstrel's neck. 'I've learned my lesson, Hugo. Never again.'

CHAPTER

43

The clouds are dark on Saturday evening but Derek, loading the last of the warm and fragrant pretzels into the ute, reassures Greta the rain will hold off until early tomorrow.

Greta, who has barely left her kitchen for the past two days, wipes her hands on her apron as we walk back to the house. 'It is good you can walk, liebchen, but can you dance?'

'Not in heels. What should I wear with my sneakers?'

'Your blue shirt will be suitable for selling the pretzels, and for the dancing.'

'It's Hugo's shirt.'

'When Hugo was this big,' she holds her hand at hip height, 'he recycled my plastics and paper. If he were here tonight to see his shirt, he would be proud.'

I haven't heard from Hugo since he called on Wednesday night. And he won't be there this evening. I sit on the steps to ease Greta's gumboot off my foot.

'I don't want to let Gus down. I could wear a skirt with the shirt.'

Her eyes open wide. 'Gus is a vigorous dancer, liebchen, shorts are better.'

As Gus predicted, the pretzels are popular, but when I refuse to leave the stall until the last one has sold, Greta corrals the Honey girls, bribing them with the chicken croquettes she's added to the menu.

'Gus is waiting,' she says, flapping her apron as she herds me out of the stall.

The barn dances are called over the microphone and, with enthusiastic instructions from Gus, I get the hang of the steps after the first few sets. Some women wear diamanté-studded shirts with jeans and boots, others wear dresses and heels, but my outfit of sneakers, checked shirt and frayed blue denim shorts isn't at all out of place. Gus and I have danced for almost two hours when the barn dances finish. With a bow, he graciously kisses my hand before joining farmers and other locals sitting at tables near the bar.

Almost the entire population of Horseshoe seems to be here—women, men, children, toddlers and babies. A DJ takes over the music and plays a mix of country and pop. The music isn't as loud as it was, but the hall buzzes with laughter and chatter. I find a table and chair between the bar and the dance floor, sitting gratefully as I take the weight off my foot.

Matts Laaksonen, tall and ridiculously handsome with brown hair and eyes, holds two-month-old Amélie in the crook of his arm. He puts a bottle of mineral water and a glass on the table in front of me.

'Patience,' he says, nodding politely. 'The drink is from Gus.'

'Thank you.'

'May I join you?'

'Of course.'

Careful not to disturb the sleeping Amélie, he takes the chair next to mine. I met Matts at Phoebe's wedding, and in the past few weeks we've exchanged pleasantries in Horseshoe, but this the first time I've seen him with his daughter. It softens his edges.

Amélie is tiny and delicate. When a pink-booted foot escapes from her wrap, I tuck it in. 'Hello, baby girl. You look nice and cosy.'

Matts kisses the top of Amélie's head. 'Sapphie says you'll care for her when we dance. Would you like to hold her now?'

'Yes, please.' Matts stands, carefully depositing Amélie in my arms and settling her comfortably. She purses her mouth, as small and perfect as a rosebud. Her eyelids flutter but close again as Sapphie appears.

'Gus wants to speak to you,' she tells Matts, touching his shoulder before taking his chair. She smiles at her daughter, and then she smiles at me.

'Is Hugo coming?' she asks.

Amélie snuffles against me, her little body warm against my chest. 'He was going to, but ...' I risk a nonchalant shrug. 'He had to work.'

'Being with Greta and Derek again,' she says. 'I imagine it brings back memories.'

'About Hugo?'

She bites her lip. 'Was I prying?'

'You're close friends. You must know what happened between us.'

'Hugo rarely talked about it, but it was clear he'd made a mess of things. The trouble was, he had no idea how to fix it.'

'I wouldn't let him.'

'He'd hurt you.'

'I couldn't see how much I'd hurt him.'

The words hang between us. Sapphie smiles sadly. And then she looks over my shoulder. 'Speak of the devil.'

Hugo, his khaki shirt half tucked into his jeans, stands near the open double doors. His hair is damp and pushed back as if he's just showered, but his boots are work boots, worn and mud splattered. Our eyes meet.

'Sapphie?' Matts kisses Sapphie's cheek before taking her hand. 'Our song is next.'

Ignoring my hammering heart, I do my best to focus on Matts, who pulls Sapphie to her feet and slings an arm around her shoulders. As the opening bars of Frankie Valli's 'Can't Take My Eyes Off You' comes over the speakers, he finds a space on the dancefloor. Sapphie laughs as he spins her around, catching her hands before pulling her close.

'Imp?' Hugo's eyes are dark and dull. He's pale beneath his tan. My breath catches. 'What's the matter? What's happened?'

He sits and leans forward, forearms on his knees. 'Nice shirt,' he says gruffly.

'Hugo?' When I touch his arm, he tenses. 'What's wrong?'

His eyes press closed, just for a moment. 'Headache.'

'A migraine? You have to go home.'

He rubs around the back of his neck. 'Headlights.'

I push my glass across the table. 'Have a drink.'

'I'll throw up.'

'It's only water.'

He looks at Amélie. A fleeting smile. 'Hey, little Sapphie,' he whispers.

I touch Amélie's hair. 'Isn't she beautiful?'

'Imp?' He moves his foot so we're toe to toe. 'Why'd you push me away? How'd you get hurt?'

Amélie's eyelashes are long and spiky, crescents on her cheeks. Her nails are pink and smooth, little semi-circles. Arcs, radius, diameter. I know a lot of formulae.

But not the one for Hugo.

Matts is a very good dancer, and he's clearly in love with his wife. As he expertly spins a laughing Sapphie around the floor, the other dancers stand back and watch. Some clap and cheer.

I raise my voice. 'I'll take you home, Hugo.'

'Your home?'

'Yours.'

He opens his mouth, shuts it again. And then he sways, gripping the chair either side of his legs to steady himself. He presses his teeth together, swallows compulsively. Greta is only two tables away. When I stand and wave, holding Amélie close with one arm, Greta bustles towards us.

'Hugo has to go home,' I say. 'I'll drive him.'

Greta puts her hand on Hugo's shoulder and searches his face. 'My poor son. It is a migraine, yes? Have you taken the tablets?'

He presses fingers against his temple. 'I thought it'd pass.'

'Patience?' Greta takes Amélie out of my arms and rearranges her wrap, efficiently parcelling her into a neat little bundle. 'You will take Hugo to the farm, yes?' She settles the baby on her shoulder. 'Derek drinks his beer and cannot drive, and we have to pack the stall and load the ute. When this is done, I will ask Matts to drive us—'

'No,' Hugo croaks. 'I'm okay at home.' Leaning forward, he puts his head in his hands. 'I don't need nursing. You and Derek stay here.'

'You can't drive like this,' I say.

He swallows again. 'No.' He's so very pale.

'Patience collects your tablets on the way,' Greta says worriedly. 'Then you come to the farm.'

He lifts his head. 'Imp?' He frowns as he collects his thoughts. 'Take me home in my car and bring it back here. I'll come and get it tomorrow.'

'You should not be alone,' Greta argues. 'Someone must—'

'I'll stay.'

Greta takes my hand. 'You have first aid training, yes? In the navy.'

'Of course.' The music is suddenly much too loud, the lights are far too bright. 'Don't worry, Greta. I'll take care of him.'

Hugo refuses to lie down in the passenger seat, but as we cross the bridge he opens the window and slumps against the door. Arrow and Lavender are lying down, but Lavender scrambles to his feet and walks jauntily to the gate. I haven't even turned off the engine when Hugo opens his door, staggers out of the car and dry retches into the gravel. The front door key is the only other one on his keychain. I flick on lights before running back. As he straightens, I take his arm.

'Your bedroom is upstairs, isn't it?'

'This is fucked.'

'Maybe lie on the sofa in the living room? It's closer to the bathroom.'

He puts an arm over his eyes. 'Turn off the lights.'

Last time I saw him like this, he would have been eighteen or nineteen. It was the annual Octoberfest party and, until he'd owned up to having had a headache all afternoon, Greta suspected someone had slipped vodka into the punch. Around ten of us were staying at the farm, the girls in one room and the boys in another, so it was impossible for him to hide how sick he was.

Things are no better tonight. Sitting with his head in his hands, pacing the floor, propped up on cushions with a fist against his temple, he can't escape the pain in his head. When he wants heat, I warm dampened hand towels in the microwave. When he wants cold, I take hand towels out of the freezer. I keep the lights low, encourage him to hydrate, and shadow him to the bathroom whenever he throws up. I barge in when the soap container crashes to the floor. He's sitting on the tiles, knees bent with his head down.

'Hugo?' My voice wavers. 'Can't you take something?'

'Not till I stop throwing up.' He rolls onto all fours and pulls himself upright.

I take his arm. 'There can't be anything left.'

It's after one o'clock when, exhausted and shaking but finally calm, he lies on his side on the sofa. I tuck a cotton blanket around him and push back his hair before sitting on an armchair and curling my legs to the side.

'Imp?' I must have dozed off, because he's sitting on the edge of the sofa, a stack of hand towels piled at his feet. He's still pale and shaky, but his eyes are clear. 'Can you go to my bedroom?' he says. 'There's a box of tablets in the second drawer of the side table near the window.' It's the longest sentence I've heard from him all night.

I close the doors to the living room before switching on the light to the staircase. Notwithstanding the missing railing, the treads seem solid enough. As the windows of the rooms at the front of the house are boarded up, I presume he doesn't sleep in them. I follow the hallway to the open door at the end.

His bedroom is built into the gabled roof at the side of the house and has a steeply pitched ceiling. The bedhead, side tables and blanket box are the colour of driftwood bleached by the sun. A built-in bookcase with different sized compartments is filled not only with books, but photographs. Most are of native plants, rivers and wetlands, but a group of three photos share a shelf of their own. One is of Greta, Derek and their three little fair-haired boys, and one is of Remy on Lavender, with Ryan holding the lead rope. In the third photo, there are eleven smiling faces. Hugo, shirtless and with spiky sun-bleached hair, would be fourteen or fifteen, a similar age to the rest of the squad. Their arms are around each others' shoulders and they're laughing into the camera. I peer more closely. *There are twelve in the photo.* I hadn't had my growth spurt—for what it was worth—so would have been twelve and I'm looking to the side, as if I've been pushed into the frame. Phoebe used to plait my hair tightly the night before training, so it didn't get in my way as I swam. Was she too busy to do it that night? Did I forget to remind her? In the photo, it's curling riotously down my back.

Hugo called it wheaten.

'Imp!' Hugo shouts.

I jump. 'I'm coming!'

Double doors in the bedroom open out onto a balcony. I lower the blinds, grey like the walls but with a vertical dark blue stripe. Opposite the bed, on the third wall, is an oil painting in myriad shades of blue—cobalt and navy, blue-green and aqua. What percentages of the primary colours would be in each stroke?

'Imp!' Hugo shouts again, this time from the bottom of the stairs.

After swallowing the tablets, Hugo leans against the armrest. 'I'll take a shower, then sleep it off.'

'How often does this happen?'

'Once a year. Maybe twice.'

'You're supposed to take the meds before it gets too bad, aren't you?'

He aims for a smile. 'I'll be okay tomorrow. You don't have to stay.'

'I'll have a shower after you.' My shirt was tied at my waist for the dance, but I undid it hours ago—it falls below my shorts when I stand. My legs have goosebumps and my feet are cold. 'I saw clean clothes in your laundry basket. Can I borrow a few things?' I fold the cotton blanket. 'I'll sleep here.'

He doesn't seem to be in pain any more, but after his shower he doesn't object when I take his arm and, keeping him confined to the middle of the staircase so he stays clear of the missing railing, walk with him up the stairs. Then, keeping a hand on the wall to steady himself, he walks to his room. When he gets there, he looks around as if he's not quite sure where he is.

'Lie down, Hugo,' I say, as I switch on the lamp on the far side of the bed and turn off the overhead light. 'I'll be back to check on you soon.'

I wash my underpants while I'm in the shower, rolling them dry with a towel before putting them on again. The smallest of Hugo's T-shirts stops short of my thighs, so I put a creased grey shirt over the top and button it up. There's a new toothbrush next to the sink, so I clean my teeth before combing through my hair with my hands. The only socks I can find are black, and they reach up to my knees.

I walk silently up the stairs, and peek through the gap in the door. Hugo is sitting on the end of the bed with his head in his hands, just as he was at the dance. I knock and he stiffens.

'Just checking up on you.' I crouch at the side of the bed. 'What can I do?'

He lifts his head. 'Too tired.'

'So why aren't you in bed?'

'I don't have a spare room. No blankets.'

'I'll be comfortable downstairs on the sofa. I've had far worse.'

He *almost* smiles. 'A hammock?'

'They're not so bad.'

He sways a little. 'Sleep with me.'

My throat is suddenly tight. I shake my head. 'No.'

He searches my face. 'What time is it?'
'A little after two.'
'I'm eighty-two kilos. What do you weigh?'
'About forty-eight.'
'What's the difference?'
'You're sixty-three per cent heavier than I am.'
'I won't take the extra thirteen per cent of the bed.'
'What?'
'I'll stop short of the mid-line. I promise.'

CHAPTER 44

Hugo must've been more exhausted than me, but I think I fell asleep before he did. And I'm still too drowsy to open my eyes. Rain taps on the windows and drums on the roof. A soft dawn light finds its way through the blinds.

I was lying on my left side, curled up with my back to Hugo, but now I'm on my right. I must have rolled over. I prise open my eyes and—

'Hey.' Hugo is on his half of the bed, just as he said he'd be. He's facing me and his eyes are wide open.

'Were you watching me?'

He smiles through the shadows. 'Not in a creepy way.'

'How do you feel?'

His hair is tousled. His stubble is dark. He considers the question. 'Hungry.'

This should feel awkward, but somehow it doesn't. I talk through a yawn. 'Should I get you something?'

'I'll cook breakfast later.'

'What were you thinking, driving like you did? What if you'd had an accident and—'

'When I left Nyngan, it was only a headache. I got here, had a shower. The migraine hit as I drove into town.'

'You shouldn't have driven at all.'

'I wanted to see you.'

My breath catches. My heart squeezes. When I lie on my back and tug, he climbs into my arms.

'It's not like I was going anywhere,' I whisper.

He finds my hand and kisses my wrist. 'Thank you for staying.'

His shoulders are broad and muscular; his body is strong. But right now, he's vulnerable. He needs me. I stroke his lion hair.

'Phoebe looked after Prim and me when we were sick. She refused to go to school.' When he looks up, I push back his fringe. 'I wanted to stay with you like that.'

'Will you stay tomorrow?'

I like the weight of him, the warmth. 'Months ago, when I came to the farm with Rick, Greta said you didn't bring your girlfriends to Horseshoe. That's why I was surprised when Lisa ...'

'It didn't feel right to have them here.'

'Because the house isn't finished yet?'

His leg crosses both of mine. 'That was part of it.'

'Can I ask you something else?'

'Anything.'

'When I moved into the granny flat, you told Greta I'd like to have baths in the bathing room, didn't you?'

'Greta picked up the ball and ran with it.'

'A few days ago, she told me you were kind. And you are.'

When he sighs, I feel the warmth of his breath on my breast. 'I need more than kind, Imp. Way more.'

'For my one of my baths, Greta used bubble bath you'd given her—a recent gift. On the card, you thanked her for something. It was for taking me to the farm, wasn't it?'

'You wouldn't let Prim look after you. There's no way you would've put up with me. I delegated to Greta.'

'She's very persuasive.' I touch his hair where it kinks at the back of his neck. 'I won't turn my back on her again.'

A hesitation. 'How about me?'

'You taught me about groundwork and helped me ride Minstrel. That was kind.'

'Stop using that word.'

A bubble of laughter. 'You used to make me laugh.'

'I could do that again.'

'Your frogs can be funny.'

He yawns. 'Our frogs.'

'I've been taking Minstrel to Arrow, and they've been chatting over the fence. I think they might be friends now. Can we ride together today?'

'Might be too wet,' he mumbles.

'You'd better rest before we ride.' I kiss the top of his head. 'I'll talk about something that'll send you back to sleep.'

It seems to be a struggle, but he gets up on an elbow. 'Impossible.'

I look up at the ceiling—the corners and planes. 'I'm teaching Ryan about angles this week. That could work.'

He runs his finger down my nose. 'Do your best.' He rolls onto his back and takes my hand, threading our fingers together.

With my other hand, I point through the shadows. 'Acute. Right. Obtuse. Straight. Reflex. Complementary. This room is rich in angles.'

'I haven't done geometry in years.' He talks through another yawn. 'What's a complementary angle?'

'Two angles that add up to 90 degrees. See the sloping sections above the doors to the balcony? And there are two shelves in the bookcase that …'

Within a few minutes, his grip on my hand isn't as firm as it was. And, by the time I turn onto my side, his eyes are closed, his breathing deep. Freeing my fingers, I lay my hand on his chest.

In February, we stood on the beach near the jetty, and I held his hands. Now it's August. Six months to be as hopelessly lost as I was at nineteen. Just like he did to me, I loop my leg across his thighs to bring him closer.

'I love you, Hugo. I always did.'

When I wake, I'm alone in the middle of the bed. I remember mumbling complaints as Hugo freed his limbs. I recall the brush of his kiss on my mouth. He dressed quietly. He tucked me in and smoothed my hair. I think I heard wheels on the gravel.

The crash of pans. I smell bacon. My tummy growls. I can't hear the rain on the roof any more. I reach for my watch.

'Nine o'clock!'

Standing in front of the bathroom mirror, I comb my fingers through my hair and clean my teeth again. And, as there was no sign of my clothes in the living room, I refasten the buttons on Hugo's grey shirt. He has his back to me when I walk into the kitchen. Faded jeans, black T-shirt and boots. He's at the stove and flipping eggs.

He turns. 'Hungry?'

His eyes are green and bright. His T-shirt pulls across his chest. I open my mouth, but nothing comes out. Then,

'Why didn't you wake me? Where are my shorts?'

He openly looks at my legs. 'When you sleep, you make snuffling noises.'

I pull my shirt down over my bottom before I sit at the table. 'Like a truffle pig?'

'Like a siren.' His gaze is amused. 'I was afraid I'd trespass on your side.'

'I was ...'

He holds in a smile. 'Lying on top.'

I focus on smoothing my napkin over my lap as he places a plate in front of me. The eggs—sunny side up, hard whites, soft yolks—sit on a piece of toast. The bacon is fried to a crisp.

'You remembered.'

He lifts his plate out of sight. 'Mine?'

'Eggs flipped. Bacon pink.'

'You got it,' he says as he sits opposite.

'Did I hear your car this morning?'

'I told Greta we might go for a ride.' He points to a bag near the door. 'Your clothes are in there. Boots outside.'

If he did get to eat dinner last night, he would have thrown it up. I must've eaten my weight in pretzels and croquettes, but consume almost as much as he does. As he finishes the last slice of toast, I stand.

'I'll clean up. Do you want to rest this morning?'

He blinks his surprise. 'No way.'

I put a hand on his shoulder and turn him towards me. I run a finger under one eye and then the other. I press my hand against his jaw and feel his pulse against the palm of my hand. I burrow under his shirt and find his skin. My breasts ache.

'You're still pale.'

'I want to be with you.' When he opens his legs, I slip into the space, and he pulls me onto his lap. He kisses my mouth, takes my bottom lip and softly bites. Then, 'Last time you were here, you ran.'

When I stiffen, he tightens his hold on my waist. A jumble of thoughts, disconnected numbers, toss patterns through my—

'Imp? Why?'

What if we hadn't met on the beach? If he hadn't got me to the hospital in the helicopter? If it wasn't a migraine last night but something worse? What if we wait even longer? What if I lose him for good?

'My reasons ...' I put my arms around his neck and link my hands. 'They don't seem so important any more.'

He stays close behind me as we walk up the stairs, as if to make sure I don't trip, but we walk down the hall side by side. We sit on his bed, me cross-legged and him with his feet on the floor. Clouds scatter through the sky, but the sun finds gaps and throws sunbeams on the sheets.

'Imp?' he says quietly. 'You okay?'

'Could you close the blind?'

When he comes back to the bed, he sits close, circling a leg around me. He opens the buttons of my shirt one by one and with the back of his hands, slowly but deliberately, he brushes my breasts through the T-shirt.

'My clothes look way better on you.' He runs his hands down my legs as he watches my face. He smiles when my skin warms. 'You're so beautiful.'

When I tug, he takes off his shirt and I spread my fingers over his chest. 'You, too.'

He takes my hand, kisses my fingers, looks up through sea-green eyes. 'You know what this means, don't you?' He's serious, intent.

'Sex?'

'More.' He lets go of my hand. 'And that's why we should settle things before—'

'I know how I feel. I want this.'

He looks at me suspiciously. 'What if Gus and Mandy turn up this afternoon? Or Greta and Derek. Can I kiss you in front of them?'

'If you want.'

He lifts my chin with his thumbs. 'I want.'

'I'm not on the pill.'

'Kiss me, Imp.'

I do my best to keep up as he peels off my T-shirt and eases down my underpants, as he yanks off his clothes and throws them on the floor. But it's not too long before his kisses go from hard and hot to gentle and careful. As if he knows. *He must know.*

'Imp?' He lifts his head. 'What's the matter?'

I put my hand over his mouth. 'Can't we just do it?'

He mutters a string of curses before shuffling back on the bed, leaning against the bedhead and hauling me into his arms. 'Talk to me.'

I shut my eyes. 'I'd much prefer not to.'

'Did I go too fast?' He brushes back my hair. 'Did I hurt you?'

'How could you? You haven't done anything.'

He runs a hand down my side. 'You're a crap communicator.'

'Please don't make this worse.'

He takes a few deep breaths. Six deep breaths. 'On the beach,' he finally says, 'you said home was where you laid your hat.' He pushes my hair aside, kisses my neck. 'Maybe you haven't left your hat in too many places.'

Mathematics won't let you down because it makes perfect sense. C equals the square root of A squared plus B squared. *Pythagoras's theorem.* Find two sides of a right-angle triangle and you can find the length of the third. In a right-angle triangle, the hypotenuse is greater than the other sides, but less than their sum. The hypotenuse is opposite the right angle.

I link my hands in my lap. 'You always had girlfriends when we were young, and from what I've seen that hasn't changed.'

'I want you, Imp. No one else.' He puts his hand on the side of my face. 'I want you longer and harder than even you can count.'

'I feel like that too, but …' I look past him, to the painting opposite the bed. The shades of blue and green, the ocean and the rivers and the creeks and the ponds. Countless colours. Countless? 'Can't we just get it over with?'

'No.'

'Don't I get a say in this?'

He pulls back. His eyes narrow. 'No.'

I push against his shoulders. And when he finally lies down, I lie next to him and pull up the sheet. I put my head on his chest.

'Are you listening?'

'When you talk?' He wraps his arms around me. 'Every word.'

'I'm attracted to you, much more than I've ever been attracted to anyone.' I trace his collarbone, the ridge where it was broken. *Broken saving me.* 'I get hot when you look at me, let alone touch me. I ache and …'

He tips up my chin. He kisses my nose. 'I'm not going to rush you.'

'It'll be different with you. It's different already, the way you kiss me, and everything else.' I come up on an elbow. 'When you touch me, I *feel* it differently.'

'That's good.' He puts hair behind my ear. 'That's a start.'

'It's more than that. It's …' Scrambling upright, I sit with my legs to the side. I consider his body and face. He's perfectly naked. Perfectly proportioned. Perfectly confident. The sheet sits low on his hips. *A merman.*

His lip lifts. 'What?'

From the top of my head to the ends of my toes, I want him. 'I feel you through my skin.'

He runs his hand down my arm and takes my hand. He kisses the inside of my wrist. He flicks my pulse with the tip of his tongue. He looks up. 'I'll take that.'

I study his photographs, of the trees and the rivers and the wetlands. 'Frogs are permeable. Some of them even breathe though their skin. If I do the same when I'm with you, it's got to mean something.'

He laughs a groan. 'Not now, Imp.'

'Female frogs can choose a mate and carry him around, no matter the size difference. They can select which one they want. I'm like that.'

'You're nothing like a frog.'

'When you touch me, I feel it everywhere.' I lie down and face him. 'Can we try again?'

The blind is down but I can still see the colours in his eyes, the flecks of green and grey and gold. When I press between his lips with a finger, he takes the tip and blows on the dampness. He cups my breast, lowers his head and kisses my nipple, open mouth, circling tongue. My skin heats, my toes curl.

He looks up. 'Can I kiss you?'

'You already are.'

Smiling, he sweeps his hand down my side to my hip. 'I haven't kissed you here.'

He crawls down the bed and kisses his way up my body. And in between kisses he asks me questions. 'Like this?' He studies my face. 'Or this?' He feels for the pulse at the back of my knee. 'Maybe this?' He puts his hands under my thighs; I bend my legs. His breath is warm on my skin as he kisses and touches between my thighs, long and slow, fast and deep.

He looks up and smiles. 'You okay?'

My toes are curled into the mattress; I'm coiled as tight as a spring. I pant. 'Please don't stop.'

He kisses until I climax, and then he crawls up the bed. He holds me close, rubs across my shoulders and down my back. A minute? Ten? The tremors subside, my breathing steadies. I open my eyes.

His eyes are bright. I touch his face. 'Can we try now?'

After he rolls on a condom, he lies on his side again. He presses against me, nudging gently, feeling his way.

Do not tense up. Do not tense up. Do not—

He stills. His jaw clenches. 'Imp?'

I swallow. 'Keep going.'

His jaw is set. 'Sweetheart?'

'It might be better if I count.'

Groaning against my neck, he trails his lips along my collar bone, nuzzling my throat.

He kisses my mouth, sweet kisses, hard kisses, long kisses, deep. His erection is hard, but his movements are gentle. I soften against him as, one tiny number at a time, he slides inside me. Tenth, hundredth, thousandth, millionth, billionth, quadrillionth.

When our stomachs touch, he groans his relief. 'Imp?'

Sensation, temptation. My nerve endings sparkle and zing. Millions of them. Billions. Trillions. Googol—

He kisses my temple. 'Are you all right?'

I rub his back, slick with sweat. 'Yes.'

He smiles against my mouth. He kisses me again—hard and possessive. He rolls so he's on top of me, up on his forearms. 'Can I move?'

I wrap my legs tightly around him, press my heels into his back. 'I'd like that.'

Long even strokes. Fast and slow. Gliding and stroking. Slippery bodies. Late nights and early mornings. Sun on our backs, sun-bleached hair. Tumbling and breathing. Limitless. Fathomless. Infinite.

When he climaxes, I hold him close. The pulse at his throat, the hair at his nape, his ragged breaths and unsteady heartbeats. Our bodies cool, our breathing settles. He rolls onto his back and I lie on his body.

I kiss his throat. 'You taste of salt.'

'At the beach, you had salt on your skin.' He lifts me by the shoulders and brushes a kiss on my mouth. 'In the rose garden, you smelt of lavender.'

I want you longer and harder than even you can count.

CHAPTER 45

He said I made snuffling noises when I slept. Lying on his stomach, his handsome face turned towards me, he makes no sound at all. It's almost midday. Should I wake him?

I trail my fingers across his shoulder. 'Ten more minutes.'

His eyes open and he kicks off the sheets. He stretches like a lion and rolls onto his back.

'Imp?'

I drag my eyes from his body. My face warms. 'We'd better go to the horses.'

He comes up on an elbow and kisses my nose. 'What time is it?'

I press into his arms, my head on his chest. 'Late.'

He runs his hand down my side and cups my bottom. He kisses my nipple, strokes with his tongue.

'The horses can wait.'

As Minstrel hasn't been ridden since last weekend, Hugo insists on cantering him around the paddock before we ride, so by the time I groom and saddle his horse, mine is puffing and sweating. Tipping his Akubra to the back of his head, Hugo slips from Minstrel's back and leads him to the water trough.

'Can we ride on your neighbour's property?' I ask.

'I guess,' he says unhappily, as he checks the fittings on my helmet.

I laugh and capture his hands. 'I fly in helicopters. I scuba dive. I know how to fasten a strap.'

When he kisses my mouth, it sends butterflies straight to my heart. 'Humour me.'

He adjusts the stirrups before giving me a leg-up onto Minstrel. I dampen down fear as I gather the reins, slide my feet into the irons and press down my heels.

'I'd clip a lead rope on Minstrel,' Hugo says, 'but Arrow wouldn't tolerate it. He likes to be up front.'

'We're happy to follow.' My voice isn't as confident as I'd like it to be, but when I guide Minstrel to the track that leads towards the Horseshoe range, he follows Arrow's lead. The sweat on Minstrel's neck dries as we walk across the paddock, but the salt leaves streaks on his coat.

When we turn off the track and take a cross-country route, the horses pick their way over the uneven ground. Hugo turns, his Akubra shading his face, and rests a hand on Arrow's rump.

'Are you okay?'

I'm tempted to tell him how many times he's asked 'are you okay' and 'are you all right' since I walked into the kitchen this morning but, as quite a few of those times involved us having sex, I hold back.

'How come you work on this property as well as your own?'

'Trevor's family run sheep and grow crops, but he's open to regenerative agriculture. He asked for my help.'

'There's plenty of grass.'

'The paddocks are rested, the crops and stock rotated. Rehabilitating the creek was a natural progression—we planned the work before I started at home. Slowing the water improves the supply and quality of what I get downstream.'

Minstrel's feet make squelching noises on the ground. I lean over his neck to make sure his legs aren't sinking too far into the—

I jerk upright.

'Imp!' Hugo swings Arrow around and pulls in close to Minstrel. Not for the first time since we left, he looks ready to jump to the ground and grab Minstrel's rein. 'Are you okay?'

I grip the pommel and take deep breaths. 'I didn't think before looking down.'

'You shut your eyes.' He steadies Arrow when he skitters and champs at the bit. 'We've done enough. Let's go back.'

'No.' I focus on the line of trees that signals the creek. 'I need to practise for when we do field work. Anyway, we're almost there.'

His lips firm. Then, 'You'll stay tonight, won't you?'

'After I help Ryan with his homework, I'll come back.'

'What about tomorrow?'

'You're supposed to be back at the marshes.'

His eyes are on my mouth. 'We can take leave.'

'I could stay up late tonight to finish Rick's work.'

'I haven't had a day off in months.'

A sturdy fence separates the paddock from the wide strips of land either side of the creek. Hugo leans over Arrow's neck to open a gate, manoeuvring Arrow out of the way so Minstrel can pass through.

'This fence is to keep out the stock, isn't it?' I say. 'They pollute the water and erode the soil.'

'We're at the furthest edge of the Horseshoe range, where streams come together to form the creek. If land is overstocked and over-cropped, it can't repair and rehydrate. Native plants and animals have no chance.'

He jumps from Arrow's back and takes his reins over his head as I swing a leg over Minstrel's rump and slide to the ground. We tie the horses far enough apart that Arrow won't be flustered, then I take off my helmet and we walk hand in hand to the creek. The trees, mostly gums, are immature, but the reeds and grasses are tall, dense and lush.

'You started this off?'

'Before we planted it out and built the weirs, water flowed downstream too quickly to soak into the ground. It washed soil and vegetation away.'

'Ground and surface water bring back the frogs.'

He squeezes my hand. 'Biodiversity, Imp.'

The further we walk towards the creek, the soggier the ground becomes. I tread lightly from one clump of grass to the other. Hugo curses when his boot sinks down to his ankle.

I laugh. 'This is like a wetland.'

'When it rains, the creek level rises and floods the banks, and the logs and other material captures it. Water will stay in the landscape, even in drought.'

'Are there tadpoles in the creek?'

He laughs. 'Thousands.'

'There are none in your part of the creek. I've looked.'

'Water was pumped out for the brewery. After that, the land was overstocked and cleared. Over decades, sediments, nutrients, soils and plants—entire habitats—were lost. The creek was like a drain.'

'Will your weirs work like this one?'

'I need another excavator.' His smile is tight. 'That's expensive.'

'You prioritise the creek over the house. And you should have a garden.'

He frowns. 'What?'

'There should be a garden where everyone parks their cars. Hasn't Greta mentioned it? I guess she thinks a kitchen is more important.'

'I'll plant natives eventually, not Greta's geraniums.'

'You could mix it up.' I'm careful of my foot as we scamper down the bank towards the water. 'Mum had roses, and spring flowers like freesias. She has them in New Zealand now. They smell nice. Bees like them. You could also have a pond. When we were kids …'

'Imp?' He's lower down the bank than me, so when he stops and blocks my path, our heights match up. 'What were you going to say?'

I shake my head. 'I don't remember.'

He takes my hands. 'In the granny flat, when you told me you'd cried about your mother, you said you had a pond.'

I nod stiffly. 'It was a long time ago.'

'That doesn't mean you forget it.'

'It was …' I look over his shoulder to the creek.

'Were there tadpoles in your pond?' he asks quietly.

'It wasn't even a real pond, it was just a plastic shell, but I thought …' My voice wavers. 'I thought they were magical tadpoles, because of the tooth fairy.'

'Maybe they were.'

I shake my head, blink back tears. 'Nope.'

'How do you know?'

'Because, Dr Halstead,' I squeeze his hands, 'I now know what species they were. *Limnodynastes dumerilii*. They not only live in ponds, they've also been found in outdoor toilets.'

'The eastern banjo frog?' He grins. 'Definitely magical.'

I keep hold of his hand as we walk the last few steps. 'Just like unicorns.'

A mound of boulders, like a cairn, splits the creek in two, but a bridge of smaller rocks creates a route across the water. When I sit on a boulder and pull off my boots, Hugo crouches next to me. He holds out his hands for my socks.

'Do you always have to wet your ...'

I follow his gaze to my foot. My instep is still pink from the surgery, but it's the bruise on the top of my foot that he's focusing on. I plunge it into the water.

'It's cold.'

'Imp.' Calm, considered. 'What happened?'

When I kick my legs, droplets of water shoot into the air. 'I'd like to know more about the landscape.'

'As a third alternative ...' He picks up the end of my plait, wraps it around his wrist and gently tugs. 'We could talk about us. Our history.'

A shoal of fish, slender and golden, swim through the shallows. I loved him. I love him. 'Go on.'

'You said you didn't want anybody else,' he says quietly. 'You never would.'

I place my hands neatly on my lap. 'You said I was impatient.'

'I'd waited until you'd finished school. Even after that, I thought I should hold back till you'd chosen what, and where, you wanted to study. I was older. I'd known what I wanted, the life I wanted, since I was sixteen. But after we kissed by the river ...' he takes one of my hands, 'I thought, "fuck waiting"'.

'Did you know about the promise Greta had made to my mother?'

'Not then, or I would have told you. As it was, Greta gave me a shitload of guilt, telling me what I already knew. You were young, your father was abusive, you'd never had a boyfriend or been to university. When I said I was thinking forever, she didn't believe it. She told me she had to keep you safe.'

'She took the promise to heart.'

'Dad chipped in. He told me if I took advantage, I wasn't the son he thought he'd raised.'

'You told me no.'

'I told you to wait.'

Tadpoles, tiny little tadpoles, dart in and out of the reeds. 'I only trusted Phoebe, Prim and you.'

'I thought we had time.' He sandwiches my hands between his. 'And then you were gone.'

My eyes sting; I blink. 'Prim said we remind her of a Jane Austen novel. Have you read *Persuasion*?'

'No.'

'Captain Wentworth went to sea like I did.'

He tips up my chin, searches my face. 'Why did he do that?'

'Anne had accepted his offer of marriage, but her family convinced her that he wasn't suitable. She broke it off.'

He traces my jaw with his thumb. 'And?'

'Wentworth came back many years later, but he was still angry. He thought Anne had been too easily persuaded and refused to have anything to do with her.'

'Fuck Wentworth.'

I laugh. 'After they spent time together, he got to know her better, even better than he had before. He forgave her.'

'Good job.'

'It wasn't only me who was angry, Hugo.' When I draw back a little, he reclaims my hand. 'At the beach, and afterwards, you wanted nothing to do with me.'

'It hurt to even look at you.' Serious. Sincere. 'I didn't trust you. I didn't trust your reasons for joining the team.'

I'm suddenly lightheaded. Chilled.

He was right not to trust me. *He can't trust me now.* I free my hand and put my foot back in the water. *Hide the bruises. Hide the lies.*

'Is that Minstrel?'

He frowns. 'I didn't hear anything.'

'We've been away a long time.' I pull my socks from my boots and shake them out. 'You go ahead. I'll be there in a minute.'

He's leaning against a tree when I join him. Thoughtful, reflective. Dappled light and tawny hair. I walk past his outstretched hand, wrap my arms around his waist, lift my face and find his throat. I press my mouth against it.

After we've stored the saddles and other gear in the shed, I run back to the horses with their carrots. Hugo is already at the house when I walk into the kitchen. He's washed his face; his hair is pushed back. Looking up from the kettle, he smiles into my eyes.

His phone rings. 'Lisa. Thanks for calling back. Is it okay to cover for me tomorrow? Same goes for Patience. She'll let Rick know.'

The pipes clunk as I lean over the old concrete sink and wash my hands. *Please, Lisa, keep quiet about seeing me with Charles.*

Hugo walks from the bench to the back door. 'She's here with me now,' he says.

Please, please, please—

'Are you sure it was him?' He turns on the threshold, facing me. Creased brow. 'I'll ask her.' A few more monosyllables. *No. Yes. No.* He pockets his phone.

The green and white striped teapot matches the crockery Greta uses for special occasions. *From Gmunden, where my mother was born.* I carefully measure teaspoons of tea. One, two, three.

'Imp?'

I don't know why I fill the milk jug or stand on my toes to take two mugs from the shelves. We're not going to be sitting at the table drinking tea. Or sharing the biscuits Greta gave Hugo this morning. He walks to the sink. He turns.

'You had lunch with Charles Tedeschi last Wednesday,' he says quietly. 'How do you know him?'

Hugo won't punish others for what I've done wrong. He won't lash out or throw things. He won't bully me or set me up. But … I'm glad we have a table between us.

I put a plate next to each mug. 'What did Lisa say?'

Three long strides. He grips the back of a chair. 'You and Tedeschi were holding hands.'

'His hand was on mine.'

His eyes narrow. 'Why were you there with him?'

'There's nothing between us. I can't tell you more.'

'You hurt your foot on Wednesday. That injury has nothing to do with slipping off a kerb.'

'You don't know that.'

'You met the son of a colleague, our colleague, for lunch. Why not tell me about it?'

'He asked to meet me, and I said yes. I had a good reason. And him taking my hand …' A shiver passes through me. 'There was nothing in it, there's nothing to be jealous of.'

He rubs around the back of his neck. 'Jealousy is straightforward. This is worse.'

'I can't tell you more, Hugo. And you …' I collect the plates, stack them. 'What else did Lisa say?'

'She had a call with the professor last Friday. That's when the lunch came up.'

'But she didn't tell you about it then?'

'It mightn't have been relevant until today.' He changes his grip on the chair. 'Knowing we both wanted leave, she would have joined the dots. She's a friend. She'd care if I got hurt.'

'She wants to be more than friends.'

'That's irrelevant!'

I bite my lip, try to think more clearly. 'I don't want Charles to know about you and me. Not yet.'

'What the fuck?'

'It's important! Important to Rick and the team.'

He briefly closes his eyes. And when he opens them again, they're hard. *Green and hard like emeralds.* 'This has something to do with your secondment.'

'I have orders. I can't tell you more.'

'The team's environmental work is valuable. It also pays my mortgage. You gave your word. You told me you wouldn't cause trouble.'

'I don't want to.'

'Within weeks, Rick was rattled.'

'That wasn't my fault.'

'I've backed you. So have Lisa and Professor Tedeschi. We didn't replace you when you were sick, we've made allowances. You owe us an explanation.'

'I can't give you one. My work won't allow it.'

'You work on our team.'

'You can't talk about this. You can't ask questions about Charles.'

'Bullshit.'

'Please, Hugo—'

'I'll brief Lisa. I'll hassle Rick. I'll call Professor Tedeschi and demand an explanation. Captain McCarthy recommended you for the secondment. I'll drive to Jervis Bay and confront him.'

'Wait a week. Maybe two.'

'Charles Tedeschi.' His eyes narrow. 'I'll take the fucker to lunch.'

He watches silently as I pour milk from the jug back into the carton. I open the fridge and place the milk on the shelf. The door seals with a thump as I take my phone from the table and scroll.

'I'll contact the base,' I say. 'I'll set up a call.'

CHAPTER 46

Hugo leans against the old concrete sink while I call the base. Silent and watchful, he's far paler than usual and he has shadows under his eyes. Instead of convincing him to take me riding, I should have sent him to bed and told him to rest. Immediately I disconnect, he steps forward, clunks his glass on the table.

'What's happening?'

'Captain McCarthy will be on the call, and possibly Commander Ruddock, the officer who followed you down to the beach. When I tell them what this is about, they'll want to talk to you. It'll be a video call. Can I use your computer?'

'It'll have to be upstairs.'

As I follow Hugo down the hall towards his bedroom, I bite my lip, only releasing it when he opens a door to one of the rooms facing the front of the house. The room is large with high ceilings, but deeply shadowed because of the board that covers the windows. There's a desk, office equipment and a couple of chairs. When he moves the board to the side, light floods into the room.

'Oh!'

The window space doesn't have glass, a timber surround or windowsill, so the red gum, the river and trees either side of it, and the park and town, are framed by sandstone blocks. It's like …

A scene from a jigsaw puzzle.

In Greta's rose garden, Hugo said *I missed you like the piece of a puzzle.* This morning we glimpsed a future together. Now?

My eyes sting. I swallow. 'It's beautiful.'

Sitting at Hugo's desktop, I key in a string of numbered passwords to access my account. Ruddock has already emailed a link. Hugo, hands in his pockets, stares out of the window. I turn in the chair.

'I have to speak to Captain McCarthy privately first.'

He nods stiffly. 'I'll wait outside.'

When the door closes, I click on the link and Captain McCarthy appears on the screen. 'Are you there, lieutenant? What's the urgency?' Ruddock leans over McCarthy's shoulder and adjusts the screen view.

'Dr Halstead knows Dr Lipman has been hiding something, and we've both refused to talk about it. He's just found out I had lunch with Charles Tedeschi, and I can't explain that either. If he's not briefed, he's threatened to talk to Tedeschi—senior and junior.'

Captain McCarthy purses his lips. 'This will be over in a fortnight.'

'He's not satisfied with that.'

'Is he linked to Charles Tedeschi in any way?'

'He's a colleague of Professor Tedeschi. Other than that connection, no.'

'Can he be trusted to keep quiet?'

'If you explain everything, I think so.'

'Is he there? Bring him in.'

After a brief greeting, Captain McCarthy warns Hugo the information he'll be given is sensitive and highly confidential. 'You'll be told what's required to keep your silence,' McCarthy finishes. 'Nothing more.'

Hugo leans back in his chair. 'I want information relevant to my project and,' he glances at me, 'my team.'

Captain McCarthy nods brusquely. 'You applied to the navy for an operative. The officer nominated was not only highly skilled and knowledgeable, but decorated through service in—'

'Patience wasn't what we requested,' Hugo interrupts. 'Why send her?'

'Dr Halstead,' Ruddock says, 'kindly let Captain McCarthy—'

McCarthy holds up a hand. 'Lieutenant Cartwright was available, and could satisfactorily perform most of the specified tasks.'

'I suspect you gave her additional tasks,' Hugo says. 'What were they?'

'A government department suspected, rightly as it turned out, financial irregularities on the water security project. Lieutenant Cartwright was asked to keep her eyes open.'

Hugo stares at my profile. 'Can you expand on that?'

At McCarthy's nod, I speak up. 'I found out that a consultant, one that didn't exist, had issued invoices for work supposedly carried out for the Macquarie team. Rick became aware of it and alerted Professor Tedeschi, who said the errors were administrative in nature and could be remedied. In the meantime, I reported these matters to Captain McCarthy. Subsequent investigations led to Charles Tedeschi.'

'That's why you went to lunch?'

'Without authority,' Ruddock snaps.

'If I hadn't gone, he would have questioned why.'

Hugo nods abruptly. 'Does this explain Rick's behaviour?'

'He was supposed to have checked the invoices. He felt guilty that he hadn't, but he thought the professor could sort it out. Things got messy when Charles appeared.'

Hugo opens his mouth, but then slams it shut. Then, 'Go on.'

'Professor Tedeschi worked out I knew more than I should. He said Charles could explain the errors, and we should meet.'

'The lunch last Wednesday?'

When I hesitate, McCarthy jumps in. 'Weeks ago.'

Hugo stiffens. 'Right.'

'Dr Halstead?' McCarthy says. 'I understand you know Charles Tedeschi.'

'I've met him once, at a social event.'

'He claims to be an environmental lobbyist,' McCarthy says. 'But it appears he has links to organisations with questionable motivations, primarily in the US. The police are attempting to trace money he's taken in the hope of catching bigger fish offshore.'

Hugo mutters under his breath. 'Fuck.'

'Charles assisted Professor Tedeschi with spreadsheets and other admin tasks,' I say. 'When the invoice anomalies came to light, the professor chose to believe Charles's version of events. Subsequently, he covered for him.'

'You said the Macquarie team was invoiced. Was money paid out? Will it be recovered?'

'This is now a secondary consideration,' McCarthy says.

'Professor Tedeschi is not only the head of the project,' Hugo says, 'he's on the Macquarie team. If he's crooked, there'll be consequences.'

'I'd imagine so,' McCarthy says. 'Nevertheless, you'll appreciate our need for discretion.'

'What's the timeframe?'

Ruddock is behind McCarthy, but almost out of view. He says something I can't hear, but McCarthy shakes his head.

'The police are building a case,' McCarthy says. 'Charles Tedeschi will be arrested sooner rather than later. Following that, Professor Tedeschi and Dr Lipman's culpability will be investigated.'

'Rick knows nothing about this!'

'We're aware of your views, lieutenant.' McCarthy looks to Hugo. 'What's your assessment of Dr Lipman?'

'He might've been distracted. He's not dishonest.'

McCarthy lifts a brow. 'And Professor Tedeschi?'

'As a scientist, I can't fault him.' Hugo studies my profile again. 'You were the one working undercover, Patience. What do you think of him?'

My fingers are linked. When I tighten them, a knuckle clicks. 'Charles took advantage of his father's trusting nature. Professor Tedeschi will be afraid for his son, but I suspect he's also afraid of him.'

Hugo's eyes narrow. 'How did you hurt your foot?'

I keep my voice steady. 'I don't—'

'Tell him,' McCarthy says.

'Last Wednesday, after lunch, Charles was with me when I climbed into my car.' I rest my good foot over my bruised one. 'He slammed the door.'

'Deliberately?'

'Yes.'

'What the fuck?'

McCarthy clears his throat. 'She didn't get to where she is by threading daisy chains.'

'The secondment,' Hugo finally says. 'What happens with that?'

'Sir?' I say quietly. 'I'm useful here.'

'You've served your time.' McCarthy peers over his glasses. 'Come back to the base.'

My chest cramps. 'Immediately?'

'We'll send a replacement.'

'But—'

'Report to me tomorrow,' Ruddock snaps. 'That's an order.'

After the call disconnects, Hugo stands. 'I'll take you to the farm for your gear.'

I nod. And swallow. I force my thoughts into some kind of order. 'I'll drive the Landcruiser to Dubbo tonight and pick up a hire car.'

'Right.'

I push in my chair, carefully checking the wheels on each side are parallel. 'Can I go to your bedroom to get my things?'

'I'll see you downstairs.'

I put my shorts, underwear and sneakers into the bag Greta packed for me this morning. As I fold the blue checked shirt I wore to the dance, my throat tightens and tears blur the colours. Sniffing hard, I stuff the shirt into the bottom of the wicker basket in the corner of the room.

My boots, the expensive boots he bought, are side by side at the back door. But there's no sign of Hugo as I walk to the shed to find treats for the horses. Eyes stinging again, I feed Minstrel an apple.

'I'll call Mandy,' I tell him. 'You can have a holiday with her ponies for a while. She'll know what will work out best. I'll let you know what's going to happen as soon as I can.'

I'm feeding apples to Arrow and Lavender when Hugo walks down the verandah steps. Looking at his phone, he leans against his car. I run back to the house, collect my bag and throw it in the back.

'I told Greta you're leaving,' he says. 'Ryan is there.'

'I'll help with his homework before I go.'

His door slams, then mine. We fasten our belts. If he ever makes a garden at the front of the house, will he grow vines up the verandah posts? The banksia roses in Greta's garden have canary-yellow flowers for most of the year.

I cling onto my belt, search for words. 'I'm sorry you have to keep this from Lisa and others in the team.' The red gum at the bottom of the driveway is a blur. 'Rick was afraid that, if he'd told you about it, you'd ask too many questions. Professor Tedeschi thought the same way.'

'Rick will have to deal with me now.'

'I'll do a handover, and make sure someone is assigned to the team as quickly as possible. I don't think—'

'Think?' His fingertips are white on the wheel. 'You're the smartest person I know, Imp, but sometimes you don't think.'

He slows for the bridge. Clunk, clunk, clunk. Twenty-two metres, six horizontal planks per metre, one hundred and—

'Will you drive back to the team?' I ask.

'While we have funding, I'll work.'

He accelerates past the park, where the red gums line up on the banks of the river.

We pass the general store, the doctor's surgery, the community centre. He stops at the T intersection.

'Look at me, Imp.'

I imagined his eyes were green like the ocean. Now it's rivers and gumtrees and streams.

'The misappropriation,' he says. 'You didn't suspect me, did you?'

'You wouldn't do that.'

'And I wouldn't tip anybody off. That makes this worse.'

'I tried to push back.'

'I asked about your foot. You lied about it. You've lied to me all year.'

'I tried to slow things down between us, but …'

He checks his mirrors and the road before he turns right. Careful. Considered. Controlled.

'From the moment I saw you on the beach, I was fucked.'

'I didn't know about the secondment then.'

'Within a week, you did. You knew we'd be together.'

'All I knew was that you didn't want me!'

'And now?' he says quietly. 'What do you know now?'

I ball my hands into fists in my lap. 'You have a right to be angry.'

'I promised myself I wouldn't do this again. You'd made your life, and I wasn't in it.'

'I didn't want to go back.'

'You know what, Imp? In my whole adult life, I've had one lousy secret. I had a broken heart that wouldn't mend.'

'Please, don't.'

'You'd prefer to change the subject? Talk about regrets?' His jaw is set. He speaks through his teeth. 'What'd make the top of your list? Getting involved with my work? My family? The horses? Or spending the night in my bed?'

My eyes sting; I squeeze them shut. 'I'm sorry.'

'I'm angry.' He slows at the crimson letter box. 'We'll talk when I'm not.'

I saw pieces of a puzzle from his window. The red gum at the end of the driveway. The single lane bridge. The river, the park and the town. A tumbling creek, an ocean of doubt. Hope and loss and heartache. Greta is standing at the top of the steps. She unties her apron, pulls it free of her dress and waves it aloft like a flag.

CHAPTER 47

Hugo and I look anywhere but at each other as he takes my bag from the back of the four-wheel drive and places it at my feet. Greta smooths the creases in her apron as she runs down the steps.

'Why do you leave us, Patience?' she asks. 'This navy, it is not fair.'

'Not always, no.'

She turns to Hugo. 'Why do you let her—' She searches his face, rests her hand on his arm. 'My poor boy.' When Hugo smiles tightly, Greta, clearly flustered, rests the back of her hand against his forehead. 'This is better, yes?'

'I slept it off.'

He has lines between his brows and at the sides of his eyes, and his shirt is half hanging out. After kissing Greta's cheek, he mutters something about borrowing Derek's drill and nods stiffly in my direction.

'Let me know when you get there.'

When Soxy walks stiff-legged down the steps, I crouch to pat him. Clearing my throat, I force out words.

'Sorry I'm late, boy. Have you and Ryan been waiting on the day bed?'

Ryan, just as he did at the start, rolls his eyes with every new question, but now he breaks them down into manageable parts and offers suggestions about how to solve them. After an hour, he untangles his legs and turns another page of the book. He opens it wide and bends back the spine.

'Farmer Jenny has bought another property,' he says. 'She's sinking fence posts again.'

'She must be doing better than we thought.' We calculate angles with a protractor as Ryan writes notes in the margin.

'I reckon you know about angles because you count fence posts,' he says.

My hand stills on the book. *I don't count them as often as I used to.* Because they don't always go in lines? There are gaps where cows push through? Or rivers bend? Or—

There are fences to keep things in, and fences to keep them out. On what side of the fence do I belong? The ache that's been sitting in my chest bubbles to my throat. I swallow. Swallow again. I love Hugo's family and Horseshoe. I love my horse and Soxy. I'm in love with Hugo, even though he's angry and hurt and might never want to see me again.

'Patience?' Ryan points to the diagram. 'Boundary fences are never as straight as that.'

Blinking fiercely, I look at the diagram more closely. 'We have to assume this fence is in a straight line because that's what the question tells us to do. Jenny has divided her paddock into four. What will the angles that come off the straight line add up to?'

'One of those angles is way too sharp to get a tractor in.'

'Describe it.'

'Twelve degrees. Acute.'

'Maybe she grazes stock in that paddock?'

'It's too small, even for sheep.'

'What do all the angles add up to?'

'They come off a vertical line, so a hundred and eighty degrees.'

'Good.'

'I still don't get the small paddocks.'

'Jenny likes to rotate her herds. That way the land has time to recover.'

'Uncle Hugo's been talking to you about regenerative agriculture, hasn't he?'

I blink. And nod. 'What do we call the point where the boundary lines meet?'

'A vertex.'

'Excellent.'

Immediately I close the book, Ryan flips cushions, finally locating a handmade card. On the front he's drawn a manga illustration of me sitting on a horse and juggling numbers. Inside is a note: *Thanks, Patience. You're the best. Ryan*

Teary again, I study the picture. 'That looks exactly like Minstrel. And a picture of me on a horse? I love it.'

He flushes and mumbles. 'Thanks for putting up with me.'

'Farmer Jenny and I have loved every minute.'

'I would've coloured the drawing, but I only found out you were leaving when I got here.'

'It surprised me too.'

'Uncle Hugo tried to help with maths, but he couldn't understand how I didn't see things like he does—patterns and stuff. He doesn't explain it like you.'

Soxy stretches and yawns when I kneel and line up cushions. 'Email your homework at the end of the week. You can sit here on

Sundays like you always do, and we can talk over the phone or on Zoom.'

'If you're in the navy again, why would you want to do homework?'

A small herd of brown and white cows, many with calves by their sides, graze in the home paddock. Behind them, the sleepy orange sun sets behind the trees.

'It'll bring me closer to things I care about.'

A car door slams. A shout. Hugo's four-wheel drive pulls out onto the driveway, a line of dust behind it. Remy shoots around the corner and stumbles to a halt. He has tear tracks down his face.

'Remy.' I scramble from the day bed. 'What's the matter?'

He sniffs and splutters. 'Uncle Hugo said you're going away.'

I hug him tightly. 'I wasn't expecting to go so suddenly, but I'll come back and see you, I promise.'

'When?'

Greta calls out from the verandah, asking for someone to feed the chickens, and I shout back. 'I'll do it!'

'When are you coming back?' Remy asks again, lifting a shoulder to wipe his runny nose.

'As soon as I get leave, seeing you and Lavender will be at the top of my list.'

He wipes his nose again. 'Minstrel should be *right* at the top.'

'I agree. But since he'll go to Mandy's stud to stay with her ponies, I'll visit him on my way.'

'Why can't he stay with Uncle Hugo?'

'Hugo has enough to do looking after Arrow and Lavender. It wouldn't be fair to ask him to care for Minstrel as well.'

Remy chatters nonstop as I strip the bed in the granny flat and pack up my clothes. Besides riding boots, a new pair of sneakers and a few T-shirts, I haven't accumulated much. I look around. *Everything was already here.*

'Patience?' Remy sticks his tongue through the gap where his front teeth should be. 'Can we play horse shows?'

Remy is cantering figure of eights and I'm scoring his flying changes when Greta finds us in the garden. Smiling sadly, she hands over a container of food scraps for the chooks.

'Your Opa will drive you and Ryan to Uncle Hugo so that you may see your pony,' she says to Remy. 'It is time to get ready.'

I look straight ahead as I walk past Greta's rose garden. *Hugo kissed me here.* Derek, after bolting the shed doors for the night, jogs ahead to open the gate to the chicken coop. His Akubra shades his face as he shoos the birds away and shuts the gate behind us.

'We'll miss you,' he says gruffly.

'I'm sorry to leave so suddenly.'

'You'll be back to see your sister in Warrandale.'

'I can help Greta with the pretzels at the Christmas fete.'

'There you go, then.'

The coop is fully enclosed to keep out foxes and eagles. Two hanging baskets, filled with red and pink geraniums, are attached to the wire by hooks. As Derek empties the water bowls into the baskets, the chickens, led by Greta's big black matriarch, gather around my feet.

'Derek …' My voice wobbles. 'I'll miss it here.'

He shoos the chickens away, clearing a path as he searches the boxes for eggs. 'We're not going anywhere.'

'I've let Hugo down.' My words come out in a rush. 'I've let his team down.'

Derek holds up three eggs, one brown and two white. Three of the smaller chickens, two brown and one white, follow a curly trail of apple peel to the fence.

'You've got a job to be getting back to,' he says. 'Greta and I respect that and, when Hugo gets over his disappointment, he'll do the same.'

I tip the container upside down to empty the last of the scraps and when Derek hands me the eggs I put them in the container, keeping a hand on them so they don't roll around too much. Derek and I walk side by side towards the house.

'You enjoyed your peace and quiet in the granny flat, didn't you, love?'

'Very much.'

When we say our final goodbyes at Derek's ute, Derek takes off his hat and hugs me. Remy neighs and throws his arms around my hips. Ryan and I tap fists.

'Send me your homework or else.'

As the ute drives away, I walk to Greta at the top of the steps. *Thank you. Goodbye. Sorry.* It's impossible to adequately express any of these things, but I should have left an hour ago.

'Greta. I—'

She links her arm through mine. 'You will take a bottle for your bubble bath.'

'I'll only have a shower at the base.'

'Then you will have soap.'

As always, the bathing room tiles are sparkling. Fresh fluffy towels hang from the rails and the plug of the clawfoot bath sits near the taps. I lift it, examine the rubber, the brass, the ring at the top.

'You've done so much for me, Greta. I'll never forget it.'

'Phooey,' she says, as she wrestles with the top drawer of the whitewashed chest of drawers.

'Can I help?' When she stands back, I put my knee against the edge of the chest and yank. The drawer opens wide.

'Bravo!' Greta says.

The inside of the drawer is lined with old-fashioned paper, printed with roses. The soaps, most of them wrapped in floral paper, seem to be arranged by scent. Lavender, gardenia and rose. Citrus, lemongrass and patchouli. Sandalwood, vetiver and pine. Like the bubble baths, many have gift cards attached. Greta carefully considers which soap might be best.

'Ah,' she finally says. 'I remember.' She takes an intricately wrapped blue package with a French perfumery logo from the drawer. There's no tag attached, but as every other scent Greta has put in my baths has come from Hugo, I suspect it's another one of his.

'I don't think Hugo would want—'

'It is mine to give, liebchen.'

'Yes, but—'

'Jasmine, mimosa, orange blossom. It is called *Baum des Lebens*, the tree of life.' She presses it into my hand. 'This scent is like the sunshine. It is for the land, and also for the water.'

The sob that's simmered softly rises to the surface. I hiccup. A tear escapes. Another. I reach blindly for the tissue box.

'I'm sorry.'

Taking back the soap, Greta places it on the windowsill, plucks a wad of tissues from the box, pushes away my hands and dabs at my tears.

I sniff and snuffle. 'I'm not like this, not usually.'

'Never a tear,' Greta says. 'When you were a child, so thin and alone at the pool. When you fell from the horse. When you ran away. You did not cry.'

'I've changed, Greta, haven't I?'

'Yes, liebchen. You have seen the world and many people.'

I blow my nose. 'And I rode Minstrel.'

She smiles gently. 'Hugo, he is a different animal, I think.'

'I've hurt him.' I take a shaky breath. 'You saw that straight away, didn't you? I can't believe you're even talking to me.'

'You care for my son as he cares for you.'

'Sometimes that's not enough though, is it?' I blow my nose again. 'Before I came to Horseshoe, I thought I knew what I wanted.'

Greta kisses one cheek, and then the other. 'Must you go today?'

I nod jerkily. 'My job …' I shove the tissues in my pocket. 'I have responsibilities.'

'The navy carries you very far away.' She gives back the soap. 'But one day, liebchen, you will find your home.'

CHAPTER
48

I've been at the base for a week when I'm called to Captain McCarthy's office. Two middle-aged federal policemen, one with a shaved head and one with a cleft in his chin, question me about Charles. When Commander Ruddock takes them aside, I wait with Captain McCarthy by the full-length windows. The view is uninterrupted; the sun is bright on the bay.

'The government likes to see collaboration between the military and other agencies,' McCarthy says. 'We'll get a pat on the back.'

'I wish they'd arrest Charles and get this over with.'

'Softly, softly, lieutenant. Leave this to the police.'

Two naval vessels, medium-sized boats used for dive training, rock on the swell. 'Charles can't be doing the reputation of the environmental movement any favours.'

'Undoubtedly true.'

'When I was fourteen, my little sister and I used boltcutters to break into a barn. We released hundreds of battery hens, but most of them had to be destroyed. It was terrible, sir, the conditions in which they were kept.'

'Assuming you didn't hack into the owner's bank account, or blow up the barn, I'll overlook that piece of intelligence.' He glances at me before turning back to the window. 'I believe that wasn't the only disclosure you omitted from your naval application.'

I endeavour to breathe evenly. 'Sir?'

'Your childhood was problematic.'

'That didn't mean I couldn't do my job.'

'You've gone head-to-head with several senior officers. It was only a matter of time before you were disciplined.'

'Lieutenant Commander Grantham assaulted me. And he set me up.'

'Tread carefully, lieutenant.' He looks towards Ruddock, then back at me. 'You have yet to lodge a formal complaint.'

'Without substantiation, sir, that's difficult.'

'You spoke to no one about it?'

'Contemporaneously? Only my sister, Phoebe, who'd be accused of taking my side. Anyway, she's been through enough.'

He nods stiffly. 'When not swearing at your superiors, your judgement is sound. You're well regarded by your peers and junior officers, and you've performed well on the secondment. Next year, I'll send you back to sea.'

Every morning for the past seven days, I've swum laps from the beach to the breakwater. The pull of the tide, the crystal-clear water, the slap of the waves on the sand. The sun on my back, the salt on my tongue.

I'm always reminded of Hugo.

Captain McCarthy told him to keep quiet. Which could explain why, besides acknowledging my text that I was safely back at the base, I've heard nothing.

Two kookaburras fly towards the beach. Will they sleep in the grey gum? The branches reach high above the shrubs, but I'm too far away to see the colours of the trunk. Could I perch in the tree like a bird, watch the waves reach the sand from afar?

'Captain, lieutenant.' Ruddock and the police officers stand back from the desk as the captain sits in his chair. The officer with the shaved head insists I sit in the chair on the other side of the desk, while he and the other men stand to my right.

'Charles Tedeschi took a calculated risk,' the officer with the cleft chin says. 'Long term, the fraud would likely have been discovered, but short term, unless the professor or Dr Lipman stumbled on it, there was little chance of being found out.'

'Even when he was found out, Charles controlled the fallout,' the other officer says. 'Lieutenant Cartwright, an unknown quantity, threw a spanner in the works.'

'Charles is afraid.' I wriggle my toes. 'That's why he's dangerous.'

'And he gets around,' the officer says. 'Commander Ruddock here had a hunch Charles might've been behind the banners strung up earlier in the year. Turned out they had his fingerprints all over them.'

The officer with the shaved head crosses his arms. 'Handing over the banners wasn't a crime, but it led us to Charles Tedeschi's local associates. We're building up quite a dossier.'

'If you've got so much evidence, why don't you arrest him?'

'He's still at his father's house in Mudgee,' he says defensively. 'We're tracing his movements.'

'The professor lives there too.'

'We appreciate your assistance so far, lieutenant, but it's best that you leave this to us.'

I'm halfway across the parade ground when Ruddock calls my name.

'Sir?'

'At the captain's request, I've found you something to keep you occupied until your next posting.' He flicks through screens on his phone. 'You've been appointed to a high school program. Careers counselling.'

'What?'

'Recruitment, Cartwright, at school careers events.' He considers his phone again. 'As you're familiar with inland NSW, you can spend your first week there.'

CHAPTER 49

My sixth school visit in the past four days is at Gulgong High. I enjoy talking to the kids, particularly the ones who remind me of Ryan, but I'm left with a lot of time on my hands. Hugo and others in the team are based in Wellington, only an hour from my motel, but as I've been warned to stay clear of anyone connected in any shape or form to Charles Tedeschi, it's not like we can meet.

Hugo doesn't even know that I'm here.

I dress in uniform to look the part. Grey and white camouflage naval fatigues. Black shoulder epaulettes with gold braid—two stripes, one with a circle. Neat hair tied back. Thick-soled lace-up boots.

Hugo gave me riding boots.

I'm not due at the school until seven o'clock tonight, and it's only just gone six when I turn off the highway. A call comes through. *Professor Tedeschi*. Hugo knows that I've been taken off the secondment, but as far as the others are concerned I'm back with the navy and stationed at HMAS Creswell temporarily. So why would the professor call? He's been working with Hugo and Rick. He must know I'm unavailable. The call rings out.

He calls again.

'Hey, professor.' My *everything is fine* voice.

'Patience!' His voice is a high whisper. 'Please. I need your help.'

'What's the matter?'

'I don't know who else to ask. Charles isn't well. He's been up all night. He believes there's something untoward going on. He told me the errors had been corrected, but now—'

'Dad! Where are you! Dad!' Charles's voice.

'He's in a rage, he's not himself.'

'Besides Charles, is anyone with you?'

'You were kind enough to meet him, to talk to him. You might be able to calm him down, to reassure him that all will be well.'

'Dad!'

'Please, Patience. Can you call him directly? He wouldn't like it if he knew I'd had a part in this.'

'I'm in Gulgong.'

'What?' He mutters a prayer. 'You're barely half an hour away. Could you come to us? Charles would be reassured. I'm sure of it.'

'Can I confirm you're alone with him?'

'He won't leave the house. I'm not allowed to leave the—'

A banging sound. The bathroom door? 'Dad!'

'It's all right son! Won't be long!'

Silence.

'Professor?'

'I'm here, Patience.'

'Is there a lock on the door? Can you stay in there?'

'I can't lock him out. I can't. He needs me.'

Like Phoebe insisted our father needed her.

'What's your address?'

'From Gulgong, take the turn-off to Mudgee.' I strain to hear. 'Lot 2 Stradbroke Lane.'

'I'll get there as soon as I can.'

'Please hurry. Pl—'

'Professor Tedeschi? Are you still there?'

A crash. A clunk. The professor cries out. Nothing.

I pull over to the side of the road. And when I can't get onto Captain McCarthy, I ask for Commander Ruddock.

'Call the police. Get them to the professor's house. He's in trouble.'

'You were ordered to leave this matter to—'

'Professor Tedeschi called me two minutes ago. He said Charles is in a rage. He won't let the professor leave the house.'

'I see.' Silence. Then, 'We've been dealing with the federal police. It will take time for them to get to Mudgee.'

'Then get them to brief the local police.'

'I'll get advice.'

'Warn them Charles is dangerous. They've got to get the professor out of the house.'

'I don't want to send the police on a fool's errand.'

'Do it!' Gravel sprays beneath my car as I pull onto the road. 'Call them now!'

The setting sun is masked by clouds when, twenty-two minutes after leaving Gulgong, I turn into Stradbroke Lane. On one side of the lane there's a vineyard with a long low house and a tasting room. Lines of grapevines supported by posts and rails march towards to the road.

Sixty-six rows. How many glasses of wine?

The professor's neat and tidy house is the only other one in the lane. I recognise Charles's car from when I saw it at the pool at Dubbo, and I presume the other one belongs to his father. No sirens. No flashing lights. No baton-wielding, taser-firing officers.

'Shit.' I call the professor, hoping he can come to me, but his phone goes straight to voicemail. I'm about to phone Ruddock again when his call comes through.

'The federal police will take two hours,' he says. 'But the local police have been notified.'

'When will they get here?'

'They needed vests, protection, but one of the units is on its way. It could be thirty minutes.'

'I'm outside, and the professor's not answering his phone. He might be hurt.'

'Use your judgement, Cartwright.'

She didn't get to where she is by threading daisy chains.

After parking on an angle behind both cars so that neither can leave before me, I step away from mine. Standing on the concrete driveway, I consider my camouflage shirt and pants, sturdy black belt and reinforced steel-capped boots.

No sandals, no floaty dress. And most importantly, no underestimating Charles.

I'll hold the fort until the police arrive. Nothing more, nothing less.

Within seconds of my knock, a curtain twitches. Charles, dressed in runners, loose fitting jeans and a T-shirt, answers the door.

'Patience.' His pupils are dilated. He shoves his hands in his pockets. 'What's up?'

Spying 101: Stick to the truth whenever possible.

'Professor Tedeschi said if I was ever in the neighbourhood, I should drop by.' I look past Charles, down the dimly lit hall. 'His car's outside, so I'm guessing he's here.'

'What's the neighbourhood?'

'I was roped into school recruitment in Gulgong.' Forcing a smile, I run my hands down my sides. 'Naval smart casual.'

'I'll tell Dad you came by.' He crosses his arms, blocking the door. 'He's busy.'

'I won't stay long.'

'Charles?' The professor calls out. 'Who is it?'

'Professor!' I shout. 'It's Patience Cartwright.'

Charles is forced to step back when the professor appears in the hallway. His face is flushed, and there's a graze on his forehead. His cardigan buttons don't line up. 'Lieutenant Cartwright,' he says with an attempt at brightness, 'what a lovely surprise. Come in, come in.'

'Sorry to arrive unannounced.'

The living room is small and cramped, with a long leather sofa, two matching armchairs and a rectangular coffee table. I take one of the chairs and the professor perches on the sofa. Charles stands sentry at the door.

'Can we offer you sustenance?' the professor asks. 'Coffee? Tea?'

I'm too wired up to drink anything, but ... 'I'd love a cup of tea.'

'You said you can't stay.' Charles favours his leg as he walks into the room. Half standing, half sitting, he props himself against the back of the sofa behind his father.

'Now, now, Charles ...' The professor's voice runs up and down octaves. 'As Patience is here, it might be best for us to have a little chat.'

'Shut up, Dad!'

'Unfortunately,' the professor says, glancing nervously at his son, 'it wasn't as easy to fix the problems with the invoices as we'd expected.' He pins his shaking hands between his knees. 'Thankfully, Patience understands.'

Charles looks from me to his father. His fists are clenched. 'What are you talking about?'

I stand, brush my hands down my pants. 'Maybe Friday night isn't the right time for chats. Hugo and Lisa have been working out Wellington way. We could see if they can join us at the pub.'

Charles looks pointedly at my foot. 'Off you go, then.'

The professor stands, but then he tilts forward, touches his head. 'We need help, son. Why can't you—'

'Shut up!'

'Have you bumped your head, professor?' I grip his arm. 'You can put your feet up in the car. Can I get you something before we go? A glass of water? Ice?'

'He doesn't need anything!'

'Charles,' the professor says, 'you haven't left the house in days. Why don't you come with us? I'll call Hugo, I'll tell him what time to expect us.'

Charles frowns, distracted, before backing slowly away. Gripping the door frame, he leans back and looks into the hallway. Professor Tedeschi fumbles to switch on his phone.

'Hugo?' the professor says. 'I'm with Charles and Patience in Mudgee. As you're relatively close by, we thought—'

'What are you doing?' Charles retraces his steps.

'Calling—'

'You stupid bastard!'

The professor jerkily presses buttons, disconnecting. 'I was going to—'

Charles points to the graze on his father's head. 'Have you forgotten already?'

The professor blinks and sways. 'It was an accident, Charles, a misunderstanding. We've had difficulties before. We can—'

'I'm not going anywhere,' Charles says. 'You're not going anywhere without me.'

The professor's face is parchment white. 'I'd hoped we could have a chat, Patience.' He touches the graze. 'But I think it might be best that you leave. Charles is under pressure with work and—'

'This is a set-up,' Charles says. 'She knows something. She *knows*.'

If the man with the shaved head and the man with the cleft in his chin can't come quickly, where are the local cops? The sirens, the lights?

I keep my eyes on Charles as I move around the table to the sofa. 'Let's go, professor.'

'Fuck off!' Spit sprays from Charles's mouth.

'Your medications, Charles ...' The professor's voice is thin. 'It's putting words into your mouth, words you don't mean to say.'

'I'll drive us to the pub, professor, so you can have a glass of wine.' Taking the professor's arm, I wedge myself between him and his son. 'You have a vineyard close by, don't you?'

'Fuck you!' Charles slashes the air with an arm. 'Get your hands off him!'

'I don't take orders from you!'

He barks a laugh. 'We could've had a good time, Patience, I knew it. You've got spirit.'

'What drugs are you on?'

'Who says I'm on anything?'

'Cocaine? Ice? Prescription?'

'Fuck off!'

The sofa is on one side of the professor and me, the table is on the other. Charles stands between the sofa and door. 'Professor?' I say quietly. 'Is he armed?'

'With his fists.'

'What's that, navy girl?' Charles takes a couple of steps towards us, holding his hand to his ear as he leans over the sofa. 'Doesn't your uniform make you tough? Are you worried about something? You scared?'

'I don't want your father to be hurt, and you shouldn't want that either. Get out of our way.'

Charles cocks his head, appears to consider my words. 'Who said I'd hurt him?'

'Please, Charles, don't do this.' The professor pleads. 'I'll make an appointment with your specialist and—'

'It's her,' Charles says, up on his toes and jabbing a finger. 'Why can't you see that?'

'Patience is doing her job, just as you do yours. I know there's been a mix-up, but that's all in the past. The lieutenant understands that.'

'I want to leave,' I say calmly. 'As does your father. Stand back so we can pass.'

He shouts a laugh. 'Are you giving me orders, pretty little Patience?'

'I'm asking you to move out of the way.'

'And what'll you do if I don't?' His eyes dart around the room.

'Charles,' the professor says. 'This is the drugs talking, not you.'

'I told you to get rid of her!' Sweat dampens Charlie's shirt. His hands shake; he wraps them around his body. 'You don't understand! She *knows*!'

The professor holds onto the arm of the sofa. 'I genuinely hoped that …'

'What?' Charles says. 'That I'd be like you? Bogged down in bureaucracy. You have no idea what I've done, what I've achieved.'

'Since your accident—'

'There was no accident!' Charles pokes the air. 'They ran me down! Why won't you admit that!'

'The driver didn't see you.'

'You stupid old—'

'Leave him alone!'

Charles smiles unpleasantly. 'You got a temper after all, navy girl?'

I bite back a retort. Endeavour to speak quietly. 'Move aside. Let us go.'

He's suddenly still. Too still. 'If you know,' he says quietly, 'who else knows?'

'I don't know what you're talking about.'

Steps deliberate, eyes intent, he looks me up and down. 'Pretty little Patience is a liar,' he says flatly.

The professor puts one hand on my shoulder. He leans across me, holding out his other hand.

'Stop this, Charles,' he says. 'Stop it at—'

Charles lunges and I jump back. But the professor is in my way. Within a moment I have my balance, but Charles is waiting. He grabs me by the throat with both hands. A vice around my neck.

'Bitch!'

I grab his forearms as he pushes me backwards, barging past his father, knocking him down and trampling over the top of him. As the professor cries out in pain, Charles bales me up against the wall. His mouth is contorted; his breath is sour.

'How much do you know?' He tightens his fingers. 'Tell me!'

I gurgle a warning. And then I kick out, kneeing him hard in the thigh. 'Get off me!'

Charles grunts and swears, taking one hand from my throat to grab my shoulder. He yanks me forward and then backwards, banging my head against the wall. My vision blurs. How many stars?

Too many.

The professor shouts at Charles to let me go, but Charles lifts a knee, shoving it into my stomach. One of his hands is still around my neck. I claw at his wrists and his hands. The backs of his fingers are rough with wiry hair.

'You wanna play rough, navy girl? Is that what you're into? I like that too.' His pupils are so dilated, I can't see the colour of his eyes. He brings back his leg, shoving his knee into my stomach again.

I suck air through my teeth. 'Can't breathe.'

'Hypoxia.' He loosens his grip a fraction. 'It heightens the pleasure.'

I gasp a breath, take another. 'Haven't tried it.'

'I could be your first.' Stroking my neck, he leans back a little, presses his thighs against mine. 'How about it, pretty little Patience?'

For the count of three I go limp. And then, bending a leg to kick off the wall, I strike his chin with the top of my head. When he falls back, releasing his grip on my throat, I drive my elbow into his teeth.

Spitting with fury, he swings a fist and hits the side of my face, throwing me backwards. He wipes blood from his mouth before lifting his fist and—

I kick out again, ramming my boot into his hip.

He screams. But then, mouth wide open, he charges again, grabbing my hair and shoving me back against the wall. Butting his head against my chest to pin me down, he claws at my clothes.

Brutal. Brute. Bully.

I smash my knee into his groin. His legs tremble. He staggers. He tilts on his axis like a skittle. I smash his groin again.

Retching and groaning, he crumples to the ground. I drop too, kneeling on the small of his back to take his hands and bring them behind him.

Professor Tedeschi, out of sight, is crying. 'It's okay, professor.' It hurts to breathe, let alone speak. 'It'll be okay.'

Charles spits and coughs. 'You fucking bitch.'

'You said no more dates.' When I push his head to the side, giving him space to breathe, his lip bleeds into the carpet.

'Police! Open up!'

'Get in here!'

Crashing. Splintered wood. Shouts and thumping footsteps.

CHAPTER 50

Professor Tedeschi, incoherent with shock, has a suspected broken wrist and a gash on his chin. I stay with him while the paramedic makes him comfortable, telling him Charles has been restrained but is safe, and the police will let him know when and where he can be contacted.

'He'll get the help he needs,' I reassure him.

After the first ambulance has turned onto the road, the paramedic from the second ambulance, a woman in her forties with thick black hair and a radiant smile, leads me to a chair.

'Your turn now,' she says as I sit.

'Just bruises.'

'I'll be the judge of that.'

Yet another vehicle joins the queue of police and other cars. *Hugo.*

My breath catches. 'Ow!' I wince and grab my throat. 'Sheesh.'

'Strangulation will do that to you,' the paramedic says, as she eases the elastic from my hair. 'Look down. I'll check out the cut on your head.'

I lean forward, my hands on my knees, as she parts my hair. The sun has gone down, but the police car and other lights illuminate the house and front garden. I hear Hugo's steps before I see his boots, splattered with mud. His khaki pants are worn at the knees. He crouches.

'Fuck.'

When I hold out my hand, he takes it.

The paramedic feels around the bump on my head. 'To fix this cut properly, I'd steri-strip it closed, but I'd have to get out the shaver to do that. It's not deep. Mind a scar?'

'I'll never see it.'

When she taps my shoulder, I look up. She pushes back the hair on my forehead. 'You've got scars in here already.'

'I fell from a horse.'

Hugo squeezes my hand. Our eyes meet. Blue on troubled green. 'What the fuck?' he says.

'Stop swearing.' I swallow. And wince. 'And don't you dare make me cry.'

'No point starting now.' The paramedic forages in her boxes of equipment. 'I'll anaesthetise the cut and clean it up.'

I thread my fingers through Hugo's. 'I missed you.'

'Yeah.'

'I was trying to find a way to distract Charles. When I suggested we meet you and Lisa, the professor dialled your number and—'

'Shhh, Imp.' He lays his cheek against mine. 'I don't want to be anywhere else.'

The paramedic clears her throat. 'No excitement allowed until you get scans done,' she says strictly. 'Neck and skull.'

I feel for the bruise, the size of an egg, at the back of my head. 'I didn't hear a crack.'

'Medic's orders. As for this …' She's already unfastened two shirt buttons, but unbuttons another. She opens the panels.

Hugo sucks in a breath. 'Fuck.'

'At twice her size,' the paramedic says, 'it was lucky he didn't damage the larynx.' When her radio sounds, she excuses herself and goes to the cabin.

'Imp?' Hugo, hand unsteady, puts hair behind my ear. 'Aren't warships enough? Are you in the SAS now?'

I aim for a smile. 'After the professor called the first time, I couldn't get onto him. I didn't know what Charles was up to, the police were delayed and—'

'You did great.'

'How did you work out where we were?'

'The professor said Mudgee, so I guessed it was here.'

The federal police officer with the shaved head walks around the ambulance. 'How're you doing?'

'Pretty good.' I follow his gaze to Charles, slumped against the door inside the police car. 'How is he?'

'His scrotum won't forget you in a hurry, but nothing too serious.'

'He shouldn't have hit his father.' I tentatively touch my throat.

'According to the local cops, you had him facedown on the floor when they broke in.'

The paramedic whistles brightly. 'Clear the decks, gentlemen.'

As the police officer mock salutes, telling me that the least he can do is drive me back to Jervis Bay when I'm ready, Hugo reluctantly stands back. The paramedic waves him in again when she's finished.

'Given the police escort to Nowra Hospital, I'll clear you to travel,' she tells me. You …' she smiles at Hugo, 'have five minutes more while I do my paperwork.'

Hugo crouches again. 'Five minutes isn't enough.'

'You'll look after the professor, won't you?'

'His sister and niece are coming up from Sydney.'

'Yes, but ...' I stand and touch his arm. 'He'll need support from his colleagues, friends like you and Rick. His reputation is important. He really didn't mean to ...'

His gaze goes to my throat. 'It could have been far worse.'

'I'm fine.' I fasten the buttons on my shirt. 'I *will* be fine.'

He takes my hand, kisses my thumb. 'Who'll look after you?'

'I'll get the scans done, and then I'll rest at the base. My friend Kat is there, and there are medics.'

'Greta's expecting you next month.'

'I'm going to see Minstrel, too.'

'Let me know how you go with the tests.'

'Captain McCarthy said I can go back to sea.' The words come out in a rush.

He opens his mouth, shuts it again. Then, 'That's what you wanted.'

My throat was sore. Now it's worse. 'I didn't know how you'd feel.'

'Your career is important.'

'The secondment, and everything else. You were so angry.'

'Anger doesn't mean ...' He thinks through his words. 'It doesn't mean relationships end. Sometimes, very occasionally, I might get angry.' He picks up my other hand. 'But that won't change what I feel.'

'No. I mean, yes.'

He searches my face, holds my gaze. 'I'll wait.'

My heart thumps. 'For what?'

'You don't have to live in Horseshoe. I wouldn't expect that.'

'But ...' My eyes sting. 'You wouldn't?'

'My condition has nothing to do with your career.'

'What condition?'

He puts his hand on the side of my face. He strokes my cheek with his thumb. 'I want a commitment.' He kisses my mouth, swiftly and sweetly. 'I need you to prove you won't run.'

My hands flutter like butterflies. 'How do I do that?'

'No variables, possibilities, probabilities.' He squeezes my hands. 'There's only one answer.'

'I don't …' My voice wavers. 'I don't know where to start.'

'You're brave and resourceful,' he says quietly. 'You know where I live. You come and find me.'

CHAPTER
51

It's two am by the time Kat Stevens, on shore leave for the weekend, meets me in the waiting room of the hospital near the base. I'm so tired and sore, it's an effort to walk to the car.

'Thanks for staying up so late.'

'What?' After lifting her bottom to smooth her sparkly blue dress over her thighs, she reaches for her belt. 'I had to leave early.'

I yawn a laugh. 'I hope I get to sleep in tomorrow.'

'No way.'

I blink. 'I have to report early?'

'Nah, but the base knows what happened.' She pats her chest. 'Above and beyond the call of duty, Fernando. I reckon you're due a medal.'

'This had nothing to do with the navy.'

'Shame about that.'

When I flick on the light to my room and lean against the door, the picture of my sisters and me stares back. Ryan's thank you card is on the top shelf. *Me and my horse.* Taking a deep breath, I push off the door and sit on the bed. I put on a Spotify playlist. 'Ring Ring'.

First a shower, then I'll message Hugo.

The steam that fills the tiny bathroom mists the mirror and masks the bruises. Stepping under the spray, I gingerly touch the back of my head. I tip up my chin and let the water cascade over my head and down my back. I wash and condition my hair before reaching for the soap.

Greta said the scent was sunshine, for the land and for the water. *Jasmine, mimosa, orange blossom.* The water is warm, as are my tears. Floods and floods, sobs and sniffs and shakes. I've had a shitty day. My throat aches. I miss Greta and the farm. But most of all, I miss Hugo.

When I send him an email, I'm sitting in bed drinking chamomile tea, my phone resting on my knees.

> *Thank you for driving to Mudgee. My scans were clear and I'm back at the base.*
>
> *I forgot to tell you about Able Seaman Poppleton, who you've probably heard from already. He'll be in Wellington next week (he has your number). I know he'll be working with Rick all month, but I thought you might like to do the introductions. He's an experienced mechanic, originally from the country, and excited about joining the team.*

Even though it's almost three, Hugo responds immediately.

> *Thanks, Imp. Poppleton's called. Leave it with me. Hope you sleep okay—give me an update tomorrow.*

Captain McCarthy's EA sends through details of a posting on the *Adelaide*, the same class of ship I was on last year. It won't start until January and until that time ...

I'll be assigned to the base.

For the past week, I've drafted policy documents on safety management governance. When a call from reception comes through, I welcome the interruption.

'I have Dr Richard Lipman with me,' Ai says. I hear Rick's voice in the background. 'He insists he has to see you urgently.'

'What?' My heart rate doubles. I close my laptop and stand. 'Has there been an accident? Is someone hurt?'

More conversation. Then, 'Dr Lipman finds Popeye unsuitable.'

'What?'

'I presume ...' there's a smile in Ai's voice, 'Dr Lipman is referring to Able Seaman Poppleton.'

Rick always dresses the same—four am on the river, at Greta's for lunch, mid-morning in a park in Dubbo, and at four pm on a naval base. Hair neatly cut and parted, a shirt tucked into his pants, sensible walking shoes.

And I haven't been happier to see anyone since I got back. His stance is stiff, but he initiates a very brief hug.

'You're six hours away from where you're meant to be,' I say.

'You are aware of my schedule, lieutenant?'

'As I drafted it, yes.' When we walk across the parade ground, he's on my left. 'What are you doing here?'

'Popeye is unsuitable.'

I laugh. 'Able Seaman *Poppleton* is eminently suitable, and you know it. He's a mechanic, and he grew up on a farm. If he can ride a bull, I'm sure he'll have no trouble with a horse. If he's very careful, and Minstrel doesn't mind, maybe he could borrow him?'

'Popeye would need two carthorses and a wagon to carry his weight, lieutenant. Hugo shares my concerns.'

'He's muscular, yes. Which means he can pull kayaks over mudflats, carry fifty kilo packs, maintain outboard engines and—'

'He talks incessantly. In the evenings, he listens to wrestling bouts. He's clumsy and unreliable.'

'Rick! He's friendly and prodigiously fit, exactly the person you advertised for. And what do you mean he's clumsy and unreliable? I don't believe it.'

When Rick sits on the left side of a bench overlooking the bay, I sit on the right. 'His fingers are too wide to type accurately. He sleeps through his alarm. I'm forced to wake him.'

'He might not like working all day, then rising at three in the morning.'

'Hugo said the same. He was most unsympathetic.'

I smile. 'There you are, then.'

'Hugo blames you for exceeding expectations. He said it is time we faced reality.'

'We?' I link my hands in my lap. 'Hugo as well?'

Rick continues to stare straight ahead. 'I believe he also regrets your departure.'

'Soon I'll go and see Minstrel at Mandy's stud. Afterwards, I've promised Greta I'll come to Horseshoe for lunch.'

'My immediate problem, lieutenant, is Popeye. What will you do about him?'

'Nothing whatsoever.' My hand goes to my neck, the faded bruises. 'Have you heard anything about the funding for the project?'

'Until the finalisation of the inquiry, it will continue.' Rick nervously taps his fingers. 'Charles Tedeschi sent government funds exceeding $500,000 to America.'

I whistle. 'Can they get the money back?'

'That's most unlikely.'

'The professor didn't benefit.'

'He's been removed from the project. Like me ...' Rick taps his fingers again. 'He was careless.'

'Once you found out, you alerted the professor. They'd have to take that into consideration.'

'He didn't correct the anomaly immediately.' More tapping. 'I told the authorities I was to blame. I have answered questions truthfully and provided a statement.'

'It won't be a criminal offence, Rick, so try not to worry too much.'

'Eliza has asked me to move in with her again.'

'Oh!'

'You are surprised?'

I blow him a kiss. 'I'm delighted! I hope you said yes.'

'If I lose my position with the university, Eliza said I will have time to paint her house, but I'd prefer to work in her garden.'

'Oh, but ... What's happening with your job, Rick?'

'Hugo assures me that, as Charles Tedeschi's behaviour was systematic and calculated, I'll keep it. A senior academic, an assistant vice chancellor, has been appointed to Professor Tedeschi's role.'

'Is the professor okay?'

'His primary concern is his son. Hugo is less forgiving.'

'He was angry we didn't tell him what was going on.'

'If I had spoken up, you would not have been harmed. Hugo pointed this out most forcefully.'

'Hugo would have talked to the professor, who would have protected his son. Charles might have got away with much worse crimes than stealing. He could have got to the US and disappeared.'

'Hugo believes the costs exceeded the benefits.' He frowns, considering his words. 'Your injuries. There is no permanent damage?'

'No.'

'Accordingly, Hugo's argument cannot be supported.'

Holding in a smile, I stretch my legs and consider my shoes. 'I hope the project's funding will continue. And now you have Poppleton—'

'Popeye lifts weights, lieutenant. This accounts for his inability to rise as directed.'

'If you're confined on a ship, even a large one, it's good to have a physical outlet. Many sailors work out at the gym.'

He glances at me, then away. 'Hugo says you will go back to sea.'

'I've been offered a posting on the *Adelaide*.'

Rick stands and looks over my shoulder. 'Thank you for the work you did on the project, lieutenant.'

'I'm sure you'll get used to Poppleton. I learned so much when I was with you, about rivers, creeks, biodiversity ... lots of things.'

He glances at me and then looks away. 'I spoke with Eliza this morning.'

'And ...?'

'When I communicated Hugo's regret, she suggested it might be thoughtful to enquire after your own feelings. Is this an appropriate time?'

'As a matter of fact, Rick, I could do with your advice ...'

An hour after I say goodbye to Rick, I'm back in my room on a Zoom call. Prim, blurred by motes of dust, is in a cavernous corrugated-iron shed.

'S ... sorry I can't ... stay long,' she says. 'I've got a hundred head of cattle waiting.' Her ponytail has been pushed to the side by her Akubra. When she smiles into the screen, her dimple flickers. 'I'm loving the bump, Phoebe.'

Phoebe, her fair hair neatly tied back, pats her rounded stomach. She turns to Sinn, sitting next to her on the sofa, and kisses him tenderly.

'Could you make me a mug of hot chocolate?'

He smiles, obviously aware she wants to get rid of him, and nuzzles her neck before turning to the screen.

'We will see you soon,' he says to Prim and me.

'You bet,' Prim says.

As soon as Sinn leaves, Phoebe's tone switches. 'What's going on, Patience? Why haven't I heard from you?'

'You're a witch, Phoebe. I swear it.'

'Prim said you went to the hospital for scans. You haven't had a relapse with your foot, have you?

'Just a few scratches. I'm back at work.'

'Navy work, right?' Prim grins. 'I'll miss your frog blogs.'

'Hugo might keep them going.'

'Was he okay about you leaving so ... suddenly?' Prim asks. 'Have you heard from him ... since you got back?'

'We've sent a few texts ...' I smile bravely. 'He knows I'll be visiting Greta soon.'

Phoebe frowns. 'You're off the secondment?'

'We found a replacement for the role I was doing, and—'

'Phoebe?' Prim lifts her hands above her head and fixes her ponytail. 'Remember how I studied Austen's *Persuasion* for my final exams? In the letter Captain ... Wentworth wrote at the end of the ... story, he ... said he was half agony and half hope, not knowing whether he'd be rejected again.'

Phoebe looks worriedly at me. 'Patience?'

'I wish Prim would shut up about Captain Wentworth.'

Prim grins and says something else, but I can't hear what it is because when a stocky man opens the doors to the shed, the bellowing noises intensify. He shouts her name, and she slams on her hat. 'Gotta go!'

As Prim disappears from the screen, Phoebe looks questioningly at me. I open my mouth to speak, to say *anything,* but nothing comes out.

'You were happy at the Halsteads,' Phoebe finally says. 'You were enjoying the work and you'd even started riding again. Why leave so suddenly? What's going on?'

'Minstrel is staying at Mandy's stud,' I say, 'and I'm having trouble getting onto her. Have you spoken to her lately?'

'I haven't,' Phoebe says, 'but maybe I should.'

'Why?' I say suspiciously.

'Last year, when you were being harassed by that creep on your ship, I told Mandy about it. She reassured me that you might look like a gazelle, but you had the spirit of a lioness. I wouldn't want you to lose that.'

I form a triangle with three pens. 'It's hard to be a lioness all the time.'

'When Prim talked about Hugo just then, I'm not sure what I saw. How're you feeling right now?'

I smile reluctantly. 'You really are a witch.'

Her face is fuller, but her smile is just the same. Loving, concerned. 'Tell me what's going on.'

Whatever the shape of a triangle, the internal angles will equal a hundred and eighty degrees. Certainty. Predictability.

'Before I left Horseshoe,' I tell Phoebe, 'Hugo and I had an argument. I saw him again last week, and it was okay. Sort of okay. But then ...' Another breath. 'It's complicated, and I'm not sure what to do next.'

'Maybe I can help.'

'He said he needs to know I won't run.'

'Oh.'

'What do you mean, oh?'

A delay. Then, 'The jacaranda tree in our garden in Dubbo. You and Prim used to run around it while holding out your school dresses. Remember that?'

'We tried to catch the flowers.'

'When Mum was still with us, even afterwards, you ran everywhere, just for the fun of it. You'd do a hundred things at once. Sort peas into fractions in your highchair. Catch blossoms. Swim lengths of the pool. Skip through textbooks in the first week of term. You'd protect me, defend me, from our father.' She tips her head to the side. 'You were fearless, determined, impatient.'

'Hugo still calls me Imp.'

'You would have been,' she counts on her fingers, 'ten years old when he first did that. I remember him shouting it from the stands at swimming competitions. He and Greta, even Derek when he could make it, they'd cheer until they were hoarse.'

I take a deep breath. 'Greta made a promise, Phoebe. I should tell you about it.'

When Sinn leans over Phoebe and puts a cushion behind her back, she looks up at him gratefully.

'You'd better go.'

'No, Patience.' She waves Sinn away again. Then she sits forward a little, looks seriously into the screen. 'Half agony, half hope. You've never wanted anybody else but Hugo, have you? Is that why Prim quotes *Persuasion*?'

'I wish she wouldn't.'

'I thought he'd broken your heart forever,' she says quietly.

'The trouble was, I broke his heart too. Which is why he needs to know I won't run.'

'If he loves you, if you love him, you won't want to.'

I rearrange the pens and line them up. *Like a fence.* 'When I joined the navy, I wanted to leave him behind. But it wasn't only that. I wanted to test myself. I wanted adventure.'

'Like a lioness, but ...' Phoebe changes position, curls her legs. 'There are other adventures too. Other things you can try.'

'In Horseshoe?'

She smiles. 'That's for you to decide.'

CHAPTER 52

'Cartwright!'

Almost seven months have passed since Commander Ruddock and I were last on the beach. Tonight, I turn and face him. 'Sir.'

'Your email warrants discussion.'

Waves scatter to the shore behind me. 'Here, sir?'

'I've been posted to Sydney for a month, commencing,' he checks his watch, 'an hour ago.' He adjusts his glasses. 'The email, Cartwright. Explain.'

I tug down the sleeves of my wetsuit. 'Last time we were here, you said numbers couldn't save me, and maybe you were right about that. But I looked at Lieutenant Commander Grantham's history and—'

'Statistics, Cartwright. You sent reams of statistics.'

'In over two decades, no woman has served under Grantham for more than two years, and usually far less. Compare that with every other officer of his seniority and—'

'Get to the point.'

'From what I can work out, women tolerate Grantham's behaviour for the sake of their careers. Others say no to the harassment, and he backs off, but it never ends there. He undermines them. He bullies them. They invariably ask for a transfer.'

'Why would he slip up with you?'

'I kept to myself, and I didn't have powerful friends. Maybe I was less likely to be believed. But mostly, I think he got sloppy.'

'Why pursue this now? What changed your mind?'

'Bullies, sir. Grantham, and others like him, should be held accountable.'

'These statistics. You believe they can help?'

'They demonstrate a pattern of behaviour that, together with the complaint I'll lodge, justify further investigation. Other women might come forward.'

'Why send the statistics to me? Why not Captain McCarthy? Do you imagine you could have kept your position in the past twelve months without his support?'

'You're a senior officer with appropriate authority. You do things strictly by the book.'

He looks at me suspiciously. 'What else?'

'You dislike me. It suggests my allegations have merit.'

He peers critically through his glasses. 'I don't dislike you.'

'I stand corrected.'

He frowns. 'I stand corrected, *sir*.'

'Sir.' A flutter of hope. 'Will you support me?'

'Formalise your complaint,' he says brusquely. 'You'll have my support.'

The next seven days drag slowly, and the closer I get to my visit to Horseshoe, the more difficult it is to communicate with Hugo. Often, he's out of range. Or he's been up all night. How do I word my texts when we haven't had the chance to see each other face to face?

I swim most evenings, walking past the grey gum, picking a leaf and folding it in half. *The smell of eucalyptus, the sharp and the sweet, always takes me back.* On Friday night, I leave my room later than usual. An owl hoots from somewhere in the distance. A cast of crabs skip across the sand at my feet. The bay is smooth like a pond.

I wade to my hips and dive into the echoes. A hundred and twenty metres, two hundred and eighty-two freestyle strokes. When I reach the breakwater, I flip I onto my back and study the stars. *Dots of exclamation points.* The water holds me up; my hair floats all around me. I imagine Greta's bathing room.

Same, but different.

Carefully clambering over the rocks, I walk along the bitumen strip to the two sets of poles and the banners. *HMAS Creswell. Welcome to Jervis Bay.* Open sea on one side, a sheltered bay on the other. When Hugo was here, I took his hands. I used him as a shield. To hide me.

To find me.

The soap Greta gave me smells of sunshine, the sea and the land.

It's finally time to go home.

CHAPTER 53

Early in the morning, a hopeful golden sun peeps over the horizon, but before too long thickening clouds hang low in the sky. Pulling off the highway, I park my rental at a truck stop. On my second call, Mandy picks up.

'Did you get my message?' I ask. 'I should be there by eleven. I can't stay long, but tell Minstrel I have carrots and apples and—'

'Didn't I call back?' Mandy interrupts. 'You're going to Horseshoe for lunch, aren't you? Can you come to me afterwards?'

I hang onto the phone more tightly. 'I planned to visit Hugo after lunch.'

'Late afternoon then.'

'Greta has asked Gus for dinner, so she wants me to go back there. I might stay the night.'

'In that case,' Mandy says brightly, 'I'll see you in Warrandale on Sunday. Send me a text when you leave Horseshoe.'

I'd have preferred to see Hugo *before* lunch, but his gift won't be delivered until early afternoon. Will he want it? His response to the text I sent last night was prompt, but merely courteous: *I won't be at Greta and Derek's tomorrow. See you here later. Hugo.*

He needs to know I won't run. *No variables, possibilities or probabilities. There's only one answer.*

I've turned off the loop road to Horseshoe when I see Mr and Mrs Hargreaves's van at the side of the road. In front of the van is a truck that must have taken the bend too fast—six wheels in the ditch and six on the road. As I pull over, Fiona Hargreaves, in her late sixties with a troublesome knee, limps towards me.

'Patience! Patience!' She waves her hands above her head. 'Thank goodness you're here. The driver's been hurt, but the ambulance is an hour away. Can you help?'

The driver, a middle-aged man with a beer gut, has a cut on his brow that bleeds steadily into his eye. He also has a gash on his arm, which I wrap in Mrs Hargreaves's cardigan.

'How bad is it?' he asks.

'You'll need stitches.' When Mrs Hargreaves hands me an old T-shirt, I press it against the man's head. 'Try to stay still so you don't lose more blood.'

I dressed in a way I thought both Greta and Hugo would appreciate— a short pink dress and new white sneakers. But by the time the police and ambulance arrive, my dress is grubby, my shoes are filthy, and I've scraped my knees on the bitumen. I have streaks of dried blood on my arm.

The paramedic, the same woman who looked after me in Mudgee, rolls her eyes. 'Naval personnel really get around.'

I clean myself up as best I can before Mr Hargreaves walks me to my car. 'When Fiona called Greta to tell her you'd be late,' he says, 'she was at Hugo's place. As it's closer than the farm, she said she'd wait for you there.'

I've been away from Horseshoe for only three weeks, but everything seems to be brighter. The flowers at the cenotaph in the park. The greens of the gum leaves, the slow-flowing river. The narrow metal strips around the letter box keg. By the time I turn off the road to Hugo's, it's almost two o'clock.

The red gum's low hanging branches throw dappled light as I bump over the cattle grid. Hugo, wearing his customary work jeans and boots, and a faded blue shirt with the sleeves rolled up, stands next to Derek on the slope to the creek. Behind them, parked between row upon row of grasses and saplings, is a sparkling yellow excavator.

Hugo, shading his eyes with a hand, walks down the middle of the driveway towards me. His gold-brown hair is shorter than it was. His expression is serious. I tear my gaze away and—

The house looks the same—the honey-yellow bricks and smart grey roof, the broad verandah with thick timber posts—but the circular driveway, mottled brown gravel with double brick edges, is new. In the middle of the circle is a mound of dirt like a miniature mountain. Along the front of the house, where the cars used to park, there's an excavated strip of land piled high with dirt and mulch.

He's making a garden.

He opens my door. We stare at each other. Is he tongue-tied like me? Unsure of the order that the words should come out? I fumble with my belt, swipe at the stains on my dress. Stepping out of the car, I brush my knees. I link my hands at my waist.

'There was an accident.' My voice is squeaky.

'Greta told me.'

'She said I should come here.' Even looking straight ahead, I see the yellow excavator. My skin warms. 'Where are your horses?'

'Around the back. I have to re-fence.'

'You've been busy.'

He lifts a hand and drops it. 'What's with the excavator?'

'It's a present.' I scuff my sneakers in the dust. 'Can I have a shower?'

He hesitates, then presses a kiss to the top of my head. 'You okay?'

'He bled on me.' My voice hitches.

When I open the passenger door for my bag, Hugo leans over my shoulder and takes it. We walk to the house in silence, close but not touching. Derek, a tool belt hanging from his hips, is attaching wire to a verandah post.

'G'day, Patience.' He smiles as he tips back his hat. 'Good to have you home.'

Remy, sitting sideways on Lavender's back, appears on the far side of the house. 'I know a secret!' he calls out.

I grasp Hugo's arm. 'He might fall.'

As Remy's smile slips, Hugo takes my hand. 'Face the front, mate,' he says calmly, 'and walk Lavender to the paddock. We'll tell Patience the secret later.'

I reassure myself that jeans, a collared T-shirt and riding boots are more appropriate than the clothes I'd selected carefully this morning. My hair, washed with Hugo's shampoo, is tied back in a ponytail, and my face is free of makeup. Crickets click a welcome as I walk down the steps.

Derek watches on as Hugo, lying flat on his stomach on the verandah, looks over the edge of the boards. I skirt around mounds of dirt where the garden bed will be.

'What are you doing?' I ask.

'We need to get power to the pond,' Derek says.

'Patience!' Remy's boots, a smaller version of mine, clomp on the boards as he gallops across the verandah. He jumps down the steps, takes my hand and tugs. 'Oma's making schnitzel and potato salad and I picked the tomatoes. Then we've got strudel. I'm starving!'

I crouch and hug him. 'I've missed you.'

'Can we play horse shows?'

'I'd love that, but I haven't seen Greta yet. Where is—'

Greta, holding a basket in one hand and untying her apron with the other, rushes around the side of the house. Flicking the apron free of her dress, she drops the basket and holds out her arms.

'Liebchen!' She hugs me tightly. 'They did not tell me you are here.' When she claps her hands, Hugo and Derek look our way. 'Zur eile antreiben! We must go!'

'Go where?' Hugo asks.

'Not you.' Greta holds out her hand like a traffic policeman. 'It is Derek and Remy. They are to come.' She bustles towards the ute. 'Quickly, Remy.'

'I don't want to—'

'Derek!'

'What's the hurry?' he asks.

'If you do not drive, I will have to do it.'

'Since when do you drive on the left-hand side of the road?'

'Before today, I have not had the need.'

'What's the big deal about—'

Holding up her hand again, she looks pointedly at me, and then at Hugo. 'Patience will teach Hugo to drive the machine.'

Derek glances at the excavator. 'Why would she do that?'

My skin warms. 'I'll come too, Greta. Remy said there's schnitzel for lunch and—'

'Schnitzel is better for dinner.'

'But I promised to help Ryan with his homework.'

'I am familiar with Farmer Jenny's many difficulties,' Greta says. 'I will assist her today.' Shading her eyes, she considers the sky. 'There will be rain. It is best you put the excavator under cover.'

'I've never operated one.'

She waves a hand dismissively. 'You drive a warship, liebchen. This machine will not be a trouble for you.'

Hiding a smile, Hugo ruffles Remy's hair. 'Patience and I will be there for dinner.'

Remy hangs off Hugo's arm. 'I want to stay here.'

'Best to do what your Oma says.' Derek puts an arm around Remy's shoulders. 'I've got chores to be getting on with, so you can keep me and Soxy company.'

Rain peppers the ground as the ute drives away. A magpie lands on the mound in the middle of the circle and pecks at the dirt. Kookaburras call out a song.

'Imp?' When I turn, Hugo holds out a hand, indicating the steps. I sit and he sits next to me. A raindrop falls on the toe of my boot. And another. 'The excavator.' He leans forward, forearms on his knees. 'What the hell?'

'You looked after Minstrel.' I study a line of ants, marching up a post. I *try* not to count. Twelve centimetres of ants approximately one point three millimetres long. Point six of a millimetre between their little bodies. Sixty-three ants. 'You helped me ride again.'

'Remy scared you.'

I rest my hands on my knees. Three weeks away from chickens and horses and work on the farm. My nails are clean.

'I understand my fears better than I did. Being scared shouldn't stop me doing what I want.'

'Imp?' He studies my profile. 'What do you want?'

I meet his gaze. 'I want to buy you an excavator.'

'It's brand new.' He frowns. 'Expensive.'

'I'll give you the paperwork.'

'You can't buy me equipment worth $60,000.'

'You bought me boots.' I point my toes.

'Four hundred bucks.'

'Maybe I should've purchased a second-hand machine, one that didn't stand out like a sunflower.'

'There are other things to spend your money on.'

'I can afford it. It's a thank you present.' The rain beats a tattoo on the corrugated roof. 'The works on the driveway. Did you borrow equipment?'

'I got a contractor in.'

'That would have been expensive.'

'I have assets, Imp. Besides the mortgage for this place, I'm not in debt.'

'You rely on continued funding for the project. What if it's delayed while they look into Professor Tedeschi?'

'I'll get other work.'

'You have unpaid work at the creek. The excavator might be useful for that.'

With a muttered curse, he gets to his feet. He paces in front of the steps, pushes a hand through his hair. One of his sleeves has unfolded; he rolls it up before sitting again. He's closer than he was. His knee bumps my thigh.

'Tell me what you're thinking,' he says quietly. 'Are you saying goodbye with the excavator?'

I study my hands. 'If I'd said goodbye in February, I wouldn't have had to lie to you.'

He searches my face. 'I knew you were hiding something. I wanted you to stay anyway.'

A whinny. Arrow? 'Are your horses in the paddock where you kept Minstrel?'

When he jumps to his feet, I stand too. Raindrops on his shoulders, circular drips. *Lines through the centre of a circle form lines of reflective symmetry.* 'Yes,' he says.

'I'll see Minstrel at Mandy's stud tomorrow.'

'I wouldn't let her take him.'

'What?' I step to the side to look around him. 'He's still here?'

Taking my hand, he tugs until I face him again. 'It's where he belongs.'

Longing wraps a band around my heart. Warm aching need seeps through my veins. I lay a hand on his chest and loop my finger through a gap between his buttons. His skin is firm and heated. My legs weaken.

'I have an answer to your question.'

'Yes?'

'I belong with you too.'

He dips his head. Breath warm, bristles rough. 'I love you, Imp.'

I force myself to push back, to order my thoughts. 'When I took your hands on the beach, you said you don't pretend.'

With his thumb, he wipes raindrops from my cheek. 'You're a piece of my puzzle. The missing piece.'

I step even closer, feel the strength of his body. 'After our picnic at the river, I said I'd only ever want you. Do you remember what else I said?'

Half agony. Half hope. I see it in his eyes. 'You said that you loved me.'

I stand on my toes and wrap my arms around his neck. 'I still do.'

CHAPTER
54

How long do we kiss in the rain? A moment? A lifetime?

I pull at his shirt, yank it free of his jeans. I tug at the buttons to search for his skin. I push my fingers through his hair, find his nape and stroke. His mouth is hard. His hands are possessive. Seeking, finding, keeping.

'Imp.' He mutters my name repeatedly—into my mouth, across my cheeks, against my neck. Our clothes are wet, our bodies warm. And, by the time he grasps my hand and pulls me up the steps, we're shaking and panting with lust. But when I trip, he hauls me against his body again. He runs his hands up and down my sides and groans into my mouth. 'I want you.'

We kick off our boots before we run into the house. Plaster archways, roughly patched walls, skirting boards, picture rails, a broad timber staircase. He's careful that I keep to the middle of the treads, but when we reach the top, he takes my hand and—

'Oh!' Bricks and rubble are heaped in a pile in the middle of the hallway. 'What's happened?'

He pushes back his hair. 'You'll come here when you're on leave, won't you?'

I hesitate. 'I guess.'

Cupping my face, he kisses my mouth. 'Good.'

The furniture has been cleared from the room where he used to have his desk. Pipes jut out of the walls and through the floorboards. Pale blue tiles, hundreds of them, lean against a wall. Long planks of timber and buckets of nails are stacked behind a workbench.

'What are you building?'

When he slides back the boards on the window, the trees and river are a watery blur. 'In a couple of years,' he says, 'I'll budget for more water tanks. I'll build a lap pool behind the house.'

'But …' As I look around the room again, words bubble up. 'This is a bathing room, isn't it?' I hold out my arms and turn a circle. 'It's enormous.'

He grasps my hand, laughing as we walk to the window. He stands behind me and pulls me against his body, my back against his front, his chin on my shoulder. He kisses my neck.

'The bath will go here.'

I swallow the lump in my throat. Two of them. Ten. Twenty. A hundred. 'Last time I was here, I imagined a scene from a jigsaw puzzle—the red gum and the river, the park and the town.' Twisting in his arms, I kiss his throat. I run my mouth across his collarbone and the lump where it was broken. I blink back tears; a smile pushes through. 'Will my bathing room have shelves for towels? Will it have bubble bath and salts?'

The oil painting, ocean and mountains and sky, hangs at the foot of the bed. *Home.* The alphabet's eighth, fifteenth, thirteenth and fifth letters. Forty-one. The sum of two squares (4^2 and 5^2) equal forty-one.

'Imp?' He tugs at the button at my throat. 'You're counting, aren't you?'

His buttons are already undone. I roll down his sleeves and tug off his shirt. I splay my hands on his chest. 'Not strictly.'

He pulls my shirt over my head and throws it onto the floor. He cups my breasts over my bra.

'You counted aloud when we picked you up for swimming.' He kisses a trail down my cleavage. 'Statistics, percentages, fractions, patterns.'

'Why didn't you tell me to stop?'

He looks up. 'You took my breath away.' He kisses my mouth again, hard and possessive. 'You always will.' Shining eyes and a flash of white teeth. He sits me on the bed and crouches at my feet. He peels off my socks and tugs at my jeans before adding his clothes to the pile on the floor. He's so much taller and heavier than me, and broader and stronger, but our bodies fit together like the pieces of a puzzle.

Sweet and shallow, deep and slow. Whispers on the breeze, lightning in the storm. I wrap my legs around his back to bring him close. His mouth and mine, soft skin, hard limbs, tenderness and craving. Warm wet bodies, limbs tangled up, strokes and sweeps and tumble turns. Summer heat and winter chills, flooding rivers, flowing streams, swaying grasses, eucalyptus.

No variables, possibilities, probabilities.

I belong with him.

My head is on his chest and he's stroking my hair. I can't hear the rain on the roof any more.

'Hey,' he says, smiling when I look up.

'Did you sleep?'

He puts down his phone and rubs across my shoulders. 'I researched.'

I stretch against his body. 'What time is it?'

'Five.'

'Tell me what you were looking at, then I'll call Greta. I'd better let her know we'll be late.'

Rolling me onto my back, he props himself up on an elbow. 'There's a female admiral in the navy.'

I smile. 'So?'

He kisses my neck. 'She has a white jacket, gold buttons, and studs on her shoulders.'

'That's her dress uniform.'

He smooths hair from my face. 'I could do what her husband does, stand to the side while you inspect the troops on the deck of a ship.'

I rest a fingertip against his mouth. 'Have you forgotten I'm trouble? They'd never make me an admiral.'

'You could be anything.' He takes a lock of my hair, curling from the rain, and wraps it around his wrist. 'I can come to you.'

'Yes, but—'

'Marry me.'

My heart stills. 'What?'

'I want a ring.' He picks up my hand, takes the third finger and kisses it. 'Do it for me.'

I take a deep breath. Then push against his chest. 'We'd better talk.'

He grumbles when, after we sit and face each other, I pull the sheet over our laps. When he lifts a hand to run it through his hair, I capture it, holding it tightly between us.

'What if I leave the navy?' I finally say. 'Then I could live here all the time.'

He shakes his head. 'That's not the deal.'

'You don't want me to live here? Or you won't marry me if I do?'

He threads our fingers together. 'Don't give up your career.'

Another deep breath. 'I like helping Ryan, but I don't think teaching would suit me. Standing behind a lectern and writing journal articles would drive me nuts, so I don't want to be an academic. Commerce, finance, banking, none of that interests me.' I stroke the soft hair on his forearm. 'When Rick came to see me at the base, I asked for his advice.'

'He knows about this?'

'Rick, Lisa, everyone on your team, want governments to support environmental initiatives. To get that support, you need to demonstrate short- and long-term benefits. For political and financial reasons, governments will change policies only if there's evidence that change will make a difference. The skills I have, compiling data and analysing it, projections and modelling, can be useful to the kind of work you do.'

'You're a sailor, Imp. A navigator and—'

'For example, if we can demonstrate it's more cost efficient, long term, for farmers to manage land in a way that facilitates water retention, the government is more likely to fund or subsidise rehabilitation of land, or allow tax breaks and—'

'Imp.' *Agony and hope all over again.* 'What are you saying?'

'My commission is up in February. I could return to the secondment so Minstrel and I could join you in October, but even if I didn't get permission, I have weeks of leave owing and I could take that.'

'But—'

'In the past four weeks, you haven't done a single post on the frog blog. You clearly need my help.'

'I don't—'

'I told you Captain Wentworth forgave Anne for rejecting him, didn't I?'

Smiling, he lifts my hand and kisses my palm. 'You did.'

'I'm not sure I have Captain Wentworth's fortune, but I've got investments and savings. Greta told me what you paid for this property. I could pay off your mortgage.'

'What?'

'Probably twice your mortgage.'

'Imp, you—'

'I'd like to have flowers in my garden.' I kiss his hand like he kissed mine. 'I'd also like windows in my bathing room. And we can't have children …' I search his face. 'Do you want children?'

He puts hair behind my ear. 'Our children.'

I wave towards the door. 'We can't have them tumbling down the stairs. You've also got hundreds of metres of creek to rehabilitate, and—'

He's laughing as he kisses me, a crazy heartfelt passionate kiss. 'You'll marry me?'

'You still want that?' I wind my arms around his neck and talk against his mouth. 'Even though I won't be an admiral?'

He pulls back a little. 'Don't rush your decision.'

'Don't be impatient?' I draw a line from his forehead to his bottom lip. 'I know where I belong.'

'But—'

'And I don't need gold epaulettes.'

He stills. Then forages under a pillow. He pulls out the shirt I left behind. *His shirt.*

'You'll always have this,' he says quietly.

The tears spring too quickly to blink back. 'You kept it.' When the blue checks blur, I take the flannelette, wipe my eyes and shrug into the shirt. I fasten two buttons. Muttering complaints under his breath, he pushes my hands away.

'I didn't want you to put it on.'

I sniff and laugh. 'I missed it.'

When he leans against the bedhead, taking me with him, I sink into his arms. He kisses the top of my head.

'You have so few possessions.'

'I learned about the things Greta valued. Her window boxes, crockery, the gifts she's never opened.'

His arms tighten. 'We'll fill this house together.'

I take his hand and examine his palm. 'Some frogs develop a textured surface, a nuptial pad, so they can cling to their mate.'

'Don't talk about frogs when we're in bed.'

'When they come to our creek,' I smile into his eyes, 'I can count the tadpoles.'

He doesn't return my smile. His eyes are bright and green. 'I love you, Imp.'

Sunshine, rain clouds, brisk country dawns. Cockatoos, kookaburras, sheep dogs and horses. A river, a creek and a sandstone house. A shelter from the storm, a place to call home.

I push back his hair. I kiss his salty lashes. 'You're the missing piece of my puzzle.'

ACKNOWLEDGEMENTS

Shelter from the Storm is my seventh novel published by HQ/HarperCollins so, when people ask what I've been up to since leaving the law, I'm now reasonably confident in responding 'I'm a writer'. But the more books I write, the more I appreciate that what makes me a writer isn't a publishing contract, or books on the shelves, but the readers who enjoy the stories I tell. So, thank you, dear reader, for finding this book. This story is written for you.

Many thanks to my HQ/HarperCollins publisher, Jo Mackay, for your continued advice, encouragement, and support. My books are so much better for your remarkable insights into what might work, and what might not. To senior editor at HQ/HarperCollins, Annabel Blay, thank you, thank you, thank you (deliberate repetition). You are not only a brilliant editor, but you make me laugh. It's been a joy to work with you again. And to the sales, marketing, publicity and cover design teams at HarperCollins, I genuinely appreciate all that you do to ensure that my books are sent out into the world of readers.

My novels involve a considerable amount of research, but as I tend to write characters with occupations that fascinate me, I have only myself to blame for that. Patience not only has a gift for numbers, but she's a naval officer. Many thanks to Stephen Basley, Australian naval captain, for his invaluable insights. While working with Steve has its challenges (he says 'no, no, no' a lot), we always find a way around what I'm trying to achieve in terms of character and plot. Any errors are mine and mine alone, and creative licence.

Readers of my fifth novel, *Starting from Scratch*, will recognise Hugo Halstead as Sapphie's good friend. And they might also recognise (a fleeting glimpse, I acknowledge) Patience Cartwright. I had no real idea who Patience was when I wrote the scene in which she appeared, but something kept her in my mind (I now know what that was—she needed a happy ending). Yet ... a whole novel about Patience and Hugo? I had a lot to learn about biology, herpetology and frogs.

Dr Jodie Rowley is the Curator, Amphibian & Reptile Conservation Biology at the Australian Museum Research Institute, Australian Museum & Centre for Ecosystem Science, UNSW Sydney, and also Lead Scientist at Frog ID (the Australian Museum's Citizen Science project). She is not only a talented scientist, but a wonderful communicator on biodiversity conservation. When I contacted Dr Rowley, she introduced me to Victoria Patterson, who is a technical officer with Frog ID and a passionate 'frogger'. Thank you so much, Victoria, for your expertise on frog identification, characteristics, habitat and distribution. For readers curious about croaks in their own backyards, and also for those who would like be part of Frog ID (an important initiative for the protection and conservation of frogs) the website www.frogid.net.au is a great place to start.

To Vani Gupta, a committed speech pathologist and talented writer, thank you for your valuable insights into neurodiversity and so much more. Your generosity and patience are greatly appreciated.

Thank you Dr Margaret Janu. In addition to your sisterly support, your insights into all things medical were, as always, essential (though any errors are mine, and creative licence). To John Nelson, thank you for straightening out the Fibonacci sequence. And to Peter Janu, your everyday burden of checking my maths has extended to my fictional world—thank you for your help.

Being a writer means having writer friends, for which I am eternally grateful. Many thanks to members of the Turramurra Writers group, Carla, Isolde, Elizabeth, Kandy, Cynthia, Cindy and Carol, for your insights into the all-important Chapter One. Thank you to Victoria Purman and Cassie Hamer for your remarkable friendship and encouragement. And last but never least, thank you my writing group, the Inkwell, comprised of Pamela Cook, Terri Green, Michelle Barraclough, Joanna Nell, Laura Boon, Rae Cairns and Angela Whitton. You continue to be inspirational, hilarious, intelligent, informative and all-round blue balls brilliant, and I love you to the libraries of the world and back.

Finally, thank you to my family. To Mum and Dad, I love that I make you proud. Thank you to English teacher and PhD candidate Philippa, for being my *literal* literary go-to girl and tapping into the exact detail I needed for the *Persuasion* references in *Shelter from the Storm*. Thank you, Tamsin, for (yet again!) sharing the ups and downs of writing. Thanks to Michaela for being my back up girl across the world, and to Gabriella for asking after my characters and sharing my books with your fabulous friends. To my sons Ben and Max, thank you for your support (and tea, chocolate and cake). Finally, thank you to Peter, not only for your love and generosity, but for giving me the gift of Paula and Otto, our children's Oma and Opa, without whom I would never have found the fictional yet very real characters of Greta and Derek.

Turn over for a bonus sample chapter from Phoebe's story, *Clouds on the Horizon*.

Clouds on the Horizon

by

PENELOPE JANU

Available now.

CHAPTER 1

Stripes of silver hang in the air and rivers of water crisscross the track, but Camelot, black as the clouds, treads confidently over the uneven ground. Leaning forward in the saddle, I stroke his rain-soaked neck. I breathe in eucalyptus and the dampness of the earth.

My face is wet, as is the hair that's come loose from my plait. Between the tops of my knee-high boots and the leg flaps of my oilskin coat, my jodhpurs are sodden. I run a finger inside my collar and re-fasten a press stud, shivering as we skirt around the tree roots. Notwithstanding my gloves, pins and needles prickle my fingers as I clench and unclench my hands. When I push Camelot into a trot, my body warms, but the wind is cold on my cheeks.

Camelot, as happy as a platypus swimming in a stream, breaks into a canter at the top of the rise, and I laugh as I pull him back. 'Not today, boy.'

A rumble of thunder sounds in the distance as we pass Mr Riley's shearing shed and sheep pens. The water tank is shrouded in mist.

When Camelot shies, edging off the path and into the bush, I increase the pressure on my outside leg to bring him back to the track. He complies but tosses his head as I guide him towards the copse of gums and the narrow dirt road that leads to the churchyard and home. He shies again, skittering sideways. I steady him, patting his neck, when he takes a tentative step.

'What's the—'

A long dark shape lies across the track, blocking our path. I kick my feet free from the stirrups and slide to the ground, my heart thumping hard. I bring Camelot's reins over his head and loop them through my arm.

The man lies on his front with an arm thrown out to the side. One of his legs is bent at the knee and the other is straight. His pants are dark; his white shirt sticks to his skin. Kneeling at his side, I touch his shoulder. Even through the rain, my gloves and his shirt, I feel his body stiffen.

He spins and rolls onto his back.

'Oh!' I sit back on my heels.

He's in his late twenties, maybe early thirties. He has a straight nose and a strong jaw. Blood trickles from his temple to his ear. 'Hvem er du?' he whispers.

I lean over him. 'What?'

He's shivering so hard that his whole body trembles. His eyes flutter closed. 'Who are you?'

'Phoebe. Who are you?'

His eyes open again and he blinks as if trying to focus. 'Phoebe Cartwright.'

'How do you know that?'

He lifts an arm and drops it. He shakes his head. With a shuddering exhalation, he passes out.

I pull off my gloves and rest my fingertips against his neck, counting carefully through the fear that tightens my chest. His pulse is faint. Breathing laboured and shallow. Skin cold and pale. Sight, hearing, touch, taste and smell. It's my job to know about the senses, but this is beyond me.

When his eyes spring open, I jump. 'Telefon,' he mutters.

'There's no reception here.'

He's cleanly shaven. His thick, dark hair looks recently cut. He's wearing a business shirt and suit pants. His shoes are city shoes, leather with narrow eyelets and long thin laces. Why is he in the middle of nowhere, alone and icy cold?

How does he know my name?

I touch his cheek and he flinches. 'Who are you?'

He shakes his head. 'No.'

'You've bumped your head. You're freezing. Tell me your name.'

He utters a string of words I don't understand. Danish? Swedish? I *think* it's Scandinavian. Another shudder takes over his body. He stares at me and swallows. 'Get my phone.' He lifts his hand, but just like before it drops back to his side. 'Find it.' His voice disappears but I read his lips. 'Pocket.'

'We have to get out of the rain.' I look towards my home, a kilometre away. And then I look up at my horse. Now that the shape on the path has taken human form, Camelot is curious. When he lowers his head, only half the length of the rein separates us.

I turn to the man again. 'I don't suppose you can ride?'

'Motorsykkel?'

'A thoroughbred.' By the time I indicate Camelot behind me, the man's eyes have drifted closed again.

He shakes his head. 'No.'

'I don't think you could get onto him anyway. Can you stand? Can you walk?'

His eyes open and his brow creases, as if he's considering my questions. And then, as if in slow motion, he rolls onto his front. He moans as he comes up on his hands and knees. He's slender but his shoulders are broad. The muscles on his arms and chest are clearly outlined through his shirt. I'm average in height, but there's no way I could carry him. I don't think I could drag him either.

Mr Riley hasn't sheared in his shed for years, but he keeps winter hay, tools and other paraphernalia here. It's likely to be weatherproof and even if it isn't, it'll be safer than being outside. I put my hand on the man's shoulder.

'There's a shed twenty metres away. We can go there. Otherwise, I'll have to ride home and call an ambulance on the way.'

'Telefon.'

A bolt of lightning splits the sky and thunder breaks it open. 'That settles it.' Getting to my feet, I take hold of the man's arm with both hands and pull as hard as I can. 'You have to help. You have to stand.'

It takes a minute at least for the man to get off the ground. I pull his arm around my shoulders. Even stooped over, he's tall. When Camelot nudges my back with his nose, I stumble.

'Cut it out, boy.'

'Telefon,' the man whispers, as blood drips on his shirt. Another bolt of lightning, closer than the last.

'Why won't you tell me your name?'

'Nei.'

I don't know what he's up to or where he's from, but he's far too weak to cause trouble. I adjust his arm over my shoulder. 'Let's get out of the storm.'

When I take a step, the man stays rooted to the spot. He holds out a hand and Camelot sniffs it.

'Vakker hest.'

He speaks nicely enough, but I have no idea what his words mean. When he sways towards Camelot, I pull his arm more tightly around my shoulders.

'You have to walk.'

Leaning so heavily on me that I'm forced to brace my legs to stay upright, the man takes slow, leaden steps to the shed. Camelot, his footfalls soft on the rain-soaked track, walks patiently behind us.

The shed isn't locked, but the bolt is stiff and I can't work it while supporting the man. I balance him against a wall. 'I won't be long.'

A moment after I release him, his knees buckle. I shove my shoulder against his chest to support him as he slides to the ground and slumps against the wall, his head tipped onto his chest. Another flash of lightning illuminates the bolt, but even two-handed I can't pull it back, so I rifle through the grass and find a brick. I whack the curved end of the bolt until it slides clear of the barrel. I pull against the doors and they swing outwards. The shed smells of hay, wool and dust and it's even gloomier in here than it was outside. Camelot baulks at the doors, but after I double back and pat his rump firmly, he walks tentatively over the threshold. When I loop his rein through a sheep pen on the far side of the shed, he stares back with big black eyes.

By the time I return to the man, he's facing the wall, pressing both hands against it as he works his way up. He leans on me as we inch towards the shed, but when we get to the doors, he reaches out and grasps the frame. He looks inside. Sways.

'Nei.'

'Yes!'

When I push him through the doors, he staggers towards a stack of hay bales, dropping to his knees just before we get to it. The doors crash shut, plunging us into darkness.

A whimper works its way up my throat.

I swallow compulsively, stilling the memories, the old, relentless fears.

'It's not locked,' I say aloud, my voice thin and high.

My eyes adjust. The windowpanes are filthy but rain streaked. I can see the outlines of gum trees through the glass. Light filters through the six half-doors behind the shearing platform. Shearers would have pushed freshly shorn sheep through the doors to scramble down the ramps and quiver in the pens.

I can breathe.

Camelot's bit jangles. When he shifts a leg, his shoe scrapes the concrete. I make out a stirrup iron, glistening dully in the darkness. Another gust of wind rattles the doors on their hinges.

I can get out.

I step carefully to the doors and push them open, ignoring the gusts of icy wind and rain as I kick the half-brick under one of the doors, creating a wedge. By the time I get back to the man, he's flat on the concrete. Concussion? Hypothermia? Either way, he has to warm up. Dragging six bales of hay off the stack, I lay them out like a bed.

'Can you get up there?'

He doesn't have the strength to stand, but I yank until he kneels and, pushing and shoving, roll him onto the bales. He lies on his back, groans and loses consciousness again. My hair sticks to my face. Rain or sweat? When I feel for his pulse, even weaker than it was before, I see a card through the pocket of his shirt and slide it out. The cardboard is wet through but the words, black on white, are clear enough.

United Nations First Committee
(Disarmament and International Security)
Sindre Tørrissen

He doesn't have a title, but the string of initials next to his name suggests scientific qualifications. There's a UN email address and two telephone numbers.

'Sindre?'

His eyes briefly flicker open. 'Sinn.'

Whoever he is and wherever he's from, he won't warm up if he's wearing wet clothes. My fingers are stiff and clumsy as I pull his shirt free of his pants. After I fumble over the top two buttons of his shirt, I grasp the front panels to rip the remaining buttons through the holes.

'Sorry about that.' I undo his cuffs before rolling him onto his side to pull off the shirt, then push him onto his back again. Thunder rattles the roof and lightning brightens the shed. His chest is firm, his abdominal muscles clearly defined.

When I exhale, my breath is white. 'Your pants are wet too.'

I peel off his socks and tug at his shoes. I undo his belt buckle and button, and unzip his fly, exposing his underpants. 'I'm not looking. I promise. And those can stay on.'

I focus on the hay as I pull off his pants, dropping them onto the pile with his other wet clothes.

Opening the press studs of my oilskin, I shake off the worst of the moisture. I pull the man onto his side, spread the coat out behind him and, brushing off the hay that's stuck to his skin, roll him onto the coat. I draw the thick cotton lining around his body. The coat covers most of his legs and torso, but isn't wide enough to wrap around his chest, so I take off my sweater and smooth the wool, warm from my body, from his waist up to his neck. I gather the coat around his sides. A drip from his hair rolls down his cheek, joining a trail of blood trickling across his throat.

Taking off my T-shirt, I fold it in half and rub his hair, shivering when drips fall from the end of my plait and down my spine. He blinks.

'Du er vakker.'

'I can't understand you,' I say as I hastily pull my T-shirt back over my head. The fabric is damp. I shiver again and rub my arms. 'I'll see what else I can find.'

Camelot's saddle blanket is warm and mostly dry. I remove his saddle and rest it over a railing before wrapping the padded rectangle around the man's feet, tucking it under his heels to secure it. I frantically search the perimeter of the shed before finding a stack of hessian sacks on the shearing platform. They're clean and thick, rough against the insides of my arms when I pick them up. I shake them out and layer them on top of the man, then I free the cape of the oilskin from under his shoulders, lift his head and lay a folded sack beneath it, positioning it like a pillow.

He's trussed up like a mummy, but he'll be warmer. So why, all of a sudden, is he so frighteningly still? Shivering is the first stage of hypothermia. After that, the body preserves energy for the vital organs—the lungs, heart, brain and kidneys. I burrow through the sacks and coat and touch his side. His skin is as cold as marble. I search for the pulse at his throat but can't find it.

'Please don't—'

Feathery beats. One. Two. Three. Four.

I take a shaky breath. 'Thank you.'

I feel down his side again. He's dry now. Any heat he produces, he should keep.

When his head jerks towards me, I jump. He murmurs something unintelligible and I put my hand on his cheek. I push back his hair. 'Sinn?'

'Ja.'

'Are you Swedish?'

'Norge.'

'Norway?'

He swallows. 'Telefon.'

I pick up my phone from a hay bale and hold it out. 'I've already told you. No reception. That's why I have to ride home.'

He grasps my hand. 'Satellitt.'

'I think you have hypothermia. If you warm up too quickly or move around, you could go into cardiac arrest. I should get a signal around five minutes from here, and I'll call an ambulance. It'll take an hour for it to get here from the hospital, but Camelot and I will race home. I'll get my car and come back with blankets and something warm to drink. You can't move while I'm gone. Do you understand?'

'Satellitt.'

'There are no doctors in Warrandale, so the ambulance will be the quickest way for you to get help. I'll be back in thirty minutes, maybe less.'

I try to prise my fingers free, but he holds on. He opens his mouth and shuts it again. Besides 'telefon', I haven't understood much of what he's said since I brought him into the shed. I put my other hand over his.

'You have to let me go.'

He shakes his head. 'Nei.'

I pull my hand free. 'I'll be back as soon as I can. Don't move. Please.'

'I have ...' His brow furrows as he whispers the words. I bend closer to listen. 'I have a satellite phone.' His dark gaze focuses on my face. He swallows. 'I have reception.'

When he does speak in English, he barely has an accent.

I use the torch on my phone to find his clothes and lift them to the hay bales before feeling the weight and shape of his phone through his shirt. The phone is zipped in a pocket that must have sat at his hip. It's not chunky like the satellite phones I'm familiar with, but black and slender like a regular phone.

The hessian sacks lift as he raises his hand. 'Here.'

When I give him the phone, he holds it up. It glows, highlighting his features. His face is attractive. Exceptionally attractive.

He doesn't dial or do anything else. I don't know that he'd be capable of it. His hand drops heavily to his chest and he closes his eyes.

'De vil komme,' he whispers.

I roll his shirt into a ball and press it against the gash on his head. 'I don't understand.'

He mutters. 'They will come.'

I didn't hear anyone on the other end of the phone, so how does he know that they'll come? Who is 'they'?

When his eyes close, the phone slips from his fingers. I make sure my sweater covers his chest, wrap the oilskin up and over his sides again, and secure the hessian sacks. I press the edges of the cape around his ears and brush back his hair.

'I wish you'd stop moving around.' I lean a hip against the hay bales as I pick up his phone and push the buttons at the side.

'Phoebe.' He croaks my name. When I look down, it's straight into his eyes. A shudder passes through him. 'Leave it.'

I put the phone back on his chest. 'I can't get anything on the screen anyway.'

He frowns as if he's lost his train of thought. 'Go home.'

'Leave you here? After I've gone to all this trouble? You said they were coming. Will there be a doctor?'

'Forget this.'

Camelot's shoes scrape on the concrete when he pivots and faces the rear of the shed. I run to him, afraid he'll pull back, dislodge the pen and panic. I put my hand on his neck, quivering with tension. 'Easy, boy,' I say as I untie him. 'What's the matter?'

Rain pounds on the roof and the wind howls through the trees. But there's another sound as well. At first it's a whir. Then it's a roar. The incessant thump of helicopter blades directly above us.

I tighten my grip on the rein and lead Camelot, toey but compliant, to the hay. *They will come.* Who are they? Who is he?

'Sinn?'

He opens his mouth before closing it again.

'That is your name, isn't it? Sinn Tørrissen. You work for the UN.'

Silence.

'You know my name. Why can't I know yours?'

He shakes his head. 'No.'

The helicopter isn't overhead any more, but it's still very loud. Mr Riley grows corn and canola crops on cleared land to the west of the shed. A helicopter could easily land there.

I touch Sinn's arm. 'Has the helicopter come for you? Should I go outside and tell them that you're here?'

He's shivering again. He attempts to roll onto his side, but when I put a hand on his shoulder and gently push, he collapses onto his back. I lean over him, securing the hessian beneath his arms.

'You have to stay still.'

When another shiver passes through him, he clenches his teeth. They're even whiter than his face, and perfectly straight. I press the backs of my fingers to the skin at his neck. He swallows and shudders again. But I'm certain he's warmer than he was. I rewrap his feet with the saddle blanket.

'Do you come from Norway? That's what you said before.'

'Gå hjem.'

'I don't understand.'

His eyes are brighter than they were. 'Go home.'

The doors open wide and I jump. Squinting, I try to look past the broad shaft of light that spills into the shed. Camelot skitters, his reins rushing through my fingers. One of the men standing on the threshold is extremely broad-shouldered and dressed in city clothes. The other man has brutally short hair and is wearing grey fatigues. He has embroidered patches on his arms and a badge on his chest. When he shines the light into the shed again, I turn away and hold a hand above my eyes.

'Who are you?' My voice isn't as steady as I'd like it to be.

'Lower the torch.' A woman's voice. Dressed in black and carrying a bag, she says something else to the men before pushing past them and striding confidently towards me. Her hair is short and fiery red and her face is peppered with freckles. 'Sorry that took a while.'

I stand between her and Sinn. 'Who are you?'

'I'm not here.' She smiles and holds out her hand. 'Who are you?'

My hand lifts automatically. 'Phoebe.' We shake briefly. 'What do you mean—'

She jerks her head towards the men. 'Politics.'

Sinn's eyes are closed; he's deathly white.

'Are you a doctor?'

'I'll check him out and then we'll get him to one.'

I step aside but stay close to Sinn as she drops the bag at her feet and pulls out a stethoscope, blood pressure equipment and a lunch box–sized container that rattles as she puts it on the hay bales. She pulls on gloves and pushes aside the hessian to take Sinn's hand and feel for his pulse. When she addresses him, she tips her head to the side.

'This'll teach you to jump from a moving van.'

He grunts before looking from the woman to me. 'No names.'

'I got the directive,' she says, listening to Sinn's heart before pressing both hands down his arms, torso and legs. She moves the shirt from his head and touches the cut before lifting his eyelids and shining a torch into each of his eyes. She places a thermometer into his ear.

'He slips in and out of consciousness,' I tell her. His head is bleeding again so I press his shirt against the cut. 'He can walk and doesn't seem to be in too much pain, so I guess no broken bones. He was freezing. I took off his clothes to warm him. I think he's better than he was, but he could have concussion. You'll take him to hospital, won't you?'

'We'll do what needs to be done.' The woman squints at the thermometer. 'Thirty-five point six. Could be worse.'

The broad-shouldered man walks towards us, looking cautiously at Camelot as he skirts around him. 'Okay to butt in here?' he says in an American accent, smiling as he runs a hand through his dark blond hair. He'd be in his early thirties.

'Looks to be a superficial head wound,' the woman says, 'but I'll sort out a scan just in case.'

'I found him on the track,' I say. 'He wasn't making much sense.'

'Being cold and wet in freezing temperatures will do that to you,' she says. 'You did a great job with him.'

'Did he really jump from a van?'

She glances at the broad-shouldered man. 'Eight hours ago.'

The man, still keeping well clear of Camelot, stands at Sinn's head and squeezes his shoulder. 'Hey, buddy. You gave us a hell of a fright back there.'

Sinn swallows. 'They didn't see me.'

The man and woman wrap a large silver blanket around Sinn. By the time they've finished, his eyes are closed. His breathing is deep.

'Is he going to be okay?' I ask.

A sleeve of my sweater peeps out from the top of the blanket. The woman moves it aside to check the pulse at Sinn's neck before tucking it in again. She smiles reassuringly. 'All good. Exhausted, that's all.'

The man at the door calls out. 'Stretcher is on its way, lieutenant.'

As he brushes hay from my oilskin, the broad-shouldered man considers my T-shirt and jodhpurs.

'You must be cold yourself.'

I reach for my coat. 'Yes.'

He smiles. 'Thanks for your help. Really appreciate it, but …'

'You weren't here, right?' I shrug into the coat and fasten all the press studs. 'I can't know your names and I get no explanation.'

He smiles apologetically. 'You got it.'

I lay the saddle blanket over Camelot's back before turning to the woman. 'You were addressed as lieutenant. Are you in the navy?'

The woman and man exchange looks. 'No comment,' she says.

'My sister Patience is in the navy. She wears the same camouflage as the sergeant over there.'

'Is that right?'

'Are you in charge?'

She grimaces as she glances first at Sinn, still asleep, and then at his colleague. 'Not the boss of these two, that's for sure.'

'Sinn's with the UN, isn't he?'

The other man attempts to hide a frown. 'Did he tell you that?'

When Sinn mumbles, I put my hand on his arm. His lashes, inky-black crescents on his cheeks, open for an instant before they drift closed. He probably has a family that cares about him. A wife or partner. What if he'd died so far from home? Repressing a shiver, I bunch my hands into fists and put them into my pockets. I stamp my feet, suddenly frozen.

'I offered to call for help, but he only wanted you. Why was that? Why so secretive? Why can't I talk? What is he hiding?'

The woman's face is expressionless as she peers closely at the bruise on Sinn's forehead. The hair at his temple is thickened with blood.

'Take it from me,' she says, 'you can trust him. He'll be grateful for your help.'

'What was he doing all the way out here? How did he know my name?'

The American's brows lift. 'What *is* your name?'

'Phoebe Cartwright.'

He whistles a breath. 'Is that right?'

'Have you heard of me too?'

'Can't really say.'

I pull Sinn's card from my pocket. 'Are you from the UN like him?'

The man plucks the card out of my hand. 'Where did you get this?'

'Besides his phone, it's all he had on him.'

'We'd really appreciate your cooperation with keeping a lid on this.' The man's smile is strained.

'Because you've finished here? I won't see you again?'

'Say nothing, Phoebe.' The man looks at Sinn, still asleep. 'When he's back on his feet, he'll be in touch.'

talk about it

Let's talk about books.

Join the conversation:

 facebook.com/harlequinaustralia

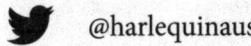 @harlequinaus

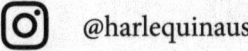 @harlequinaus

harpercollins.com.au/hq

If you love reading and want to know about our authors and titles, then let's talk about it.